On a Turning Tide

On A Turning Tide is Ellie Dean's sixteenth novel in her Cliffehaven series. She lives in a tiny hamlet set deep in the heart of the South Downs in Sussex, which has been her home for many years and where she raised her three children.

To find out more visit www.ellie-dean.co.uk

ELLIE DEAN

On a Turning Tide

arrow books

1 3 5 7 9 10 8 6 4 2

Arrow Books
20 Vauxhall Bridge Road
London SW1V 2SA

Arrow Books is part of the Penguin Random House
group of companies whose addresses can be found
at global.penguinrandomhouse.com

Penguin
Random House
UK

First published by Arrow Books in 2019

www.penguin.co.uk

A CIP catalogue record for this book is available
from the British Library.

ISBN 9781784758134

Typeset in 11.5/14.5 pt Palatino
by Integra Software Services Pvt. Ltd, Pondicherry

Printed and bound in Great Britain by Clays Ltd, Elcograf S.p.A.

MIX
Paper from
responsible sources
FSC® C018179

Penguin Random House is committed to a
sustainable future for our business, our readers
and our planet. This book is made from Forest
Stewardship Council® certified paper.

Acknowledgements

Due to the tragic turn of events in *On a Turning Tide*, I had to turn for advice to those whose medical knowledge far outreaches mine. To Dr Paul Frisby MBB, neighbour and friend, thank you so much for spending the evening before going on holiday sending me links to the appropriate websites, and for discussing with me the aspects of what I was trying to achieve. You're the kindest, most generous man, and certainly know how to make a party go with a swing!

Dr Keith Maybury FRCS, retired Consultant in General and Vascular Surgery, and his lovely wife Sara. Thank you for a wonderful day at Henley – Ollie and I thoroughly enjoyed ourselves and through Keith's vast knowledge of rowing, actually managed to learn something! Thank you, too, for listening to my questions about the medical problems relating to my character in the book, and then introducing me to your colleague and friend, Brian Livingstone.

Dr Brian Livingstone FRCS, retired Consultant Orthopaedic Surgeon. I am hugely indebted to you for your enthusiastic approach to the task in hand. I so appreciated your correspondence setting out the medical situation I was writing about, and the great deal of research you undertook into how the treatment would have been in 1945. These letters included passages from medical books and journals written at the time; photographs and advice on the medicines and treatments available – and the ultimate prognosis. You have been the most marvellous help in all this, patiently dealing with what were probably silly questions, and treating my patient as if he were real and in your care. Thank you too for your very pleasant company at Henley. Any mistakes I've made are my own, which I hope you will forgive.

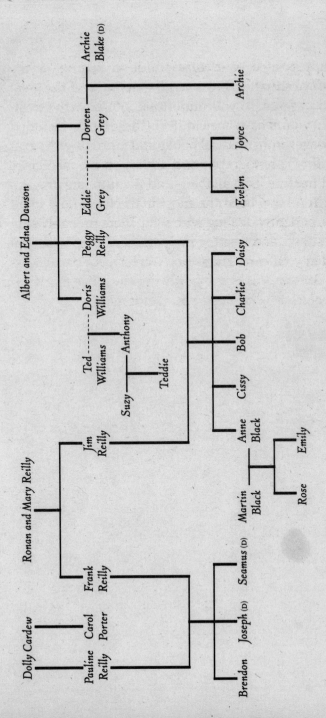

The Cliffehaven Family Tree

1

Cliffehaven
1944

Life had been hectic at Beach View over the past few weeks, so Peggy appreciated the fact that Solly Goldman hadn't pestered her to come to a decision about his very tempting job offer at the factory. Now it was late October – time to make up her mind once and for all.

Peggy had agonised over what to do about it as the war news had at first brought hope and then huge disappointment. It would definitely be a step up to oversee the shop floor, and the increase in her pay would make a massive difference to her situation at home now that Ron was about to move into the Anchor with Rosie. Then again, if the war did come to an end – however impossible that seemed at the moment – it would mean spending less time with Jim and her family when they eventually came home.

She gave a regretful sigh as she finished sewing the bell-bottom trousers and cut the thread. The mood amongst the women in the busy uniform factory was solemn, and mirrored her own, for there had been such excitement and hope when the Allied airborne assault on the Netherlands had begun. Operation Market Garden had been expected to open the way over the Rhine and into the heart of Germany, thereby bringing an end to the war in Europe before Christmas. The news that it had been an unmitigated disaster with thousands of Allied troops killed, in retreat or taken prisoner, was a bitter blow – compounded by the fact that the Polish Home Army's uprising had ended in surrender to the Germans, the Japanese were still fiercely defending their foothold in Burma, and a second attempt by the legendary 617 Bomber Squadron to destroy Hitler's fearsome battleship *Tirpitz* had failed.

Emerging from her dark thoughts, Peggy realised she was due her mid-morning break. She gathered up her coat and string bag, and pushed back from her machine. She decided to take her flask of tea outside rather than sit in the noisy canteen, for the sun was bright and she needed some fresh air after the dry atmosphere of the factory, and time to think.

There was a definite breath of autumn in the light breeze. Peggy found a sheltered sunny spot and lit a cigarette, her thoughts still occupied with what this setback in the advance of the war would mean to her and her scattered family – and how it would affect her decision about the job.

Hitler's V-2s were continuing to rain down in great numbers over the south-eastern counties, despite the sterling efforts of the Allied forces to find and destroy the launch sites that were hidden on the other side of the Channel, and although travel restrictions had been lifted and the blackout changed to dim-out, it still wasn't safe to bring her daughter, two young sons and the grandchildren home from the farm in Somerset.

Peggy had determinedly plastered on a smile and tried to stay positive throughout the five long years of struggle to keep the home fires burning in the face of shortages, ever-tightening rationing and the constant threat of death from the skies. However, there had been days when she'd barely managed to keep her anguish contained, and many a night when she'd cried into her pillow, fearful for her Jim, and desperately yearning for her absent family. Now another Christmas was looming without them – there wasn't a glimmer of hope that this war was even close to ending – and her spirits were at their lowest ebb.

Peggy sipped her tea and watched the little ones racing about the small playground behind the crèche. Since the V-1s and V-2s had started causing mayhem, many more children had been sent away until it was safe for them to return, and there were times when she wondered if she was being reckless in keeping Daisy with her. But life was hard enough, and selfish or not, she clung to Daisy in the desperate hope that nothing bad would happen to her.

Daisy would be three in December, and although Jim had managed to see her as a babe in arms before he'd been posted to India, the child had no memory of him. Peggy had told her stories about Jim and made sure there were photographs of him around the house, but she suspected Daisy didn't really understand who and what he was – and when he did finally come home, he'd be a stranger to her.

Daisy wouldn't be alone in that dilemma, she thought sadly. The majority of those children in the playground had fathers fighting abroad and had become used to just being with their mothers, and the sudden appearance of a man in the house would come as a shock.

Peggy puffed on her cigarette and frowned as it occurred to her that as much as she longed for Jim to come home, it wouldn't be easy to return to the routine of their life before the war. In fact, she wasn't at all sure she wanted to go back to that now she'd tasted the heady freedom of life beyond the walls of Beach View, and her own money. If she took Solly's job then she'd be reluctant to give it up – and that could cause no end of trouble.

Jim was a man who believed that a woman's place was in the home and, as the breadwinner, he expected his tea on the table at six; to always have clean shirts and pressed trousers; and to reserve the right to go to the pub whenever he wanted – usually without her. In this, he was like every man she knew, and she suspected there would be ructions in most

Cliffehaven homes once the men returned home expecting nothing to have changed – and finding a very different set-up.

Impatient with these uncomfortable thoughts, she took a last puff of her cigarette and stubbed it out. There was no point in being gloomy about things. Jim's experiences in Burma must have changed him too, and when he did come home, they would work together to steer their way through the difficulties and find a new order.

Peggy drank her tea and watched the gulls hover above the rooftops, their mournful cries lost in the roar of the planes that seemed to be a constant background noise now they were flying sorties day and night. Even if, by some miracle, the war did end soon, it could be weeks, or even months before Jim could get home, so she might as well accept Solly's offer while she had the chance – and deal with any fallout later.

Having finally come to a decision, she felt her spirits lighten. She replaced the cap on her Thermos and went back inside to climb the stairs up to Solly's office. There was no sign of Madge, his secretary, but his door was ajar, and she could see he was alone at his desk.

'Hello, Solly. Have you got a minute?'

Solly's smile was warm as he eased his large frame out of the leather chair. 'Oy, vay, Peggy. I always have time for you, you know that. Come in, come in.'

Peggy had known Solly most of her life, and although some might find his large presence and big personality daunting, she'd always been comfortable with him, for beneath that façade of wealth and power beat a soft and understanding heart.

'How are you, Peggy?' he asked, lighting her cigarette and watching her intently.

'Struggling on,' she replied. 'At least my Jim's still safe in that hospital in India and not having to face the Japs in Burma.' She regarded him with great sympathy. 'I was so sorry to hear about what happened in Poland, Solly. Is there any news of your family?'

He shook his great head, his dark eyes shadowed with pain. 'It's difficult to get any news out of Poland at the moment – and what has emerged is so horrifying, it's almost better not to know what's going on. How has young Danuta taken the defeat of the uprising?'

Peggy gave a sigh as she thought of the Polish girl who'd returned from her dangerous missions behind enemy lines to come and live with her again at Beach View. 'She's being stoic as usual, but she's bitterly disappointed it all came to nothing.'

Solly nodded thoughtfully, and then changed the subject. 'I hope you've come to tell me you'll take up my offer, Peggy. There have been developments, and despite the fact this war looks as if it's going to drag on into a new year, there are plans afoot and I need to get things organised.'

Peggy frowned. 'What developments? I thought you were planning to go back into the ladies' wear trade again?'

'I am, but I've just been offered something rather more lucrative than frocks and with a guaranteed income.' His dark eyes shone with excitement, for there was nothing he relished more than a promising new business venture.

Peggy chuckled. 'Spit it out, Solly, before you burst your boiler.'

'I tendered for another government contract and, because they're pleased with the quality of our uniforms, they've awarded me a healthy slice of a new commission to make suits for the servicemen when they're demobilised. Every man Jack of them will get a suit, Peggy, so the contract is worth a fortune.' He leaned back in his chair with a beaming and very self-satisfied smile.

'Goodness,' breathed Peggy. 'So the idea of making dresses is out of the window, is it?'

'We can put that on hold for now. The winter's coming and I need to get going on these demob suits so we have a good supply when the war ends. Montague Burton has the lion's share of the contract because he's a bigger outfit than us, but I'm determined we'll match him in quality and speed of supply.' He sat forward. 'Are you with me on this, Peggy?'

'I've thought long and hard about it, Solly,' she confessed. 'And it hasn't been an easy decision.

But with the fiasco of Operation Market Garden and the continuing trouble in the Far East, I've realised it could be ages before any of my family comes home.' She took a steadying breath. 'If you really think I'm up to managing the shop floor, then I'd love to give it a go.'

He pushed himself out of his chair and came round the desk to pull her into an enthusiastic hug. 'I knew I could rely on you,' he said, almost squeezing the breath out of her.

It was like being engulfed by a very large, soft cushion, and Peggy rather liked it, for it had been too long since her Jim had held her like this. She reluctantly pulled away from him, aware they could be seen through the large window that overlooked the factory floor. 'I've yet to tell anyone at home,' she said breathlessly, 'so don't say anything to Ron or Danuta before I do.'

'I shall be discretion itself,' he said, returning to his chair and making the springs groan beneath his bulk. 'But don't take too long. I want you up here on Monday morning all ready to make a start.'

Peggy felt a stab of alarm. 'This Monday? It's a bit soon, isn't it?'

'This is a big operation, Peggy. Thousands of off-the-peg suits and flannel trousers will have to be made in every size imaginable, and what with the uniforms we'll still be making for the regular servicemen, we'll have to start recruiting extra cutters and tailors, and sound out the machinists about their future plans.'

'And where do we find skilled cutters and tailors when most of the male population is in the Forces?'

'I have it on good authority that the government already has a plan for demobilisation which will begin around Christmas time. Servicemen and women will start to be released from duty according to their age, theatre of war and the length of their service, and I'm sure we'll find the skilled people we need amongst them.'

Peggy felt a dart of hope that Jim might be one of those released from duty, but it was quickly extinguished when she realised it was highly doubtful with so much going on in Burma and the Far East.

She pulled her thoughts together. 'Are the service women getting suits as well?'

Solly shrugged. 'There was no mention of such a thing, but I doubt it.'

Peggy felt this was unfair, but she kept her thoughts to herself. 'How do we get the material to make the suits when clothing rations are so tight?'

'The government is dealing with all that, and I can assure you, it will be of the finest wool cloth, so to start with we'll only use the best machinists and cutters.' He gave a sigh. 'I wish young Gracie could be persuaded to come back. She's a fine cutter and proved to be an excellent teacher.'

'Gracie's not coming back, Solly,' Peggy said quietly. 'Clive will be leaving the Dover hospital for

East Grinstead soon, and the restructuring of his face could take months. He still can't accept what happened to him, but Gracie's determined to stay at his side. She understands how frightened he is and why he keeps pushing her away, but their marriage seems strong enough, thank goodness, to weather this awful storm. At least she has her mother's support and doesn't have to worry about little Chloe on top of everything else.'

A cloud seemed to shadow Solly's dark eyes. 'Oy, vay, Peggy,' he sighed. 'It's a terrible world, isn't it? You'd have thought we'd all have learned from the last shout that war is not the answer to anything.'

'I'd better get back to work,' said Peggy, not wanting to dwell on the horrors of war. 'Talking of which, you do understand that I won't be able to do any extra hours? I still have Daisy to look after and my responsibilities at home.'

'Of course, of course,' he said airily. 'We'll discuss all that on Monday.'

Peggy regarded him sharply. 'I mean it, Solly. I won't be doing weekends or night shifts.'

Solly heaved a sigh. 'I have taken your family circumstances into consideration, Peggy. My niece Loretta will share the hours with you until she leaves in November, by which time Mavis Whitlock will be here.'

'And who is Mavis Whitlock?'

'She's a very capable woman who's been helping my brother run his factory in London. Born and bred in Cliffehaven, she's had enough of the city and now she's been widowed, she wants to come back here.' He smiled at her. 'I'm sure you'll get on just fine.'

Peggy had lived in Cliffehaven all her life, but had never come across a Mavis Whitlock. 'What was her maiden name?'

'Anderson,' he replied, his gaze sliding away. 'You might remember her from school.'

Peggy's spirits sank. Mavis Anderson had been head girl and two years senior to Peggy, and she remembered how vindictive and bossy she'd been. She could only hope that age and experience had made her more likeable.

Solly seemed to sense that Peggy wasn't too happy about the arrangement, and heaved himself out of the chair to signal the end of the meeting. 'How are the wedding plans coming along?' he asked, escorting her to the door.

Peggy dragged her thoughts from Mavis. 'Rosie has a long list of things for poor Ron to see to before the big day, and I suspect he's beginning to realise that there's more to a wedding than just buying a new suit and turning up on time.'

Solly grinned. 'My Rachel was the same before our wedding. Ron should take a leaf out of my book: agree with everything, say nothing – and get on with it if he wants a quiet life.'

Peggy smiled back at him. 'That's what he's doing, but I can tell he's not finding it at all easy after spending most of his life following his own dubious path.'

Solly laughed. 'I'll see you on Monday, Peggy. You'll be shadowing Loretta for a while until you get the hang of things.' His eyes were kindly as he regarded her. 'They're not so difficult, Peggy, and I have every faith in you, so there's no need to look nervous.'

Peggy nodded and returned to her sewing machine. She wasn't nervous exactly, just a little wary about the added responsibility and the prospect of having to work with Mavis – but there was excitement too for the challenge ahead – and as there was nothing Peggy enjoyed more, she couldn't wait to begin and prove to Solly that he'd made the right choice.

It was a bright, brisk day, the wind carrying a chill as it blew across the hills from the sea, and Ron was congratulating himself on having escaped the Anchor and the endless list of jobs Rosie had presented him with. He loved the very bones of that woman, but she was firing on all cylinders at the moment, and he was wondering what it was about weddings that turned women into whirling dervishes. After all, he reasoned, it was simply a matter of getting his suit cleaned, buying a ring, sorting out a bit of grub and some decent drinks and turning up on the day – he really couldn't see why so much fuss had to be made of it all.

He was tramping along the hill with Harvey and Monty galloping ahead of him, the ferrets snugly curled up asleep in the deepest pocket of his poacher's coat. They'd been out for most of the morning and Ron had netted four rabbits, as well as a canvas bag full of mushrooms he'd found on the edge of the woods belonging to Lord Cliffe, and a paper bag filled with juicy blackberries he'd gathered from a hedgerow.

Ignoring the nagging pain in his lower back from the shrapnel that had become embedded there during the First War, he stomped across the gently undulating grassland, unperturbed by the ever-present thunder of the planes returning from their bombardment of German airfields and industrial zones. There were fewer aircraft at Cliffe now, for the much-depleted Luftwaffe no longer came across on raids and were kept busy by the Allied Air Forces who'd set up bases all along the northern shores of France, the Netherlands and Belgium to concentrate their firepower on German targets and V-2 rocket sites.

Ron's granddaughter Cissy had at first feared she'd be relocated to another aerodrome far from Cliffehaven and her mother, Peggy, but she'd been assured that her WAAF posting at Cliffe was secure for the immediate future. The girl was worried about her American flyer, Randolph Stevens, who'd been captured some time ago and was now in a POW camp somewhere in Eastern Germany, but at least she knew he was out of danger. Which was more than could be said for Rita's Australian chap,

Peter Ryan. He'd been sent to an Allied airfield in Belgium, and from his brief letters to Rita, it seemed he was flying endless sorties over Germany and coming under constant fire.

Ron paused to dig his pipe out of his pocket and take in the view as he filled it with tobacco and got it alight. Ugly gun emplacements lined the clifftops, but they were no match for the V-2s which came across silently and far too high to be seen, let alone shot down, and this southern corner of England had once more become a dangerous place. Hundreds of them came across every day, undetected until they went pop and then exploded mightily on contact with the ground, causing death and destruction to the villages and farming communities – as well as poor old London. The newspapers were calling it a second Blitz, and it certainly felt like it at times when all the sirens went off.

Ron tried to ease his aching back as his thoughts turned to the women at Beach View. Being the most senior man in the house, he felt responsible for them, and he was rather worried about how they'd cope without him once he moved into the Anchor with Rosie. Peggy would miss the rent he paid her, and elderly Cordelia Finch would have no one to banter with over the breakfast table, or carry her home after she'd enjoyed a sherry or three at the Anchor.

As for the girls in his and Peggy's care, Sarah was doing well at her new office job, but she was worried sick about her father and fiancé who hadn't been heard of since the fall of Singapore and their incarceration in Changi prison. Rita fretted over Peter Ryan as well as her father who was fighting with the army in France; and little Ivy was just as worried about her older brothers who were with the Atlantic convoys, and her parents and sister who'd refused to leave the East End of London despite these recent attacks. Danuta seemed content enough now she'd settled into her job as district nurse and assistant midwife, but he suspected the latest news coming out of Poland had dashed any hope for her country's liberation.

He heaved a sigh, thankful that now Peggy's snobby sister Doris had seen the error of her ways since moving into Rosie's rental bungalow, the calm atmosphere at Beach View had been restored. Doris had surprised him by how much she'd changed – both in her outlook on life and her attitude to the people she'd once looked down on – and he was secretly pleased that she and Peggy had mended the rift between them, for he knew how much it meant to Peggy. How long that would last was anyone's guess, but it seemed Doris was settled and content and making a new life for herself following the death of her estranged husband and the V-1 attack which had destroyed her home.

Ron set aside these thoughts, determined to focus on more pleasant things. Fran would be all right now she had the stalwart Robert to stand by her. The newly-weds had returned to Beach View, all starry-eyed from their honeymoon, to set up home in the large bedroom on the top floor. His smile was wry, for they emerged from that room only to leave for work, join the others for their meals or help about the house. They seemed to be blissfully happy despite the fact Fran's family had banished her from their lives, and Ron thought their registry office wedding had been perfect.

Rosie, however, had other ideas for their own wedding. She thought a registry office service was too short and lacked any sense of real occasion, so despite Ron's distinct lack of faith in any sort of religion, he'd reluctantly let her have her way and they'd booked St Cuthbert's for the 9th of December. The wedding celebrations were to be catered for in the private function room at the Officers' Club, which would no doubt cost him an arm and a leg, but if that's what Rosie wanted, then that was what she'd get. If he'd had his way, the ceremony would take place next week at the Town Hall, with the wedding party in the large community hall next to the council offices – but Rosie had turned up her nose at that idea and seemed determined to have a really big do.

He gripped the stem of his pipe between his teeth. He really couldn't blame her for they'd waited long enough to tie the knot, and he didn't have it in his heart to deny her yearning for what she saw as a proper wedding with all the trimmings, but there was an unexpected price to pay.

It didn't involve money, but it was at a cost to his conscience, and as time had gone on it had begun to trouble him.

Ron puffed furiously on his pipe. Because the wedding would be in church, he'd been forced to make an appointment to see Father O'Leary this afternoon, which he most definitely wasn't looking forward to. The old priest had been around for years and seemed determined to bring Ron back into the Catholic fold – even though he'd never seriously been in it once he'd passed puberty.

He and Father Peter had had many heated religious discussions over the years, helped along by a dram or three of whisky, and Ron had steadfastly refused to be a hypocrite by attending Mass or playing any part in the church's affairs – especially after he'd come back home from the trenches in 1918. Now it seemed the old man had the upper hand, for he'd made it plain that Ron must attend Mass every Sunday leading up to the wedding, go to confession and brush up on the catechism, or he wouldn't marry them in his church.

Ron had found himself wedged between the devil and the deep, and knew he'd be damned if he stuck to his principles, and damned if he didn't. But that didn't mean the wily old priest would have things all his own way.

He checked his watch and whistled to the dogs before hitching the string of rabbits over his shoulder and half-heartedly making his way towards the ancient church of St Cuthbert which sat in a fold of the chalk hills and overlooked the sea.

The square Norman tower and delicate Gothic spire rose towards the clear blue sky, and the rough stone walls which had been there since Saxon times seemed to hold the echoes of all the generations who'd come before. Ron pushed through the lych-gate, the dogs racing past him as he slowly walked up the path. Lichen-covered headstones stood on either side, so worn by age and the elements that the epitaphs were illegible. Ron looked across the carefully tended cemetery, noting that the winter pansies he'd planted were nodding their bright heads in the breeze, and that the grass had recently been given its final cut of the year.

He suspected Father O'Leary was having his usual afternoon nap, so it wouldn't matter if he was a bit late – and he needed a moment to think again about what he was doing.

Ron walked past the memorial for Danuta's heroic brother, Aleksy, who'd been shot down and killed during the Battle of Britain, and the stone cherub that had been placed for her baby, Katarzyna, who'd barely lived long enough to take a breath. The shadows of the yew trees stretched across the peaceful garden of rest, and as Ron took the path towards the back of the church he was rewarded by the sight of the sea stretching between the chalk headlands, and out to the horizon where, on this clear day, he could see the faint smudge of the distant French coastline.

Reaching into his poacher's coat pocket, he whistled to the dogs and clipped the leashes to their collars. Both looked at him with disgust as he firmly tied the ends to a sturdy bench and ordered them to stay. With disgruntled sighs, they settled down, experience telling them they were in for a long wait.

Satisfied they couldn't get up to any mischief, Ron followed the meandering path through the headstones until he came to where his wife, Mary, had been laid to rest over forty years before. A carpet of pansies covered her, and the roses he'd placed last week in the stone urn at her feet were still quite fresh. He pulled out a couple of weeds, and then rested his grubby hand on the sun-warmed headstone he'd lovingly carved for her.

'Well, Mary,' he murmured, 'it seems you and Father O'Leary have your way at last. The black sheep will darken the doors of your church again. To be sure, I'm not easy with it, but 'tis all for a good cause, wee girl – and you know me, acushla, it won't last.'

Ron could almost hear her laughter as a sudden memory returned of her looking up at him, her dark hair flying in the winter's wind, her cheeks bright with cold and her eyes sparkling with love and happiness as they'd emerged from this church on their wedding day. She'd known then that he'd never be a regular churchgoer, but that hadn't really bothered her, for she had her own faith and was certain it was strong enough for both of them.

'Ach, Mary,' he sighed, remembering all that youthful exuberance and joy in life slowly ebbing away as the sickness took her and he was left alone to raise their two small boys. 'You were too young for your God to take you from us, and to be sure I still find it hard to forgive Him for that.'

Closing his mind to the terrible struggle he'd had to raise his sons and put food on the table while he grieved, he patted the headstone and then headed for the church. He'd visited Mary regularly over the years and told her all about Rosie, even though he didn't really believe in life after death. Yet having her to talk to and confide in when things troubled him was comforting, and he liked to think that Mary approved of Rosie and was glad that he wasn't alone any more.

The dogs looked up at him hopefully as he passed and then slumped back down with sighs of disappointment when it became clear they were to remain tied to the bench.

Ron lifted the heavy iron latch and the studded oak door creaked ominously as he stepped into the dark, chill interior of the church and closed it behind him. The familiar smell of incense, snuffed candle wicks, damp stone, woodworm and musty prayer books greeted him along with that echoing and rather intimidating hush that all churches seemed to possess.

Ron hung up his coat so the ferrets couldn't escape, dumped the string of rabbits and canvas bag on the floor, and then stuffed his old cap into his trouser pocket before bypassing the stoup of holy water to make his slow way up the aisle.

The white altar cloth gleamed in the flickering light of candles and the glow from the eternal flame in the small brass tabernacle which had been placed beneath the simple wooden cross. Beams of sunlight poured through the stained glass of the windows where motes of dust danced and shimmered in the blue and red, and the only sound to break the silence were his footsteps on the flagstone floor.

'You're late!'

The voice of doom resounded through the church and up into the high rafters.

Ron nearly jumped out of his skin, and his heart skipped a beat before it began to hammer wildly against his ribs. And then he saw the dark-clad figure standing in the shadows by the pulpit. 'To be sure, Father, I thought God himself had come down to strike me,' he managed. 'Is it a heart attack you'll be wishing on me?'

Father O'Leary smiled as he stepped from the shadows in his long, rusty-black cassock. 'If you didn't have such a guilty conscience, you'd not be afeared of a voice in the stillness, Ronan Reilly.'

Ron refused to let him see how rattled he was, and he met the Dublin man's amused gaze squarely. 'Is it not said, Father, let him who has no sin cast the first stone?'

'Well remembered, Ronan,' replied the priest. 'I'll make a believer of you yet.'

'I wouldn't count upon it,' he retorted gruffly. Father Peter O'Leary was at least eighty-five, but his face was barely lined, his brown eyes were lively and his mind was as sharp as a tack. Short and stout, he had to look up at Ron, but strangely, Ron always felt small and intimidated in his presence.

Ron broke the eye contact first. 'Well, I'm here now, so let's get on with it, eh? I've things to be doing.'

The priest regarded him from head to foot, and clucked in disapproval at the old corduroy trousers held up with garden twine, the faded shirt and ragged sweater. 'You could have made an effort, Ronan.'

'I've been out ferreting with the dogs,' he replied shortly. 'No point in dressing up to kill your God's creatures.'

The other man sighed in acceptance that Ron was a lost cause, especially when it came to his attire. 'When was the last time you made a confession, Ronan?' He held up his hand as Ron opened his mouth to reply. 'And I don't mean all the times you've confessed your shenanigans to Rosie or Peggy, either,' he said sternly.

'Well, now, it seems to me that me sins are me own to be dealing with – and although I know you enjoy hearing all the wicked things your parishioners tell you, I'll not be adding to your entertainment today. Besides, it would take too long.'

'I have all afternoon,' Father O'Leary countered, undeterred.

Ron shook his head and, reaching into his trouser pocket, drew out a quarter-bottle of whisky. He saw the priest's eyes light up as he'd known they would. 'This is good twenty-year-old malt. Why don't we share it while I listen to your usual lecture? I'm sure your God already knows all me sins, so we can cut out the middle man, and I'll rattle off a couple of Hail Mary's as penance. What do you say, Father?'

The priest tore his gaze from the bottle and shook his head, his expression mournful. 'You're the very divil for tempting me this way, Ronan Reilly. To be sure, there's little point in you pretending to do penance when you lack an ounce of remorse and have absolutely no intention of mending your ways.'

Ron chuckled. 'Aye, temptation's a terrible thing, and I've always found it easy to give in to it.' He turned the bottle so it caught the coloured rays of light coming from the windows. 'But it would be an awful shame to turn down fine malt whisky when it's so hard to come by these days.'

Peter O'Leary raised a bushy eyebrow, his gaze once more returning to the bottle. 'I'll not be bothering to ask you where you got it,' he said in defeat, 'but if you promise to come with Rosie to Mass every Sunday, I'll forget about listening to your confession for now.'

'Good wee man,' said Ron, giving him such a hefty pat on the shoulder that the little man sagged beneath the weight of it. 'To be sure, I'll do me best – but I'll not be promising, mind.'

The priest held up a warning finger. 'You'll be here every Sunday,' he said sternly, 'and I will test you on the catechism before we go much further. If you fail, I will be forced to inform the cardinal, and he will have no choice but to put a stop to the wedding.' He regarded Ron from beneath his heavy brows. 'And 'twill be you having to explain why to Rosie.'

Ron experienced a sharp stab of panic and covered it up by turning towards the vestry. 'Ach,' he said airily, 'that's no bother. To be sure, it was drummed into me well enough as a wee boy, so I've not forgotten a word of it.' He rummaged about in the vestry cupboard. 'Where have you hidden the glasses?'

'Where they always are,' the priest replied dryly, reaching to the shelf below the small washbasin.

Ron opened the bottle and was disconcerted to see a glint of something approaching triumph in the other man's eyes. He knew then that his ruse hadn't worked, and if he didn't do some very thorough homework, he would be in deep and terminal trouble with Rosie. But how to get hold of the necessary books without having to admit he'd forgotten nearly everything he'd learned as a boy?

To his consternation, he found his hand was shaking as he poured generous measures into both glasses. '*Sláinte*,' he said, before downing his in one.

Father O'Leary smiled and repeated the Irish toast. He savoured the whisky in silence, his brown eyes all too knowing as they regarded Ron. 'I could test you now, if you'd like,' he said, after draining his glass.

Ron's gaze slid away as he poured more whisky. 'To be sure, 'tis not the time, Father. Not with us full of the demon drink.'

'I expect you're right,' the priest murmured. He took a leisurely drink, his gaze drifting to a pile of books on the desk below the small window. 'And it's a lot to remember after so many years.'

'Aye. I could be a bit rusty on a few of the finer points,' admitted Ron, following his gaze to the cat-echism books, relieved that the other man was offering him a way out of his dilemma.

'You're welcome to borrow one,' said Father Peter, 'but I shall need it back for Sunday School.'

'That would be grand, so it would,' said Ron. 'Just to brush up on a few of the minor things, you understand,' he added hastily.

Father O'Leary smiled a knowing smile and said nothing.

2

Peggy had mulled things over during the afternoon and decided she'd take Mavis Anderson as she found her and focus on the exciting prospect of her new job. She was still feeling positive about things when she went to the crèche to pick up Daisy at the end of her shift. It was Fran's turn to cook the tea, Ron had promised faithfully that he'd sort out the dripping overflow from the upstairs washbasin as soon as he'd been to see Father O'Leary, and Sarah had planned to do the shopping during her lunch break – so if all that had been achieved, she had only to get Daisy to bed after tea and then put her feet up. If there were any letters in the post, then that would be a bonus.

She pulled up her coat collar as she waited impatiently for someone to open the door to the nursery, for the wind had strengthened and become quite cutting.

'Ah, Peggy,' said Nanny Pringle as she opened the door. 'You'd better come in.'

Peggy was a little alarmed at the other woman's serious expression. 'Why, what's the matter? Daisy's all right, isn't she?'

Nanny Pringle stepped aside and closed the door behind Peggy before replying. 'I'm sorry to report that we have an outbreak of nits,' she said, bristling with disapproval.

'Oh, is that all?' said Peggy, relieved. 'I thought there'd been some sort of crisis.'

Nanny Pringle's usually pleasant smile was not in place as she regarded Peggy sternly. 'Being infested with nits is very serious,' she said. 'With so many children, they are inclined to spread like wildfire. I've had to telephone for Sister Danuta to come and deal with it all. Daisy is still waiting her turn, so I'm afraid it might be a while until you can take her home.'

Peggy felt duly chastised and bit down on a smile as she followed the bustling figure into the large, pleasant room at the back, which was now crowded with anxious mothers and fractious children. Nanny Pringle's bark was worse than her bite, but at times she made Peggy feel five years old again.

Nanny Pringle started issuing orders to one of her two young helpers to clear away the scattered toys, and then firmly separated two small boys who were tussling over a toy truck. The other girl was trying to bring some order to the line of children who were waiting for Danuta to comb their hair and apply the nit powder.

Danuta caught Peggy's eye and grinned as she handed over a box of powder and fine-toothed comb to the mother of the child she'd just treated, and then turned her attention to the next in line. Peggy saw that Daisy was right at the end of the queue, so she dumped her bag and coat and went to see if she could help in any way.

'I'd appreciate it if you could keep that little lot amused until we've finished here,' Nanny Pringle said, tipping her head towards a cluster of toddlers who'd already been treated and were getting raucous. 'They aren't due to be picked up for another hour or so.'

Peggy rounded them up, took them to the far end of the room and got them sitting in a semi-circle. Plucking a colourful book from a nearby shelf, she settled down to read the story and show them the bright pictures which accompanied it.

As she read, she kept an eye out for Daisy. One by one the children were treated and sent home with their mothers, the room quietened, and order was restored.

Daisy came running up to her just as she'd finished the story. 'Nuta put powder on my hair,' she complained, dumping the box of powder and a comb in Peggy's lap before scratching furiously at her head. 'Don't like it.'

Peggy gave her a hug. 'But everyone else has got powder – look.' She pointed at the other children. 'You don't want to be the only one without, do you?'

Daisy shook her head, but still looked doubtful.

To ward off any tantrum, Peggy quickly fetched their coats, noting that Danuta was packing away her things and reaching for her cloak. 'Come on, Daisy, let's see if Danuta will walk home with us for our tea.'

To Peggy's mind, Danuta was still far too thin after her long weeks of recovery in the Memorial Hospital, but despite what the Gestapo had done to her, she'd never lost her fighting spirit, and having beaten all the odds and survived, there was now a healthy glow in her face, and her hair was a glossy dark brown beneath that fetching little starched cap.

'I'm sorry, Mamma Peggy,' she said as they headed for the door, 'but I have to return to surgery first to check I am not needed. There is a mother expecting her baby very soon, and I might have to visit her before I can come home.'

'Oh, dear,' sighed Peggy. 'I do worry that you're doing too much after all you've been through. Have you eaten yet?'

'I had lunch,' said Danuta, leading the way outside, 'and a biscuit with tea just before I was called here.'

'Well, that's not enough to keep you going until teatime.' Peggy scrabbled in her string bag. 'I didn't get around to eating all my sandwiches today,' she said, handing over the small packet. 'Do try and get those down you before you go rushing off again.'

Danuta smiled, her green eyes lighting up with affection. 'You do not practise what you preach, I think. Why you not eat at lunchtime?'

'I had my mind on other things and simply for-got,' Peggy replied, grabbing Daisy to stop her from running into the road.

'Is something the matter, Peggy?' the girl asked with a frown.

Peggy explained about her new job. 'I'll have to tell the others tonight,' she said, 'and I'm rather dreading what Ron will say.'

Danuta gave a little shrug. 'It is not his decision,' she said. 'And it is good that Solly thinks so highly of you. Well done.' She placed the packet of sand-wiches in her basket, gave Peggy a hasty kiss on the cheek and tethered the bag and box on the rack of her bicycle. 'I will bring the powder for the rest of the household with me when I come home,' she promised. 'And thank you for the sandwiches.'

Peggy watched her cycle away, and with a sigh, began the walk home, tired now after a long day and ready for her tea.

The overflow pipe was no longer dripping, she noted with relief when she arrived home at last. Climbing the concrete steps from the scullery to the kitchen, she found it wonderfully warm and welcoming after her chilly walk. The atmosphere was calm and happy as everyone sat around the table eating their tea and the two dogs snored contentedly by the range fire. There was no sign of Queenie the three-legged cat, but as it was her time to prowl the neighbourhood, Peggy wasn't too concerned.

Daisy ran straight to the elderly and much-loved Cordelia to have her coat and hat taken off. 'I got nits, Gan-Gan,' she declared proudly, whipping off her woolly hat to show her the powder in her dark curls.

There was a general groan, and Fran got up from the table to fetch Peggy and Daisy's supper plates which had been put in the warming oven. 'Ach well,' she sighed. 'These things happen. At least it's not an outbreak of measles or mumps.'

'They'll come soon enough,' said Peggy, admiring the golden crust on the pigeon pie. 'My goodness, that does look lovely,' she praised.

'It tastes all right too,' Ivy said with her mouth full.

'It is *not* made of paste and glue,' said Cordelia crossly. 'Really, Ivy, do think before you speak. Fran has done a lovely job.'

'I never said ...' Ivy made winding signals with her hand. 'Turn yer hearing aid up, Grandma Cordy. You ain't makin' sense.'

'There's no need to shout,' the elderly woman retorted. 'I should think they could hear you in Scotland!'

'Only if they remember to turn up their hearing aids,' Ivy muttered, rolling her eyes and stuffing down more food.

'What's that? What did you say?' Cordelia fiddled with her hearing aid and winced as it screeched.

31

Rita and Ivy stifled their giggles and bowed their heads over their plates to hide their amusement.

Ivy and Rita were a couple of naughty imps and Peggy shot them a glare of warning to behave – for all the good it would do. She then settled Daisy in her chair and made sure her food wasn't too hot before she tucked into her own meal.

Once the initial pangs of hunger had been satisfied, she turned to Fran who was looking very pretty in a moss-green cardigan she'd knitted that enhanced the colour of her lovely Irish eyes. 'No Robert tonight?'

'He's working late up at Castle Hill Fort,' Fran replied. 'There's some sort of flap on as usual, so if it isn't resolved, he'll probably have to spend the night up there.'

Robert's work for the MOD was a complete mystery to all of them, and it wasn't unusual for him to stay at the Napoleonic fortress overnight, but Peggy understood how difficult it made things for the newly-weds. She cleared her plate and gave a sigh of satisfaction. 'That was delicious and very welcome, Fran,' she said. 'I don't know how you managed it, but the potato topping was scrumptious.'

Fran went pink with pleasure. 'I just made up a little dried egg and mustard powder with some water and a smidgeon of grated cheese and brushed it over the really thinly sliced potato,' she said. 'It was a trick I learned from Mammy when we had no butter or flour to make pastry.'

Peggy saw the sadness in Fran's eyes and reached for her hand. 'I don't suppose you've heard anything from Ireland?'

Fran shook her head, her copper tresses glinting in the firelight. 'All me letters have been sent back unopened,' she replied. 'To be sure, they meant what they said, and I'll not be hearing from them again.'

'Oh, Fran,' sighed Peggy. 'I'm so sorry to hear you say that. Is there really no hope they'll come round to you having married Robert?'

Fran tossed back her hair in an effort to appear defiant. 'I've made me bed, and now I must lie in it,' she said firmly. 'But once this war's over, Robert and I have decided to go to Ireland and make them face up to the fact that I'll not be cast out of their lives just because they're so blinkered and cruel – and we'll fight to make them understand that the old ways are not always the best.'

A heavy silence fell, for no one knew what to say in the light of such a desperately sad situation.

Ron clattered his cutlery on his empty plate. 'It strikes me that religion is the cause of too many troubles,' he said grumpily. 'And we'd all be better off without it.'

'I take it things didn't go too well with Father O'Leary,' Peggy teased.

'We had our usual exchange of opinions, so we did,' he replied sourly. 'I'm thinking he gets lonely stuck out there and is enjoying making me life a misery. To be sure, he can argue the legs off a table given half the chance.'

'He's not the only one,' Peggy replied, trying not to laugh. 'Especially if there's whisky involved,' she added with a glint in her eye.

'Oh, aye, we might have had a drop or two,' he conceded. 'To help oil the wheels so to speak – but the man still talks a lot of drivel if you ask me.'

'So you'll be going to Mass from now on?' Peggy continued. 'That'll be nice. We can walk up there together for the early service on Sunday mornings.'

Ron glared at her and heaved himself out of the kitchen chair. 'Don't be counting your chickens just yet,' he rumbled. 'There's time enough for all that palaver – for now I'm taking Monty home to Rosie.'

Peggy eyed him sharply. 'You're not having second thoughts, are you, Ron?'

'If I am, then you'll hear about it soon enough,' he muttered.

'But you can't let Rosie down,' she gasped. 'You know how much store she's set on having a church wedding.'

'Aye, and that's the rub,' he said on a deep sigh. 'Leave it be, Peggy. Me head's pounding with it all, and I'm in no mood to be answering any more questions on the subject.' He grabbed his army issue greatcoat he'd kept after the First World War and dragged it on over his tweed jacket and smart trousers, his expression making it clear the conversation was at an end.

Peggy knew that when Ron was in this sort of mood she'd get nothing more out of him – but it was all very worrying. She could only pray that he wouldn't do or say anything to throw a spanner in the works when everything seemed to be going so smoothly after what could only have been called a roller-coaster courtship of many years.

She watched him pull his new tweed cap over his thick salt and pepper hair, and remembered she'd yet to tell him her news. 'Before you go there's something I need to tell you,' she said quickly.

He eyed her from beneath his brows, his bright blue eyes suspicious. 'Oh aye?'

Peggy met his gaze and told him about her new job. 'And before you say anything, Ronan Reilly, he's paying me six guineas a week.'

The blue eyes widened and there was a chorus of gasps from the others. 'Well now, that's a fine amount of money,' he replied, 'but what sort of hours is he expecting from you for that?'

'The same as always, although I might go in an hour earlier than usual once we get busy,' she admitted. 'It's a godsend, Ron, and will more than make up for the rent I'll be losing when you move out.'

He nodded thoughtfully. 'Aye, that it certainly will. I was worrying you'd be left short.'

'I'm concerned that you're trying to do too much,' said Fran. 'I'm sure Robert and I can pay a bit more rent if that would help.'

'You're paying quite enough,' said Peggy firmly. 'And I'm looking forward to doing more at the factory, so don't worry on my behalf.'

Sarah, who'd remained silent throughout all this, leaned forward and took Peggy's hand. 'It's wonderful news, Peggy, and we're all delighted for you.'

'I know it's asking a bit much to expect you to help about the place and so on, but with Jim and the rest of the family away, I'd go mad sitting about here doing nothing.'

'Hmph,' snorted Ivy. 'Chance'd be a fine thing. You're never still.'

'We'll help out whenever we can, you know that,' said Rita, 'but what will you do when this war finally ends? Will you carry on working?'

Peggy shrugged. 'I have no idea,' she replied, 'but once I get used to earning that much money, I doubt I'll give it up in a hurry.'

'Jim won't like it,' said Cordelia.

'He's not in a position to have an opinion,' said Peggy with rather more defiance than she actually felt. 'He and I will discuss all that when he comes home,' she added firmly, thereby bringing the subject to a close.

Rosie had spent the afternoon with the dressmaker having a second fitting for her wedding outfit, and she'd returned to the Anchor with a gorgeous hat she'd purchased in Plummer's department store that would complete the outfit perfectly.

She ran up the stairs to her rooms above the Anchor, rather surprised to find no sign of Ron or Monty – which meant that either Ron was still at the church or he'd taken Monty home to Beach View whilst he fixed Peggy's leaking pipe. Whichever was the case, she was quite glad to have the place to herself, for she was eager to try on her hat again.

Shedding her coat and scarf, she hurried into the bedroom and opened the hatbox to carefully draw out the scrumptious confection of velvet, lace and net. It was half a hat, really, and had cost her a whole guinea, but as she regarded her reflection in the mirror, she knew it was worth every brass farthing.

The broad, dark blue band of velvet sat perfectly over her crown amid the curls and waves of her platinum hair; the clusters of pale blue lace rosettes on either side lifting it out of the ordinary – as did the delicate, bird-cage netting which veiled her face and added a touch of mystery and glamour. 'Perfect,' she breathed. 'Just perfect.'

Rosie had taken great care in choosing what she'd wear for her big day, for she was in her early fifties and it was an awkward age for any woman – especially one who was about to walk down the aisle. There was always the danger of overdoing things and ending up looking like mutton dressed as lamb, but on the other hand she had a real dread of turning into a frump.

She put the hat back in its box and stowed it away on top of the wardrobe in the spare room. Today's fitting had pleased her, for the pale blue jersey dress and coat bridged the gap between mutton and frump, and with her white fox fur stole and the new hat, she'd be a sophisticated and very glamorous bride. Ron couldn't fail to be impressed, and she could barely contain her excitement at the thought.

Returning to her kitchen, she discovered she had enough time to make a cup of tea before she had to open up for the evening session, so she put the kettle on and went to get changed into the black skirt and white blouse she always wore behind the bar. She had two identical skirts and blouses which had become her uniform over the years, and although they were definitely showing their age now, they saved her good clothes from getting spoiled from beer splatters and the general wear and tear of running a busy pub.

She made the tea and went into the sitting room to stand by the window to drink it. It was after five-thirty, but Camden Road was still busy with straggling queues of last-minute shoppers hoping to find anything useful or edible from the sadly depleted shop shelves. A cluster of children were kicking a can about with noisy enthusiasm in the road, and a large ginger tom was sitting hopefully outside Fred the Fish's shop, tail twitching in anticipation that Fred would relent for once and throw him a morsel – which was most unlikely, for the housewives wasted nothing these days and everything went into the pot to make stock or soup.

Rosie sipped her tea and her thoughts turned to Ron. She'd been glad to have the distraction of going to the dressmaker this afternoon, for she'd been fretting over how he was getting on with Father O'Leary. The two men had never seen eye to eye when it came to religion, but there was a certain mutual respect that made them enjoy each other's company, even if it did often descend into heated debate. Rosie suspected they'd reached a compromise by accepting that they'd never agree on the subject, and as the whisky went down, so did the heat in the arguments.

Rosie's smile was soft as she thought about her darling Ron. They'd had more than their fair share of ups and downs over the years, and although he could be maddening at times with his habit of going his own way, and disappearing for hours without explanation, she'd never stopped loving him. He'd proved that he was deadly serious about wanting to marry her, by smartening up his appearance and taking her out and about like a proper suitor, but she had been very surprised when he'd agreed with hardly a murmur to a church wedding.

She finished the tea, checked the time and lit a cigarette, her thoughts suddenly and unexpectedly troubled. Ron had never been a religious man, and having heard something of what he'd been through in the trenches, she could understand why. And yet, he was willing to go through the service because it was what she wanted.

A cold rush of realisation washed over her. She'd been so caught up in the excitement of planning the wedding she'd dreamed of for so long, that she'd lost sight of what she was asking of Ron. He might have agreed to it all, but was he really happy to play along with the charade? And that's what it would be, for he didn't possess a religious bone in his body, and although the vows he made would come from his heart, the rest of the ceremony would be meaningless to him.

Rosie sat down with a thump. Ron had certainly been rather quiet of late, but she'd put that down to him being a bit grumpy at having to decorate these rooms, put up sheds in the back garden for his ferrets and his clutter, and see to all the repairs at Beach View. But what if he was regretting his decision to go along with her plans, and didn't know how to tell her?

She tried to get to the bottom of her own feelings on the matter. The dream of marrying Ron in a church filled with beautiful music and the aroma of incense and flowers had been with her for so long that she'd never considered the alternative. Her Catholic upbringing had certainly coloured her life, but it hadn't ruled it, and as the years had gone on, she'd let things slide. She didn't go to church very often, couldn't remember the last time she'd made her confession, and no longer felt she was worthy of taking communion. So why on earth had she been so adamant about getting married at St Cuthbert's?

Her troubled thoughts were shattered by heavy rapping on the pub door as the mantel clock struck six.

She stubbed out her cigarette and ran down the stairs to open up. Plastering on a smile to hide the turmoil in her heart and mind, she welcomed the group of impatient factory girls, took the towels off the pumps and began to pull pints. She and Ron needed to have a serious talk before their wedding plans went any further.

Ron couldn't face Rosie yet, so instead of going to the Anchor, he took the dogs for another walk in the hills in the hope that the exercise and cold air would clear his mind and bring him some sort of peace.

Harvey and Monty were delighted at this unexpected treat and shot off to hunt rabbits, whilst Ron settled down on a fallen beam in the ruined farmhouse and stared out at the darkening landscape, his heart heavy, his thoughts in a whirl. He was barely aware of the RAF planes going overhead, or the booms and crumps as yet more V-2s exploded somewhere to the north and shook the very earth beneath his feet despite being so far away. He watched the orange glow of fires suddenly light up the black sky and looked away, unable to bear the thought of more lives lost to this endless bloody war.

He lost track of time as he wrestled with his conscience and watched the sickle moon rise serenely over the water to drift towards the apex of the black sky which was filled with stars, the sweep of the Milky Way like a vast, silvery brushstroke above the silent land. This was his cathedral, more magnificent than any church made by man, and it instilled in him a sense of awe at how immense it was, and how small and insignificant his troubles were compared to what was going on in the world.

Ron's inbuilt clock eventually warned him it was getting late, so he got to his feet, whistled up the tired dogs and headed back down the hill. He dropped Harvey off at Beach View, and with no explanation for a startled Peggy, reluctantly continued on his way with Monty to Camden Road and the Anchor.

His heart was heavy, his mood dour as he reluctantly approached the pub, for he knew that before the night was over, he could very well find himself without the woman he loved so dearly, the future they'd planned shattered forever.

Closing time had come and gone, but to Monty's confusion, Ron didn't go straight in, but remained in the shadows to watch Rosie through the diamond-paned window as she moved with her usual sinuous grace behind the bar to clear the dirty glasses and wipe down the counter.

Her platinum hair gleamed like a halo in the soft light above the bar, her neat hourglass figure enhanced by the tight skirt and white frilly blouse that gave tantalising glimpses of the curve of her peachy breasts. Rosie was like a film star to his mind and he adored the bones of her – had waited for years to make her his own – so why couldn't he just go ahead with this wedding and be done with it?

It was a rhetorical question, for he knew the answer – had been plagued by it ever since they'd booked the church – and if he didn't do something about it now, he'd never be at peace. He moved from the window and took a deep breath before he went into the pub by the side door.

Rosie had decided during the busy evening that she'd see how the land lay with Ron before she said anything, for it had suddenly – and rather shockingly – occurred to her that it might not be the church he was being moody about, but the actual fact of getting married. If he was getting cold feet, then she had no idea how she'd cope.

Hearing the side door slam and the scamper of Monty's claws on the bare stairs as he raced to his bowl of food, she forced a smile and turned to greet Ron who was looking decidedly disgruntled – which was not a good sign.

'Well, it's about time you got back,' she teased, kissing him on the cheek. 'I thought you and Father O'Leary were either making a night of it, or murdering one another.'

'We had a few drams, to be sure,' he confessed. 'And although there are times I'd like to strangle him, the old divil was still alive when I left.'

'I'm glad to hear it,' she said, regarding him more intently for any sign of what he might be thinking. 'So who won the debate this time?'

''Twas no battle, Rosie,' he said gloomily. 'He thinks he has me where he wants me and I let him believe it – but to be sure, it's a hollow victory on both sides.'

Rosie frowned and folded her arms. 'You're talking in riddles, Ron. Just what happened between you today?'

'Rosie,' he began, his expression very serious as he reached for her hands. 'Rosie, let's turn off the lights and go upstairs where we can talk properly.'

Her heart skipped a beat and a cold trickle of dread slithered down her spine. 'We can talk down here just as well,' she said, rooted to the spot.

'This is no place for what I have to say, Rosie,' he said, his face creased with anxiety. 'Please, wee girl, do as I ask.'

Rosie could scarcely breathe. 'You're frightening me, Ron,' she managed. 'What is it you're trying to tell me?'

Without replying, Ron stepped past her and switched off the light above the bar, then steered her towards the narrow hallway and the stairs leading up to the apartment.

Rosie's legs were threatening to give way as she climbed the stairs, and her hands trembled as she switched on the light and quickly drew the curtains. Was this the end? Did he really mean to call off their wedding? His expression certainly boded ill – but perhaps it was something entirely different, she thought with a surge of hope – after all, her own focus had been centred on the wedding, so it was logical she'd jump to the conclusion that his had too.

Impatient with her swirling thoughts and heart-sick with anxiety, she kicked off her high heels, took a breath for courage, and turned to face him. 'Has something happened to one of the family?'

Ron reached for her hand, kissed the palm and held it to his heart. 'Nothing like that,' he said, his voice rough with emotion as he avoided looking into her eyes. 'But to be sure, what I have to say will not be easy for you to hear, Rosie.'

Her heart thudded as she snatched back her hand and folded her arms tightly about her waist. 'Then you'd better get on and say it,' she said, lifting her chin, determined to be brave and keep her emotions in check.

'I can't marry you, Rosie – not ...' His voice broke with emotion.

'Why not?' she demanded, the pent-up anxiety making her temper flare. 'Is it because you can't face getting married to me – or just a general dislike for marriage in particular?'

He opened his mouth to reply but the stresses and strain of the past few hours meant she was too fired up to stop now. 'Is there someone else?' she stormed. 'Have you been cheating on me, Ronan Reilly? Because, if you have, I'll kill you!'

'No, no,' he cried. 'That's not it at all. What I meant was, I can't marry you in that church.'

She stared at him, the fury abating as swiftly as it had risen. She expected to feel relief, but instead she was overwhelmed by a burning desire to get her own back on him for frightening her so badly. 'But you swore to me you were happy to go through with a church ceremony.'

'I know I did,' he said, 'but I realised today that my conscience won't let me.' He seemed to sense that this was not the moment to approach or touch her, so kept his distance. 'It's hypocritical when it all means nothing to me, and as much as I adore and cherish you, I cannot go through with it.'

Rosie regarded him for a long, silent moment and then, to play for more time, went to the side table to mix a large gin and tonic. She continued to say nothing as her mind raced and she battled against the need to punish him for giving her such an awful scare, and not being man enough to have told her sooner. She gulped down half of the strong drink. 'You married Mary in that church, so why not me?' she asked finally.

'Because when I married Mary I was little more than a callow youth who was already having doubts about God and the Church and the part it was supposed to play in my life,' he replied. 'But Mary was already in the family way and a church wedding was what everyone expected of us, so I went along with it to keep the peace and make Mary happy.'

Rosie felt a stab of jealousy which she dismissed instantly as unfair and indecent. 'So why can't you do it again for me?'

'Because I'd be living a lie. I'd be spouting prayers to a God I can't believe in, in a church where I no longer belong, in front of a priest who can see into my soul and knows me for the unrepentant sinner that I am.'

Rosie felt her heart melt with love at this raw honesty, but she wasn't finished with him quite yet. She turned to face him, the drink forgotten in the need to see the truth in his eyes when she asked him the question that had plagued her since this afternoon. 'Is it really the church service you can't face, or the thought of getting married again that's brought you to this moment?' she asked.

'Oh, Rosie,' he groaned. 'How can you even think that of me? I'd marry you in a heartbeat. It's what I've longed for ever since we got together. Please don't ever doubt the feelings I have for you.'

She wanted to feel his arms about her, to tell him that she'd suspected his reluctance and was ready to accept it. But a quirk in her character wouldn't let her.

'You should have said something before we booked the church,' she said. 'I knew you were only agreeing to it to please me, but I had no idea you felt so strongly. Didn't you trust me to understand?'

'I could see how set on it you were and didn't want to spoil things,' he admitted. 'But as time went on I felt more uneasy about it, and then today with Father O'Leary I realised the whole thing was turning me into a liar. And that's not the way I can live, Rosie.'

Rosie saw the anguish in him as he hung his head and couldn't bear it any longer. She reached out to him and lightly lifted his chin until he was looking at her again. 'We said back in the summer that there would be no more secrets between us,' she reminded him softly. 'And yet you've kept this to yourself for weeks. Why today, Ron? Why tell me now when the banns are about to be read and all the arrangements are in full swing?'

He clung to her hands like a drowning man. 'I thought I could ignore the doubts and silence the voice of my conscience, but it got louder, the doubts multiplied, and as much as I love you and want to give you everything you desire, I simply couldn't live that lie.'

He pulled her towards him. 'Do you still love me, Rosie? Please say you love me and want to marry me even though I've let you down so badly.'

Rosie's heart swelled with such love she thought it would burst. She held him close. 'Of course I do, you silly man,' she murmured, the tears rolling down her face. 'And if the only way we can get married is in the registry office, then so be it.'

She pulled back from him and saw that his eyes were brimming too. 'But you'd better see to it that there's music and flowers and the whole kit and caboodle.'

Ron drew her back to him and kissed her passionately. Then he swung her into his arms and carried her into the bedroom until they were standing by the uncurtained window. 'I'd give you the moon if I could,' he murmured against her damp cheek, 'but for now you'll just have to make do with those stars.'

Rosie looked out to the crescent moon and diamond-studded sky and knew then that it didn't matter where they got married, for as long as they had each other, they possessed the world and were complete.

3

Peggy's older sister, Doris, was also looking up at the stars. It was almost midnight, but the letter that had been delivered by hand today had disturbed her to the point where she was finding it impossible to sleep. Wrapped in a thick dressing gown and sheltered from the wind in a corner of the back garden of her rented bungalow, she sat on the bench Ron had made for her and wondered why she hadn't just destroyed the letter the moment she'd realised who'd sent it.

It had arrived at her home whilst she was at work in the factory estate office with her neighbour and friend, Colonel John White. Addressed in a bold, unfamiliar masculine hand, it contained a single page of expensive notepaper that bore the Chumley coat of arms. Shocked that Sir Walter was writing to her at all, she'd had to sit down to read it, and when she'd got to the end, she'd spent a long while wondering what had prompted it, and if it held some hidden agenda she'd yet to understand.

Doris reached into the dressing-gown pocket and drew the letter out to read again by the flickering light of the lantern that sat on the garden table.

It was quite brief and shockingly direct but, against her better judgement, she was intrigued by it.

My dear Mrs Williams,

I hope this finds you well and happily settled in your new home. I apologise for not writing earlier but felt it wouldn't be appropriate so soon after losing my dear wife and your own recent bereavement.

I have always admired you, Mrs Williams, not only for your stalwart help with all my late wife's charities, but for the gracious manner in which you have conducted yourself. Your absence has been sorely felt, not only by the good ladies of the charity committees, but by myself. To this end, I was wondering if you would do me the honour of having dinner with me at the Officers' Club this Saturday evening?

I await your reply in the hope we may renew our friendship and become better acquainted.

Most sincerely,
Walter Chumley, KBE

Doris returned the letter to the envelope and shoved it back into her pocket, her emotions mixed. Wally Chumley had a nerve. Did he expect her to jump at his invitation just because he had pots of money and a title, and was used to getting his own way? They'd been merely passing acquaintances when Lady Chumley was alive, and although he'd been kind to her on the day of the memorial service,

51

he had no right to assume that because they'd both been widowed, he could take liberties.

However, she couldn't help but be flattered by the invitation and the possibilities it opened up for revenge on those vicious women in Lady Aurelia's circle. What a coup it would be to be seen having dinner with him at the club. It would certainly ruffle feathers and stoke gossip, perhaps even cause some alarm amongst those who were angling to be the next Lady Chumley – and there were several of those, she was sure.

The thought made her smile, for they'd shown their true colours on the day of the memorial service for Lady Chumley and the women who'd died in the V-1 blast, making it all too plain with their sneering remarks and cold eyes that she wasn't, and never would be, a part of their elite set.

That day had been one of the worst in her life, but it had also been a revelation, and she'd turned her back on the lot of them, handed in her notice to the WVS and all the other committees she'd been on and set about making a new life for herself. She'd vowed then that she'd have nothing more to do with any of them – but this invitation had shaken her resolve.

Doris lit a cigarette, closed her ears to the RAF planes flying over, and contemplated the vast sweep of the Milky Way. Wally Chumley was a bit of a rough diamond who'd never quite shaken off his lowly beginnings as a miner's son, but, rather like Solly Goldman, had a good eye for the main chance and enough charm and gift of the gab to sell any-thing. He'd made his fortune in the First War by dealing in armaments, and was adding to his coffers in this one. Wally had been awarded his life peerage for services to his country, and his pomposity had grown along with his waistline as he'd settled into the smaller of Cliffehaven's two manor houses and taken up the reins of running the estate.

Doris knew that Wally yearned to be like Lord Cliffe whose family had owned Cliffe estate and most of the land on the eastern side of Cliffehaven for generations, the ancestral title handed down from father to son. Wally's title would die with him, and for all his money, he couldn't escape the fact he would never be classed as true landed gentry – and Doris suspected he found that a bitter pill to swallow.

She sat there in the brief lull between the planes taking off, enjoying the stillness of the night as she watched the moon slowly traverse the sky. The wind had dropped and despite the late hour it was very pleasant to sit out here and let her thoughts drift.

This year had been traumatic, changing her life beyond all recognition, but oddly enough bringing her a sense of peace she'd never known before. First had come the V-1 attack which had destroyed her beautiful detached house in Havelock Gardens, kill-ing Lady Chumley and some of her friends and leaving her with only the clothes she'd worn that day along with her mink coat and diamond ring.

Then within days had come the news of her estranged husband's death, and the devastating revelation that Ted had married again, borrowed against the house, and therefore wiped out any government compensation she might have been entitled to, as well as his generous monthly allowance.

Her shock and grief had been compounded by the cold reception of those women she'd once thought of as friends, and she'd been made to realise that she'd been chasing shadows in her pursuit of trying to be someone she was never meant to be. And in that respect she was rather like Wally, which didn't sit at all well.

Doris stubbed out her cigarette. She'd had harsh lessons to learn this year – not least, humility and a deeper understanding of the people she'd once looked down upon. If it hadn't been for her sister Peggy's love, and the support of Ron, Rosie and the girls at Beach View, she doubted she'd have coped.

She gave a sigh of contentment. Her work in the office was satisfying; her friendship with Colonel John White blossoming into something unexpected and really rather lovely, and she'd become closer to her sister Peggy than she'd ever thought possible. She still might not possess much in the material sense, but Rosie's bungalow had become her haven, and she'd discovered great joy in the mundane, everyday things like tending the garden under the watchful eye of Colonel White, and taking care of the second-hand furniture which now gleamed with polish.

The old Doris would have accepted the invitation with alacrity, seeing it as a chance to step up the social ladder, and perhaps even snare a title – but the new Doris was more circumspect. Chumley might be rich and titled, but he couldn't hold a candle to John White – not in his looks or his character. If she accepted the invitation to dinner she could be putting everything she now held dear in jeopardy – and yet she couldn't deny she was curious as to the reason behind that invitation.

Doris considered asking Peggy's advice, but knew in her heart what it would be. She certainly couldn't discuss it with John, and if young Ivy got wind of it, it would be all round the town in five minutes. There again, if she did go to dinner with Chumley, everyone would soon know about it and she'd have a lot of explaining to do. The Officers' Club was a favourite venue for some of the town's more well heeled, and that included John White. The thought of deceiving him made her feel quite ill, for he'd been so good to her and these past months had shown her how marvellous it was to have someone at her side who was unfailingly reliable and attentive.

The thought of John sleeping innocently in the bungalow next door while she dithered about Chumley's invitation made up her mind. She dug in her pocket for the letter, set it alight and watched it burn to nothing in the ashtray. Curiosity was a dangerous thing – especially when it involved men like Chumley, and although it would have brought some satisfaction to poke one in the eye of those women he surrounded himself with, she was not about to be drawn back into that vicious circle.

Doris blew out the candle in the lantern and went indoors, tired now, but with an easier mind, and ready for her bed.

She rose at her usual time the next morning and wrote a short note to Chumley, politely and very firmly turning down his invitation. Posting it on her way to work, she hoped that would be the end of any contact between them, and she could forget him.

Two evenings later there was a knock on the door, and thinking it was John coming earlier than usual for their nightcap after his game of billiards, she hurried to answer it.

A late middle-aged man with a lugubrious expression stood there in a chauffeur's uniform, an all-too familiar gleaming Rolls-Royce sitting at the kerb beyond the gate. He was carrying a basket of fruit the likes of which she hadn't seen for five years.

'With Sir Walter's compliments, Mrs Williams,' he intoned, holding the basket out to her.

Doris's mouth watered at the sight of the oranges, peaches, apricots and bananas which must have come from the manor's hothouses. The temptation to accept the gift was almost too much but she managed to resist. 'Please return them to Sir Walter,' she said stiffly.

He looked startled. 'But you won't see the like again,' he gasped.

Doris put on her most imperious voice. 'I have no wish to receive gifts from Sir Walter. Take them away.' She shut the door before he could protest further, thankful that John was still at the club and therefore hadn't witnessed that little scene. Yet she couldn't help regretting having to deny herself the pleasure of eating that gorgeous fruit.

The next day the chauffeur arrived in the teeming rain, armed with a large umbrella to shield himself and the enormous box of Fortnum and Mason's chocolates which was tied with silk ribbon and bore an envelope. Doris barely gave it all a glance before sending the sour-faced man on his way back to Chumley with a terse order to his employer not to bother her again.

Her message was ignored and the chauffeur duly arrived on the wet, blustery Thursday evening with a joint of ham. Doris gave him her most withering glare.

'Yeah, I know,' the man said wearily. 'You don't want it. There's some that'd be only too pleased to have such a thing.'

'Some might,' Doris snapped. 'I'm not one of them.' She slammed the door in his face and went into her sitting room to watch from behind the curtains as he drove the Rolls-Royce out of the cul-de-sac.

It was with great dismay that she saw other curtains being twitched. There was little doubt that speculation amongst her neighbours was growing over the regular appearance of that damned car which couldn't fail to be recognised as Chumley's. If this went on for much longer then John would get wind of it, and that was the last thing she wanted. But what to do about it? That was the rub.

Chumley was playing games – for she was sure he wasn't seriously trying to court her – but what was behind it? Was this all about him using his money and position to get her back to run about after those women and do all the hard work? If so, he'd discover he'd chosen the wrong woman, she thought crossly.

But it had got to the point where it was becoming intrusive, and even a little sinister. All she could really do was hope that once it became clear to him she wouldn't be turning up for dinner on Saturday night, he'd admit defeat and leave her alone.

To her great relief, there was no sign of the chauffeur on Friday night, and Doris was able to sleep through for the first time all week.

It had rained solidly for days and was still hammering down as Doris left the bungalow early that Saturday morning. She'd received a letter from her son, Anthony, in the first post and was looking forward to reading it once she'd prepared the office for the day's work.

Having shaken the worst of the rain from her umbrella and coat, she set about giving everything a good dust, switched on the two-bar electric fire, sharpened the pencils, put the kettle on for tea and checked that the morning's post was ready for John to go through. She was feeling a bit on edge, despite the fact there had been nothing from Chumley the night before, and she'd slept well. She could only hope that once today was over, things would return to normal.

There was still time to spare before John was due to come in, so she sat down and eagerly opened Anthony's letter. To her joy, it contained photographs of Teddy, her beloved grandson, who was growing fast and changing into a really handsome little boy. Doris pored over the snapshots with longing, and then read what Anthony had to say.

It seemed his wife, Suzy, had gone back to nursing, and Teddy was being looked after in the hospital crèche – which Doris certainly didn't approve of, for she firmly believed that mothers should stay at home with their children. But then Suzy had always been wilful, and Doris had found it very difficult to get on with her, especially as Anthony was so deeply in her thrall he took her side in everything. The days when Doris had any influence over him were long past, and the knowledge was rather galling.

Anthony was working flat out with the MOD, but of course couldn't say what he was actually doing, and with Suzy working too, it seemed they had little spare time to make the journey down to Cliffehaven to visit her – but there was no invitation for her to visit them, she noted sadly.

She tucked the letter back into her handbag, accepting that they all had busy lives, and until this war was over, she'd have to be content with letters, photographs and the occasional telephone call.

'Good morning, Mrs Williams,' said John White cheerfully as he came through the door moments later.

Doris smiled back at him, delighting as always in his cultured voice and gentlemanly manner. 'Good morning, Colonel,' she replied, keeping to their agreement to remain formal whilst in the office. 'There's some correspondence to see to before you have your meeting with the security personnel, but there's plenty of time to have a cup of tea and get warm first.'

His handsome face lit up in a smile which made his eyes a brighter blue. 'Thank you, dear lady,' he said quietly, shedding his wet coat and umbrella. 'You must have read my mind.'

They sat in companionable silence to drink their tea, and then went through the correspondence and the endless memos that had been delivered to the office from the various factory managers. Doris took dictation, and when he'd left to attend the meeting, she typed the letters and put them on his desk to be signed on his return.

She busied herself by making more tea and stood at the office window to watch the rain pouring down. She saw Peggy hurrying away with Daisy from the Red Cross Distribution Centre to join Kitty and Charlotte, but they were too far away to be called, and none of them looked up so she didn't wave.

Peggy never liked to disturb Doris when she was working, and seeing that the office light was on, she didn't call in after her voluntary shift at the Red Cross Distribution Centre, but accompanied Kitty and Charlotte to their little cottage in Briar Lane. They'd been working in different areas of the vast centre this morning and hadn't been able to catch up, and as it was such a miserable day, she was looking forward to spending some time with them and their darling babies before she had to walk home to Beach View.

Both girls had been in the ATA, delivering planes of every size and type from the factories and repair shops to the airfields, but when Kitty had lost part of one leg following a nasty crash, she'd spent a long time at the Memorial Hospital learning to walk again on her prosthesis. Peggy had come to know and admire her during those stressful weeks, for the girl's courage had never faltered, and when she'd been discharged from the hospital, Peggy had taken her home to Beach View where she'd become an intrinsic part of the family.

Kitty's romance with Peggy's son-in-law's wing-man, Roger Makepeace, had blossomed, and following their wedding ceremony in the chapel at Cliffe aerodrome, she'd climbed into the Oxford plane, taken the controls and flown them both off for their honeymoon in the Lake District.

Charlotte had continued flying throughout, and had married Kitty's charming rogue of a brother, Freddy. Once both girls discovered they were pregnant, the four of them had bought Briar Cottage, which stood at the end of a rutted lane to the north of Cliffehaven. It was a tiny, long-abandoned cottage which had taken weeks to repair, extend and make habitable. Now it looked cosy beneath its newly thatched roof and trailing wisteria, the sprawling back garden a riot of vegetables and fruit trees.

Peggy hitched Daisy onto her hip to keep her out of the puddles as the girls negotiated their large, well-sprung prams over the mud and deep ruts. The three babies were fast asleep and snug beneath their blankets, and everyone was eager to get indoors out of the rain.

The cottage was kept warm by a range in the kitchen, and once the prams were stowed in the large new extension that ran along the back of the cottage, the babies were left to sleep whilst wet coats and umbrellas were shed, tea was brewed and soup heated through for lunch.

Daisy was fascinated by the babies – especially the twins, David and Hope, who lay top to tail in the pram – and was trying to clamber up to watch them. Peggy stopped her from jolting the pram and lifted her up so she could see without disturbing them.

Charlotte's twins had Freddy's thick black hair, dark eyes and light olive skin – but if they'd also inherited their father's lust for life and strong will, then poor Charlotte was in for a rough ride. Kitty's little Faith had a shock of brown hair, her skin was pale and her eyes were a shade of blue that was almost violet. She would be a heartbreaker when she was older – rather like her mother.

Peggy joined the girls at the kitchen table, settling Daisy down with a cup of milky tea and a picture book until the soup was ready. 'I take it neither of you have heard any more from Freddy or Roger?' she said.

Charlotte grimaced whilst she stirred the soup. 'Kitty got a couple of letters, but they were so heavily censored they were almost impossible to fathom. As far as we know, Freddy is still in a POW camp somewhere near the Polish border with your Cissy's American flier. I can only pray that the pair of them have given up trying to escape, because there's a very real danger they'll get shot now the Germans have their backs to the wall.'

'Cissy telephoned from the airfield last night, and there's been no word from Randy since he's been moved there,' said Peggy, 'so it seems the tighter security at that camp means they've no choice but to behave.'

'We've heard nothing from the Red Cross,' said Kitty, 'so I have to assume Roger's still with Martin and the others.' She regarded Peggy across the table. 'I don't suppose your Anne's heard anything to the contrary?'

Peggy shook her head. 'She's said nothing in her letters, and I'm sure that if she had heard anything new about Martin, she'd ring and tell me.'

'What about your Jim?' asked Kitty, slicing up the loaf of wheatmeal bread. 'Is he on the mend?'

'He seems to be,' she replied, taking the steaming bowls of soup from Charlotte. 'He's writing more regularly now, and says he's enjoying being fussed over by all those Australian nurses.' Her smile was wry. 'But that's typical of my Jim. He always did enjoy being the centre of attention – especially when it comes from a bunch of young women in nurses' uniforms.'

She blew on Daisy's soup and handed her a spoon, warning her to take care. 'But I dread the day he's sent back to his regiment,' she confessed. 'Which is rather wicked considering it will mean he's fit and healthy again.'

'Understandable, though,' murmured Kitty, squeezing her hand in sympathy.

A heavy silence fell as they drank the delicious vegetable soup and became immersed in their own thoughts. Peggy could just imagine Jim lapping up all the attention while he enjoyed sitting on that veranda in the Indian sunshine, far from the noise and dangers of war. Of course she wanted him to recover, and was eternally thankful that he hadn't been as badly hurt as his friend Ernie, whose spinal injury meant he would never walk again.

Peggy didn't know why Jim blamed himself for Ernie's plight – he hadn't gone into any detail in his letters – but she knew it preyed on his mind, and wished there was something she could do or say to ease that worry. But apart from writing most days, sending snippets of news from the local papers and enclosing photographs of Daisy, there was nothing she could do. Distance and the lack of any real communication was the reality of this war which had scattered loved ones to the four corners of the world, and those that were left behind just had to keep faith that the family ties were strong enough to weather the separation.

As if to remind them that life went on regardless of what was happening beyond these four walls, Faith started crying, soon to be followed by loud demands from David and Hope.

Once nappies had been changed, Kitty put Faith to her breast, and as Charlotte didn't have enough milk to feed both twins, bottles were warmed and peace was restored.

Peggy took little Hope into her arms to feed her, and her heart swelled as long dark lashes feathered against sweet cheeks, and little hands tried to grasp the bottle. She was so like Daisy had been at this age, but as she smiled at her little girl who was leaning against her knee watching the baby feed, she couldn't help noticing how much she'd grown. Daisy's features were losing their baby softness and becoming stronger; her eyes and hair dark, her little nose straight like Jim's, the set of her chin rather too determined at times which betrayed a strong will. And yet she could be so charming, with her big eyes and winning smile. There was no doubting she was Jim's child, for they shared the gift of knowing how to get their way.

Peggy finished feeding Hope, held her against her shoulder to wind her, and then enjoyed a few minutes of cuddles as Daisy cooed and stroked her tiny feet and hands.

'By the way,' she said once the babies were asleep and in their prams again, 'Ron and Rosie have decided to hold their wedding at the Town Hall. It's the same date, as Rosie needs time to get things ready for the big day.' She gathered Daisy onto her lap. 'And Daisy is going to be a bridesmaid, so I've got material to find and some sewing to do.'

'I'm sure Ron's relieved,' said Kitty with a glint of humour in her blue eyes. 'He never struck me as someone who felt easy in a church. And talking of sewing, are you getting nervous about taking on that new position at Solly's?'

'A bit,' Peggy confessed. 'There are one or two women there who might take umbrage over my promotion. They've been there for years and will probably think they should have got it.'

'Solly had his reasons for picking you over them,' said Charlotte. 'I shouldn't let their jealousy get to you.'

'I'll try not to, but the first week or two could be tricky. Winnie Holman and Gladys Bright are a force to be reckoned with if you get on the wrong side of them. I'll have to watch my back.'

'I'm sure you'll cope admirably,' said Kitty. 'I remember when I was flying there was a girl who was always sniping at me for no real reason, and I found that if I just kept on smiling and ignoring what she said, she soon got tired of it and gave up.'

'Do you miss flying?' asked Peggy.

'Yes,' the girls chorused before sharing a chuckle. 'We'd both love to be back in the air, but now we have our babies, it's out of the question,' said Charlotte.

'That doesn't mean we've given up on the idea completely, though,' said Kitty. 'Once Roger and Freddy and the others come home, we thought we might start up our own charter business – delivering people and goods all over the country. With four fliers in the house, we can take it in turns to mind the children and do the runs. It seems too silly for all of us to be grounded, and the men will need something to do to keep them out of mischief once they get back – especially Freddy.'

'Goodness,' breathed Peggy. 'What a very exciting idea. But won't it be expensive to set up?'

'Probably,' said Kitty on a laugh, 'but there are bound to be unwanted aircraft lying about once this war's over, and I wouldn't mind betting we could find some bargains. We'd start with one plane and see how we go, but the plan is to have a small fleet eventually, and to take on more pilots.'

Peggy's smile was warm with affection as she hugged each girl in turn. 'Well, I wish you all the luck in the world,' she said. 'But for now, I'd better get home. Ivy's in charge of tea, and if I don't keep an eye on her, she'll burn it to a cinder.'

The Colonel returned after an hour, and having signed the letters, he sat back in his chair and regarded Doris with some concern. 'I don't wish to pry, Mrs Williams,' he began tentatively, 'but you've seemed rather distracted these past few days. Is something troubling you?'

Doris was startled by his astuteness, for she'd thought she'd hidden her concern over Chumley rather well. 'It's this war,' she said lightly. 'There seems to be no end to it, and it's getting rather wearing.'

His gaze remained steady. 'It's tiring us all,' he murmured. 'But now Rommel's committed suicide and the Allies have liberated Athens, things are improving by the day.'

'You're right, of course, but this weather doesn't help lift the spirits much.'

'It certainly doesn't,' he replied, staring gloomily out of the window to the damp and dreary sprawl of grey factory roofs beneath the leaden skies. 'Perhaps we should cheer ourselves up by having dinner at the club tonight?' he said. 'There's a rumour the chef will be cooking roast beef with all the trimmings.'

Doris felt a stab of alarm that even the temptation of roast beef couldn't quell. 'That sounds heavenly, but I can't, I'm afraid,' she said rather too quickly. 'I promised to have supper with my sister Peggy tonight.'

'Oh, that is a shame,' he murmured. 'Another evening then?'

Doris nodded, feeling the colour rising in her face at the lie she'd told him. 'I look forward to it,' she replied, turning her attention to the pile of invoices. 'Until then, we have these to go through for the government auditors who'll be coming on Monday,' she said briskly.

They worked through the rest of the afternoon and it was almost five o'clock by the time they left the office. The Colonel offered his arm and they shared his large umbrella as they walked through the factory estate and past the guard at the gate.

There was an uneasy silence between them for once, and to break it, Doris pointed to the building works going on to restore the dairy which had been flattened some months ago by a doodlebug. 'It looks as if Mr Jenkins will have his dairy up and running properly again soon,' she chattered. 'It must have been an awful bind having to milk his cows by hand every day.'

'I suppose it must,' he murmured, clearly not that interested in the Welshman or his dairy.

Doris wasn't looking where she was going and stepped in a puddle. 'Damn and blast it,' she muttered crossly as icy water splashed her good stockings and soaked through her best shoes.

The Colonel came to a halt and turned to face her. 'Are you sure there's nothing bothering you, Doris?' he asked. 'Only you seem very out of sorts.'

'I'm fine, really,' she retorted sharply. 'Please don't fuss.'

He regarded her questioningly.

'Sorry,' she said, realising she'd been rather abrupt. 'It's just that these are my best shoes and stockings, and this rain is really getting on my nerves.'

He said nothing, merely tucked her hand more firmly into the crook of his arm and set off again, but Doris could tell that he was puzzled by her edginess.

They left Mafeking Terrace and began the steep descent into Ladysmith Close. The view of the town and the Channel was lost in the low cloud and sweeping curtains of rain which came in from the east – but nothing could mask the sight of the distinctive Rolls-Royce which was parked outside Doris's bungalow.

'I say,' murmured John. 'Isn't that Chumley's Rolls? I wonder what it's doing here?'

'I can't imagine.' Doris felt like a rabbit caught in the light of a poacher's lamp, but somehow managed to keep walking, praying all the while that the chauffeur would drive away as she was with John.

But the Rolls-Royce stayed where it was, and as they approached, the chauffeur leapt out, opened an umbrella and the back door.

Doris thought her heart would stop as Walter Chumley emerged armed with an enormous bunch of hothouse flowers.

'What's all this?' murmured John.

'Nothing. It's nothing,' she managed. 'Just ignore him.'

But Wally Chumley was not a man to be ignored. He stood beneath the umbrella and blocked their way. 'Mrs Williams, at last,' he boomed. 'You are a difficult lady to please, so I thought I'd bring you these in the hope they'd brighten this gloomy day before we go to dinner.'

Doris felt John tense, was aware of his confusion as he looked to her for an explanation, but her whole focus was on Chumley. 'I'm not coming to dinner,' she blustered. 'Not tonight, or any other night.'

Chumley blatantly ignored John and thrust the flowers at Doris. 'Lovely flowers for a lovely lady,' he said with what he clearly thought was a winning smile. 'I do enjoy the cut and thrust of the chase, Mrs Williams, and although I'm disappointed that you'll not be dining with me tonight, I'm sure we'll see each other again very soon.'

Doris clutched the flowers to her bosom as he doffed his hat, climbed into the car and was driven off. She was almost numb with shock at his audacity, and unable to think or even speak.

'I understand now why you couldn't have dinner with me tonight,' John said gruffly. 'I didn't realise Chumley was on the scene.'

'He's *not* on the scene,' she snapped, completely unnerved. 'Never has been.'

'But this isn't the first time his car has been seen outside your door,' said John, holding her gaze. 'What's going on, Doris?'

She swallowed and tried desperately to get her thoughts in order and her panic under control. 'Absolutely nothing on my part, I assure you. Suffice it to say, Chumley has been pursuing me for some reason and sending me unwanted gifts to try and bribe me into having dinner with him. I've turned him down flat, having no wish to get involved with him or his silly games.'

'I see,' he said softly, his steady gaze fixed upon her. 'So you weren't lying to me about having supper with Peggy tonight?'

Doris swallowed, and looked away. 'No … well, yes, I was, but I …'

'There's no need to explain,' he said sadly. He tipped his hat to her. 'I'll see you in the office on Monday.'

Doris stood in the rain clutching the flowers as John turned and walked swiftly up his garden path, taking the umbrella with him. The door closed behind him and the only sound in the street was the splatter of raindrops on the pavement and the chatter of the wind through the remaining leaves on the trees.

Suddenly aware that everything was being eagerly watched from behind nearby curtains, she dug her key out of her coat pocket and ran indoors.

Once the door was closed behind her, she let the flowers drop to the floor and burst into tears of anger, shame and frustration. Everything was ruined, and John would never believe a word she said from now on – and all because that bastard Chumley wouldn't take no for an answer.

Eventually she stopped crying and dragged off her sodden coat and headscarf. Furious with herself for letting Chumley get under her skin and reduce her to tears, she picked up the soggy flowers which had been crushed and broken during the exchange, and threw them out in the general direction of the compost heap.

Feeling much calmer, she made a cup of tea and sat down at the kitchen table to think about how she could convince John that she wasn't a liar – that she'd only fibbed about Peggy because she hadn't wanted to go to the Officers' Club in case Chumley was there. And to work out why Chumley was pursuing her – once she knew that, she could find a way to put a stop to it.

4

The piece of shrapnel in Ron's back was giving him real gyp this Sunday morning, and he put it down to the cold, damp weather and the fact he really should remember he wasn't eighteen any more. Rosie weighed very little, but lifting her up like that did him no good at all – especially when followed by a night of enthusiastic lovemaking.

He'd left the Anchor whilst it was still dark so as not to set the gossips' tongues wagging, and had returned to Beach View for a hot bath in the hope it would ease the pain. However, one bathroom in a busy household could never be a haven of peace, and it wasn't long before Fran was urgently knocking on the door.

He emerged from the bathroom wrapped in his old dressing gown, muttered a good morning to Fran who was due to start her shift in the hospital theatre within the hour and made way for Cordelia as she came bustling out of her bedroom.

'What are you doing, lurking about here in a state of undress?' she demanded crossly.

'Waiting for you to get out of my way so I can get downstairs,' he replied. 'What's bitten you this morning? You're not usually this nice to me so early.'

Her expression was scathing. 'Sarcasm is the lowest form of wit, and the highest form of vulgarity,' she retorted.

'Ach, yes, Cordelia, but a smile costs nothing, and you're awful pretty when you smile,' he teased.

She swiped at his arm. 'Get away with you, you old scallywag,' she said, trying not to laugh. 'Soft words don't impress me.'

Cordelia headed for the stairlift contraption that Rita and Peter Ryan had built for her so she had the freedom to come and go about the house as she pleased. Picking up Queenie who'd taken to sitting on it every morning for a free ride, she tucked her onto her lap and strapped herself in. Pushing down the handle to engage the motor, she gave a regal wave of her walking stick and sailed slowly down the stairs to the hall, the cat sitting like a masthead on the good ship Cordelia.

Ron followed, admiring the engineering of the stairlift, and the huge benefit it had brought to Cordelia. He went down to his basement bedroom to get dressed in his oldest clothes, for after walking the dogs and visiting his son Frank, he would be giving the Anchor's chimney a good sweep before painting the ceiling in the bar. In between, he'd be visiting Father O'Leary, but he was trying not to think about that.

The rain had stopped, so after a breakfast of tea and toast, he left Beach View, and was soon tramping up the hill with the dogs haring ahead of him.

His back didn't like it and, unusually, he had to stop frequently to ease it before he could carry on.

He'd never given much thought to his age, and certainly never considered himself to be old, for he'd always been fit, the shrapnel a minor niggle he'd learned to live with. But today the shrapnel was really bothering him and he felt every one of his – how many years? He paused to add them up and was shocked to discover that he was sixty-seven.

'Bloody hell,' he muttered. 'I never thought I was that ancient. 'Tis no wonder I'm falling to pieces.' He squared his shoulders and strode out, determined not to let that unwelcome knowledge slow him down. He was about to get married to a lively and rather demanding, sensual woman – he'd have to look to his laurels if he was to continue to keep her happy.

At last he crested the hill and made his way across the flatter ground to the steep track that led down to Tamarisk Bay. There had once been a number of fishing boats beached on the shingle, but now there was only one, and the lobster pots and trawling nets lay idle beneath tarpaulins.

Three cottages nestled beneath the cliff, well above the high-tide mark, facing the arc of the tiny bay and the sharply sloping shingle beach. Two of them had been abandoned at the start of the war and were showing marked signs of neglect as the elements ate away at them, spiders weaved their webs across the mouldy windows, and wild ivy and brambles took over. The house on the end was in better shape, the wooden planking of the walls freshly painted, the roof, gutters and chimney in good repair and the windows neatly shuttered from the wind and rain – proof, if needed, that Frank had too much time on his hands.

Ron stood for a moment on the bank at the top of the rutted track where the tamarisk grew in abundance amid the long marram grass and sea sedge. This was the house his father had helped him buy just after Frank had been born, and where he'd raised him and his younger brother, Jim, after Mary had died. It held a lot of memories – not all of them good – and he'd gladly handed it over at a peppercorn rent to Frank on his marriage to Pauline, and moved in with Jim and Peggy at Beach View.

Yet, as his gaze trawled the beach which the army had declared too small to be mined, he could still remember the pleasure of foraging the shore for rock samphire, wild fennel, sea beet, lovage and spinach to eke out the meals when the catch had been poor. To the uneducated eye a shingle beach held only weeds, but to Ron it was a storehouse of nutritious vegetables – the rock pools a source of shellfish – and he knew Frank went foraging to this day.

The dogs raced ahead of him and he found Frank sitting in the wheelhouse of the last of the family's fishing boats staring out to sea. There was no sign of his moody and difficult wife, Pauline, which was a relief, for Ron found her tiresome in the extreme.

The shingle crunched beneath Ron's boots and Frank leaned out of his shelter to watch his approach as the dogs hurtled past him and into the shallows. 'Hello, Da. What brings you down here on a Sunday morning?' he boomed.

'To be sure, 'tis a lovely day and I needed to get away for a wee while.'

Frank grinned. 'Rosie finding you too many things to do, is she?'

'Aye, she is that,' replied Ron, clambering into the boat to sit beside him. 'If that's tea you've got brewing, I'd be glad of it,' he said, eyeing the spirit stove and whistling kettle.

Frank was still smiling as he poured the tea into two tin mugs and added generous slugs of whisky. 'To chase away the cold,' he said with a wink.

'Pauline's not here, then,' said Ron, returning the wink.

'She's gone to work for the morning,' Frank replied, 'so what she doesn't see won't hurt her.' He regarded his father with gentle pleasure. 'It's good to see you, Da.'

Ron took the tin mug and breathed in the aroma of whisky and good, strong, milkless tea as he regarded his eldest son with deep affection and pride. Frank was a big, handsome man of few words who'd just turned fifty. He had an expressive face and a thoughtful disposition which Pauline found infuriating, and Ron considered to be wise as he was married to the sort of woman who took umbrage at the slightest thing.

Frank had fought in the First War and done a couple of years' service in this one, and Ron knew he was finding it hard to settle down again now he was at a bit of a loose end, and had time to worry about his only surviving son, Brendon, who was with the fleet in the Mediterranean. The two other boys had lost their lives in the Atlantic on one of the family's large trawlers which had been requisitioned as a minesweeper – and their loss still cast a long shadow over everyone.

'How are things with you?' asked Ron, after taking a tentative sip of the scalding drink and burning his lips in the process.

'The same as always,' Frank rumbled. 'Pauline's still on edge over Brendon, but she's less fraught because that office job at the Red Cross place has given her something else to focus on, which can only be a good thing. We're rubbing along a bit better now we share our thoughts and talk things over.'

'That's good,' murmured Ron, thankful that his son was having a quieter, more settled life since Pauline's mother, Dolly, had come down for a visit. 'Dolly must have pulled her up short,' he added thoughtfully.

'Aye, Dolly saved our marriage. I don't know what she said to Pauline before she left, but it worked, and life has been a lot easier since.'

Ron's heart warmed at the thought of Dolly Cardew. She'd been a friend since he was a youth of thirteen or so, and had turned from tomboy into the most intriguing woman he was ever likely to meet. Always glamorous and vivacious, she seemed to breeze through life without a care – although he was privy to the heartache and regrets she'd suffered along the way. She was now in her sixties but could easily pass as someone at least a decade younger, and Ron knew that behind that sophisticated air of being rather empty-headed and frivolous, she possessed an extremely sharp mind, a keen eye and ear for detail, and a lethal knowledge of hand-to-hand combat and sabotage which she'd put to good use in both wars.

He glanced at his son surreptitiously, wondering how he and Pauline would react if they knew the truth about Dolly. Everyone in the family thought she'd retired from her office job in London to a flat in Bournemouth where she was ruffling feathers amongst the good ladies of the local WI – whereas, in fact, she was working for the Special Operations Executive which had been formed back in 1940.

The secrecy surrounding the work and the agents of the SOE was absolute, but Ron had performed similar covert missions in the First War and had learned of her involvement in that side of things during an unexpected meeting in France where they'd both been sent to sabotage a German communications centre.

This covert experience had led her to be recruited, and as he was also still involved in a very minor way, he knew that Dolly had played a key part in Danuta's recruitment and training for the dangerous missions behind enemy lines which had almost cost the girl her life – and had supplied the necessary paperwork to secure her the post as district nurse and assistant midwife once she'd recovered from the injuries that had been inflicted on her by the Gestapo.

Ron dragged his thoughts from the delectable Dolly and blew on his tea. The family would remain ignorant of the parts they'd played, for each of them had signed the Official Secrets Act – and he didn't mind at all that they all thought he was just a grumpy old man who told tall war stories, moaned about the shrapnel moving in his back to avoid work, and did his bit with the Home Guard – or Dad's Army as the wags called it.

He turned his attention back to his son who was gloomily staring out to sea. 'What about you, Frank? You look a bit down in the mouth, if you don't mind me saying so.'

Frank grimaced. 'I'm still waiting for the compensation to come through for all our boats that were requisitioned. I'm managing all right on what I earn at the tool factory, and Pauline's wages help – but I need to get back to sea where I belong.' He blew out his cheeks. 'You know what the government's like – they requisition your property quick enough with lots of promises, but are very slow to honour them.'

'It'll come eventually,' said Ron, blowing on the tea again before taking a tentative sip. 'And until this war's done with, and the fishing grounds and beaches are cleared of mines, there'll be no boats going out from Cliffehaven anyway.'

Frank gave a grunt of agreement and sat in silence for a while, his large hands cradling the mug as he watched the dogs dash in and out of the water.

'Brendon's been very good about writing home, so we know he's all right so far,' he murmured eventually. 'He and Betty got engaged during that short leave he had in Devon, so no doubt he'll be bringing her to meet us all when this lot's over – if it's ever over,' he added dourly.

'Aye, it's beginning to feel endless, that's for sure,' murmured Ron. He took another sip and then gave up on it to light his pipe. 'We'll just have to concentrate on the good things for now. Cordelia's birthday party is all organised at the golf club – Bertie Double-Barrelled has seen to that, so it'll be quite a bash.' He nudged Frank's arm. 'We'll have to be wearing our best bib and tucker for that one – the club's very posh and insists that men wear ties and jackets in the dining room.'

Frank grunted at this and Ron silently agreed that it was a bind, but one that had to be borne with dignity if they wanted a quiet life. 'Daisy will be three at the beginning of December and Peggy's talking about having a tea party at home with some of the other little ones from the factory crèche – so I'll be making meself scarce that day.'

He took a breath and hurried on. 'Then there's me wedding. Me and Rosie will be tying the knot at the Town Hall on the ninth of December. We've decided the church isn't for us.'

'Oh aye?' Frank regarded him evenly. 'You mean you chickened out and Rosie gave in,' he teased.

Ron grinned. 'Something like that. To be sure, she's a good wee girl, and I'm a lucky man to have her in me life.'

'That y'are,' said Frank, pulling out a tin of tobacco from his pocket to roll a cigarette. 'And what does Father O'Leary have to say about this change of plans?'

'I've yet to tell him,' Ron admitted. 'I'm going over there later, and to be sure, I'm not looking forward to it.'

'I'm surprised Rosie isn't going with you,' said Frank, cupping his hands around the match to light his cigarette.

'She thought it was best I did it, as me and the Father have a close understanding of things,' Ron replied airily.

Frank gave a bark of laughter. 'Don't give me that. You're both a couple of old divils who've never agreed on anything. Rosie's punishing you for mucking up her plans, more like, but I suspect he'll be glad not to have to perform the ceremony knowing what a heathen y'are, Da.'

'Aye, you could be right,' muttered Ron. 'To be sure, 'tis a relief I'll not be going through all that rigmarole, and that Rosie's been so understanding about it.' The tea had finally cooled enough to drink, so he raised the mug in a toast. 'Here's to weddings, birthdays and Christmas and the hope that 1945 will bring peace.'

Frank raised his mug in agreement. 'You always were an optimist, Da.'

Ron slowly drank the cooled tea, relishing the fire of the whisky warming him through and dulling the pain in his back. 'There's no point in being down in the mouth about things we have no control over,' he said. 'But I have to confess 'tis a worrying thing having to face Father O'Leary again. The wily old so-and-so will no doubt make me pay for spoiling his fun.'

Frank chuckled. 'Better that than going through something you know isn't right.' He eyed his father quizzically. 'It must have taken a lot of courage to tell Rosie.'

'Aye, it did. To be honest with you, son, I thought I would lose her.'

Frank nudged him with his shoulder. 'But you didn't, so everything turned out just right, didn't it?'

'Aye,' breathed a happy Ron, holding out his mug for more tea and whisky to give him courage to face the priest.

They sat in companionable silence as the dogs grew tired of their game and came to shake themselves dry before slumping in a panting heap by the side of the beached fishing boat. Frank was the first to break the silence.

'I got a letter from Jim yesterday. He seems to be on the mend, but I'm not sure I believe his injuries were so superficial. They wouldn't have kept him this long in hospital if they had been. And the tone of his letters isn't right, either. It's too matter-of-fact and overly cheerful – and when Jim's in that frame of mind it means he's hiding something.'

Ron had come to the same conclusion a while ago. 'I'm thinking he's putting it all on for wee Peggy's sake, so she's not worried about him. If his injuries were that light he'd have been treated in the field hospital and then sent back into the fighting again by now.'

'Aye, that was my thought too.' Frank regarded his father solemnly. 'At least we know for sure it wasn't bad enough to send him home like his mate Ernie. That poor wee man will not be walking again, and Jim blames himself for putting him in the line of fire.'

Ron nodded. 'Ernie's wife wrote to Peggy, telling her how grateful she was that Jim had saved Ernie's life that day – but it seems neither man is willing to talk about what happened, so I reckon we'll never get to the bottom of it.'

He swallowed the last of his tea. 'I'd better be getting on. Mass will be over and I want to catch Father O'Leary before he has his lunchtime tipple.'

Frank followed him as he clambered awkwardly out of the boat and eased his back. 'Is the shrapnel bothering you, Da?' he asked with concern.

'Ach, it's nothing,' Ron fibbed. 'Just old age and creaking bones.'

Frank eyed him sternly. 'It looks more than that. You should take the family's advice and go and see a doctor about it.' He held up his hand to wave away Ron's protest. 'I know the army surgeon said he couldn't do more to get that last bit out, but I'm sure things have moved on since then and there's something they can do to be rid of it once and for all.'

'To be sure, the medics have enough to do without bothering them with my troubles,' Ron replied, cross with himself for having let Frank see he was in pain. To ward off further discussion, he took his son in his arms and hugged him. 'I'll see you at Cordelia's party, if not before,' he said, trying not to flinch as his son hugged him back with great fervour.

He could feel Frank watching him as he left the beach and walked determinedly up the steep slope, the dogs trailing after him. Frank's strong embrace had made his back feel even worse, but he was damned if he'd let it show.

By the time he'd reached the presbytery his back was easing somewhat, so he tethered the dogs to the gatepost and walked up the gravel drive to the front door, his mind working furiously on what to say to the old priest that wouldn't offend him. For all his faults, Father O'Leary was a good man at heart, and his unwavering faith in what he believed had earned Ron's respect.

The priest's house was an enormous red-brick barn of a place that had been built in Victorian times to house several priests and three members of staff. It was set behind the cemetery trees in a large garden that was forever in shadow, and since the other priests had either retired or gone into the services, Father O'Leary lived there in almost solitary splendour, but for an elderly housekeeper called, rather appropriately, Miss Thorn, who resided in a couple of rooms behind the kitchen and fiercely guarded him against all comers.

Ron's rap of the knocker was answered almost immediately, which told him she'd seen him coming, and the door opened to reveal her sour, wrinkled face and unwelcoming glare.

'Good day to you, Miss Thorn,' he said, taking off his cap and giving her his friendliest of smiles. 'Would the Father be in?'

'He's about to have his pre-luncheon sherry,' she replied. 'You'll have to come back.'

'Ach, now, Miss Thorn, I've come a long way and 'tis urgent I speak to him now. Would you be after telling him it's Ronan Reilly?'

A lesser man would have quailed in the force of her glare, but Ron had faced the might of the Hun and stood firm.

'I know who you are,' she snapped. 'I'll see if Father wishes to speak to you.' She slammed the door in his face.

'Old witch,' Ron muttered. How Father Peter put up with her, he couldn't fathom, but he supposed the old boy needed someone to look after him and he'd unfortunately drawn the short straw.

When the door opened again it was Father O'Leary standing there. 'I hope this is important, Ronan. My sherry's waiting.'

'This won't take long, Father,' he replied quickly. 'Rosie and I have had a long talk, and we've decided to get married at the Town Hall,' he said in a rush. 'I appreciate all you've done for us, and we're sorry if it's an inconvenience to cancel things, but we both agree it's for the best.'

Father O'Leary eyed him for a long moment and then broke into a chuckle. 'I wondered how long it would take you to see the error of your ways. But at least it shows you do possess some moral fibre.'

'Well, thank you, Father,' he replied, a little nonplussed by his reaction. 'You and I both know it wouldn't have been right, and me conscience is much easier now things are sorted.'

The little man looked up at him keenly. 'I'm glad to hear you have a conscience, Ronan – it shows you're not a completely lost cause. But what I'm asking meself, is, why does a man who is not a believer have a conscience about going through a ceremony before God in church? You think on that, Ronan. Now good day to you.'

Ron stood on the step as the door was once more closed on him, albeit softly. The older man's reaction had come as a pleasant surprise, but his parting words lingered with him all the way back to Beach View and throughout the rest of the day.

5

Doris had rather hoped John would call in to ask how she was after that distressing scene with Chumley, and to give her a chance to fully explain. But as he hadn't – and what was left of her pride stopped her from going to him – she'd eaten the remains of the potato and corned beef hash she'd made the day before, and spent a miserable evening listening to the wireless as she knitted a cardigan from the unravelled wool of an old sweater.

The knowledge that if it hadn't been for Chumley's interference and her silly fib she could have been sharing a roast beef dinner and pleasant evening with John at the club hadn't made her feel any better, and she'd gone to bed early in the hope that a good night's sleep would help her see things in a clearer light.

Sunday had dawned with brighter skies and a brisk wind. The absence of rain was heartening even though she hadn't slept particularly well and was feeling a bit groggy. However, as she finished her solitary breakfast, she was able to clarify her thoughts on what must lie behind Chumley's aggressive and unwelcome attentions, and to take a more reasoned look at her relationship with John.

He was a good man who'd offered friendship and delightful company at a time when she'd needed it most – and through her loneliness, she'd been drawn to his warmth and kindness, perhaps even falling a little in love with him. She was still finding her feet in this new life she was making, and coming to terms with the loss of Ted and everything she'd once taken for granted, so perhaps it had been wishful thinking that had made her see more in his friendliness than was really there?

If so, then she'd been in danger of making an utter fool of herself by imagining he was in love with her, thereby risking not only his companionship, but her job too. In a way, she thought, she should be grateful to Chumley for bringing things to a head.

Doris cleared away her breakfast dishes and went into the pristine bathroom to wash and prepare for the day. Pride was all very well, but there were times when one had to push that aside and do the right thing – and this was one of those times. She would write a letter to John, telling him everything, and slip it through his letter box so he'd find it when he came back from his usual round of Sunday morning golf.

She'd just finished the letter and was reaching for her coat when there was a knock at the door. John would still be at the golf club, so it had to be that damned chauffeur – or worse, Chumley. Fired up and ready to give either man an earful, she yanked the door open.

John White swiftly took off his hat and took a step back, startled by her furious expression. 'I'm so sorry,' he stuttered. 'Is it a bad time to call?'

Doris almost sagged with relief. 'It's the perfect time,' she said. 'In fact, I was about to drop in a letter, thinking you were at golf,' she babbled on. 'But it's always better to discuss things face to face, isn't it?' She realised she wasn't making much sense, so she stopped talking and stood back to invite him in.

'Golf has been the last thing on my mind this morning,' he said as he stepped into the hall, his hat clutched in his hands, his expression a little wary. 'I've come to apologise for my appalling manners yesterday,' he continued. 'I should never have left you unsheltered from the rain like that – and certainly should have allowed you to explain what was happening between you and Chumley – although it really isn't any of my business,' he finished rather lamely.

'There's nothing going on between us,' she said firmly. 'And it's me who should be apologising for being untruthful.'

'I'm sure you had a perfectly good reason,' he replied, running his fingers through his thick silvery hair.

'Shall we go into the sitting room where there's a fire and we can talk more comfortably?' At his nod, she led the way, and gave the meagre fire a prod with the poker to liven it up. 'I could make some coffee, but I warn you, it's more chicory than anything, and doesn't taste very nice.'

His eyes were very blue as he smiled down at her. 'I think I'll pass up the offer for now,' he said.

'A wise decision,' she replied, taking one of the armchairs by the fire and indicating he should take the other.

John drew a silver cigarette case from his jacket pocket, opened it and offered it to her. When he'd lit both cigarettes he remained tense and upright on the edge of the chair, as if he was on parade.

'I've had the feeling something has been bothering you all week, and it's clear to me now that it has to do with Chumley,' he began hesitantly. 'Would it be impertinent of me to enquire what has brought this about?'

'Not at all,' she replied, feeling rather foolish, for if she'd been straight with him right from the start they wouldn't be having this awkward conversation now. 'But it's a long story, and I really don't know where to begin.'

'Why don't you tell me how you became acquainted with Chumley?' he encouraged. 'I've always found it's easier to begin at the beginning so the flow of things goes in the right order.'

How wise he was, thought Doris, beginning to relax at last in his calm, caring presence. She took a breath, marshalling her thoughts, then began to tell him how the Chumleys had taken over the manor fifteen years ago, and how it had soon become clear that Lady Aurelia was a force to be reckoned with when it came to raising money and setting up charities. She went on to tell him about her own charitable works at the time, and how flattered she'd been to be invited to join Lady Aurelia's fund-raising committee.

'It was 1930, and there was terrible poverty,' she said with a sigh. 'Even here in Cliffehaven. The slums behind the railway station were pitiful, with several families squeezed into four rooms and having to share a standpipe for water and an outside lavatory between eight houses. You can't imagine how ghastly it was.'

'I've seen the slums in India,' said John, 'so unfortunately I can imagine all too well. It strikes me the fire-bombs that flattened that area must have given the poor souls a chance of decent housing.'

'Not really,' Doris replied. 'There was no alternative housing and those bombs just made more people homeless, and poorer than ever.' She thought fleetingly of little Rita whose home and father's garage business had been blown to smithereens, and the hundreds of others she and the women of the WVS had tried to find homes for following that raid – and then refocused on the tale she had to tell.

'I'm ashamed to say that at the time, I thought I was really quite something to be associating with that very smart, rich set, and I began to get ideas above my station and started to look down on those who really cared about me.'

She took a deep breath, still unable to look John in the eye. 'It took me a long while to realise that I was no better than anyone else, and that the clique of women I'd fallen into would never regard me as one of their own. I was merely there because I was useful when it came to the less glamorous tasks of organising people and events, doing the accounts and being a general dogsbody.'

She glanced up at John, saw sympathy in his eyes and was thankful he made no comment. 'Walter Chumley isn't what one would call a true gentleman – he's too brash for that – but he was always very charming on the few occasions I was invited to the manor. I never really knew him, apart from what I learned from local gossip – and I've never been one to take much notice of that.'

She bit her lip. 'But I did admire him for being such a stalwart supporter of his wife's good works. Having a title and coat of arms on all the charity correspondence helped to bring in the donations, and Lady Chumley was very skilled at using their position in society to its full potential.'

John remained silent and attentive, but Doris could see no condemnation in his expression, so she told him about the ghastly memorial service and her decision to resign from the committees and turn her back on all of them.

'It sounds as if you're well rid of them,' John murmured.

'I thought I was until I received Chumley's letter inviting me to have dinner with him at the club – and the bombardment of gifts he sent round with his chauffeur.' She knotted her hands in her lap and took a breath before meeting his steady gaze. 'I fibbed about going to Peggy because I panicked at the thought of bumping into Chumley at the club. I wasn't to know he'd have the brass neck to turn up here.'

'My dear Doris,' said John, reaching across to take her hand. 'Why on earth didn't you tell me all this right from the start? I would have understood and put Chumley straight before he caused you any further upset.'

'I realise that now,' she replied ruefully, 'but rather stupidly, I thought I could deal with it on my own.'

'That was very brave of you, dear lady, but men like Chumley don't take no for an answer – not from a woman, anyway.' He squeezed her fingers, the colour rising in his handsome face. 'And may I say, I don't blame him for pursuing you. You're a most attractive, delightful woman.'

Doris blushed furiously at this unexpected compliment and tried to calm her racing pulse. She looked down at their entwined fingers, his so strong and masculine, swamping her more delicate ones, and thought rather distractedly that she was long overdue a manicure.

He eventually released her hand and lit them both another cigarette, which broke the intimate moment that had embarrassed them both. 'I can see how distressing you've found Chumley's pursuit, and it can't be allowed to continue,' he said thoughtfully. 'Do you wish me to have a word with him?'

'If you think it might do any good,' said Doris, forcing herself to think straight. 'But I realised last night that none of this has anything to do with romance. Chumley's after something far more important.'

John frowned. 'I don't understand.'

'When I was part of that crowd I did the book-keeping for the various charities. Over the last eighteen months or so, several entries began to puzzle me. New accounts had been opened in company names I'd never heard of, and money was being deposited into them from the main account with rather alarming frequency. I began to take notes of the discrepancies, because I didn't want anyone to think I was fiddling the books.'

Doris tapped the ash from her cigarette into the hearth, disconcerted by the trembling in her hand as she remembered her encounter with Lady Chumley. 'I tackled Lady Chumley over it as she was the treasurer and always did the banking, and showed her my notes. But she assured me these new accounts were quite legitimate, and that they offered a much better rate of interest. She ordered me – rather forcefully – to burn the notes and forget all about it.'

John leaned forward, his attention fully engaged. 'But you still had your suspicions?'

She nodded. 'I was not wholly convinced by Lady Chumley's explanation. There were no accounts for these companies, no paper trail at all as to where the monies were being spent. So I made copious notes about what I suspected, listing the names of the companies and so on, and the amount of money that was disappearing. To safeguard my own back, I lodged them in a safety deposit box at my solicitor's. And thank God I did, because if I'd taken them home, they'd have gone up in smoke along with everything else.'

She paused momentarily, seeing again the awful flames that had devoured her home and killed so many people. 'Shortly after that conversation those books disappeared and she presented me with new ones that just showed the income, expenses and donations that had gone through the usual bank account. There was no sign of any of the previous account books, and our income had fallen quite alarmingly.'

'So the Chumleys were siphoning off the money into their own accounts?'

'That's my suspicion. I was reluctant to believe it at the time, as I considered Lady Chumley to be a good friend, and I'd always had the highest regard for her, but something inside me wouldn't let it go. But without those books, I can't prove anything – and Lady Chumley was killed before I had the chance to question her again.'

She had a sudden memory of the distressing inquest that had followed the fire. 'Lady Chumley's body was found in what had been my bedroom,' she murmured. 'I wondered at the time what she'd been doing up there, but now it occurs to me she might have been trying to get into my wall safe. I remember mentioning it to her when I had it installed shortly after my husband left me. I was so shocked and grieved by her death, and the deaths of all those other women, that I didn't give it any further thought.'

'Mmm.' John sat back in the chair, deep in thought. 'Do you still possess those notes, Doris? Are they what you think Chumley's after?'

Doris was too ashamed to admit that at first she'd been flattered by his attentions, and seriously tempted, but once she'd given it a great deal of thought, she'd realised what he was really up to, and was furious with herself for being a deluded fool. 'I do have them, and yes, I'm sure that's why Chumley's bothering me.'

'But how would he know they exist?'

'Lady Chumley must have told him I'd questioned the accounts and made notes which she'd ordered me to destroy. She probably thought I was dazzled enough by their position in the town, and daunted by her strong personality, to do as she'd asked – and I have to confess that I was a bit – but the seriousness of my suspicions outweighed the danger of upsetting them both. Walter Chumley hasn't got where he is by taking things on chance – and the annual audit is due any time now. Which I'm now quite sure is why he's suddenly started turning up here.'

'If Chumley is helping himself to the charity money, then he must be a very worried man,' said John.

Doris shivered. 'Do you really think he'd go so far as to try and steal them from me?'

John took her hand again. 'I didn't mean to frighten you, Doris. I'm sorry. But I wouldn't put anything past that man.'

Doris gained some strength from his clasp and felt a little better, but the knowledge that Chumley might bring real trouble to her door was disturbing to say the least. 'You talk as if you know more than I about him,' she said.

John squeezed her fingers before settling back into his chair. 'There are rumours going round that all is not well with the Chumley finances,' he said with a serious expression. 'He has a large house in Mayfair, and it's said that he stretched himself financially when he bought that run-down manor, spending twice as much again on the repairs and refurbishment. He entertains on a grand scale, has bought hunting and race horses and likes to gamble in the London casinos and on the stock market. There is talk that he has huge gambling debts, and I know for a fact that his bar bill at the Officers' Club has not been paid for months.'

'I had no idea,' she gasped. 'But how on earth did you get to know all this?'

He smiled. 'I keep my eyes and ears open, and there are people at the Officers' Club who have good cause to know that Chumley is strapped for cash, and doesn't pay his debts. He owes Bertie Grantley-Adams fifty pounds on a wager they made several months ago, and he never did pay Major Radwell after losing to him at cards. I could go on, but you get the picture.'

'Good grief,' muttered Doris. 'The man's a crook.'

'He's a complete bounder, and an absolute cad,' said John with distaste.

Doris was still finding it hard to absorb what she'd learned. 'And here's me thinking he was regarded as someone to look up to,' she breathed.

'I wish you had those notes here, Doris. This would be a good time for us to go through them.'

'Oh, but I do,' said Doris. 'I collected all my papers from the solicitor's after I moved in. I'll go and get them.'

She was still feeling a little shaky after all those revelations, but she went into the bedroom and took the cardboard box from the wardrobe. It was filled with letters from Anthony and her younger sister Doreen, and all the paperwork relating to the lease on the bungalow and her divorce from Ted. Nestled in the bottom of the box were two secretarial note-pads filled with shorthand and columns of figures. She plucked them out and sat for a moment, rifling through the pages, wondering what can of worms she was about to open – and if she had the courage to go ahead.

Deciding Chumley deserved to be exposed before things went any further, she left the bedroom and found John in the kitchen making a pot of tea. Doris hunted out cups and saucers, then realised it was almost lunchtime. Glad of the momentary respite during this distressing morning, she went to the larder and gave a cluck of annoyance.

'There's a bit of cheese and some bread for lunch, but not much more, I'm afraid,' she apologised. 'With all that's been going on this week I haven't had time to do any shopping – and I still find it rather distressing to go into the Home and Colonial now that Ted's no longer there.'

'That's quite understandable,' John said sympathetically. 'I'll nip next door for a jar of pickled onions, some chutney and more bread and cheese.'

Minutes later they were sitting at the table eating their lunch with cups of tea as she translated her shorthand for him and explained the columns of figures.

'I'm not a bookkeeper,' said John, 'but even I can see why you became suspicious. There are institutions here that I've never heard of – not that I'm an expert in such things, you understand – and the sudden drop in income is very odd.'

'I just wish I could get hold of the original books,' she said. 'But I suspect they're long gone by now.'

'Oh, I'm sure they are.' He drank the last of his tea and studied the notebooks thoughtfully. 'I think the best place for those would be the office safe,' he said. 'But before we lock them away, we're going to visit a friend of mine.'

Doris regarded him warily. 'Oh, I don't know,' she murmured. 'Is it wise to show them to anyone else?'

'If we're to get to the bottom of this, yes,' he said firmly. 'James Harcourt is a fellow officer I know and trust, and he's recently taken over as manager of Barclays Bank in the High Street. His position there means he's a man of discretion, and I'm hoping he'll shed some light on those names you've got down there.'

'But what do I do about Chumley?' she asked nervously. 'He could turn up here at any time.'

'Don't worry about Chumley,' said John with a grim set to his chin. 'I'll deal with him.'

She felt a dart of alarm. 'Oh, John, you will be careful, won't you?'

He chuckled and patted her hand. 'I was a colonel in the Indian Rifles and have faced far worse than Chumley. Please don't worry yourself on my behalf. Now, get your coat and hat, and once we've seen James, I shall treat you to afternoon tea at the club.'

She suddenly felt nervous again. 'What if Chumley's there?'

'Army tactics, Doris. Once you've got the enemy in your sights, shoot the blighter first. Puts them off their stride, don't you know.'

Doris giggled quite girlishly. He was awfully attractive and commanding when he spoke like that.

Two hours later John decided it would be kinder to Doris not to risk bumping into Chumley, and they were sitting in the lounge at the golf club. A table draped in white linen and dressed with silverware and finest bone china was before them, displaying plates of tiny cucumber sandwiches, scones and rock buns, with small bowls of strawberry jam and thick cream.

Neither of them knew what to say, for their visit to Major James Harcourt had stunned them. It looked as if Doris's suspicions had been proven correct, and that the Chumleys had taken out accounts in false company names to syphon off the money from the charities. It was frustrating that it was Sunday and everything was closed, but James had kept the notebooks, promising he'd start digging first thing in the morning, for some of those accounts were held at his bank.

Doris became aware of Cordelia and Bertie waving to them from the table by the window, and nodded back before turning away. The last thing she needed today was Cordelia twittering on about nothing whilst Bertie gave one of his hearty monologues about some endless game of golf.

'What are we going to do, John?' she asked.

'There's nothing much we can do without hard evidence,' he replied, taking charge of the silver teapot. 'James is well placed to find out more, and he'll get back to us if he finds anything untoward.' He leaned towards her, his voice barely above a murmur so he couldn't be overheard. 'However, I suspect Chumley has covered his tracks very carefully. This is theft on a grand scale.'

'But he can't be allowed to get away with it,' hissed Doris. 'He's stealing from charities to feather his own nest. He has to be stopped somehow.'

John handed her the cup. 'If James uncovers anything you can be sure he'll inform the police. We can do no more. But at least those notebooks will be secure with him.'

Doris felt quite ill at the thought of Chumley getting away with it, and even the sight of such a luxurious tea couldn't tempt her appetite. 'It's not fair,' she muttered.

'Life rarely is, unfortunately,' John replied. He reached for her hand to stop her fidgeting with the linen table napkin. 'But we're all right, aren't we, Doris?' he murmured, his gaze direct and steady.

She felt quite weak when he looked at her like that – and as it was a new experience, she wasn't sure how to handle it. 'Yes, I rather think we are,' she managed.

'Jolly good,' he said softly. 'Now let's enjoy our tea.'

Peggy had been delighted to hear from Cordelia that Doris and John White were clearly getting on very well, but was rather envious at the thought of them sharing what sounded like a slap-up afternoon tea. It seemed that even during these austere days there was always a way round rationing – if you were prepared to pay for it.

However, Peggy was even more delighted on Monday morning to hear on the early news that the Americans had at long last gained a massive German surrender at Aachen, which was the first town to be captured on German soil. It was hoped that the way would now be clear to advance into the heavily industrialised Ruhr Basin and capture a series of dams in the Hurtgen Forest which would open up the road to Berlin.

This German surrender had lifted everyone's spirits, and Peggy left Beach View that morning with a spring in her step. She kissed Daisy goodbye at the door of the crèche and hurried into the factory, eager to begin her new job.

Climbing the stairs to Solly's office, she walked in to find her friend, Madge, already busy at her typewriter. 'Good morning,' she said cheerfully. 'How are you today?'

Madge grinned back at her. 'All the better for hearing about Aachen this morning. Solly and Loretta are down in the delivery bay. The cloth has arrived for those demob suits and flannel trousers.'

'Righto. I'd better get down there then. TTFN.' Peggy ran down the stairs and weaved her way through the long lines of machines, nodding and smiling at the women working them, but not stopping to chat. She didn't want Solly to think she was dawdling on her first day.

She became aware that Winnie Holman and Gladys Bright were watching her with narrowed eyes and, although she'd given a great deal of thought over how to deal with them, she knew there would be some sort of confrontation before the day was out. She could only hope that Loretta and Solly would agree to her idea.

Winnie looked like everyone's favourite granny, with a cottage-loaf figure, rosy apple cheeks and thick grey hair fastened into a bun on the top of her head. She smiled a lot and called everyone deary and ducks, but could take umbrage in a flash, and had been known to cause a good deal of trouble amongst the other women.

Gladys was the same age, but scrawny and hard-bitten. She rarely smiled, for she thought the world was against her – which it probably was, because she never stopped complaining about the raw deal life had handed her. However, both women were stalwart union members, and Gladys had taken on the role of mouthpiece and troublemaker at the slightest provocation, and Peggy knew Solly was very wary of the power she wielded. The last thing they needed now was a strike.

Peggy kept smiling and nodding as she made her way to the delivery bay where a huge lorry was being unloaded by the storemen. Buckling under the weight of the vast bales of pinstripe cloth and grey flannel, the men hoisted them onto heavy-duty trolleys.

Solly was issuing orders and warning the men not to drop the bales on the dirty floor or scuff them against the rough walls as they wheeled them away, whilst his niece, Loretta, checked that each bale had a delivery ticket, before putting a cross beside the corresponding order number on her list.

'Ah, Peggy, my dear,' said Solly. 'Just in time. Help Loretta with that delivery list whilst I go and make sure they've stowed the cloth correctly.' He didn't wait for a reply but went bustling off to chivvy the men who already knew very well how to stow cloth properly and wouldn't appreciate his interference.

Loretta smiled at Peggy, her dark eyes soft with affection as well as amusement. 'Uncle Solly has been like a cat on hot bricks ever since he got the contract,' she said. 'Thank goodness the cloth has arrived at last so we can get on.'

She quickly explained the list as another bale was unloaded. 'We'll check each bale more closely once we've got it into the storage bay, but for now we feel the quality and check the width against this list and tick each one off as it comes in.'

She handed over two of the four sheets of inventory, a pencil and a spare clipboard. 'We can work on this together. Just shout out the number if you don't have it on your list, and I'll make sure it's on mine and tick it off.'

'And what if it isn't on either list?'

'Then it has to be stored over there,' said Loretta, pointing to a far corner just as another bale was unloaded.

The flannel for the trousers was grey, and the pin-stripe woollen cloth for the three-piece suits came in grey or charcoal. It took over an hour for it all to be unloaded and put away. The inventory matched the delivery, so Loretta got the driver to sign them off before he drove away.

'Now we'll give Uncle Solly a hand in checking that the quality is the same right through the bales,' said Loretta. 'I'm sure it is as it's been paid for by the government, but you can never entirely trust the suppliers,' she warned. 'They try to get away with cutting corners and slipping in inferior cloth to make a bigger profit. It happens all the time – especially as supplies are at such a premium at the moment.'

The morning fled past as each bale was duly checked and found to be correct. Solly disappeared back into his office, and the storemen heaved a sigh of relief and went off for a fag break and cup of well-earned tea.

'Time for a cuppa in my office,' said Loretta, leading the way to a small room off the canteen, and ordering a pot of tea along the way. She shot Peggy a wry smile. 'Just think, Peggy, this will all be yours soon.'

Peggy giggled nervously as she took in the filing cabinets, the cluttered desk and two utility chairs.

'I've never had an office before,' she said. There was a telephone and intercom on the desk, a trade calendar on the wall depicting machinists hard at work, and a sickly looking spider plant on the window ledge. The poor thing needed some water, but as she didn't want to be seen as interfering, she decided to deal with that when Loretta was busy elsewhere.

Loretta's diamond engagement ring flashed fire as she smoothed back strands of her dark hair which had come loose during the delivery inspection and tucked them back into the neatly coiled victory rolls on either side of her head. 'It's not much, I grant you, but with the door closed, it gives me a bit of peace to get on with the paperwork, and when the weather's better, this window opens to let the fresh air in.'

She noticed the spider plant and poured some water into the pot from a carafe that sat on the desk. 'I keep forgetting this poor thing,' she sighed. 'I really should take it home, but it'll probably get ignored there too.'

'I'll look after it,' said Peggy, itching to pick off the dead bits, repot it and add a bit of Ron's compost to what looked like very poor soil.

The tea arrived along with a plate of digestive biscuits and Loretta became businesslike. 'We'll go through the questionnaire I'm giving out to the machinists and cutters whilst we drink this. I wanted to see if you can spot anything I've forgotten.'

They settled down to go through the list of questions and discuss the rest of Peggy's duties – which included becoming mother hen to those who were struggling for some reason; watching out for theft; stepping in at the first sign of bullying or infringement of the strict factory rules; and dealing with complaints, incompetence or idling.

It was a bit daunting, for it was on a much bigger and more diverse scale than she was used to, but having run a boarding house and brought up a large family, she felt fairly confident she could manage. It would be a case of feeling her way at first, and seeing the women she'd worked with from a different perspective. She had few illusions about being regarded as management and therefore no longer one of the workers, but she didn't really mind. She knew the ones she could rely upon, those who might distance themselves, and some who would try to push the boundaries with a newcomer.

'I've already told the workforce you'll be taking over from me when I leave next month,' said Loretta once the questionnaire had been discussed and, after a few minor adjustments, approved and sent upstairs to have copies made. 'I can't see that it will cause any problems, but then you never know with people like Gladys and Winnie sticking their oar in.'

'They were giving me the evil eye this morning,' said Peggy, 'so I won't be at all surprised if they feel they have something to say about it.'

Loretta cocked her head, her gaze thoughtful. 'But you can handle them, right?'

Peggy stubbed out her cigarette and finished the last of her tea. 'Oh, yes,' she said firmly. 'I have long experience of dealing with Winnie and Gladys, and I've a suggestion to make that – if you agree to it – will definitely take the wind out of their sails.'

Loretta grinned. 'I'm all ears.'

Peggy told her the idea that had come to her the night before, and the younger woman chuckled. 'A stroke of genius,' she said. 'Uncle Solly will definitely approve, and I'll do the same with two of the more troublesome ones on the night shift. He was right to promote you, Peggy. You'll do very well.'

Madge came in with a stack of copied questionnaires and Peggy gathered them up, still warm from the mimeograph. 'I'll take these round so I can get a sense of how the land lies and perhaps allay any fears they may have. They'll have seen the delivery and will know something's up.'

'Uncle Solly has already informed the night shift about the new orders, and as gossip spreads like wildfire in this place, most of them in there will already know. But he's planning to make another short speech during lunch break. Go ahead and pass those out – it doesn't hurt to give the personal touch, and you're good at that.'

Peggy started at the line of machines where she'd so recently worked. Handing out the pieces of paper she explained what they were for, and how necessary it was they filled them in before the end of their shift, for it would give Solly some idea of the numbers that would continue to work for him even when the war ended.

There were some guarded congratulations on her promotion as well as more genuine smiles and good luck wishes. And as Peggy went up and down the lines, she could see that Gladys and Winnie were watching her like a couple of hawks, waiting to unsheathe their talons.

She deliberately left them until last, and finally approached their work area. 'Here we are,' she said pleasantly. 'You need to fill these in as best you can so we know if we can rely on you to continue working for us while we fulfil this latest contract.'

Winnie folded her meaty arms beneath her large bosom and sat back from her machine. 'How come you got the job, then? Me and Glad have been here for years, and never got a sniff of promotion.'

'Yeah,' snapped Gladys sourly. 'It ain't right. You've only been here for five minutes.' Her expression became sly. 'But then I seen you cosying up to Solly the other day – all friendly and intimate like. You and him got something going? Is that why you got the job?'

'No, Gladys, it isn't,' Peggy said firmly. 'And I don't like what you're implying.'

'I got a right to be suspicious when I seen what I seen,' she replied belligerently.

'Indeed you have every right to think what you like, but it wouldn't be wise to cast aspersions – not

if you want to keep in with Solly – or more import-
antly, Rachel.'

Gladys's mouth shut like a trap, for if Rachel got
wind of her remarks, she'd be out on her ear quicker
than she could blink.

'Oh, yes?' snapped Winnie. 'Are you threatening
Gladys?'

'Not at all,' said Peggy calmly, all too aware that
they were now the centre of attention. 'I'm just
advising Gladys that it would be wise to keep her
thoughts to herself in the light of your new positions
on the factory floor.'

Both women's eyes narrowed. 'What new position?' demanded Winnie with deep suspicion.

'You're to be promoted to senior machinists who
will be in charge of the new intake, and those still on
probation. There would be a pay rise of an extra ten
bob a week each, starting today.' She looked at the
stunned women. 'What do you say? Are you both
up for it?'

'Well, I . . .' Winnie was clearly lost for words.

Peggy looked at Gladys who shrugged as if she
wasn't that bothered. Then, with bad grace, she said,
'Yeah, why not?'

Winnie unfolded her arms and gave a nod. 'I could
certainly do with the money,' she muttered. 'But I'm
not doing extra hours, I'm telling you straight.'

'You won't have to,' Peggy assured her. 'Thank
you for agreeing to do it. Solly regards you as the
best and most experienced machinists, and will be

very happy to know you're willing to do your bit for the war effort.'

Realising she was laying it on a bit thick, she plucked two questionnaires from the stack in her arms and handed them over. 'I'll catch up with you in the lunch break to explain your duties, but if you could fill in those, I'd be grateful.'

She turned away to sweep a stern gaze across the women sitting idle and earwigging at their machines, and within seconds work was in full flow again. She'd got over the first major hurdle, but she was sure there would be many more in the coming weeks – especially once Mavis put in an appearance.

6

India

The air was full of beautiful birdsong, and Jim could hear the scamper and chatter of the monkeys as they ran across the roof gathering the fruit that had fallen from the mango trees growing behind the hospital. It was the first day of November and barely past sunrise, but the heat was already rising, and by noon it would be unbearable – the sun glaring from a molten sky until every living thing was silenced and stilled into torpor.

Jim had spent almost three months in the military hospital – most of it dead to the world under heavy sedation – but it felt as if he'd been here for half a lifetime. Now he was at last on the mend, he was becoming bored and restless; eager to be with his regiment again even though it meant leaving this peaceful, orderly haven for the chaos and noise of battle.

He stood naked to the waist at the basin in the large communal shower room and ran the razor over the dark stubble on his chin. When he'd first recovered enough to get out of bed, his legs had been so weak he could barely walk, let alone stand for any length of time, and he'd had to rely on the nurses and a walking stick to help him get about the place. It had come as a terrible shock to see himself in the bathroom mirror that first time, for the fever had ravaged him and he hadn't recognised the gaunt old man staring back at him with sunken eyes in a drawn face, his skin the colour and texture of old newspaper, the bones of his skull visible beneath it.

Now, as he looked in the mirror, the sight wasn't quite so shocking, and he was almost back to the old Jim despite the glints of silver in his black hair and the cobwebs of fine lines at the corners of his eyes. He'd filled out and could no longer count his ribs, although the muscles he'd been so proud of still needed a good bit more work, and the scars on his back were inclined to itch.

He finished shaving and washed his face before easing off the light bandaging to check on the progress of those scars. The main one ran in a thin arc from beneath his armpit and over his ribs to his hip bone; the lesser one branching off at an angle towards the base of his spine. They were still a little red, the scars left by the stiches like punctuation marks on either side, but they looked impressive enough to show off to the girls when he finally got back home, and prove to his father that he too could have an operation to retrieve the shrapnel that still bothered him.

Yet Jim doubted Ron would heed his advice, for he was a stubborn old devil and seemed attached to that shrapnel for some strange reason. He replaced the dressing, dropped the towel from around his waist and pulled on pants, a singlet and shorts – the customary attire for all the patients in this heat. The surgeon had told him that not all the shrapnel could be removed at the field hospital due to the infection he'd picked up whilst waiting to be airlifted out. It had therefore been necessary to perform the second operation on his arrival here. He'd had a lucky escape, that was for certain, and if he hadn't been poleaxed by that damned septic fever and kidney infection, he'd have been out of here weeks ago.

His mellow mood dimmed as he thought of Ernie, whose luck had run out through Jim's carelessness and gung-ho belief that nothing could touch them after they'd survived those torturous weeks of the Japanese barrage. The shrapnel had severed Ernie's spinal cord, and the poor wee man would spend what was left of his life in a wheelchair. The knowledge that Ernie didn't blame him, and his wife had written to thank him for saving him that day, simply made him feel all the more guilty.

He shoved his bare feet into the rubber sandals that everyone wore – apart from the nurses – and headed back into the ward where the nurses were attending to those who were still bedridden. The injuries were many and varied in severity, and he knew from his time here that not all of them would survive.

It was a depressing thought, and as he walked through the French doors that opened onto the veranda he wanted nothing more than to fall into a dreamless sleep – something that had been denied him ever since he'd been taken off the heavy medication. Yet he knew that if he slept the nightmares would come, and he'd be haunted by the sounds, smells and horrors of that flooded battlefield in which so many of his comrades now lay buried. Asleep or awake, the images came anyway, and he'd yet to discover how to blot them out. Perhaps once he was discharged and fully occupied with something useful again, he'd find respite.

Jim greeted the other injured men who were lounging in rattan chairs beneath the ceiling fans, playing cards, reading or listening to the wireless. There were others playing croquet on the lawn with rather more enthusiasm than skill, whilst Indian servants chased away the thieving monkeys, and the orderlies tended the potted plants and hanging baskets which swung gently in the draught of the spinning fans.

The orderlies were mostly late middle-aged Italian POWs who'd been captured in Africa and brought to India for the duration to assist the overworked nursing staff in the many military hospitals that had sprung up since the start of the Burma campaign. Despite the fact that Italy had changed sides the previous year and declared war on Germany, they were now stuck here, but they seemed happy enough to carry on their duties, and Jim suspected they were relieved not to have been roped into the British Army to rejoin the fighting.

He headed for his favourite chair, which was placed at the end of the veranda beneath a fan and in the shade of a vast palm tree.

'Oh, no you don't,' said Staff Nurse Fitzpatrick in her broad Australian accent as she bustled up to him with purpose before he could put his behind on the chair. 'You're supposed to be at the parade ground for your morning exercises.'

Jim gave her his most appealing smile. 'Do I have to?'

The plump little nurse looked up at him, her grey eyes warm with humour. 'There's not much wrong with you, Jim Reilly, that a good dose of exercise wouldn't cure.'

He wiggled his eyebrows suggestively as he admired her deliciously rounded figure. 'I can think of better ways of getting exercise than running round a track with an army PT instructor bellowing at me.'

She shook her head, the twinkle in her eyes still present. 'I'm sure you can, but if I had a quid for every time that's been suggested to me, I'd be rich and living the high life in Sydney. Now move that skinny backside and get out from under my feet.'

'You're a hard woman, Sarah,' he sighed. 'What's a man got to do to get any sympathy around here?'

She chuckled. 'You've had all the sympathy you need, so don't try and pull a fast one. Get to the parade ground.' With that, she turned on her heel and sashayed off, the starched apron crackling as her well-rounded hips moved delightfully beneath the thin cotton dress.

Every man on the veranda watched her appreciatively until she went out of sight, and then returned with some lethargy to what they'd been doing before. It was incredibly hot, even in the shade, and the fans were making little headway in lowering the temperature.

Jim drank a cup of tea and then reluctantly went to fetch his plimsolls and a towel before heading for the parade ground which fronted the nearby army barracks. He'd have preferred to stay on the veranda than go through the torture of these morning exercises, but at least he was capable of doing something physical, which was more than could be said for most of the other men in the hospital, and he knew that once he'd begun the seemingly endless round of running, jumping and press-ups, he'd feel a lot more positive.

The barracks served as a staging post for men coming off sick leave to prepare them for their return to the jungles of Burma and Siam. Discipline was rigidly enforced by the officers who understood the necessity of getting the men fighting fit again before they were sent back into action. There was even a curfew at sundown to keep them from the bars and dubious delights of the nearest town which was a half-hour truck ride away.

Jim paused in the welcome shade of towering trees to lace up his plimsolls and regard the barracks which he suspected would soon be his home. The wooden huts that housed the lower ranks ran in an orderly line along a cinder path edged by big, white-painted boulders and a low picket fence. A large mess hall and ablutions block stood between the huts and the administration offices, which had garages, stores and workshops behind them; and the officers' quarters and mess were isolated at the far end by a magnificent hibiscus hedge, ablaze with plate-sized scarlet and yellow blooms. A broad, verdant lawn ran the length of it all and was constantly manicured and watered by a small army of Indian servants.

The parade ground was an unshaded, stark square of flattened, baked red earth which seemed to shimmer with the heat, even at this early hour – and waiting impatiently there was Sergeant Major Bourne in full, pristine tropical uniform.

Seeing the other men leave their quarters at a run, Jim hung his towel on the nearest tree branch and went to join them as the sergeant major began to roar at them to get a ruddy move on. It seemed rank didn't count when it came to physical jerks, for Jim recognised a first lieutenant, two captains and a major lining up with him.

Bourne was a robust Yorkshireman of indeterminate age, with a bristling moustache and brutal haircut, a voice like a foghorn and a bearing that defied any disobedience or show of aggression. He'd been an army physical trainer for most of his career, was the holder of several prestigious boxing titles, and well known for his lack of humour. He was, therefore, not a man to mess with.

Jim stood to attention with the others, and once Bourne was satisfied they were all present and correct, the torture began.

Bourne marched back and forth bellowing orders, a swagger stick tucked beneath his muscled arm, seemingly untouched by the rising heat or the swarms of flies that pestered everyone as they sweated and strained through the exercises.

An hour later saw Jim drenched in sweat and out of breath, but the ache in his muscles felt strangely rewarding, and as he flexed and stretched them out, he knew he was definitely on the way to a full recovery.

The fifteen men stood to attention trying to ignore the buzzing insects that crawled over their sweating faces as they waited to be dismissed.

'Warrant Officer Reilly, you will stay at attention,' shouted Bourne. 'The rest of you are dismissed.'

Jim wondered what he'd done to attract this unwanted attention and tried not to flinch as a fly explored his face and tried to crawl up his nose.

'At ease,' rumbled Bourne, coming to stand almost toe to toe with Jim, who was in fact his senior in rank. 'Get showered, changed into uniform and have a haircut,' he barked. 'The CO is expecting you in his office at eleven hundred hours prompt.'

'Yes, Sergeant Major,' said Jim, perplexed by this summons. 'Any idea what he wants me for?'

'I am not privy to my superior's thought processes, Reilly,' he replied tersely. 'You'll find out soon enough. Dismissed.'

Jim watched him march smartly away as if he was at some military parade. 'Pompous ass,' he muttered without rancour as he grabbed his towel and headed for the hospital showers, his mind still occupied with what his CO might have in store for him. With any luck it would be a discharge from the hospital and a new posting – but if he'd heard about his illicit dealings in whisky with the local Indian trader, he could be for the high jump.

Feeling cool and relaxed after a cold shower, he pulled on a fresh uniform shirt and clean, knee-length shorts. The long socks and heavy boots were cumbersome after being free of them for weeks, and he was sweating again as he grabbed his battered, sweat-stained slouch hat and went back to the barracks for a haircut.

Jim suffered the indignity of the army barber's enthusiasm for almost scalping him and, emerging back into the glaring sun, he rubbed his hand ruefully over what was left of his hair before ramming on his hat. He tried to ignore the enticing smell of curry and the rumbling of his stomach as he walked to his CO's office. Hopefully the old man wouldn't keep him for too long, for it had been hours since breakfast, and he was starving.

Jim had only seen the brigadier from a distance, but he'd become quite a legend around here if the stories about him were true. Brigadier Ffaulkes-Hubert was tall and lean with the leathery complexion of a man who'd spent his life in the tropics. He'd come out of retirement at the age of sixty to release a younger officer for battle duty and to take command of this out-of-the-way military post where any ambition for promotion was doomed.

Ffaulkes-Hubert was regarded with great affection by everyone other than his junior officers, who found his absent-mindedness and leniency towards the men extremely tiresome. He was not a man who stood on ceremony and could often be found sharing a curry and beer with the Indian servants and lower ranks. And yet he was tolerated because his military record was exemplary, and he told the most wonderful stories of his youthful adventures during the Second Boer War.

The brigadier's door was open to garner the slightest breeze, and as Jim's shadow fell across his desk he looked up from the tea tray before him and smiled. 'Come in, come in,' he encouraged with a wave of his hand. 'It's far too hot to be standing out there.'

Jim stepped inside and stood to attention beneath the whirring ceiling fan as he saluted. 'Warrant Officer Reilly reporting, sir.'

The brigadier saluted back rather distractedly, his focus returning to the tea tray. 'Sit down, young man,' he said. 'Would you like a cup of tea and a ginger biscuit?'

'Thank you, sir, that would be very welcome,' he replied, taking off his hat and sitting cautiously on the edge of the rattan chair. He took the delicate cup and saucer, helped himself to a biscuit, and waited for the old boy to tell him why he'd been summonsed.

The brigadier drank his tea and then spent some time lighting his pipe. 'So, young man,' he said between puffs, 'what was it you wanted to see me about?'

'I do believe, sir,' said Jim carefully, 'that it was you who wished to see me.'

Grey eyebrows shot up and faded blue eyes widened. 'Did I? Now why would that be, I wonder?' His pipe was discarded as he shuffled through the drift of paper and folders on his desk, seemingly at a loss. 'What was your name again?'

'Warrant Officer James Michael Reilly,' said Jim, returning the empty cup to the tray and trying to see if he could spot his name on anything amidst the disorder.

'Ah, yes. I seem to remember that I have some interesting news for you,' said the older man, still hunting through the mess. 'Now what was it?' he muttered crossly.

Jim swallowed his impatience and was finally rewarded with a beaming smile from the brigadier as he unearthed a brown cardboard folder.

'Here we are,' he said triumphantly. 'I knew it was somewhere.' He opened the folder, perched his glasses on the end of his nose and peered short-sightedly at the papers inside it. 'Ah, yes,' he murmured. 'Now I remember.' He took off his glasses and stood, offering his hand to Jim. 'Congratulations, young man. Thoroughly deserved, I'm sure.'

Jim quickly stood to shake the proffered hand, still none the wiser as to what the old boy was on about. 'Thank you, sir,' he said, 'but what is it exactly that I've earned?'

'Oh, didn't I say?' The brigadier shook his head. 'It's the heat, you know. After fifty years in India and Africa, it's inclined to addle the brain somewhat.' He stood there smiling at Jim, having once again lost his train of thought.

'May I know why you're congratulating me, sir?' Jim persisted.

'Oh, yes, of course. You've been mentioned in dispatches for showing extreme courage whilst under enemy fire, with a recommendation that you be commissioned immediately to Second Lieutenant – a position I believe you held during the First World War.' He gave Jim a beaming smile. 'Jolly good show, eh what?'

Jim nodded without great enthusiasm as the brigadier began opening and shutting his desk drawers. An MiD was really something to write home about, and as it would be announced in the newspapers, the whole of Cliffehaven would hear about it. But despite the substantial pay rise that went with the promotion, he was not looking forward to rejoining the officer ranks – in fact he'd turned down the offer when he'd been called up and had been avoiding such a thing ever since.

His thoughts were interrupted by the brigadier slamming a drawer and advancing on him with a couple of shoulder tabs bearing a single 'pip' and a small box. 'You'll have to get these sorted out,' he said gruffly, handing over the tabs. 'Now stand still, my boy. It's my duty to pin this on you. Don't want to stab you, what?'

Jim stood to attention again, his alarm rising as the unsteady fingers fumbled to open the pin on the back of the bronze oak leaf award.

'May I offer to help with that, sir?' he asked.

'It is fiddly, and my eyes aren't what they used to be,' the older man muttered, handing it over. 'Probably best you do it.'

'Thank you, sir.' Jim pinned it to his shirt collar and stuffed the box and epaulettes into the pocket of his shorts. 'It's an honour to wear it.'

The older man stood in dreamy silence as he admired the badge.

Jim realised he was off in his own world again, and if he didn't say something, they could be here all day. 'Permission to leave, sir?'

The brigadier snapped out of whatever he was thinking about. 'Um, no, there was something else ...' He leafed through the folder and drew out a very important-looking certificate and a sheaf of papers.

Jim stood there in a lather of impatience as the older man unearthed his glasses again and took forever to read through everything.

'Ah yes,' he said eventually. 'This is the certification of your MiD, and these are your new orders. You'll see that you are to take two weeks' leave from tomorrow at six hundred hours and return here for training before you rejoin your regiment which I believe is still in Burma.' He handed over the paperwork and smiled. 'Marvellous place, Burma. I was stationed there for a while back in 1913, and I remember ...'

Jim listened politely to the rambling reminiscence and when the brigadier paused for breath, he broke in. 'That's very interesting, Brigadier. Thank you for taking the time to tell me about my award and commission.' He nodded towards the desk. 'But I can see you're very busy, so I won't keep you any longer.'

The brigadier blinked as if surprised to see the mound of paper on his desk. 'Goodness me, so I am. Well, it was a pleasure to meet you.' He pumped Jim's hand again with surprising firmness. 'Good luck and Godspeed, young fellow.'

Jim saluted and finally escaped to a quiet, cool corner of the hospital gardens to admire the citation which had been signed by the King himself, and to read through the orders. Transport had been arranged to get him to a hotel that had been requisitioned by the army for the rest and recuperation of injured officers. The name of the place was unpronounceable, but he would be free to come and go as he pleased – which was a huge relief, because he didn't fancy being holed up with a bunch of upper-class twits for two weeks.

He read the citation again which had been awarded to him for his valour in saving a comrade whilst under fire during the Japanese bombardment that had seen him hospitalised and Ernie crippled for life. Jim gave a deep sigh. He hadn't earned the damned thing – if anyone deserved it, it should have been Ernie.

The siren scents of the lunchtime curry drifted from the veranda. Jim unpinned the badge and returned it to its box. He would say nothing to the others, he decided, for there was no point in bragging about something he hadn't deserved. As for the commission, it would probably be wise to keep that to himself, too. Officers had been the butt of all their jokes, and he didn't want to spoil his last night here by revealing that he'd been forced to change sides.

He reached the veranda and of course there were questions, for it wasn't every day that one of them had to wear uniform and get a haircut. He replied that he'd been passed fit and was going on leave the following day, which seemed to satisfy them.

He went to his locker and tucked away his orders and citation along with the box containing the oak leaf badge, and then changed back into his singlet and shorts. Arranging with one of the more senior Indian servants to sort out his uniform shirts so the epaulettes could be attached, he slipped the man a few rupees to ensure his silence.

Once he'd achieved all this, he returned to the veranda to tuck into the spicy curry and delicious saffron rice, which he washed down with icy cold Indian Pale Ale. The heat was at its fiercest and the talk was desultory, each man too drained of energy to engage in conversation, and it wasn't long before they drifted off to take their siestas.

Jim was quite happy to eat alone, and as he mopped up the remains of his meal with the warm flatbread chapattis, and called for another beer, he planned the rest of his day.

He felt energised suddenly, and knew he wouldn't sleep despite the debilitating heat, so he'd go to the surprisingly well-stocked hospital library and dig out a map of Burma to try and find the place he was going to. It was probably up in the hills where the temperature wasn't quite so fierce, or if he was really lucky, it could be on the coast and he'd get to swim in the sea. There would be time before supper to write to Peggy with his news, and then he'd pack his few belongings, sell off the last of his illicit stock of whisky, shower again and enjoy several more beers once the sun went down.

He rose from the table and stretched luxuriously. It would be a very early start tomorrow, but he doubted he'd sleep much, for there was an excitement in him for what lay ahead that he hadn't felt in months, and he was eager to be on the move and feel useful again.

7

Three weeks had passed since Peggy had taken up her new position at the factory, and she was enjoying her Saturday off despite the fact the November rain was lashing down in a strong wind, and all her washing had to be hung from the suspended airer in the scullery.

It was nice to get up a bit later than usual and to eat breakfast at leisure without having to rush off to the factory to deal with the numerous problems that always seemed to be awaiting her. Not that she wasn't enjoying her new position – she was revelling in it – but now Loretta had left, she found that managing a lot of women who were inclined to fall out with each other over the slightest thing was a little wearing.

She poured another cup of tea and idly watched Daisy playing with her doll as she shared the hearth rug with Queenie in front of the glowing fire. It was peaceful for once, but she knew it wouldn't last, so was making the most of it whilst she could.

Ron was out with Harvey, Sarah was doing overtime at the council's offices and Ivy was having a lie-in after coming home very late last night and waking everyone by falling up the stairs to land in a heap on Cordelia's stairlift which she sent up and down whilst singing very loudly and out of key.

Peggy chuckled. It had taken some time to shut her up and get her into bed, for she'd been very tipsy – and she suspected she'd have one heck of a hangover when she did finally surface.

There had been no sign of Fran and Robert, who were no doubt enjoying a rare few hours together upstairs before Fran had to start her late shift at the hospital; Cordelia was getting ready to go out to lunch with Bertie; Rita was on duty at the fire station; and Danuta had gone out on her district nursing rounds. The only thing other than the weather marring this morning was the fact that neither the paper boy nor the postman had put in an appearance. But at least Mr Jenkins had his dairy up and running smoothly again, and the milk had arrived in bottles on the doorstep before anyone was up and about.

As if her thoughts had conjured them up, the letter box rattled and she hurried into the hall to find the papers and a stack of mail in the wire basket. She quickly opened the door to offer the two lads a momentary refuge from the weather with a cup of tea, but they were already cycling away.

Shutting the door against the wind and rain, she discovered that everything was damp, the pages of the newspapers curling up and a bit ragged from where the boy had shoved them rather too carelessly through the letter box. Peggy gathered everything together and took it all into the kitchen. She placed the papers on the chair by the fire to try and dry them out a bit, and then sifted through the letters. Some of the ink had run, but the writing was legible enough to sort them out according to the recipients.

There were two letters from Canada for Cordelia, three airmails from Sarah's mother in Australia – which would no doubt upset the girl with even more airy-fairy plans for her and Philip when he and her father were released by the Japs.

Peggy clucked in exasperation. When would the stupid woman realise it would be an absolute miracle if either of them had survived, and that the pressure she was putting on Sarah and her sister Jane was immensely selfish and unfair?

She placed the letters on the mantelpiece, wishing she had the nerve to write to Cynthia Fuller and tell her straight to stop living in a fantasy world and face reality. There again, she reasoned, the poor woman was clinging to hope, and it would be too cruel to snatch it away. But the time would come when she'd be forced to face the truth, and like Sarah, Peggy dreaded what it would do to her.

Peggy returned to sorting the letters. Ivy had one from her younger siblings who'd been evacuated to a tiny market town near Salisbury, and one from her mother. Rita's father had written, as had Peter Ryan, and Peggy knew the girl would be thrilled to hear their news, for there hadn't been any letters for over a week and she'd begun to get worried.

Peggy's hand stilled as she came to the letter for Fran, and hope flared that it might be from one of her family – but it bore a London postmark, and was therefore probably from one of her nursing colleagues who'd gone up there at the start of the war.

She set it aside and quickly plucked out the bills from the gas and electricity board – she'd see to them later – and finally found Jim's letters. There were two each for her and Ron, plus a large and intriguing stiff brown envelope addressed to both of them.

She was about to open it when Ron came stomping through the door with muddy boots and a streaming poacher's coat, followed by a soaking wet Harvey who bounded in and shook himself vigorously, sending dirty splatters all over her lovely clean kitchen as well as Daisy and Queenie.

'Get him out of here and dry him off,' she said crossly as Queenie bolted for her shelf above the sink. 'Look at the mess he's made – and you're no better – you're dripping all over my clean floor.'

Ron blew out his cheeks, grabbed Harvey by the collar and plodded back down to the scullery muttering under his breath and leaving a trail of muddy footprints behind him.

Peggy abandoned the post and cleaned up Daisy, who didn't seem at all fazed at being drenched but objected strongly to having her clothes changed and let Peggy know it by yelling and thrashing about.

Peggy wrestled with her and got her dressed again, and to the accompaniment of Daisy's temper tantrum, fetched the floor cloth and bucket from under the sink.

In the middle of all this Cordelia arrived in the kitchen and took charge of Daisy, who shut up immediately and smiled at her with beatific innocence. 'I see Ron and Harvey have come back,' she said, plonking Daisy in a chair and handing her a colouring book and crayons. 'You should make him clean up the mess, Peggy, not do it yourself.'

'I would if I thought he'd do it properly,' she replied, running the cloth over the floor with rather more vigour than was necessary. 'Unfortunately, he usually makes more mess than we started out with.' She wrung out the cloth as if it was Ron's neck. 'There's some letters for you, by the way,' she added. 'And the papers are on the chair drying out.'

'Oh, good,' said Cordelia. 'The local paper is supposed to be doing a piece on the golf club today, and Bertie is rather hoping he'll be mentioned as he's just been elected as club president.'

'Goodness me,' breathed Peggy, giving the floor a final wipe over and then resting back on her heels. 'I didn't realise he was even up for it.'

'He's extremely well thought of at both clubs,' said Cordelia proudly. 'In fact, there has been talk of him taking over as chairman at the Officers' Club – which would be a real coup.'

Cordelia settled down next to Daisy at the table to read the local paper. She started at the back as usual to see who'd died before going on to the

announcements of requests for probate, court app-
earances and bankruptcies – she liked to keep up
with all the local goings-on.

Peggy tipped away the dirty water and returned
the bucket and cloth to the shelf beneath the sink
just as Ron emerged sheepishly at the door with
Harvey restrained in a tight grip.

'Is it safe to come in now? We're both dry and I've
cleaned Harvey's feet.'

Peggy's flare of annoyance died and she smiled.
'Of course it is. Sorry I shouted, Ron, but the pair of
you really are the limit.' She reached for the kettle.
'I expect you'd like a cup of tea after being out in
that,' she said. 'And we've both got letters from Jim.'

'Good heavens!' yelped Cordelia. 'I don't believe
it!'

'What's got you all stirred up, old girl?' asked
Ron. 'Someone died and left you a fortune, have
they?'

'Look,' she said, stabbing a finger at the paper.
'Look there and see for yourselves.'

Ron and Peggy crowded round her to see what
she was pointing at and they gasped when they
saw Jim's photograph below the headline on the
front page.

LOCAL HERO MENTIONED IN DISPATCHES

Local hero, Second Lieutenant James Reilly, has
been mentioned in dispatches for his bravery in

rescuing a comrade whilst injured and under enemy fire during a fierce battle in Burma.

James Reilly, known locally as Jim, has lived in Cliffehaven all his life and was the projectionist at the Odeon cinema, escaping injury when it was firebombed in the early stages of the war. James saw action in 1917 as a very young man and returned to the Royal Engineers to fight for his country when war broke out again.

He was subsequently drafted into the Chindits, which is a specialised branch of the 14th Army that has been highly trained in jungle warfare, and has seen action in India and Burma since 1942. Following his discharge from hospital, James is expected to rejoin his regiment in the fight to drive the Japanese out of Burma.

Second Lieutenant Reilly is married to the highly regarded Peggy (née Dawson) who is running Beach View Boarding House as a haven for evacuees as well as working at Solomon Goldman's factory and caring for their youngest daughter, Daisy.

The editor and staff of the *Cliffehaven Gazette* are extremely proud to make this announcement, and I'm sure our readers will join us in wishing Second Lieutenant Reilly Godspeed and a safe return home to his family.

'Oh my,' breathed Peggy, sitting down with a thump and taking charge of the newspaper. 'What wonderful news; and look how handsome he is. I'm so proud of him I could burst.'

'He won't appreciate being an officer again,' said Ron, unable to hide his own pride. 'But he wouldn't have been commissioned if he hadn't earned it.' He reached for the large brown envelope. 'I bet I know what this is,' he said, slitting it open.

Peggy and Cordelia gasped as Ron carefully placed the certificate on the table. 'It's signed by the King,' breathed Peggy in awe, not quite daring to trace her finger over the signature and very important-looking seal.

Daisy went to grab it and Ron snatched it out of her reach. 'I'll find a frame for it before it gets damaged,' he said as Daisy's expression became stormy. 'Ach, Daisy, this is a very special thing about your da,' he soothed. 'You can look, but you mustn't touch, wee girl.'

'Dada?' Daisy frowned as she eyed the certificate which clearly meant nothing to her.

Peggy quickly showed her the picture of Jim in the paper. 'This is Dada, Daisy. He's a very brave soldier – so brave the King has given him an award.'

'Dada!' Daisy clapped her hands and looked at the photograph. 'Dada come home now?'

Peggy drew her close and had to swallow the lump in her throat before she could reply. 'Not yet,' she managed, kissing the top of her daughter's head. 'He's very busy, you see – but he'll come home soon.'

Daisy lost interest, wriggled from her mother's embrace and returned to her colouring book, so Peggy carefully placed the certificate on the mantelpiece, propping it up against the large framed photograph of the King and Queen so that everyone could see it.

Ron cut the report from the newspaper and tucked it between the photographs on the mantelpiece before going out to his shed to see if had any wood he could use to make frames for those two precious bits of paper.

'Well, Bertie got his name in the paper too,' trilled Cordelia, 'but Jim's news is far more exciting. Do hurry up and open his letters, dear. I can't wait to hear what he has to say about it all.'

Peggy swiftly opened the earliest of Jim's two letters, and after another glance at the newspaper photograph, began to read.

My darling Peggy,

Thank you for the letters, cards and photographs you've all sent to me over the last months, they certainly helped cheer me up, and I can't believe how much Daisy has grown. I had hoped I'd be at home for her birthday, but of course that's impossible, and all I can do is pray that I shall be with you for her next one. Give her a kiss and cuddle for me and tell her I love her, even though she will have no memory of me. It makes me sad to think of the years I've lost with her and the others, but this war has to be won if they're to have a secure future, and I shall make it up to all of you when I get back.

I'm not sure I'm entirely happy about you getting more involved at Solly's, although it sounds as if the pay is very good, and I'm proud that Solly thinks so highly of you. Still, you clearly feel you need to do your bit, as they say, but once the war's over and the volume of work slows down to a trickle, he won't need you as much and you can spend more time at home looking after me and the rest of the family. We've all been apart for too long, it will be wonderful to be a real family again, and to get to know the grandchildren.

I'm writing this on my last night in hospital, as I will be discharged first thing and sent on leave for a couple of weeks before I return to my regiment. I have no idea where I'm going, but I'm looking forward to getting out of here and away from the depressing sight of injured men and the smell of disinfectant.

Of course I shall miss the nurses, Sarah Fitzpatrick in particular, for she's a jolly good sort and brightens everyone's day – and there are a couple of chaps I've become friendly with, who I hope to stay in touch with. But the thought of being free to come and go as I please for a couple of weeks is something I've dreamed about for so long, I can hardly wait. I have no real idea where I'll be billeted, and I doubt the censor would let me tell you even if I did. But I'm hoping for the seaside rather than the mountains, because I miss the sound and smell of the sea after being away from home for so long.

I do have some rather surprising news for you, which you might already have heard about with the post being so erratic. But I've been mentioned in dispatches and promoted to Second Lieutenant.

I'm a bit dubious about it all, to be honest, Peggy. I didn't deserve the MiD, and certainly never wanted the commission – you know how little respect I've always had for officers after those idiots made so many blunders during the first shout. But the pay's much better, which should be a real help to you, and being an officer – albeit a very junior one – I'll probably be amongst the first to be sent home once all this is over.

We get to hear the BBC World Service and the Forces broadcasts on the wireless, so I know how the war in Europe is progressing, and by the sound of it, they're doing better than us over here! Stay safe, Peggy, what with the doodlebugs and so on, and I hope both Cordelia and Daisy enjoy their birthday celebrations.

Any mail will be forwarded on, so just keep writing to the same address and it will get to me wherever I am. I love you, Peggy, and if I have a chance, I'll do some shopping when I'm on leave, and send you all presents for Christmas.

Love, kisses and hugs,
Your Jim. xxx

'Well, Cordelia, he doesn't say very much about it at all,' said Peggy, handing the letter to her. 'But he's certainly not happy about me taking on extra responsibilities at Solly's.'

'That doesn't surprise me,' said Cordelia. 'Jim's like most men – he expects his wife to be at his beck and call.' She chuckled. 'But I get the feeling he won't be the only man to have his nose put out of joint when he comes home to find his wife is enjoying earning her own money too much to spend all her days tied to the kitchen sink.'

Peggy smiled. 'Going by the number of women who've signed up to stay on at Solly's at least until the demob suit contract is fulfilled, you could be right, Cordy. But time will tell. None of us knows how we'll feel when it is all finally over.'

She opened Jim's second letter which contained several black and white snapshots. She smiled as she pored over each one, for Jim had certainly got his wish to be beside the sea, and it looked very different to what Cliffehaven had to offer.

The beach was a long stretch of pale sand shaded by palm trees, and fishing boats of all shapes and sizes and bedecked in flags and ribbons were moored in the shallows. Small stalls had been set up in the shade selling everything, it seemed, from food and drink to beach towels and umbrellas, and Peggy could only imagine how colourful it all must be.

Jim was clearly having a good time and looked very well as he grinned into the camera alongside a group of other men, or lounged in a rattan chair on a flower-bedecked veranda being waited upon by an Indian servant who looked splendid in a turban and exotic clothing. The last photograph was of Jim sitting shoulder to shoulder with a large, burly man and laughing uproariously about something as they saluted the photographer with bottles of beer.

Peggy set aside the photographs and eagerly began to read.

Darling Peggy,

Well, here I am and it's all smashing – but the very best part of it all, is that Big Bert is here too! I couldn't believe it when I saw him walking towards me as I arrived, and it was an even bigger shock to discover he'd been made up to Second Lieutenant as well!

Mind you, he deserves it after all the years he's been in the army, and I hope he doesn't do anything to be demoted again. He's lost his pips twice before, you see – once for getting drunk and smashing up the mess, and then for hitting another officer who was being obnoxious. Big Bert does like a drink, but unfortunately it brings out the worst in him, so I'm going to have to keep him on the straight and narrow and make sure we get through the next lot together.

This place is a real paradise and most of the other men are a pretty good bunch who've come up through the ranks and don't put on airs and graces. I'm feeling really fit after swimming every day and going for runs on the beach. The sand is very soft and it's hard going, but Bert's determined to get me as fit as possible and is worse than a sergeant major at issuing

*orders. He can run surprisingly fast for a big man,
and I find it hard to keep up with him, but I'm blowed
if I'll let him beat me.*

*The hotel is very posh, with huge bedrooms and four-
poster beds that you just sink into. There are more
servants than guests, so you only have to raise a finger
to get a drink or something to eat. The food is good too,
with lots of lovely fruit and curries so hot they burn
your mouth for an hour afterwards, but the air is clean,
the temperature much cooler here on the coast. There's a
very good market nearby, so I've managed to buy some
bits and pieces for everyone which I sent off today in the
hope they'll get to you before Christmas.*

*Bert and I will be sorry to leave, but the time is flying
by and we only have a couple of days left before we go
our separate ways. He's going back to our regiment, and
I have to stay in India to be retrained before I can do the
same — at least that's what I hope, but the army has its
own agenda, and they could send me anywhere.*

*I love you and miss you, and wish so much you could
be here with me to see this place — you would love it —
just as I'd love to see you in a swimsuit again!!*

Jim. xxx

Peggy sighed and handed the letter and photographs to Cordelia. Jim was clearly in his element
now he had Big Bert to join in his mischief-making,
and she could only hope the pair of them didn't get
into too much trouble. The beach and the hotel
looked wonderful and she thought wistfully of

wearing a swimsuit and feeling that sand between her toes as the sun warmed her skin.

'Fat chance of that,' she muttered, getting up from the table to hunt out raincoats and sort out the pushchair for her walk up to the Red Cross Distribution Centre.

She had just finished dressing herself and Daisy when Bertie Double-Barrelled arrived looking dapper as always in a tweed suit beneath a very smart gabardine mac. He kissed Cordelia's hand in greeting and smiled at Peggy as he congratulated her on Jim's news.

'Goodness me, I can't possibly allow you to walk all the way up there in this weather,' he exclaimed after Peggy had told him where she was going. 'You must let me drive you.'

'That's very kind of you, Bertie,' she replied. 'Are you sure it won't be out of your way?'

'Not at all, and I'd come and pick you up too, but I have an emergency committee meeting at the Officers' Club straight after lunch.'

'Would that be about you becoming chairman?' Cordelia asked.

'No, my dear, it's rather more serious than that.'

'Ooh, do tell,' twittered Cordelia who loved a bit of gossip.

'It's all rather hush-hush, I'm afraid,' said Bertie solemnly, handing Cordelia her coat and making it plain he was saying no more.

Peggy and Cordelia exchanged amused glances. Like most men, Bertie liked to have his secrets, but they'd find out eventually what it was, just as they always did.

Neither John White nor Doris had heard anything from James Harcourt since handing over her notebooks to him, which was very frustrating. In the first few days following Chumley's visit Doris had been on tenterhooks in case he called again, or sent someone to break into her house to find them.

However, Chumley had stayed away, perhaps realising that Doris had a champion in Colonel White, for they made no secret of their burgeoning relationship and were now seen everywhere together. John had been marvellous and hugely supportive, fitting good locks and bolts on both doors, and keeping her company in the evenings, but she was still a bit jumpy every time someone knocked on the door.

It was bitterly cold, wet and windy that Saturday afternoon, and she hurried home from the office, looking forward to sitting by the fire with a bowl of hot soup. John had been called to an emergency committee meeting at the Officers' Club, and would join her later, so she was planning to heat through the stew she'd put together earlier from the vegetables they grew in their back gardens.

She closed the door behind her and hurried into the small kitchen to dump her wet umbrella in the sink before it dripped everywhere, and then took off her raincoat and headscarf. Her stockings were wet through, so she peeled them off and hung them on the airer above the cooker to dry out, and then slipped her cold feet into slippers and went into the sitting room to switch on the wireless for company and light the fire.

Coal was a real luxury now, and the low-grade anthracite that was on offer proved difficult to light and, with its low blue flame, didn't really provide the warm orange glow that was so much more appealing – and yet when it did get going it gave off a really good heat, and didn't smoke like coal. Adding a few bits of kindling, she placed the fire-guard in front of it and went back to the kitchen to see to the stew and heat through the soup she'd made from the bottled tomatoes she'd harvested from her garden that summer.

As she stirred the soup she smiled at the memory of her mother, Edna, and the lessons she'd given her and her sisters as youngsters in the art of cooking good nutritious food from the most basic of ingredients, and the tricks of running a home on a shoestring budget. Those lessons had served her well in these tough times and she was quite surprised at how many of them she'd remembered after so many years of never having to watch the pennies.

She glanced across at her small larder which was stocked with homemade chutneys, jams and bottled pears; the cooking and eating apples from her trees were carefully stored in boxes between layers of brown paper that had started out as envelopes and packaging. There were dried herbs tied into bunches by the cooker, and onions strung up in a corner of the shed – and winter vegetables were now flourishing in her garden thanks to John's patient guidance. Feeling rather pleased with herself, she cut a slice of wheatmeal bread to go with the soup and carried her lunch into the sitting room.

The rain had stopped, but the wind still buffeted the bungalow as it came off the sea, and although it was barely past three in the afternoon, it was already getting quite dark. Doris drew the curtains on the dismal day, switched on a table lamp and settled down to her lunch by the fire.

Time ticked away pleasantly as the aroma of the warming stew came from the kitchen and concert music played softly from the wireless. She finished the soup and picked up her library book, but the soothing music combined with the warmth of the fire made her drowsy and she set it aside when she realised she'd read the same paragraph twice and not taken in a single word. Resting her head back and settling deeper into the armchair, she closed her eyes and sighed contentedly. John would be back soon.

The knock on the door startled her awake an hour later, and at the thought of John getting soaked on her doorstep, she groggily hurried to let him in.

'Good afternoon, Mrs Williams. May I come in out of the rain?'

Shocked out of her grogginess, Doris drew herself up stiffly and glared at Chumley. 'No, you may not,' she snapped, and made to close the door only to find his large brown brogue was blocking it. 'Remove your foot immediately,' she ordered in her most imperious tone. 'Or I shall call the police.'

Chumley's foot remained where it was. 'That's not very hospitable, Mrs Williams,' he said, his expression mournful as he stood beneath his large umbrella. 'Especially as I've come to apologise for ignoring you after our previous encounter. I've been in London, you see.'

'I hadn't noticed your absence,' she retorted, looking down her nose at him. 'And I'd appreciate it if you'd leave now and not bother me again.' She tried to close the door, but Chumley's brogue was still in the way, and as there was no sign of the chauffeur or any of her neighbours, she couldn't expect any help in getting rid of him.

'Mrs Williams – Doris – I really don't understand why you're being so hostile,' Chumley persisted. 'I thought we were friends, and I wish only to get to know you better.'

Doris knew she had to be careful, for she didn't want him to suspect she knew the true reason behind his harassment of her. 'If I've been hostile, it's only because you don't seem to be able to take no for an answer,' she replied coolly. 'I have returned your very generous gifts and made it plain that I do not wish to further our acquaintance – and yet you have chosen to ignore my wishes.' She held his gaze, determined to remain calm.

Chumley put his hand on the door suddenly and before Doris could react, he'd thrust it open, shoved her out of the way and slammed it behind him. The smile was gone – all pretence at civility wiped away in cold fury. 'Don't stick your nose up at me, you supercilious bitch,' he rasped, advancing on her.

Doris shuffled back along the hall. 'Get out,' she managed, her pulse thudding as fear threatened to overwhelm her.

'I'm not leaving until I get what I came for,' he growled, grabbing her by the throat and thrusting her against the wall. 'Where are those notebooks?'

'I don't know what you're talking about,' she gasped, clawing at the strong fingers that were threatening to squeeze the life out of her.

The fingers tightened. 'You know damned well,' he hissed inches from her face. 'Just as I know you didn't destroy them.' He squeezed a little harder. 'Where are they?'

'I burned them,' she gasped, fighting for breath and clawing frantically at his hand.

He leaned his considerable weight against her. 'I don't believe you.'

'But I did – I did,' she choked out. Spots were appearing in her eyes and a terrible darkness was beginning to fill her head as he pinned her to the wall. In that moment of blinding terror, she knew that if she didn't fight back he would kill her.

Doris stopped grappling with his fingers and rammed the heel of one hand under his nose and swiftly followed this up with a poke in his eye. As he loosened his hold on her and reeled back from her attack, she kicked him hard in the shins and then rammed her knee into his groin.

He fell to his knees and clutched his testicles, blood dripping from his nose and claw-marks showing vividly on his face. 'I'll get you for this, you bitch,' he gasped.

Doris was poised to flee for her life when the front door was kicked in and John was standing there.

Taking in the scene at a glance, he advanced on Chumley and dragged him to his feet before delivering a punch that sent him crashing back onto the floor. 'Are you all right, Doris? He didn't hurt you, did he?'

She couldn't speak, her throat was too sore, but she shook her head to assure him she was fine.

John dragged the groaning Chumley to his feet and propped him against the wall in much the same way Chumley had held Doris.

Chumley cringed and blubbered, begging John not to hit him again and accusing Doris of attacking him.

John's expression was scathing as he looked him up and down. 'Get out, and stay away from Mrs Williams. That punch was just a taste of what I'm capable of, Chumley, and I assure you, if you cross either of us again, you'll feel the full force of my many years in the army boxing team.'

'I'll have the law on you for assault,' slurred Chumley through his bloody mouth.

'I doubt that very much.'

'She's got my property and I want it back!' Chumley shouted.

John didn't bother to reply. He grabbed Chumley by the collar, opened the door and shoved him so hard he stumbled over the step and ended sprawled on the path, the rain beating down on his bloodied face. John tossed the umbrella after him, and then stood ready to boot him down the path to his car if he didn't clear off immediately.

Doris was trembling with shock as she went to John's side and watched Chumley stagger to his car and drive off. Her throat was aching, but her admiration for John was such that she had no words to express it.

John closed the door and she leaned into him as he put his arm around her and kissed her forehead. 'I'll mend that broken lock later,' he murmured, regarding her keenly. Seeing the marks on her throat, he tenderly traced a finger over the bruises. 'Did he do this?' he asked with cold, grim fury.

Doris nodded and then managed a wry smile. 'But I did worse to him,' she said hoarsely. 'Went for his eyes and probably broke his nose as well as his balls.'

John's eyes widened momentarily at this plain speaking which was so unlike Doris, and then drew her to him and chuckled. 'Clever, brave girl,' he murmured against her cheek. 'Let's sit you by the fire and I'll make you a cup of tea.'

Doris let him fuss over her, and once she'd drunk the tea and had a cigarette she at last stopped trembling and began to relax, for surely Chumley would never dare approach her again?

She remained by the fire whilst John replaced the broken lock on the front door and then, ignoring his protests, she went to clean away the smears of blood from her hall wall and floor and wash her hands. She still had no idea how she'd found the strength and courage to fight back, let alone remember the self-defence course she'd attended whilst in the Girl Guides all those years ago – and could only assume that fear had driven her and given her the clarity of mind she'd needed in that desperate situation.

Once everything was back in order, John set up a card table in front of the fire and served their supper. When they'd finished eating, he pulled his chair next to hers and held her hand whilst they listened to the wireless, and Doris was almost consumed by a deep sense of contentment that she'd never known before.

The clock chimed eleven, which was the usual signal that the evening was over, and they both reluctantly got to their feet.

'I'd better go home,' he said, not making a move.

'Do you have to?' she asked softly.

His gaze was intense as he looked into her eyes. 'Not if you don't want me to,' he murmured.

Doris could feel the electricity between them as they gazed at one another, and felt such an overwhelming need to be loved by him that she couldn't speak. She answered him by switching off the light and taking his hand to lead him to her bedroom.

8

Peggy was fast asleep and dreaming of walking on that lovely beach with Jim when she was thrust awake by an enormous explosion which rocked the house and rattled the windows. Scrambling out of bed to snatch a terrified Daisy from her cot, she almost lost her footing as a second explosion reverberated through the old walls and sent a shower of dust and plaster over them.

Thunderous gunfire from the emplacements on the surrounding hills and along the promenade swiftly followed and she gripped the screaming Daisy tightly in her arms, grabbed a blanket and dressing gown and fled into the hall, yelling to the others at the top of her voice to get downstairs.

There was no need, for within seconds she was joined in the kitchen by the five ashen-faced girls and Robert who was carrying a very confused Cordelia. As there was no sign of Ron or Harvey, Peggy could only assume they were at the Anchor with Rosie, and Queenie would still be out on her nightly prowl – but were they safe? Those V-2s had been too close for comfort.

'What's happening?' Cordelia was trembling so much that when Robert carefully set her on her feet, she almost collapsed into the nearby chair.

'It's Hitler's bleedin' rockets, Grandma Cordy,' said Ivy through chattering teeth. 'Nearly blew the bleedin' 'ouse up this time.'

'All right, Ivy,' snapped Rita, 'there's no need to put the wind up us even more. We all know how close they came.'

Cordelia still looked confused, and Peggy realised she hadn't had time to put her hearing aid in before Robert hauled her out of bed. She put her free hand on her shoulder in an attempt to soothe her, but Daisy was squirming and yelling, so Sarah hurried to Cordelia and gently embraced her – explaining to her great-aunt what was happening by talking clearly, and very close to her ear.

The big guns were still hammering away and now they were joined by the sirens which began to wail, gathering volume and pitch as they were activated all through the town.

'We ought to go into the Anderson shelter,' said Robert, gathering Fran to him.

'A fat lot of good that would be,' said Ivy, shivering in her thin nightclothes. 'If one of them things comes down, that bit of tin won't save us. We'd be better off in the cellar.'

'Not if the next one hits the house,' said Peggy, still trying to soothe a sobbing, clinging Daisy. 'We'd be buried under it.'

'If it hits the house none of us would know about it anyway,' said Danuta grimly. 'We've all seen the craters those things leave. I vote we stay in here and take our chances.'

Another blast rocked the house and the pistol shot of cracking glass made them all cower. The kitchen window had split in half.

Galvanised into action, everyone scrambled for shelter beneath the kitchen table. There wasn't much room, but they huddled there, holding each other for comfort as the sirens continued their blood-curdling moans, the guns pounded and a fourth rocket exploded in the distance.

The lights went out, and the darkness made it even more terrifying. Peggy heard the shatter of glass and china, and the clang of something heavy hitting the range before it thudded onto the floor. There was the ominous clatter and thump of things tumbling over the roof and crashing onto the front steps, and the creak of guttering as it was torn from its fixings.

Peggy could scarcely breathe for fear that her home was about to fall on top of them all, and the awful claustrophobia of being crushed in that small space as she was half-strangled by Daisy. Yet as she tried to ease Daisy's grip on her neck, the child merely tightened her hold, her knees and feet digging painfully into Peggy's stomach and ribs.

Peggy bore the discomfort, for she could feel Daisy's little heart thumping wildly against her, and although she was finding it very hard to stay calm, she knew she must for everyone's sake. She could hear Ivy's stifled sobs and Fran's quick, shallow breathing, and felt Rita trembling every time the guns boomed and something else smashed onto the floor. It seemed Danuta was the only one not to be affected, for she sat calmly next to Cordelia and didn't even flinch when something heavy hit the front wall.

'This is like the bad old days,' said Cordelia with a shudder. 'I thought they were behind us.'

'It's much worse, Grandma Cordy,' rasped a distraught Ivy who was clinging to Rita. 'At least then we could 'ear the bombs coming before they 'it.'

No one had an answer to this, so they remained silent and tense in the darkness, straining to hear anything above the sirens and cannon-fire that might herald yet another V-2. But everyone knew it served little purpose, for Hitler's new weapon brought death without warning, and there was nothing they could do to escape it should fate decree that their time was up.

Endless minutes passed; the guns stopped their thunder; Daisy's sobs quietened as she fell into an exhausted sleep and Peggy prayed for their deliverance. And then the sirens faded and the all-clear was finally sounded.

The silence was deafening and no one moved until Rita disentangled herself from the crush.

'I have to get to the fire station,' she said urgently, crawling out from beneath the table. 'Watch out!' she yelped in pain. 'There's glass everywhere.'

'Stay where you are, Rita,' ordered Danuta sharply. 'I am wearing shoes and will fetch torch from emergency box.'

'Right you are,' said Rita, 'but do try and hurry. They need me to drive the fire truck.'

'I too will be needed,' said Danuta as she bent and crab-walked out from beneath the table.

They could hear the crunch of glass beneath her feet as she carefully crossed the floor to retrieve the emergency box that had been kept by the sink since the war had begun. After fumbling around she found the torch and switched it on.

Peggy gasped in horror as the weak beam swept over the glittering shards of glass and china that had been strewn across the floor. Rita's knee was bleeding, and she stood barefooted amidst it all, not daring to move.

Danuta snatched up the broom and swept a clear path for everyone before shining the torch on Rita's knee. 'You will need to check there is no glass left in that wound, Rita, and then you must clean and dress it before you go out,' she advised.

'I'll see to that while you get dressed, Danuta,' said Fran, gingerly following the cleared path in her slippers to take the first aid kit out of the box. 'We'll both be needed at the hospital. Lord only knows how many casualties there might be.'

As if to underline her words, the urgent ringing of fire and ambulance bells came from Camden Road.

The electricity was still off, so Sarah lit all the candles she could find in the box, anchoring them firmly into any bit of china she could find before handing one each to Fran and Danuta.

Whilst Fran hurried upstairs with Rita, and Danuta shot off to get dressed, Sarah placed the candles about the room and the others slowly emerged to stare in shock at the mess. The cracked window hadn't withstood the blast of that fourth rocket, nor the thudding of the guns, and there were lethal shards of glass glinting in the sink and on the draining board.

Peggy's china had been jolted from the shelves and now lay in shattered pieces amidst the pool of porridge that was still dripping from the overturned pot – and her heavy iron skillet had dropped from its nail above the range leaving a nasty dent in the hotplate cover before it hit the floor and buried an edge in the lino.

A layer of dust covered everything and Peggy's resolve to remain calm began to falter as she eyed the large framed print of the King and Queen which had shifted on its hook to a sharp angle, knocking her mother's clock and all the photographs off the mantelpiece. By some miracle, the precious clock had landed on the fireside chair and was still in one piece, but it was the sight of Jim's certificate and newspaper cutting lying on the floor that broke through the tight hold she'd kept on her emotions for the past hour, and she burst into tears.

Robert put his hand gently on her shoulder. 'It's all right, Peggy,' he said softly. 'Sarah and I will clean up here whilst you see to Daisy.'

'I'll get Grandma Cordy sorted and then help with the clean-up,' said Ivy. 'We'll soon have it all ship-shape again, you'll see.'

Peggy nodded, unable to even thank them in case she went completely to pieces. She took a candle and carried Daisy into her bedroom to settle her into her cot, before getting dressed. It was still black as night outside, even though it was almost six o'clock. Unlike Daisy, she was far too tense and fretful to sleep.

Staring at her reflection in the dark, rain-lashed window which had survived the blasts thanks to the heavy taping she'd kept over it, her fears rose and her thoughts whirled.

Where had those rockets landed? Had RAF Cliffe and Tamarisk Bay escaped – was the Anchor still standing – and Doris's bungalow? And what about Kitty and Charlotte and their babies up in Briar Lane – and Fred the Fish and his wife Lil who lived three streets away with their adopted boys? And then there was the telephone exchange where April worked, and the little stationmaster's cottage where she lived with her baby Paula and her Uncle Stan – and ... and ...

She shook her head, knowing that if she carried on like this she'd be sent mad by it all, and would be of no help to anyone. She heard the sound of running feet coming down the stairs and across the hall and knew it was Rita, Danuta and Fran leaving to do their bit at the fire station and hospital, so she purposefully rolled up the sleeves of her cardigan and donned her wrap-around apron. It was time to be doing something useful, rather than standing about in here worrying herself silly.

Peggy left the bedroom door ajar in case Daisy woke and needed her, and returned to the kitchen to discover that Robert and the two girls had done a sterling job in clearing away the broken glass and china and stirring the range fire back into life. Ivy was on her knees scrubbing away the last of the porridge, Sarah was putting away the unbroken china she'd washed, and Robert had found a bit of hardboard – probably from Ron's shed – and was nailing it over the window to stop the wind and rain from getting in.

'No sign of Ron yet?' she asked, mournfully regarding the very few bits of china she had left before reaching for the kettle.

'I expect he's out with the wardens and Home Guard,' said Robert, the raucous sound of more fire engines arriving from the station in the next town almost drowning him out. 'There were bound to be people trapped after that raid, and it'll be all hands on deck. Once I've done this and checked on the rest of the house, I'll go out to see what I can do to help.'

'The window in my bedroom is still in one piece, so there's no need to disturb Daisy,' she replied. 'And it's still too dark to see anything outside – but I have a horrible feeling the chimney's gone. Where's Cordelia?'

'Out for the count in her bed,' said Ivy. 'Poor old duck's worn out.'

Peggy wasn't surprised to hear it, and she went to the table to inspect the pitiful stack of photographs which had once stood so proudly on her mantelpiece. They'd been taken out of their damaged frames, the broken glass carefully removed – but the sturdy frames Ron had made for Jim's certificate and newspaper cutting were still all right, and she placed them back on the mantel. Eyeing the dust and debris lying over everything, she didn't have the heart to explore the rest of the house. 'Oh, lawks,' she sighed. 'I do so hate this bloody war.'

'We all do,' said Ivy, getting to her feet to dump the filthy cloth in the sink. 'Especially when me breakfast ends up on the flaming floor.' She pushed her hair off her face with the back of her grubby hand. 'Still, at least we've got a roof over our 'eads, which is probably more than some after tonight, so I suppose we should count ourselves lucky.'

'We're all alive,' said Sarah, 'and I for one am very grateful. I think we should get dressed, Ivy, and go and see if we can help in any way.'

'Yeah, yer right, as always,' said Ivy. 'Make that tea, Auntie Peg, we'll need something warm inside us before we go out in that.' She jerked her thumb towards the sound of the heavy rain battering the hardboard, and then hurried out of the room after Sarah.

Peggy pulled herself out of the doldrums, realising she had no business to feel sorry for herself when she'd got off so lightly. After all, she reasoned silently, what were a few broken cups and picture frames compared to lost homes and lives?

There was still no sign of Queenie, which was very worrying, but she supposed she was hiding out somewhere, still terrified by those explosions. She tried not to think of her out there in the rain, alone and frightened, but it was difficult, for Queenie was as much a part of the family as the rest of them.

To keep herself busy, Peggy made the tea, lit a cigarette and quickly put some bread on the hotplate to toast before checking the contents of her larder. She doubted very much if the hens had laid any eggs with all that racket going on, but there was a packet of Shredded Wheat, and enough bread and milk to get them through until tomorrow morning when the shops opened again.

Once the tea and toast was on the table, Peggy's restlessness sent her into the hall. She would telephone round to make sure everyone was all right.

But the electricity was still off and the telephone line was dead. In growing frustration, she returned to the kitchen and began to clear away the layer of dust and debris that smothered the collection of oddments on the dresser. She'd been meaning to sort it all out for days, and as she needed something to do, this seemed to be as good a time as any.

Robert and the girls came back down, bundled up in raincoats, scarves and hats. They stood to drink the tea and stuff down the toast before hurrying out into the darkness and the teeming rain.

Peggy stood on the back doorstep calling for Queenie, but there was no sign of her, so she checked the hen house was still standing and the birds alive, then shut the door and returned to the kitchen. She wished she could do something to help in the aftermath of those rockets, but with Daisy and Cordelia asleep, she had little choice but to stay here and carry on with clearing up.

Returning to her previous task, she sorted out the top of the dresser, and gave the old battered wood a good polish before running the mop over the floor and wiping the dust and grit from the oilcloth on the table.

However, she soon found that although her hands were busy, her imagination was running wild and putting her on edge. She couldn't help but worry about where those rockets had come down, and if her friends and loved ones were safe.

Unable to stand it any longer, she grabbed her coat and headed for the front door to see if she could spot any sign of fire which might give her some idea of where those rockets had landed.

The distant sound of fire and ambulance bells echoed throughout the town, and as she opened the door, she was met by the horrifying sight of the enormous flames of a blazing inferno rising into the sky less than two hundred yards away. Two fire engines were already in attendance, but the jets of water and drenching rain seemed to be making little difference to the ferocity of those flames.

Peggy took a shuddering breath, the realisation of how close they'd all come to being killed making her pulse race. Tearing her gaze from that awful sight, she noted the rubble strewn on her steps and the glow of another fire to the west. It seemed far enough away to be on the other side of the cliffs where there was nothing but fields – but perhaps that was wishful thinking, for the dawn had yet to come and it was difficult to gauge the distance.

However, there had been four explosions, so there must be four fires. She pulled up her coat collar and was about to leave the shelter of her doorway for a better view from the end of the cul-de-sac when she thought she heard something.

Peggy stilled, straining to hear it again beneath the background noise of shouting firemen and drumming rain. She began to wonder if she'd imagined it and was about to go back indoors for her umbrella when it came again.

The faint, pitiful mewl was instantly recognisable and drew her onto the top step. She peered down into the gloom. 'Queenie? Is that you? Where are you?'

A dark shadow shifted slowly on the pavement into the reflected glow of the nearby fire, and with a heart-rending yowl, struggled to climb the bottom step to reach her.

Peggy stumbled down the rubble-strewn steps and sank to her knees beside Queenie, who'd collapsed, and was now lying panting and clearly in great distress.

'Oh, Queenie,' Peggy breathed tearfully, 'what is it? What's happened to you?'

Queenie lifted her head to Peggy's gentle touch, her eyes pleading for help and dulled with pain as she reached out a trembling paw. But even this small movement seemed to prove too much, and she collapsed again.

Peggy tentatively ran her hand over the soaking black fur, but the cat didn't respond – not even when Peggy's fingers found the cruel sliver of metal embedded in her spine.

'No! Oh, Queenie, no,' she sobbed, gathering her to her heart and burying her face in her lifeless neck.

Blinded by her tears, unaware of the rain beating down on her and the rubble digging into her knees, Peggy rocked Queenie in her arms, remembering how she'd arrived at Beach View in Ron's coat pocket – a tiny ball of fluff that fitted in the palm of

Peggy's hand. And how Harvey had tried to intimidate this intruder with his barking and snarling, only to be cowed by a swipe of her sharp claws, eventually becoming her constant, loyal companion. And how, despite her withered back leg, she'd taken to accompanying Ron and the dogs when they walked the hills, often returning home exhausted and tucked into Ron's coat pocket.

Peggy finally got to her feet and carried her indoors for the last time. Queenie had become an intrinsic part of the Beach View family, and had done her best to come home to them, so it was only right that Peggy should help her complete her final journey.

9

Ron had been on the point of reluctantly leaving Rosie's soft and enticing warmth for the cold, wet walk home when the first rocket hit. Within minutes they'd grabbed their clothes and were fumbling their way downstairs in the dark to the cellar where the dogs were already cowering in a corner.

Ron had just lit the oil lamp that hung from the rafters of the Anchor's makeshift air-raid shelter when the second explosion rocked the foundations of the centuries-old pub and the sirens started to wail, accompanied by the heavy booms of the big guns. He'd known then that he'd have to stay to look after Rosie and the dogs, but as he'd comforted a terrified Rosie, and heard the third and fourth explosions, his fears had risen for everyone at Beach View.

As soon as the all-clear had sounded, he'd been on his feet and hunting out a torch. 'I have to make sure Peggy's all right,' he said, dragging on his greatcoat. 'But I'll check everything here before I go and come back as soon as I can.'

Rosie was still trembling but making a sterling effort to keep her fear under control. 'Please be careful,' she begged him. 'I know what you're like, and I don't want you risking life and limb trying to rescue people.'

He kissed the top of her head. 'It's what I do,' he said, 'and if I'm needed, I can't just stand aside and leave it to others.' He glanced across at the two dogs which were still shivering in a huddle at the end of the couch. 'Keep Harvey with you, Rosie. He's getting too old for digging about in rubble.'

Rosie gave a snort. 'And you're not?' she retorted.

He grinned and waggled his brows. 'There might be snow on the roof, Rosie girl, but there's still fire in me belly and muscle enough to be useful.'

He gave her a hug, silenced any further protest with a kiss and went quickly up the steps. Closing the cellar door so Harvey wouldn't follow him, he did a quick inspection of the upstairs rooms and then went into the bar.

The brasses had fallen off the beam above the inglenook fireplace, dust and bits of plaster coated everything – including the old piano, which had somehow moved across the room to wedge itself in a corner. The large mirror behind the bar had been cracked during an earlier doodlebug blast, but it had not survived this time, and there were lethal shards of glass on the floor.

Ron heaved a sigh of relief that the old place had withstood the battering and went to fetch a broom and dustpan. As far as he could see there was no further damage, the beer glasses having survived because they'd been kept in a box beneath the counter, the precious bottles of spirits alongside them.

Ron cleared away the glass so neither the dogs nor Rosie cut themselves, and then spent several minutes wrestling the piano back into place. He could hear the fire engine and ambulance bells now, and so he donned his greatcoat and hat, and hurried outside to see where they were heading.

He was forced to jump back onto the narrow pavement when a fire truck came hurtling past him on the wrong side of the road and screeched around the corner towards the seafront. Catching a glimpse of Rita at the wheel, he clucked his tongue and shook his head. That girl would meet a sticky end if she carried on driving like that. And yet her very presence in that truck meant that Beach View had come to no harm, which was an enormous relief.

Ron quickly glanced back down Camden Road to where people were dazedly emerging from their homes to stand and stare, seemingly unaware that the rain was soaking through their nightclothes as they sought the comfort of their neighbours. He could make out the glow of a fire to the west, and another two to the north, but the brightest glow was coming from near the seafront.

Another fire truck came racing down the road, and as he followed it, he noted that there was glass glittering on the wet pavements from dozens of broken windows, and bits of rubble were strewn everywhere – but it seemed Camden Road had been lucky tonight and had missed the worst of it.

Reaching the end of Camden Road he saw that Beach View was indeed still standing and appeared to be in one piece, although it was hard to tell anything much in the gloomy light and the driving rain. But what was very visible was the enormous blaze three streets down that was being tackled by two fire crews and attended by an ambulance.

It looked as if an entire terrace had caught alight, and the ferocity of the fire was such that it could only have been fuelled by a broken gas pipe or an illicit store of petrol – in which case, Rita and those firemen were dicing with death.

Ron stood in a lather of anxiety, praying that the gas would be turned off at the mains before this entire section of Cliffehaven went up. And just as he'd decided to ask the fire chief, John Hicks, if he should start evacuating everyone his prayers were answered. The gas engineers arrived and within minutes the flames were being brought under control.

He was about to cross the road to check on everyone at Beach View when he saw Robert, Sarah and Ivy emerge from the alleyway at a run.

'We're all safe,' said Robert quickly. 'I've done some minor repairs, but as far as I can tell there's no serious damage.'

'Proper shook us all up, though,' said Ivy, her tearful gaze fixed to the blaze. 'I got mates living there. Do you reckon anyone got out?'

Ron took her hand. 'We can only hope, Ivy,' he said softly.

'Oh, Gawd,' she breathed through her fingers, the tears rolling down her cheeks.

Sarah put her arm around Ivy's trembling shoulders. 'Do you know where the other rockets came down, Uncle Ron?'

'One over to the west, but I think it fell on fields; and two to the north – well away from Briar Lane and the bungalows around Ladysmith Close,' he added quickly. 'It's hard to tell what was hit, but the fire crews are already on them both – and by the sound of it reinforcements are on their way.'

The distant but urgent clanging bells confirmed this, and Sarah hugged Ivy close as she turned back to Ron. 'We want to help,' she said. 'What do you suggest we do?'

Ron gathered his thoughts and led the way back down Camden Road. 'There's nothing we can do about the poor souls trapped in those houses until the fires are out – and even then, I doubt there will be any survivors,' he said sadly.

'No!' Ivy shook her head vigorously. 'We gotta stay positive. Me mates will be all right. They have to.'

''Tis sorry I am to upset you, Ivy, but I really think you should prepare yourself for bad news.'

Ivy squared her shoulders and knuckled away her tears, seemingly determined to cling to hope.

Ron's spirits lightened a little as the WVS wagon entered the street, accompanied by the men of the

Home Guard and Civil Defence, as well as council maintenance crews, and an army of willing helpers armed with blankets and an assortment of tools to help with the clear-up.

'It looks like the auxiliary services are arriving, and as there will be windows to board up, damaged roofs to be weatherproofed and blankets and hot tea to be dispensed, I suggest you and Ivy help the WVS, whilst you come with me, Robert, and make a start on the windows.'

Doris had been curled in John's embrace, blissfully at peace in the afterglow of their early morning lovemaking when the first explosion thrust them back to vicious reality. By the time the second explosion rattled the windows they were dressed and fumbling their way in the darkness to the kitchen. As the final two rockets exploded somewhere beyond the factory they were huddled in a tight embrace beneath the kitchen table.

The noise of the sirens and guns echoed all around them, and when the all-clear eventually sounded, Doris scrambled to her feet and ran to the sitting-room window which gave a panoramic view of the town. In the darkness she could see fires burning fiercely to the east and west of them, but it was the conflagration down by the seafront that made her catch her breath in fear for Peggy and the others.

John had drawn her tightly into his arms, soothing her fears by pointing out that it was too close to the seafront to be Beach View.

Feeling slightly calmer, she took another look and acknowledged he was right. 'But I still have to go down there to check on her,' she said firmly.

'We'll do that once I've made certain everything is secure on the factory estate,' he replied, giving her a hug. 'Come on, Doris, chin up.'

'But we can't leave the house together at this time of the morning,' she gasped. 'What would the neighbours say?'

John chuckled and drew her closer. 'A bit of gossip will take their minds off the V-2s.'

He must have felt her stiffen in his embrace, for he drew back and eyed her quizzically. 'But if the idea upsets you, I could always go out the back way and climb over the fence.' His smile was deeply affectionate as he added, 'Although I might not be quite so spry after this morning's delightful encounter.'

Doris blushed furiously. 'I suppose it would be a bit silly to risk life and limb,' she agreed.

'It is rather,' he replied softly, 'but if it makes you feel easier, I'm quite willing to do it.'

Doris giggled. 'I think we should go out together and to heck with them all. It's not as if we've made a secret about how we feel for each other.'

'Jolly good,' he murmured into her hair.

They pulled on their coats, blew out the candles and went arm in arm into the deep gloom, sheltered by their umbrellas, and so wrapped up in each other they barely noticed the curious faces of those watching them from every front window in Ladysmith Close.

Doris was amazed at how strong her feelings were for this lovely man, and she was positively glowing with happiness as they headed for the factory estate. And yet this profound sense of well-being was overshadowed by the sound of ambulance and fire engine bells resounding throughout the town, and the sight of the fires raging as thick black smoke penetrated the rain.

Reaching the factory gates they were met by the sight of people pouring out of the vast underground shelter, running through the rain towards their work-benches or making for home as a fire blazed on the far eastern perimeter of the factory compound and the emergency lighting came on.

Doris was gratified to see that no one gave them a passing glance, so intent were they on their own agendas – and that there was no sign of Ivy. If she'd spotted them arriving together at this hour she wouldn't have been able to resist making some crude remark about it.

John led Doris to their office, turned on the oil heater, and left her there in the warm whilst he spoke to the security team and checked that all was well.

Doris made a pot of tea and kept watch from the window as the allotment fire was swiftly brought under control. From her vantage point high above the roofs of the factories, she could make out the glow of another blaze somewhere within the eastern hills, and rather hoped it was Chumley's house going up in flames. Slightly shocked by this unchristian thought, she justified it by the fact that if anyone deserved to be blown up, it was Wally Chumley.

However, it was the blaze down near the seafront that really worried her, for Hitler's latest weapon caused devastating damage, not only at the seat of the blast, but in a wide area around it, and she knew she wouldn't rest until she was certain that Peggy and the others at Beach View were all safe.

John returned and they quickly drank the tea before setting off for Camden Road. The rain had finally stopped and the clearing-up was well underway, but it did look as if the heart of the town had escaped the worst.

'Blimey,' spluttered Ivy who was carrying a tray of tea and biscuits away from the WVS wagon. 'You two look cosy. What you been up to, then? As if I didn't know!'

Doris turned scarlet and couldn't meet those knowing eyes. 'Will you keep your voice down?' she hissed furiously.

Ivy laughed uproariously. 'If I were you, I'd be shouting it to the flaming rooftops.' She gave Doris a nudge with her elbow. 'Still life in the old dog, then?' she said, jerking her head towards John and winking at Doris.

'Ivy, behave,' Doris spluttered. Despite the embarrassment of it all, she couldn't help but find the bemused expression on John's face very funny.

Ivy grinned. 'Good luck to the both of yer, I say.'

'I take it that Peggy and everyone at Beach View is all right?' said Doris as John was dragged off by Ron to help board up a window.

'Yeah, we're all fine. Peggy's at home with Daisy and Cordelia, Fran and Danuta are at the hospital, and Rita's fighting that 'orrible fire. The rest of us are helping here.'

'Talking of help,' said the woman behind the WVS counter. 'I've not seen hide nor hair of Cecilia Bridgestock who was supposed to be here, and I could do with a break, Mrs Williams.'

Doris had resigned from the WVS some time ago, but she wasn't in the mood to be churlish. Cecilia was famous for not turning up, and she'd always quite liked Barbara Owen who worked in the library. Now she knew for sure that Peggy was all right, there really was no excuse. 'Of course I'll help,' she replied, stepping up to the large urn.

'Thank you so much,' breathed Barbara, scuttling off before Doris could change her mind.

Doris became aware of Ivy still dithering about. 'Get those teas out before they go cold – and don't stop to gossip. I need you back here.'

Ivy blew a raspberry and then grinned cheekily. 'A bit of the other ain't changed yer much. You're still the same old bossy boots,' she said before hurrying off.

Everyone worked with a will and great camaraderie despite the heavy rain which soaked them all and poured through leaking roofs and empty windows. The supply of tea from the WVS wagon was supplemented by seemingly endless cups from the grateful residents, and shelter was freely offered to those whose homes had yet to be weatherproofed.

Ron had been surprised to see Doris mucking in alongside Ivy and Sarah, and going by the glances she and the Colonel were exchanging at every opportunity it seemed things had moved on fairly rapidly between them. It quite warmed his heart, so when he saw Rosie approaching, her arms loaded with blankets, he gave her a smacking kiss and a quick squeeze.

'What was that for?' she giggled.

'Because you're beautiful and I needed a kiss to keep me going,' he replied with a wink before climbing back up the ladder to rejoin the team of men heaving a tarpaulin over a damaged roof.

Apart from broken windows, loose roof tiles and a couple of unsafe chimneys which had to be taken down, there was very little serious damage to the town centre but, as Ron had feared, not everyone had been so lucky.

The rain had stopped an hour before and as dawn had lightened the sky and the fire crews wearily returned to their station, the full horror of that blaze in Victoria Terrace was revealed.

Ron had tried to deter Ivy from going up to the factory to find out about her friends, but the girl had been adamant, and he suspected there would be tears before the end of the day. Doris was still busy with the WVS, the Colonel had rushed back to the factory after speaking to the fire chief, John Hicks, and Robert had gone to the hospital to tell Fran he had to leave for the Fort. Ivy and Sarah were back at Beach View with an exhausted Rita, and he presumed Danuta was still helping out at the hospital, for he hadn't seen her.

With a promise to return and help Rosie through the lunchtime session, Ron ignored the chill of his sodden clothes, collected Harvey, and went to find John Hicks.

He found him gloomily surveying the sixty-foot-deep crater that gaped another sixty feet across, and had once been three terraced houses. 'How many?' he asked.

'Too many,' replied John, his soot-blackened face drawn with exhaustion and sadness. 'The owners of those three houses left at the start of the war, but they rented them out, and each one was filled to the rafters with factory girls. We can only account for six of them who were on night shift. The rest ...' He gave a ragged sigh and fell silent.

Ron blanched at the depressing thought of all those young lives that had been wiped out in an instant. The only consolation was that they'd known nothing about it and hadn't spent their last minutes in terror and pain.

He took a deep breath and regarded the remaining houses, most of which were were miraculously still almost in one piece. He turned his gaze to the two on the end which were little more than shells standing like sentinels amidst the sea of destruction. 'What about them? Did everyone get out?'

John lit a cigarette and drew the smoke deep into his lungs before releasing it on a long sigh. 'Four fatalities,' he replied. 'There were some other injuries, mostly from flying glass and being crushed by heavy debris – and a suspected heart attack. They were taken to the hospital and most will probably be discharged before the day's out. But nobody will be allowed back until the remaining houses are checked and passed as safe.'

'They look all right to me,' muttered Ron around the stem of his unlit pipe.

'They might appear to be so, but we estimate that about three thousand tons of debris was blasted with massive force into the air – and that can do a great deal of damage to the fabric of any building within a certain range. The blast from this rocket was contained by the surrounding houses, so each and every one on this hill will have to be checked.'

Ron took the pipe from his mouth. 'Even Beach View?'

John nodded. 'The force of that explosion would have travelled deep into the ground, making the whole hill unstable and shaking the foundations of every house on it.' He put a consoling hand on Ron's shoulder. 'It's better to be safe than sorry, Ron.'

'Aye, that it is,' he agreed. 'How long will it be before we know for sure the auld place won't fall down around our ears?'

'Not too long, I hope, because my cottage is just at the bottom of this hill and will need checking too. I'll have a word with the county surveyor and try to chivvy him up.'

They stood in thoughtful silence and Ron puffed on his pipe. 'Do you know where the other rockets came down?'

'My colleagues from Collington station radioed through to tell me that one came down very close to the farm on Cliffe estate and blasted a copse of trees to smithereens. The debris did a fair bit of damage to one of the barns, destroying the winter stock of hay, but everyone's safe.'

John Hicks drew on his cigarette, his hand trembling with weariness. 'The other took out a corner of the allotment. Several sheds were burned down and a good portion of the crops were destroyed, but thankfully no one was there at that time of the morning.'

Ron saw the other man wince as he shifted his weight from his prosthetic leg to his good one. John had lost part of his leg when he'd joined the flotilla of little boats to rescue the men from the Dunkirk beaches back in 1940, and Ron knew the stump often pained him, especially after a night like tonight.

'And the fourth?' Ron prompted.

'That landed in Tom Potter's field on the other side of the hill, killing three sheep and maiming several others that were in lamb. Poor Tom will probably have to put the rest of the flock down – they're half-crazed with terror.'

Ron knew how hard Tom had worked to increase his prize-winning flock, and could only hope that he'd get compensation – but it would hit the man hard, for his family had farmed that bit of land for over three generations. He saw John easing his leg again. 'I'll leave you to get home and rest,' he murmured.

'It's been a long, difficult few hours,' John admitted, crushing out his cigarette and stretching his back. 'But home isn't the same without Sal and our little Harry, so I prefer to be at the fire station.'

'They're safer in Somerset with their Auntie Vi and our Anne,' said Ron, glancing again at the obscene aftermath of Hitler's latest weapon.

'They are that,' muttered John. 'But it doesn't stop me missing them.'

Ron gripped his shoulder in sympathy, then tugged on Harvey's lead and headed for home. He understood John's loneliness and the void that had been left in his life by the absence of his wife and child. There wasn't a day when he didn't long to see his family again, to hear their chatter and noise, even the tears, tantrums and mess they always left behind. But Cliffehaven was once again in the line of fire, and he was prepared to make any sacrifice to keep them out of danger.

The smell of burning hung in the damp, cold air as he regarded the front of Beach View and the debris scattered over the roof and down the steps. There was a deep scar in the brickwork where something had hit the front wall with some force, and tiles were missing from the roof.

He walked on and turned into the alleyway where he let Harvey off the lead. A swift glance took in the boarded kitchen window, the guttering that had been loosened by a lump of concrete falling on it, and the smashed roof tiles that littered the garden. The chimney didn't look too clever from this side, so he'd have to go up there later and check it over – but the chickens were happily pecking in their coop and the outside lav and shed were still standing. All in all it seemed they hadn't come off too badly considering how close they'd been to that explosion. However, he'd feel more at ease once the surveyor had been round to confirm that there was no serious structural damage.

Harvey scampered up the cellar steps to the kitchen and Ron went into his basement bedroom to check that his ferrets hadn't been too upset by all the noise. They seemed content enough, so he left them slumbering and went up the steps, his thoughts on a very late breakfast. The bitter wind had penetrated his sodden clothes to chill his skin, and he needed a bath and bit of kip before he had to be back at the Anchor for the lunch-time opening.

He entered the kitchen, fully expecting to be told off for mucking up Peggy's floor again, but was met with mournful silence. Rita, Sarah, Cordelia and Peggy were red-eyed as they tried to keep a whining and distraught Harvey from sniffing and pawing at the shoebox which stood in the centre of the table.

Since nobody seemed keen to enlighten him as to what the heck was going on, he grabbed Harvey's collar before reaching for the box and drawing back the scrap of blanket. He had to swallow the lump in his throat as he ran his hand over the stiff little body.

'What happened?'

'She got hit by flying debris,' said Peggy tearfully. 'I found her at the bottom of the front steps with a bit of metal in her back. She was trying to get home, but ... but ...'

'I know you must think us pathetic for crying over a dead cat,' sobbed Rita, 'but after what happened today, losing her is the very last straw.'

'Aye,' muttered Ron, 'that it is.' Harvey was whining and straining to get to Queenie, and it took all his strength to keep him under control.

'This war's so cruel,' sniffed Cordelia, dabbing at her reddened eyes. 'Poor little Queenie. I shall miss her sitting on my chair for a ride every morning.'

'We'll all miss her,' said Sarah. 'Especially Daisy.'

'Where is Daisy?' asked Ron, still wrestling with Harvey.

'Still asleep,' replied Peggy, 'and I'm glad, because I don't want her to see Queenie like this.'

Ron folded the scrap of blanket back over Queenie and placed the box on the high shelf she'd always favoured, which was out of Harvey's reach. He hugged the distraught dog as he sat down, his heart twisting at each whimper and whine. 'Daisy has to learn about life and death, just as we all did as children when our pets died,' he said sadly. 'We'll have a proper funeral this afternoon.'

'Who's having a funeral?' asked Doris, stepping into the room.

'Our sweet little Queenie,' said Peggy, still fighting back her tears.

Doris looked at her askance, but didn't voice her incredulity, perhaps realising that feelings were running high and any scorn at such mourning would not be well received.

'I'm just so relieved you're all right,' she said, giving Peggy a hug. 'I would have come earlier, but I've been helping with the WVS and had to get the wagon back to headquarters so it could be restocked.'

'Will you stay for a cuppa?' Peggy got to her feet, clearly eager to have something to take her mind off Queenie.

'Not this time,' said Doris. 'I have to get back to John who's at the factory.'

'On a Sunday?'

'He's got the names of those thirty factory girls who were killed in Victoria Terrace, and apart from letting the different managers know, the families will have to be informed. As John is the chief supervisor, he feels it's his duty to write to them personally.'

'Poor man,' sighed Sarah. 'I don't envy him.'

'I'll be there to help him,' said Doris. 'Now I must go and leave you to your cat's funeral.'

'It might seem ridiculous to you,' rasped Cordelia. 'But Queenie was part of the family, and although we're all saddened by the loss of so many today, my tears are for her, and I'm not ashamed of them.'

Doris very wisely made no comment and left the house.

Peggy made yet another pot of tea and some toast, and as Harvey went to sit by the sink to keep watch over Queenie, she came to a decision.

'Daisy's too young to understand why we're burying Queenie,' she said before Ron could leave the room. 'She's already had a terrible shock, and I don't think it's wise to upset her any further.'

Ron thought for a moment and then nodded in agreement – Daisy was not quite three, after all, and perhaps it was too much. 'I'll see to Queenie when I've had a bath and eaten something.'

An hour later, he'd left a distressed Harvey at home and was tramping up the hill with the shoe-box tucked under his arm and a spade over his shoulder. The wind was still cutting, but the sky was clear, and he could hear the beautiful songs of black-birds and robins as he came to the copse of trees hidden away in an isolated dip in the hill and gently placed the box on the ground.

The earth was soft and lay deep above the chalk in this sheltered dell, so she wouldn't be disturbed by foraging animals, or scented by Harvey. Once he'd finished digging, he placed the box in the deep hole.

'Goodbye, wee girl,' he murmured, filling it in with soil and camouflaging the spot with broken tree branches and large pieces of flint he'd found lying about. 'To be sure, you'll be snug and safe now.'

He made a rough cross from two bits of apple wood tied with string, and pushed it firmly into the ground. Getting to his feet, he stood by that little grave for a long moment remembering Queenie's short life, and the joy she'd brought to them all.

The tears came and he swiped them away, berating himself for being a soft old fool. It was absurd to feel her loss so deeply when others had died today, but like all his animals, he'd loved and cared for her, and would miss her trotting after him on her three legs, and the weight of her in his pocket as he'd carried her home.

He eventually turned away and headed for Beach View, knowing how empty it would feel without her.

10

Peggy had been dreading the moment Daisy asked where Queenie was, but the child hadn't noticed her absence until after she'd had a late breakfast. Peggy gently told her that Queenie had gone to Heaven, and because she was very happy there, she wouldn't be coming back.

Daisy didn't really understand and asked a lot of questions about why Queenie had wanted to go to Heaven instead of staying here, and why she couldn't play with her any more.

Peggy did her best to explain and gave her a cuddle as she'd shed a few tears, but she knew from past experience with her other children that Daisy would soon forget Queenie, and was thankful that little ones had short memories.

Ron returned from his sad task and made a huge fuss of poor Harvey, who'd been wandering through the house and garden looking for his playmate. They left shortly afterwards so Ron could help Rosie finish the lunchtime session at the pub.

The kitchen was quiet, for Fran and Danuta were still at the hospital, Sarah and Rita had returned to their beds to catch up on sleep, and the electricity was still off so they couldn't put the wireless on. Cordelia sat with Daisy on her lap reading her a story by candlelight as the boarded-up window made the kitchen so dark, and Peggy was trying to concentrate on her mending, but she was all too aware of the empty hearthrug, and kept pricking her fingers with the needle.

She gave up, lit a cigarette and read the headlines in the paper, which had only just been delivered.

But after a while she found she hadn't taken any of it in, so set the paper aside and tried to find the heart to go outside and see what was left of the houses in Victoria Terrace. However, she'd heard enough graphic descriptions from the others, and the thought of becoming one of those people who went to stand and gawp at scenes of others' tragedy made her shudder, so she picked up her darning again.

As she sewed, her thoughts turned to the clothing factory and Mavis Anderson – or Whitlock as she was now. Mavis had been due to start there today, and was no doubt already picking out the women she could boss about, and those who would stand up to her – and she'd certainly find quite a few of those on the factory floor. Back in their schooldays, Peggy had never been one of Mavis's targets, but she'd seen the harm her bullying had done to others and had fought their corner, which was probably why Mavis had left her alone. But Mavis also had a darker side, she remembered. She would sneak to the teachers, steal food from lunch boxes and demand money in return for keeping her mouth shut over some childish indiscretion. Sharp-eyed and nosy, she'd made it her business to find something she could use as a lever to get her own way and show herself in a good light to the teachers – who were taken in by her big eyes and innocent expression.

She had yet to meet her again since they'd left school, but that dubious joy awaited her tomorrow morning. She did so hope Mavis had changed for the better, but if she still had that vindictive streak in her, Peggy could only see trouble ahead. She would have to keep an eye on things, stop any fights erupting and try not to get caught up in the middle of it all. Thankfully they'd be on different shifts, and she could only hope that Mavis stuck to her hours and didn't try and interfere in hers.

Ivy came hurtling through the door to break into her thoughts by shouting out her news. 'Me two mates were on night shift, so they're all right,' she declared, dragging off her coat and scarf and plumping down into a kitchen chair.

'That's the first bit of good news I've heard today,' Peggy said with a soft smile. 'I'm so glad for you.'

Ivy was warming to her subject. 'Honestly, Auntie Peggy, I'm that relieved,' she gabbled on. 'I dunno what I'd've done if they'd bought it, 'cos we all lived in the same street since we was nippers with our arses 'anging out of our knickers, and come down 'ere together to get away from the bombs and 'ave a bit of fun.' She pulled a face. 'We got that wrong, and no mistake. It's as bad 'ere as in the Smoke.'

'Where will your friends live now?' Peggy asked as Ivy stopped talking to draw breath.

'They're going into the hostel at Collington and will get bussed in every day,' said Ivy, distracted by Daisy who'd come to lean against her knee. She ruffled her dark curls. 'Hello, love, what you lookin' so gloomy about?'

'Keenie gone to Heaven,' the child replied solemnly. 'Mumma said I can't go and play with her.'

Ivy's eyes widened and she shot a questioning glance at Peggy who nodded back. 'I'll explain later,' she murmured.

Ivy hugged Daisy and gave her a kiss before encouraging her to return to Cordelia's story-telling. Once the child was settled, she leaned towards Peggy and became quite tearful as Peggy explained what had happened.

She took a moment to compose herself, and then reached for Peggy's hand. 'I'm sorry I got carried away earlier, Auntie Peg,' she said softly, 'but there is more bad news, I'm afraid.'

Peggy's heart thudded with dread as Ivy pulled a piece of paper from her trouser pocket and placed it on the table.

'This is the list of five of the girls who died today. They all worked for Solly.'

Peggy wondered when this awful day would end, and reluctantly picked up the list to read the names with deepening sorrow. They'd been a young, jolly group of girls who'd gone everywhere together and were the life and soul of every party. They'd always been ready to tell a rather off-colour joke or start a singalong to the music on the wireless – but they'd also been hard-working, adept at their jobs and true team players. To think of all that youthful exuberance being wiped out, was almost too much to bear.

'The Colonel doesn't have their details, and the telephone lines are still down, so he wondered if you'd be kind enough to tell Solly so their families can be informed.'

Ivy bit her lip. 'I'm sorry to ask you, Auntie Peg, it's been an 'orrible day all round, but as shop floor supervisor, you're best placed to deal with this.'

Peggy took a deep breath and then got to her feet. 'If you could help Cordelia keep an eye on Daisy, I'll go and tell Solly now.'

At Ivy's nod, she pulled on her coat, tied her scarf over her head and grabbed the umbrella in case it decided to rain again. Kissing Daisy goodbye and promising to return as soon as possible, she hurried out of the house and, once she was in the alleyway, broke into a run.

She needed to escape the horrors of the day; the sadness, and the awful feeling of helplessness that threatened to overwhelm her. Tears were hot on her face, and she stopped running as she approached the factory gates, knowing it was futile, for no matter how far or fast she ran, she could never escape the bitter realities of this war. And yet, as she tried to get her breath back, wiped away her tears and gazed up at the austere red-brick building, she was comforted by the knowledge that some things never changed.

Solly would be there in his office as he always was on a Sunday which, in his Jewish faith, was regarded as a working day like any other. Friday night to Saturday night was his Sabbath, and it was the only time he stayed at home with Rachel – unless there was an emergency. And Camden Road might look a bit battered, but with everyone pulling together, there was once again the harmony of good fellowship – and that was growing stronger year by year as this war carried on.

Peggy hadn't run like that for years, and she was still quite breathless as she trudged up the long flight of stairs to his office and found him with his elegant wife, Rachel, going through the weekly accounts.

'Peggy, my dear.' Solly rose from his chair immediately, his concern clear in his face as he put his arm about her shoulders. 'What has happened to bring you here in such distress?'

Peggy couldn't answer, so Rachel pulled out a chair and pressed her into it. 'Sit down, Peggy, and get your breath back.' She regarded Peggy's reddened eyes and gently cupped her face in her hand. 'Is everyone all right at home?'

'We're all fine,' she managed, 'though the house took a bit of a battering. I ran all the way here, which was a bit silly, considering how out of condition I am,' she added with a lightness she didn't feel.

'That was indeed very foolish,' Rachel replied with a soft smile.

Peggy had now got her breath back, and she looked into their worried faces. 'But I do have some bad news and thought you should know straight away.'

Rachel had poured glasses of brandy for them all, and she set them down on the desk. 'Is it about the girls from Victoria Terrace?' she asked gently.

'I'm afraid it is,' Peggy replied, placing the list on the desk before taking a restorative sip of the warming brandy.

'Oy vay,' breathed Solly, his dark eyes bright with the ready tears Peggy had witnessed many times over the years. 'We were afraid of this when we saw the fire,' he said gruffly. 'It would have been a miracle if anyone had survived – but we'd hoped for that miracle and that they were elsewhere. I can't believe they're gone. This place won't feel at all the same without them.'

Rachel gripped Solly's hand, her expression equally sorrowful, for those girls had been very popular with everyone. 'Did *anyone* survive?' she asked.

Peggy sipped some more brandy before answering. 'Sadly, there were over thirty killed this morning; the only survivors were six girls on the night shift at the armaments factory. Colonel White is evidently dealing with everything up there, but these girls' families will have to be informed.'

'Solly and I will do that, Peggy,' Rachel murmured. 'And all the other workers will also need to be informed before the rumour mill starts grinding.'

'I suggest we do as we've always done in these awful circumstances,' said Peggy. 'Each shift is told by their supervisor before they start work, and after a short eulogy and prayer, we hold a minute's silence.'

'I disagree entirely,' said Mavis Whitlock, who'd approached so silently that no one had heard her come to the door. 'It's all utter nonsense, and totally inappropriate in a workplace.'

Peggy realised that Mavis had missed the start of what she'd been saying as she'd eavesdropped, but it seemed everyone was so shocked by her outburst and sudden appearance, they were in no mood to correct her.

Mavis bustled in, the picture of efficiency in her tweed skirt, immaculate white blouse and sensible shoes, her expression purposeful, not one hair out of place in the tight victory rolls.

'Hello, Mavis,' said Peggy without enthusiasm. 'I'm sorry you don't agree, but if you had ...'

Mavis butted in. 'You always were a milksop, Peggy Dawson,' she said briskly. 'Allowing your heart to rule your head when only discipline and order is called for.'

Peggy heard Rachel's gasp of astonishment and got to her feet to face Mavis, eye to eye. 'Five of our most popular girls were killed this morning,' she said evenly. 'It's only right we should acknowledge their passing – just as we've done for all the others we've lost.'

'Sentimental claptrap,' snapped Mavis, her grey eyes hardening beneath severely plucked eyebrows. 'I might have known *you* were behind such ridiculous self-indulgence. The dead are dead and the living have a duty to get on with helping to win this war.'

Peggy noted Solly's expression darkening and was about to reply, but Mavis clearly hadn't finished airing her views, so she let her dig herself into an even deeper hole.

Mavis squared her shoulders and looked down her nose at Peggy. 'There's no place for mawkish sentiment when we're on a very tight schedule. Wasting time with silly prayers and unnecessary eulogies will achieve nothing but provide an excuse for those half-witted women to hang about gossiping and feeling sorry for themselves instead of getting on with their work.'

Peggy felt her hackles rise as she looked at the mean little mouth, the hard eyes and stubborn chin. The years had clearly not softened Mavis, but sharpened her sense of self-importance and honed her skill for being bossy and nasty with it. She could see the storm gathering in Solly's eyes, and Rachel's look of disgust, and decided to help Mavis talk herself into trouble.

'So, what do you suggest?' she asked.

Mavis pushed Peggy roughly to one side and addressed Solly directly. 'With your permission, Solly, I shall get your secretary to type out an announcement first thing tomorrow and pin it to the noticeboard next to where they clock in and out. That way, everyone will be informed without a minute's work being lost.'

Solly rose slowly from behind his desk, his imposing height and width made all the more daunting by the fury in his eyes. 'I don't know what my brother does in these circumstances, but that is not the way we do things here,' he said flatly. 'We work as part of a team from the youngest porter to the most senior staff, sharing our joys as well as our sadness, and when one of us is taken, we mourn them as part of the family.'

Mavis took a step back as his face reddened, the storm broke and his voice thundered out.

'*No* member of Goldman's will *ever* be a name on a list tacked to a bloody noticeboard!' he roared, slamming his fist on the desk. 'They will receive the full courtesy of a short eulogy, a prayer and a minute's silence!'

He was breathing heavily as he glared at Mavis who'd taken another step back, grown quite pale beneath her make-up and was visibly trembling. 'Is that absolutely clear, Mavis?' he roared.

'Yes, Solly,' she whispered, her head bowed.

'Good,' he barked. 'Because I don't wish to have this conversation again – and while we're at it, you'll call me Mr Goldman until I tell you otherwise – and show Mrs Reilly some respect for the position she holds here.'

Mavis dipped her head even further. 'Yes, Mr Goldman.'

Like Rachel, Peggy was well acquainted with Solly's volcanic rages, and because they came and went as swiftly as a summer storm, they no longer had the power to intimidate her. But she was utterly fascinated by the change in Mavis.

It appeared that, like all bullies, she liked to dole it out but couldn't take it. The obnoxious, self-important and aggressive woman had been cowed into a quivering wreck. It would be very interesting to see how long she lasted in the job now she'd put Solly's back up on her first day.

Solly buttoned his jacket and picked up the list, his temper still simmering but now under tight control. 'Peggy, I will inform this shift and give the eulogy. I know it's your day off, but I would be very grateful if you'd stay and lead us in prayer.'

He turned his flat gaze of contempt on Mavis. 'Mrs Whitlock, you will accompany us and learn how we do things here.'

He swept out of the room, and Mavis shot a malevolent glare at Peggy before scuttling after him.

Rachel softly touched Peggy's arm as they headed for the door to the outer office. 'You're going to have to watch that one,' she murmured. 'I have a nasty feeling she's trouble.'

'You'd better believe it,' Peggy muttered. 'I don't know what Solly was thinking of to take her on.'

'He probably thought she'd improved since schooldays,' Rachel replied with a sigh. They walked through Madge's office after the others. 'It seems his brother has pulled a fast one,' Rachel continued. 'I wouldn't mind betting he's delighted to be rid of her.'

The two women shared knowing looks before going down the stairs to join Solly, who was calling for silence on the shop floor and sending someone to fetch the people who were in the warehouse, canteen and storerooms.

As they waited for everyone to assemble, Peggy could almost feel the animosity radiating from Mavis, and was relieved to know that she had Rachel on her side. Solly might think he was in charge, but it was Rachel who steered the Goldman ship both here and at home, and if she wanted Mavis gone, then she would see it done.

Doris and John had gone to the canteen for a lunch of hearty soup, and then worked through the long afternoon, sharing the sad list of those who'd been killed and writing letters of condolence.

'I feel very guilty about all this,' John admitted at one point. 'When I was in the army I knew every man under my command and could add a personal touch to my letters. Whereas, to my shame, I have no recollection of most of these women – they were just names on duty rosters.'

'At least their shop-floor managers could give us a little insight into what they were like,' said Doris, trying to read the scrawled handwriting on the notes that had been sent up to the office from the various factories.

'Yes, that helps a little,' he replied with a deep sigh. 'But I still feel guilty that I didn't make it my business to get to know them.'

'I don't see how you possibly could,' said Doris, putting down her pen and easing her aching hand. 'There are over a thousand women working on this estate at any one time. With changing shifts and all the comings and goings of personnel, it would be impossible.'

He nodded. 'I know you're right,' he said, 'but from now on I'll make it my business to visit the factories more so I can put faces to names. I might not still be in the military, but this is a sort of army – an army of men and women who are doing their bit to win this war as much as any soldier – and it's my duty to look after them.'

Doris felt a loving warmth sweep through her as she watched him begin another letter. His sense of duty and caring nature were just two of the many qualities that drew her to him.

She picked up her pen again, but sat there for a moment, her thoughts turning to Ted. He'd been kind too, and very generous throughout their marriage, especially when it had come to her divorce settlement and monthly maintenance payments. But there had been a side to him that no one outside their marriage had seen – a side she'd only witnessed after his death.

Ted Williams had been a popular man and half the town had turned out for the short memorial service that was held for him and his new wife, but the people of Cliffehaven had only known him as the cheerful manager of the Home and Colonial who was always ready for a chat and slipped them an extra ounce of cheese or a can of beans from under the counter – not the husband who'd cheated on her for years, secretly remortgaged her home to pay off his debts, and left her with nothing.

Doris still smarted from that final betrayal, and when that spike of fury threatened to unsettle her, she determinedly squashed it. She'd survived it all to find satisfying, well-paid work and happiness in her rented bungalow, and after last night, she had very high hopes of a bright future with John.

The nights were drawing in, and by four it was already dark. Doris finished the last letter, added a stamp and placed it on top of the others. Being Sunday there was no postal collection, but she'd put them in the box tonight for the early one tomorrow morning.

'I hope we never have to do that awful task again,' she sighed, collecting the pile of envelopes and slipping them into her handbag.

'It's never an easy job,' agreed John, sitting back in his chair to stare down at the dimly lit factory estate. It was raining again, the wind strengthening to blow dead leaves and debris across the deserted walkways. 'How about we have a cup of tea before we head for home? The rain may have stopped by then.'

Doris thought that was highly unlikely but didn't argue. She didn't fancy the walk home either, and a cup of tea would be welcome after licking all those stamps and envelopes. Minutes later they were sipping the tea, warmed by the two-bar electric fire and feeling cosy as the rain splattered against the window and hammered on the tin roof.

'How's your throat?' John said. 'I forgot to ask with all that's been going on.'

'It's still a bit tender, but nothing I can't deal with,' she replied, smiling to reassure him – although in all the chaos, she'd barely noticed it.

'Jolly good,' he replied. 'And you'll be delighted to hear that you'll never see Chumley again.'

'That's a comforting thought, John. But how can you be so sure?'

He leaned forward and took her hand. 'Do you remember that I was called to that emergency committee meeting at the Officers' Club yesterday afternoon?'

Doris's smile was wan. 'Was it only yesterday? It feels like a lifetime ago.'

'Certainly a great deal has happened since,' he agreed. 'But that meeting was called because some serious discrepancies were found in the club's bar records. Bottles of spirits and hundreds of cartons of cigarettes couldn't be accounted for.'

Doris stiffened and gripped his hand as she thought about the upright Admiral Falkner who was in charge of ordering stock for the bar and undertook his responsibility with meticulous attention to detail. 'Surely they don't suspect Peter Falkner?' she gasped.

'Absolutely not,' John said firmly, clearly shocked by the idea. 'It was Peter who alerted the committee to the discrepancies. He's only been in charge of stocking the club's cellars for three months, and being an honest man, rather took it as read that the previous incumbent had kept proper records of purchases and sales.'

Doris didn't interrupt. She had a fair idea where this was leading.

'Admiral Falkner might be retired from the navy, but he's a busy man with a great many other commitments, and when he finally had the time to sit down and go through the books, he began to suspect foul play. He said nothing to the committee until he'd had time to investigate. Having spoken to our suppliers and gone through the order sheets and invoices with them, the culprits were revealed and he immediately called that extraordinary meeting.'

John paused for breath. 'I can see you've already guessed who was at the heart of it all, Doris, and to be honest, it was hardly a surprise to any of us.'

'If that was the case, then why was he on the committee in the first place?' Doris asked.

'Chumley had been elected onto it some years ago because his title gave the club a certain kudos, and he was deemed upright and honest enough to be put in charge of ordering the bar stock.' John grimaced. 'It just goes to show how a title can blind perfectly sensible people into making bad judgements.'

'Chumley and his wife fooled a lot of people,' Doris murmured. 'As I know to my cost.'

John stubbed out his cigarette rather forcibly before continuing his story. 'Three months ago, the committee began hearing complaints about Chumley reneging on his debts. His club membership hadn't been paid for almost a year, and his bar bills were adding up to a serious amount. He'd been given leeway because of his wife's death, but it was felt he was now taking liberties, so we agreed that he should be voted off the committee, and relieved of his victualling duties. I must say I was glad to see the back of him, and I think most of the other committee members felt the same.'

'So, he was up to his old tricks,' murmured Doris.

'Indeed he was, Doris. During his time on the committee he'd found someone at both wholesalers who wasn't averse to making some money on the side. He'd put in an order for three cases of whisky, say, bill it to the club, and then sell one off and share a portion of the profit with the warehouseman to keep him sweet. The same with the cigarettes and tobacco. He had quite a business going until the Admiral took over.'

'He's not going to be allowed to get away with it, is he?' gasped Doris.

'Our chairman reported it to the police immediately, so I suspect he arrived home yesterday to find the police waiting there to arrest him.'

'That's marvellous news,' she breathed. 'And if James Harcourt can find evidence of him skimming the charity money, it should keep him in prison for many years to come.'

'I telephoned James straight after the meeting, so he's well aware of their decision and the reason behind it. He told me he's got enough evidence of laundering the charity monies to take to the police now. So it really is over, Doris.'

Close to tears with relief, she grasped John's hand. 'Thank you,' she said softly. 'Without your help, Chumley would have got away with it.'

John smiled bashfully at her praise and then looked out of the window. 'It's stopped raining,' he said. 'Let me get you home before it starts again.'

They turned everything off and locked the door behind them to go arm in arm through the estate. The factories were humming with activity as the shifts changed and the canteen became busy, the lights spilling from the lightly dimmed-out windows across the wet concrete and oily puddles. The sense that nothing would stop the war effort despite the terrible losses that had been incurred made Doris feel very positive – and the thought that Chumley would get his just deserts was the icing on the cake.

Having put the letters in the box, they bent their heads to the wind and hurried on to Ladysmith Close. Doris opened her front door, eager to be in the warm and looking forward to another night of passion.

'I haven't even thought about supper,' she said, shedding her coat. 'But there is some stew left over which I could heat up.'

'I won't stay for supper, if you don't mind, my dear,' he said.

The disappointment was sharp. 'Oh, but I thought ...'

'It's been a long day, Doris, and neither of us got much sleep last night,' he said, giving her a rather bashful smile.

'Yes, of course, you're right,' she said quickly, although she didn't feel at all tired – in fact, she hadn't felt this alive in years. 'It's probably better we both get a good night's sleep after ... after ...'

John took her hands and drew her close. 'It was a wonderful night, Doris,' he murmured, 'and I will hold it in my heart forever, but ...'

'But?' She pulled her hands from his grasp, her desire drenched by a cold wash of sudden doubt. 'Was last night all you wanted from me?'

'Not at all,' he said urgently, grasping her arms. 'I love you, Doris, and can think of nothing I want more than to be with you every night. But I'm not in a position to ask you to marry me, and it wouldn't be fair to you, or your reputation, if we continued to sleep together without the respectability of a wedding ring.'

Doris's heart missed a beat and then began to race – she hadn't expected him to talk of marriage. 'But we don't have to make things formal between us,' she said breathlessly. 'We could carry on as we are and to heck with my reputation – which is probably already hanging by a thread after today.'

'My dearest girl; if only we could,' he said sadly. 'Last night was wonderful – you are wonderful – but we acted in haste, Doris, without any thought for the consequences.'

Doris was beginning to wonder if he was trying to finish things between them but was too gentlemanly to say it outright. 'I'm hardly likely to get into the family way,' she said with a brittle little laugh, 'so I don't really understand what other consequences there could be.'

He seemed lost for words and she regarded him squarely. 'Are you trying to tell me you regret last night?'

'No, no, no. That's not it at all,' he replied, dragging his fingers through his thick silvery hair in agitation. 'If I could, I'd get down on one knee right now and ask you to marry me. I love you and don't want to lose you, but I have others to consider before I make such a commitment.'

Doris suddenly understood. 'You're worried about how your son would feel, aren't you?'

'That's it exactly,' he said, reaching once more for her hands. 'Michael lost his mother shortly before he was taken prisoner, and although I write regularly to him, I've only ever received a few standard POW postcards from him. I don't even know if he's received those letters, and if he hasn't, he'll know nothing of my life since I retired from the army – and certainly nothing about you.'

Doris could see the conflict of love and loyalties in his eyes and her heart went out to him as he drew her closer.

He rested his chin lightly on her head. 'Life in a POW camp must be fraught with danger and difficulty and for all I know he could still be grieving for his mother. I couldn't bear the thought of him coming home at the end of the war to find that I'd married again. He'd think I'd forgotten her, you see. They were very close.'

'I can understand that,' Doris murmured. 'There's a special bond between mother and son, which I have with my Anthony.' She didn't add that the bond had been severely frazzled since Anthony had married Suzie. This was not the moment.

'Would your son approve of you marrying again so soon?'

Doris almost smiled at the irony of the situation with her beloved son. 'Ted and I were separated for a long time before the divorce, and he married again the same weekend he and his new wife were killed. My Anthony loved his father, but he has his own life now and I doubt he'd have any objections to me finding happiness again.'

'And do you think you could be happy with me?'

'Oh, yes,' she breathed, her heart beating wildly at the idea of spending the rest of her life with him.

He kissed her passionately and then firmly drew back. 'I know it's asking a great deal of you, Doris, but we must be strong,' he said, 'and patient – and not allow our passions to rule us. Once this war is over and my boy is home, he'll have the chance to get to know you – just as your son needs to get to know me. And then we can make things formal between us.'

Doris understood that he loved his son and was only trying to do the right thing, but she was a bit miffed at the idea of having to wait until the son approved – or otherwise. And what if he was against it? What were they supposed to do then? Just forget the whole thing and walk away? The thought twisted her heart.

'But we can still share suppers and cosy evenings by the wireless?' she asked hopefully.

'Of course we can, Doris. We'll go on as before last night. Nothing has changed between us, and it never will.' He kissed her, gave her a hug and then opened the front door. 'I'll see you in the morning, and take you out to dinner at the club to celebrate Chumley's downfall.'

Doris returned his cheery wave and closed the door. He'd said that nothing had changed, but it had. She'd experienced the sweetness of loving, passionate intimacy with a man she'd come to adore, and she wanted more. But the sense of honour and correctness that had so drawn her to him was now setting them apart. Did he really mean for her to live like a nun? Could they continue to share almost every moment of every day without succumbing to the needs that had been awoken in both of them?

She gave a sigh of frustration and headed into the kitchen. Only time would tell.

11

Over two weeks had passed since the V-2 attack, and it broke Ron's heart to see poor Harvey still wandering about the house and garden looking for Queenie. He was clearly deeply puzzled by her absence, and missing her company.

Cordelia missed the morning ride down on the stairlift with her on her lap, and Peggy was finding it distressing not to see her stretched out by the fire or sitting on her shelf, keeping an eye on everyone. The girls seemed to have accepted she'd gone, and little Daisy had been far too excited about her upcoming birthday party to think of anything else.

Cordelia's eightieth birthday celebrations had been a little muted as they'd followed so soon after the devastation of that attack, but everyone had enjoyed the sumptuous meal at the golf club, which had been followed by a very lively evening in the Anchor. Bertie had driven Cordelia home and Ron had had to carry her up the stairs, for she was out for the count after too much excitement and far too many sherries.

Ron had been intrigued by the rumours that were flying about of Wally Chumley being arrested, but it seemed that anyone who was in the know wasn't talking. As Chumley had been seen with two black eyes and a bloodied nose shortly before his arrest, the gossips were having a field day; speculating on the whys and wherefores with increasing flights of fancy that often bordered on the ludicrous. It was only when his short court appearance was announced in the newspaper that anyone knew he'd been charged with theft and the misuse of charity money and refused bail – but that only ground the rumour mill even harder.

However, even that scandal couldn't eclipse the day-to-day struggle of trying to remain cheerful, keeping the larder supplied and staying warm as December arrived, and winter began to really bite with chill winds and icy rain. Coal was at a premium, and the scrappy bits of low-grade anthracite and coal dust they had managed to get barely kept the range going at Beach View, so it was hot water bottles and blankets all round in the evenings as they sat in the kitchen listening to the wireless. But at least the county surveyor had passed Beach View as habitable, and that had come as a huge relief.

The war news was the usual mixture of victories and defeats. The *Tirpitz*, which had been hiding in the Tromso Fjord, had at last been sunk by 617 Bomber Squadron; Patton had begun a new offensive in Holland; the Home Fleet had sunk almost an entire enemy convoy off the coast of southern

Norway, and the French troops had driven through the Belfort Gap to the Rhine to capture Strasbourg.

However, yesterday morning it had been reported that the political unrest which had been growing since the liberation of mainland Greece had escalated into civil war, and the Allies had placed Athens under martial law – and the 14th Army was still battling it out against the Japs in Burma.

Ron wondered if the Burma campaign would ever end, for it was being continually hampered by the monsoon, which meant that the whole thing had been dragging on for years – long before his Jim had been sent there. And yet the Allies held the advantage, even through the monsoon, for the Japanese didn't have the same reliable supply network of air and land support, and it was becoming clear that although there were still small pockets of resistance, the Japanese were slowly being weakened through lack of food, transport and ammunition.

Setting all these thoughts aside, Ron straightened his tie and regarded his reflection in the bedroom mirror. He didn't look too bad for a man in his sixties, he decided, although he felt like a trussed-up turkey in the starched collar and tie Rosie had rather firmly insisted he wear. It was Sunday, and as the Anchor was closed, they were going for a late lunch and leisurely drink at the Officers' Club to avoid the horde of small children who would be arriving later for Daisy's birthday party – although she wouldn't actually turn three until Thursday.

Shuddering at the thought of that noisy invasion, Ron picked up Jim's blue fedora. As he gave it a brush, he regarded Harvey snoring on his bed. It was all right for some, he thought without rancour.

He finished brushing the dog hairs off the fedora and glanced around his room. It was looking quite bare now he'd emptied the cupboards and stowed his fishing and hunting gear in the shed which he'd recently transferred from Beach View to the back garden of the pub. The ferrets would stay here under his bed until the day after the wedding, and then they too would go to their new home in the purpose-built housing Rosie had insisted he erect next to the shed. How the ferrets would feel about that, he didn't know, but Harvey would be all right – he'd have Monty for company and be given free rein over the Anchor.

There were only six days to go before their wedding, and things were gathering pace as all the last-minute details were attended to and fussed over. Ron was feeling quite relaxed about it all, eager to get it done with so they could start their new life together without playing hide-and-seek with the neighbours at five o'clock every morning.

But Rosie had spun into a complete tizzy: she was convinced that a rocket would fall on the Town Hall before they could have the service; or that she'd forgotten something vital in the planning; her dress wouldn't fit on the day; or her most trusted barmaid would fall ill and not be able to look after the pub.

And then she'd turned her attention to fretting over the menu for the wedding breakfast, and if the Officers' Club could get the champagne she hadn't been able to find from her usual suppliers.

Ron grimaced, for in her panic, Rosie had gone to see her arch rival, Gloria Stevens, at the Crown – but even Gloria with all her black market contacts was unable to oblige. He'd tried to ease the situation by telling her that any champagne would do, or failing that, a good white wine, which he could easily get.

That suggestion had gone down like a lead balloon, so he'd sought advice from his old friends Fred the Fish and Alf the butcher as to what on earth he could do to calm her down. They hadn't been a lot of help, merely pronouncing that women were inclined to throw a wobbly at times like this and the best way of dealing with it was to turn a blind eye and get on with something sensible – like organising an evening out with the boys before he tied the knot.

He liked the idea of a bachelors' night out but knew it would only lead to trouble with Rosie, and she'd kill him if he turned up with a massive hangover and stinking of drink on their wedding day. Perhaps he'd organise it for Thursday, which would give him a day and a half to recover.

Glad that he'd made one good decision today, Ron checked his watch. He still had some time before he had to leave to meet Rosie at the Anchor where he'd ordered a taxi to take them up to the club, but he was reluctant to go upstairs where he'd no doubt get roped into some job or other. The hurrying footsteps and excited chatter from up there signalled that Peggy, Danuta, Cordelia and Sarah were busily preparing the children's tea party whilst trying to keep an overexcited Daisy occupied.

He sank onto the bed next to the dozing Harvey, who'd also sought refuge from the chaos, and reached for the letter that had arrived yesterday morning from Jim, which he'd already read twice.

Ron had managed to get to the post before Peggy, and was very glad he had, for Jim had written it on his last night in India, and had given a fairly graphic account of his time on leave – why his recovery had taken so long, and how close he'd come to death through the combination of septicaemia and malaria as he'd waited in the field hospital on that jungle battle zone to be airlifted out.

Ron unfolded the letter and skimmed over the bits he didn't want to read again, for he could imagine all too well how helpless Jim must have felt as he'd waited at death's door for that life-saving airlift. He paused at the bottom of the page and read the last paragraph.

I'm telling you, Da, that second bit of shrapnel was so close to my spine that one careless move could have had me crippled for life. For the love of God, will you get the doctors to do something about yours before it does real damage? I know you regard it as a reminder of all the pals you lost, but it's clearly getting more painful every

year, and at your age, it can't be doing you any good. In
fact, Da, Frank and I agree that you'd be much better off
without it – especially as you're about to marry the
lively Rosie.

Ron turned the page. He didn't like the reference
to his age and certainly had no intention of letting
some half-baked quack muck about with his back.

The letter continued in a much more light-hearted
way with accounts of Jim's time off in India. There
had been heavy drinking sessions in the bars and
hotels with his friend Big Bert, which had usually
led to a jolly good punch-up and finished with them
all being pals. He and Bert had rarely made it back
to their hotel during those two weeks, often waking
the next morning sprawled on a beach with a blinding hangover that only another drink could cure.

Ron smiled at that, for it brought back memories
of some of his leaves in which he'd enjoyed getting
drunk and hitting someone before becoming pals
and drinking together in seedy foreign bars lining
even seedier waterfronts. But soldiers were soldiers
the world over and clearly nothing had changed. He
returned to the letter.

Despite the brawls, which were more about letting off
steam than anything, there was great camaraderie
between us and the Yanks, for we Brits had all witnessed
the hair-raising heroics of the USAAF pilots and crews
which had come in repeatedly under heavy enemy

bombardment to deliver equipment and carry our
wounded to safety.

I'd made a promise to myself during one of those
airlifts that I'd buy a very large drink for the first Yank
pilot I came across – and so I did just that, to thank him
and honour his courage. I must have laid it on a bit
thick, for he was a bit embarrassed by my enthusiasm.
But I knew that if it hadn't been for the brave men like
him, I would not have made it out of that jungle.

Ron was pleased that Jim had thoroughly enjoyed
his two weeks at the seaside, and not at all surprised
that it had come as a bit of a shock to have to return
to the discipline of the retraining camp where alcohol was forbidden and a strict curfew was in place.
It was a shame he hadn't been able to catch up with
Staff Nurse Fitzpatrick, but she'd been transferred to
a field hospital close to the border with Burma, so it
was unlikely he would see her again. Which was
probably a good thing; because Ron had a sneaking
suspicion his son had formed rather a soft spot for
that Australian nurse.

I shall be leaving here at dawn tomorrow to rejoin my
regiment, which I'm pleased about, because it means I'll
be with Bert and the others again. Though I dread to
think how my mates will feel about the promotion.

Officers, however lowly, are considered to be
beneath contempt, so me and Bert will have to prove
to them that you don't have to speak with a plum in

your mouth and go to Eton, Oxford and Sandhurst to make a good officer, and I'm looking forward to getting stuck into the fighting again. The men are a good bunch who work extremely well as a team. I know how they think, and where their strengths lie, and as all the lessons I learned in the first shout came flooding back, I have no fear of being able to lead them.

We get Forces Radio and the BBC World Service, and by the sound of things the tide is beginning to turn on the war in Europe, and with the Yanks beating the hell out of the Japs in the Pacific, there is real hope that this damned war will soon be done and dusted and we can all come home. Although you probably won't recognise me. I've spent so long out here, I'm darker than the natives, and if it wasn't for my uniform, I'd probably be mistaken for one!

I hope Daisy and Cordelia got their birthday presents, and there should be more to come for Christmas. Give Daisy an extra hug and kiss from me, and tell Cordelia she's still my best girl after Peggy.

I've written to Anne, Cissy and the boys as well as Peggy, but I'd appreciate it if you didn't show this to her. Unlike you, she'd get upset about things and certainly wouldn't understand about the drinking and fighting – and would only imagine that girls were involved – which they weren't. My Peggy is enough for me, as I'm sure Rosie is enough for you.

Good luck for your wedding, Da. I so wish I could be there to give you a proper Reilly send-off, but I'm sure

Frank will do the honours just as well. Just for goodness'
sake don't turn up hungover on the day.

  I love you, Da.
  Jim.

'What's that you're reading?' Peggy suddenly
appeared in the doorway.

Startled, Ron stuffed the letter into his trouser
pocket. 'Just a letter from a pal,' he said blithely,
reaching for the fedora.

'But it was an air letter,' she persisted. 'Who's
been writing to you from abroad, if it wasn't Jim?'

'Jack Smith,' he fibbed, trying to follow a skulking
Harvey out of the room.

She barred his way, arms folded, expression
determined. 'And why would Rita's dad be writing
to you?'

'He wanted me to know how it was going over
there,' he blustered. 'Just drop it, Peggy.'

Peggy wasn't about to drop anything – neither
was she going to budge from the doorway. 'And
how *are* things going over there?'

'It's no picnic,' he replied, putting on the fedora.
'I'm sorry, Peggy, but it was a confidential letter
from one man to another, and not the sort of thing
his daughter needs to know about. Now I'm going
to be late picking up Rosie, so if you wouldn't mind
shifting ...'

Peggy didn't shift but regarded him evenly. 'Is it a
common thing? This sending of letters between

men? And why is it necessary to hide them from us women? Don't you think we're entitled to know what's going on?'

Ron opened his mouth to reply, but she carried on, her steady gaze penetrating. 'Have you been keeping Jim's letters from me?'

He'd tied himself up into knots by lying and it was clear that Peggy wasn't about to leave the subject alone. He blew out his cheeks and caved in. 'When a man goes to war he sees and experiences things which he can only speak about to someone who's been through the same thing and can truly understand. He knows his wife and family are already on edge and imagining all sorts of things, so what good would it do to tell them about the stark reality of what he's going through?'

He took a breath and decided he couldn't pussy-foot around the subject any longer. 'War isn't pretty, Peggy. It's violent and bloody and cruel – as we saw only two weeks ago when that V-2 came down. Just imagine that duplicated a thousand times over with machine-gun fire, heavy artillery booming, and enemy planes swooping down over you. It's no wonder a man needs to let it all out – and he can only do that with another man.'

He paused, realising he was frightening her. 'I bet you didn't tell Jim about that V-2 and its aftermath in your last letter, did you?'

She bit her lip. 'I did mention it,' she confessed. 'But I didn't go into any detail because I didn't want him worrying about us.' There were tears in her eyes as she looked back at him. 'It seems we're all guilty of glossing over the truth, so I can hardly blame Jim and Jack for keeping things back. Is it truly so awful out there they can't bear to tell us?'

Ron put his arm about her. 'The whole damned war is awful, wee girl. And there's no escaping it wherever we are. But you and Rita don't need to know what was in those letters. They were never meant for your eyes, and I'd be breaking my word if I showed them to you.'

She nodded against his chest and then drew herself back and squared her shoulders. 'As long as I know he's alive, that's all that matters – and the same goes for Rita and Jack. I'm glad they both have you to confide in, Ron. You're a good man, and I'm sorry I gave you the third degree.'

She kissed his cheek and moved into the narrow hallway. 'Go to your Rosie, Ron, and enjoy a peaceful day.'

'Aye, I'll do me best.' He regarded her with deep affection and a niggle of concern that he was being selfish by running out on her today. 'Will you be able to cope with all those children?'

'I've got Sarah, Danuta and Cordelia to help me, along with some of the mothers, so we'll be just fine.'

Ron grinned and grabbed his umbrella, then cheerfully headed for the door with Harvey at his heels. Peggy might look delicate with her slight figure, big dark eyes and elfin face, but she was made of steel. His Jim was a very lucky man.

Peggy heard the back door slam behind him, and sank onto the bed. She needed a few minutes to herself to think about what he'd said, and to gather strength for the afternoon's party which was bound to be chaotic.

She idly smoothed the counterpane and brushed away dog hairs as she listened to the wind howling around the house, and Daisy's excited chatter upstairs. She didn't blame Ron for trying to protect her, for she'd always suspected that Jim had written to his father in a very different tone to the way he'd written to her.

At first she'd felt quite put out that neither of them seemed to trust her with the unvarnished truth, and had even gone to some lengths to try and ferret out those letters so she could read them. She never had found them, and as the war had dragged on and the newsreels at the cinema had shown graphic evidence of what the men were going through, she no longer had the desire to know more.

Peggy stretched her back and gave a deep sigh. If Jim or Jack needed someone to confide in, then Ron was the ideal candidate, for he'd experienced war on the front line and witnessed things that he'd never spoken about, but which she knew still haunted him. He'd been so right when he'd said war was ugly, cruel and bloody, and she was grateful that he and Jim wanted to shield her from it. But after the doodlebug and V-2 rocket attacks she'd had her own taste of what war could do, so she wasn't entirely incapable of imagining how bad it must be for the men caught at the very heart of the conflict.

Peggy stood and regarded the basement room which was already looking abandoned. Ron had lived here all her married life and it would feel very strange without him. There again, he was about to begin a new life with Rosie, and it wasn't as if he was moving very far – she'd still see him most days. But she would miss him. Miss his humour and wise counsel – miss the tall stories and the mess he and Harvey made – but most of all she would miss his very male presence in this house of women.

She cocked her head towards the ceiling to listen to the hurrying feet upstairs and Daisy's excited chatter, and as she did so she spotted something at the very back of the top of the wardrobe. Ron must have forgotten about it when he was clearing out his things to take to Rosie's.

She grabbed the chair and stood on it, scrabbling to reach what she discovered was a shoebox. It was covered in dust and had clearly been there for some time. Intrigued, she plumped back on the bed, blew off the worst of the dust and opened it, expecting to find shoes or perhaps old letters.

What she found made her gasp. There were four velvet boxes nestled in yellowing tissue paper alongside a jumble of loose campaign medals and a pay book dated 1918. With her hands trembling in excitement, she opened the velvet boxes one by one and stared at the contents in utter amazement. Ron had always told good stories about his war – had even made light of it at times – and the family had always taken them with a pinch of salt. But these ... These were proof that Ron's stories must have been true, and far from being an ordinary soldier, he'd been an honoured hero.

She reverently picked up each box and gazed in awe at the Distinguished Service Order medal, the Military Cross, the Legion of Honour and the Croix de Guerre. 'Oh my goodness,' she breathed. 'I can scarcely believe it.'

'Put them back, Peggy, and forget you saw them.'

Peggy whirled round as Ron came into the room and gathered up the velvet cases to toss them back into the shoebox. 'But why, Ron? These are something to be proud of. The family should know what a true hero you were.'

'There's no need for all that,' he replied gruffly, shoving the shoebox back onto the wardrobe.

'But there is,' she protested. 'Those medals are the highest honour that can be given, and you must have done something very brave to have been awarded them.'

He turned to face her, his expression grim. 'I did no more than my duty, Peggy. Better men than me died doing the same thing, and fancy bits of metal will never make up for their loss.'

'But you can't just ignore the fact those medals were awarded to you because of your bravery and the service you gave to this country and France.' Peggy was on the brink of tears. 'You've always been our hero, Ron, so why hide those medals away when so many others wear lesser ones with such pride?'

Ron let his breath out on a deep sigh and took her hand. 'Because I have reminders enough of that war,' he said quietly. 'They come in my dreams and in the twinges in my back – and now in the letters that Jim and Jack write to me from the Front. Those medals will stay where they are, and I want your solemn promise to say nothing to the others.'

Peggy grasped his rough hand, her love and pride for him making it almost impossible to speak. 'Of course,' she managed.

He kissed her forehead and began to rummage in the dresser.

'What are you doing here, anyway?' she asked. 'I thought you'd gone to the Officers' Club with Rosie?'

'I forgot my damned chequebook,' he muttered, chucking old sweaters and vests onto the floor as he delved into the drawer.

'What on earth do you need that for?'

'To pay the balance for the wedding breakfast,' he replied, waving the chequebook at her in triumph.

'You'd better make sure there is a cheque left in there,' she advised, eyeing the suspiciously thin blue book.

He flicked through it in panic and then grinned in relief. 'There's one left, so I'll not be in trouble with Rosie. She warned me I'd need this today, but in all the excitement it went out of me head.'

Peggy gave him a hug. 'You'll never change, will you?' she asked fondly.

'To be sure, I'll try not to,' he replied. He eased away from her. 'Just remember that promise, Peggy.'

She nodded and followed him to the back door. Watching him hurry down the path under the large umbrella, she smiled. Ron was a reluctant hero, but a hero all the same. She would keep his secret warm in her heart for as long as he wished.

12

Now the Allies were making excellent advances into Europe, the threat of invasion was considered to be over, so the Home Guard was stood down, much to the disappointment of those who'd relished being in a position of authority and wearing uniform again.

The King had broadcast a message of praise and thanks to these volunteers who'd given their time, and sometimes their lives, to defending their own small corners of the country. On Monday evening, there had been a short ceremony outside the Town Hall for the Cliffehaven participants, in which Ron had refused to take part unless Harvey could accompany him. This caused a bit of a stir amongst the army bigwigs, but as Ron was one of the senior officers they'd reluctantly had to give in.

The presence of his dog might have ruffled a few official feathers, but the people of Cliffehaven were delighted, for Harvey had become a local hero at finding and helping to dig out people buried in rubble after a bombing raid, and as they'd paraded up the High Street behind the brass band, he was given enthusiastic applause which he positively lapped up.

As far as Ron was concerned, his dog deserved the Dickin Medal, which was awarded by the PDSA for outstanding acts of bravery by animals, and he'd been very miffed when Harvey had lost out again this year to a couple of carrier pigeons.

The Home Guard would be officially disbanded at the end of December, and they'd all been promised a certificate to thank them for their sterling work in helping to defend the country. There would also be a medal for anyone who requested it, but Ron scorned the idea and refused to apply despite Rosie's urging.

He was relieved that he no longer had to man firewatch stations, or teach youngsters how to handle a rifle and play silly war games, for it freed up a lot of his time. However, he'd been sharply reminded on the Wednesday that he still had some military responsibilities and unfinished top secret business to deal with which he had to see to without delay.

The letter from the War Office GHQ had arrived this morning in a plain brown envelope, ordering him, as the local leading officer of the Special Reserve Battalion 203, to check over and then destroy the underground bunkers and miles of escape tunnels that had been hidden away in the hills at the very beginning of the war. The ordnance had reportedly been removed shortly after they'd been abandoned, but it was vital that the general public remain ignorant of their existence, for they were now deemed to be dangerous.

Ron had little doubt of it, for they'd been dis-used for years, but as he burned the letter to ash, he was worried that this dangerous task had been thrust on him too close to his wedding, for if any-thing went wrong, he'd really get it in the neck from Rosie. But orders were orders, and as an old soldier he was bound to obey them. In fact, he was rather curious as to how bad it actually was down there now, and quietly looking forward to blowing everything up.

He prepared for his task carefully, and as he cleaned the Sten gun and checked the sharpness of the Fairbairn-Sykes fighting knife he should have returned years before, the memories of how he'd become involved in this covert mission came flood-ing back.

Very few people knew about those secret bunkers or the specialised battalions, for the recruits had been made to sign the Official Secrets Act after they'd been approached by Colonel Gubbins who was acting commander of the newly formed Special Operations Executive.

Following the fall of France back in May 1940, the likelihood of an enemy invasion seemed inevitable, and Gubbins had been ordered by Churchill to create a special force of civilian volunteers. It had been decided that the ideal candidates should be First World War veterans, farmers, foresters, gamekeepers and poachers whose knowledge of their particular area was indisputable, and who either had, or could be trained in, the necessary skills for guerrilla warfare and the silent kill.

Their task was to operate from secret underground bases, and if Britain was invaded, to be the front line of defence and carry out attacks and sabotage against enemy targets such as supply dumps, railway lines, convoys and enemy-controlled airfields, and to harry and disrupt supplies and lines of communication. Ron had joined up with alacrity, for he'd fitted the bill perfectly and was keen to use the skills he'd learned in the trenches, and in his long poaching career, to play his part in defeating Hitler.

Ron waited until the household was asleep before leaving Beach View with Harvey. He hitched the large hessian bag over his shoulder, feeling the heavy weight of the equipment he would need to set up a string of controlled explosions that would fill in the miles of tunnels for all time with the minimum of disruption to the land above them.

Harvey seemed to sense that this was no ordinary walk, and instead of dashing off to hunt, stayed close to Ron's heels as they kept to the deeper shadows away from the skyline and skirted the few anti-aircraft gun emplacements that were still being manned by the regular army. Ron hadn't come here since the threat of invasion had waned after the Blitz, but old habits die hard and he still remembered the way as if it had been yesterday.

Walking down into the deep, dark valley and past the high wire fencing that surrounded the

Cliffe estate, they continued on into the dense woodlands where gorse grew in thick clumps beneath gnarled trees and brambles deterred walkers. Like Harvey, Ron possessed excellent night vision, and he trod carefully through the clinging goose grass and tangled tree roots, making sure he left no trace of his passage as he followed the path only a very few knew.

The main bunker had been constructed by the Royal Engineers who'd thought it was for emergency food storage. It was made of preformed corrugated iron segments, sunk into the ground with concrete pipe access and a maze of tunnels leading to other bunkers and escape routes. Well hidden by tangles of brambles as deadly as barbed wire, wild honeysuckle and sprawling gorse, it had been built so deep, the roof was simply a low mound beneath this natural camouflage, the air vents disguised as old bits of drainage piping.

Harvey sloped off to relieve himself in the bushes and Ron carried on, knowing he'd soon catch up. Five minutes later, he paused and peered into the darkness, searching for the trapdoor which had been cunningly set in the earth and hidden beneath yet more brambles.

Having found it, he began to wonder why it was necessary to destroy the place, for unless you knew where it was, it would be impossible to find. But orders were orders, and he was quite looking forward to using explosives again.

He ordered the returning Harvey to sit and keep quiet, pulled on his thick leather gloves, drew out the killing knife and wrestled to cut away the overgrown brambles, tree roots and weeds so he could get to the lever as well as clear the main air vents that were clogged with vegetation and broken piping – he certainly didn't fancy running out of clean air down there.

It took him some time, for Mother Nature had been very busy these last four years, but he at last cleared everything away and opened the trapdoor, which screeched quite alarmingly on its dry, rusting hinges. The stench of damp earth, rotting vegetation, weeping concrete and rusting iron greeted him, and he waited for the worst of it to clear before venturing further.

'Down you go, boy,' he whispered to Harvey.

The dog sniffed warily at the opening and after shooting Ron a questioning look, went slowly down the moss-covered concrete steps into the inky black of the tunnel.

Ron fumbled the torch out of his poacher's coat pocket but didn't switch it on until he'd negotiated the first two steps and closed the hatch firmly behind him. The bright light hurt his eyes after being in the darkness for so long, and he paused to let his sight adjust before making his way down to where Harvey was waiting uneasily at the bottom.

'Good boy,' Ron murmured, patting his head and then leading him along the short, narrow tunnel which took a sharp right-angled turn into a large, iron-clad cavern with a low concrete roof.

Ron half-expected to see Rear Admiral Maurice Price sitting in his deckchair, waiting for him to help relieve the boredom, but sadly, like so many of the more elderly guardians of this secret place, he'd passed away.

Maurice had been a jolly companion during those long hours of waiting for something to happen – which thankfully never had – with lots of amusing seafaring stories to tell as they'd played endless games of cards and drunk gallons of tea heavily laced with rum in the dim glow of a hurricane lamp. They'd always been aware of the huge arsenal that lay down there with them, but as long as it was out of sight, it was out of mind – although neither of them dared break the strict no-smoking rule in case they blew themselves to kingdom come.

Harvey sat at his feet as he flashed the torchlight around the cavern. The deckchairs were still there, neatly folded against a wall, the card table next to them – all mildewed and rotting from the seepage water which had been running down the corroded sheets of iron for years and now lay in murky pools on the crumbling concrete floor.

The main area was still kitted out with wooden bunks, and rusting pipes for ventilation still traversed the roof, along with the remains of the frayed wires that had once carried the signals from their wireless and connected them to HQ and the outside world. The wireless had long gone, and neither was there any sign of the boxes of rations and jerry cans of fresh water that had been down here to sustain the men for fourteen days should the invasion come. Which was a shame, for Ron could always find a use for tinned food.

He swept the torchlight over the bunker, now fully understanding why GHQ wanted this place destroyed, for it was clearly a death trap to any untrained civilian who might find their way down here. The corrugated iron which lined the earthen walls was beginning to succumb to the pressure of the tree roots which were determinedly pushing against them. There were more roots poking through the collapsing concrete roof, and wild honeysuckle and ivy had trailed through the cracks to entangle themselves in the machinery of the small generator which had once circulated fresh air from the vents.

Quite why the generator had been left behind was a mystery, and Ron made a mental note to give it the once-over before he detonated the charges to see if it would be of any use to him.

'Probably best if you stay here,' he muttered to the shivering dog. 'To be sure, I should never have brought you in the first place.'

He adjusted the strap of his heavy hessian bag to a more comfortable place on his shoulder and set off to follow the beam of his torch down the mile-long tunnel which sloped deeper into the ground and would take him to the second bunker.

He hadn't gone far when he became aware of Harvey padding alongside him, and decided not to send him back, for the companionship made them both feel easier.

Ron was tall and broad and had to bend a little, for the earthen ceiling was lower here, and crumbling. There were roots poking through on all sides and giant, rusting bolts hung loose from the flat sheets of corroded metal which leaned at precarious angles, on the very brink of collapsing.

Ron shivered and quickened his pace. He'd never liked enclosed, dark places – not since the First World War – and this low ceiling and tomb-like silence was beginning to give him the creeps.

Harvey seemed to sense this and stuck close to his heels.

Ron finally reached the second bunker and came to an abrupt halt. Cold sweat broke out and crawled down his spine as he stared in shock and growing horror. The ordnance had not been cleared.

He grabbed Harvey's collar to keep him from exploring, and his hand was not quite steady as he flashed the torch over the hundreds of cases of ammunition, plastic explosives, timing devices, detonators and grenades.

He ordered Harvey to sit and stay and took a halting step forward to examine the cardboard boxes holding the grenades and explosives, only to discover they were rotting with mildew, and had been nibbled by rodents.

Ron backed away, not daring to open anything to examine it more closely, for if the damp and foraging rodents had got to the explosives then they would be extremely unstable and any movement could set them off. And if that lot blew, he, Harvey, this valley and half the hillside would go up with it.

Standing there in a lather of uncertainty and growing dread, his first instinct was to get the hell out of there as quickly as possible. And yet there were many more tunnels and another two caverns to explore. It was his duty to find out if they too had been forgotten.

He set down the hessian bag which he no longer needed. 'Go back,' he ordered Harvey sternly. 'Go back and wait for me.'

Harvey snorted and sat down.

Ron pulled him up by the collar and forcibly turned him round to face the way they'd come. 'Go. Go now,' he hissed.

Harvey glanced at him over his shoulder and very reluctantly slunk off.

Ron waited until Harvey was beyond the reach of the torchlight and then, with his heart in his mouth, eased past the boxes and crates and crouched to follow the gently sloping tunnel ever deeper underground. There was no corrugated iron here, but thin sheets of corroding iron holding back the walls and heavy wooden beams holding up the earthen roof.

Ron knew which were the escape tunnels, so didn't waste time exploring them, but hurried on as best he could to inspect the other bunkers. The claustrophobia was beginning to make itself felt, the walls and roof closing in on him, reminding him of the tunnels he'd dug and crawled through during the First World War to lay explosives right under the feet of the enemy – shafts in which he could hear his German opposite number moving within feet of him to lay his own explosives beneath the British lines. They too had threatened to cave in on him at any moment, and when one had, it had been a matter of luck that he'd managed to dig himself out. So many others hadn't been able to.

He gritted his teeth, refusing to let those memories unnerve him even further as he pushed on and crouched lower, the torchlight wavering with every step. He'd lost track of the time he'd been down here, but the air was foul and becoming worse the deeper he went, the decay and collapse even more noticeable.

Discovering that the other bunkers were also still stocked with vast quantities of ordnance, he gingerly closed the heavy iron door to this last one and turned the wheel to lock it. If it did blow, then at least the explosion would be contained – or at least, he hoped it would.

He hurried back to the second tunnel to close that off and found Harvey waiting for him. Ron didn't upbraid him for his disobedience but patted his head; he shared the dog's unease at being alone down here in the dark and knew Harvey was attuned to his own fear of enclosed spaces – in fact he could probably smell it coming off him in waves.

He closed off the second bunker and together they started to make their way quickly back to the first one. The illuminated hands on his watch told him he'd been down here for over an hour, for it was now five in the morning. It was imperative he get out of here and reported his findings to GHQ.

The icy sweat of dread had now soaked through his many layers of clothing, and Ron turned up his coat collar to ward off the cold, but the chill came from inside him as he stooped to navigate the seemingly endless miles of low, narrow earthen tunnels back to the main bunker. He must not let his fear make him careless or allow him to forget the map of the tunnels he'd kept in his head since he'd last been down here. One wrong turn in this confusing maze would defeat even Harvey's heightened senses, and they could be down here until doomsday.

He'd gauged that they'd almost reached the main bunker when something hit the ground somewhere high above them with such force that they felt deep shock waves ripple through the earth beneath their feet.

Harvey whimpered and Ron stopped walking, his heart missing a beat until another thump from above ground sent it racing again.

The floor heaved beneath them as a deep rumble came from far behind them.

'Run!' shouted Ron, breaking into a lumbering and awkward crouched run as the rumble deepened and clods of earth began to rattle against the iron cladding.

Harvey, being smaller and fleeter of foot, was soon out of sight.

Ron tried to run faster but was hampered by his size and the sharp reminder of the shrapnel digging into his back.

The iron sheets holding the earthen walls back began to slide and slip, more clods of earth fell from the low roof and the rumble became a roar.

Ron's entire focus was on the narrow torchlight beam as he forced himself onwards. He was nearly there.

And then the boom of an explosion came from the very bowels of the earth to shake the tunnels and send iron tumbling amid an avalanche of soil, concrete, lead piping and wooden props.

Ron could see Harvey now – at the very end of the torchlight beam – barking frantically and dashing back and forth at the entrance to the bunker. He didn't have the breath to yell at him, but fought his way towards him, his fear of being buried alive giving him almost demonic strength as the ground heaved beneath him and the tunnel began to collapse behind him.

More explosions thrust him forward in a tidal blast of dust and dirt. And then, with the force of a piledriver, he was punched in the back and thrown into a terrifying whirlwind of dirt, darkness and debris that tossed him about like a rag doll until suddenly all went black, and he knew no more.

13

Thursday morning dawned with a clear sky and weak sun, and Peggy was a little put out that Ron wasn't here, for it was Daisy's actual birthday, and it had always been a family ritual to open birthday presents at the table after breakfast. Not that he was the only absentee this morning, for Fran was on night shift again, Robert was at the Fort and Rita had yet to return from the fire station.

She watched Daisy excitedly open the beautifully illustrated story book from Cordelia; the new colouring books and crayons from Ivy and Rita; the jigsaw puzzle from Sarah; and the lovely dress Danuta had hand-sewn and embroidered. There were hair ribbons and pretty slides from Fran and Robert, and Daisy was already wearing the dress, the white shoes from Ron and Rosie, and the hand-knitted cardigan Peggy had finished the night before. Like all little girls, Daisy loved dressing up, and had demanded her mother tie the ribbons in her hair as well as put in the slides.

Daisy squealed in delight at the beautiful doll her father had sent her from India. With black button eyes and plaited hair, the doll was exquisitely dressed in brightly coloured silks, right down to her underwear and tiny bejewelled slippers. There were bangles on her wrists and more jewels in her hair and dangling from her ears, and when Daisy tipped her on her back she closed her eyes and said, 'Mamma.'

Peggy would have given her eye teeth for such a doll when she'd been Daisy's age, but she'd loved her homemade Polly Ragdoll, which was so precious she hadn't passed it on to her daughters but kept it wrapped in tissue in a case up in the attic.

It was such a shame that Daisy was so rough with her things, for Peggy knew that before the week was out, the doll would be naked, her lovely clothes and jewellery scattered about the house and garden. What on earth Jim had been thinking when he'd bought it, Peggy didn't know – but then he was hardly in a position to understand what was suitable for his three-year-old daughter.

'Was that thunder I heard last night?' she asked when the fuss had died down and she'd freshened the pot of tea with more hot water.

'I didn't hear anything,' said Cordelia.

'That's hardly surprising, Grandma Cordy,' said Ivy. 'Yer bad enough at the best of times; but without yer 'earing aid switched on, you've no chance.'

'Don't be cheeky,' said Cordelia, unperturbed. 'You wait until you get to my age, then you'll see it's no laughing matter.'

245

'Well, I thought I heard the rumble of a thunder-storm,' said Peggy determinedly. 'Though it was odd considering how cold and wet it's been.'

'I thought I heard something too,' said Sarah, who was opening yet another letter from her mother. 'But it didn't sound like thunder.'

'You're right, Sarah, it wasn't,' said Rita, coming into the kitchen from the basement in her fire service uniform. 'It was a Lancaster bomber which didn't quite make it to the airfield.'

'Oh, no,' breathed Peggy. 'Did anyone survive?'

Rita shook her head, her expression grim as she shrugged off her thick coat. 'The fire team from the airfield got there at the same time as us. They'd been told it was shot up and flying on one engine – too low for anyone to bail out.'

She kicked off her sturdy boots. 'It came down right on the ruined farmhouse and exploded. They clearly hadn't ditched all their bombs, because it went off several times and fairly shook the ground beneath us. There was nothing any-one could do but put the fire out, and then retrieve the bodies.'

'Oh, Rita, how awful!' gasped Sarah. 'I don't know how you can bear to deal with things like that.'

'Someone's got to,' she replied flatly. She bent to kiss Daisy, wish her a happy birthday and admire her finery. She smothered a vast yawn and then stretched. 'I had breakfast at the fire station, so I'm going to have a bath and then get to bed to catch up on some sleep before I finish tuning Pete's motorbike.'

'You mean he's actually given in to your nagging and said you could tinker with it?' asked Ivy in surprise.

'Not exactly,' Rita replied with the ghost of a smile, 'but it seemed silly to just let it sit there at the airfield when I'm perfectly capable of getting it going properly.'

Ivy's brown eyes widened. 'But how did you get it from there? Surely you didn't just go in and take it?'

'Of course not, silly. I chatted up the guard on the gate whose bike I'd mended some time ago and he brought it out to me. I'm keeping it at the fire station.' To avoid any further discussion, she left the room and hurried upstairs.

'I am thinking she is wanting to surprise him when he comes home,' said Danuta, putting on the red beret and gabardine raincoat which was part of her winter uniform.

'He'll be surprised all right,' said Ivy. 'But I doubt he'll be pleased. Pete wanted to do the tuning himself.'

'Ah yes, but he has more important things to do in Belgium. Best for Rita to see to the bike – she is very good mechanic,' replied Danuta.

'I know she is.' Ivy pulled her thin coat on over her dungarees and belted it tightly at the waist. 'But you know what blokes are like. They can get very dog in the manger about their stupid engines.'

Danuta frowned. 'Peter has dog?'

Ivy giggled and explained before glancing at the clock. 'Oh, Gawd,' she breathed, 'I'm gonna be late again! Bye, everyone!'

'I too must go,' said Danuta, picking up her medical bag as Ivy clattered out of the house.

Sarah gave a distracted wave to her, but Peggy noticed that she was more concerned with her letter. 'What is it, dear?' she asked. 'Your mother making more plans?'

'No,' she said quietly. 'She's received a POW postcard from Pops.' She handed over the letter, her face pale and drawn with worry.

Peggy quickly scanned the scrawled writing.

I know you think I'm making too much of things and planning for this unknown future with perhaps rather too much enthusiasm, but you see I've been keeping a secret from you. I would have told you earlier, but I didn't dare tempt fate, or dash any of your hopes. Now it seems only right to tell you that I received a postcard from your father four months ago. It was sent from some POW camp in Burma. The wording made it clear that Jock was restricted to saying very little. He wrote only that he was well and gainfully employed, and that the camp was very accommodating, but not half as luxurious as Petaling Street.

Peggy frowned. 'I don't understand. What's Petaling Street?'

'It's a shanty slum area and red-light district of Kuala Lumpur,' said Sarah. 'Pops was making it clear that conditions were dire in the camp, and used the example because the Japs wouldn't know what he was talking about.'

'I can't believe your mother kept this from you all this time,' said Peggy, returning the letter to her. 'What on earth did she think she'd gain by it?'

'She explains further on in the letter that as there was no mention of Philip, she'd hoped there would be a card from him too, and then she could give me even better news. She didn't want me to lose hope, you see,' she added softly.

'Oh, Sarah,' Peggy sighed, taking her hand, lost for any words of real comfort.

Sarah squeezed her fingers in reply and pushed back from the table. 'There's nothing I can do about it, Aunt Peggy. That card was written so long ago, anything could have happened to him since.'

'At least we know he survived Changi prison,' said Cordelia. 'So we mustn't give up hope that at least one of them might come home.' She kissed Sarah's cheek. 'I wish I could do or say something to ease your worries, Sarah, but the Fullers are a strong and determined lot and my brother's son is no exception, I'm sure.'

Sarah kissed her back and pulled on her coat. 'I have to go to work,' she muttered. 'Don't worry about me, either of you. Nothing's really changed.

I'll just have to wait and see what happens when this war is over.'

There was a heavy silence in the kitchen once Sarah had left. Cordelia wiped her eyes on her handkerchief and purposefully returned to reading her newspaper, clearly not wanting to discuss her nephew's plight.

Peggy fretted about what all this was doing to young Sarah. She was already between the devil and the deep, and her mother's shattering revelation must have hit her hard. *Silly woman, keeping a thing like that to herself,* she thought crossly. *And what on earth possessed her to tell Sarah now when the news out of Burma and Siam is proving to be so horrific?*

Peggy realised she had no answer to any of it and was as much in the dark as Sarah and Cordelia, so she finished her cup of tea with a cigarette and watched Daisy playing with her new doll.

There was still no sign of Ron or Harvey by the time she'd finished the dishes, mopped the floor and made her bed, so Peggy went down to check on the ferrets. If he'd slept here last night their bedding would have been freshened before he left for his morning walk – if he'd been at Rosie's, then she'd have to do it. It really was the limit never knowing where he was from one night to the next.

Ron's bed was made and it looked as if the two ferrets had clean bedding, so that was one thing less to worry about. But had the chickens been fed? Peggy gave a sigh. It would come as a bit of a relief when he finally moved out with his ferrets, for she'd know then where she stood.

Peggy checked the bowl of chicken feed, and finding it empty, had to assume the birds had been fed – but just in case they hadn't, she gave them a couple of handfuls anyway. Hurrying upstairs to the kitchen, she tried and failed to persuade Daisy to exchange the birthday dress and shoes for something more hard-wearing, so to avoid a tantrum, she put a change of clothes in her string bag and let Daisy have her way for once. Nanny Pringle would sort her out.

'You're leaving early this morning,' said Cordelia, eyeing her over her half-moon glasses.

'I want to check that Mavis hasn't been meddling with my files,' she replied. 'I'm sure she's been poking through things that don't concern her.'

Cordelia raised questioning brows. 'Like what?'

'There are personal files on all the women who work for us, and I have special responsibility for those who work the day shifts. Loretta put those files together over the years so she could have a fully rounded picture of everyone. They contain medical reports, family history and so on, and as such could provide ammunition for someone like Mavis to cause trouble.'

'She sounds most unsavoury,' said Cordelia with a sniff. 'I can't think why Solly ever employed her.'

'Neither can I, but it seems we're stuck with her,' replied Peggy, wrestling Daisy into her coat and putting her wellingtons into the string bag. 'Production is up, and there's been very few ructions amongst the workforce so far. As long as that continues, Solly won't want to upset the apple cart.'

'So what are you worried about, Peggy?'

Peggy hunted out Daisy's woollen mittens. 'I know Mavis of old,' she said, 'and I get the feeling she's up to something. I need to find out what it is and nip it in the bud. Which is why I'm going in early.'

'Oh dear,' sighed Cordelia. 'I do hope it doesn't lead to trouble for you.'

'I can handle Mavis,' she replied briskly.

Peggy reached for her raincoat, umbrella and scarf and changed the subject. 'What are your plans for the day, Cordy? Is Bertie taking you out somewhere nice in his car?'

'Not today, dear,' she replied. 'He's saving himself for Ron's bachelor party tonight – as I shall be saving my energies for our do at the Anchor.'

'Where are the men going? Do you know?'

'The Crown and Gloria Stevens are definitely out of bounds, as is the Anchor, of course. I think they're starting at the Officers' Club, going on to the Working Men's Club, and if they're still capable, finishing off at the Fishermen's Club.' She chuckled. 'They'll probably be found fast asleep under some hedge tomorrow and in no fit state for anything.'

Peggy grinned. 'At least they're not doing it tomorrow night, so they'll have a day to get over it. Who's going?'

'The usual rambunctious crowd, plus Colonel White, Frank and Robert. Ron told me yesterday morning that there would have been twelve of them all told, but that Solly had to pull out because something's cropped up which he couldn't avoid.'

'That's a shame,' Peggy sighed. 'I know how much he was looking forward to it. Still, that's quite an army. I pity any poor barman trying to keep that lot in order.'

Cordelia shrugged. 'I'm sure they'll have seen far worse behaviour when the Yanks and Australians were in town. But what about Rosie? I bet she's getting excited now the big day is almost upon us.'

Peggy grinned. 'She's in a complete tizzy, and who can blame her after waiting so long to pin him down? We're going to give her the best send-off ever, Cordy, so you'd better have a good afternoon nap so you're bright-eyed and bushy-tailed, all ready to join in the fun.'

She glanced at the clock and gave her a kiss and a hug. 'I must go, Cordy. Have a lovely day, and I'll see you at six.' Hurrying down the steps, she waited for Daisy to climb into the pushchair with her new doll and then headed for the factory.

The sun was fairly bright, but the wind cut like a knife as she exchanged greetings with some of the women who were shivering in the long queues outside the shops, and waved to Rosie who was polishing the inside of the bar windows.

There were two sets of factory gates, and the men and women of the day shift were pouring through one to take over from the night-shift workers who were streaming out of the other. The recruitment drive had been a great success, for some of the other factories had cut down on their staff as production had tailed off, and middle-aged men had started to return as the temporary airfields and army bases had been decommissioned and closed down. Solly's factory was working at full capacity, and Peggy could feel the positive energy running through the crowd as she let it carry her through the gates.

Nanny Pringle opened the door and smiled broadly at Daisy, wishing her a happy birthday. As the toddler rushed in to show off her doll to her little friends, Peggy gave her the bag of clothes.

'Please try and change her into these,' she said. 'And if you could, I'd really appreciate it if you'd hide the doll before it gets wrecked.'

'I'll see to it all immediately,' Nanny Pringle replied. 'That doll is far too delicate for such a small child.'

'It was a present from her father,' said Peggy. 'It's very lovely, but not at all practical.'

'Don't worry, Peggy. I'll make sure it comes to no harm.'

Feeling grateful that Nanny was a woman of great common sense, Peggy went into the factory, waited her turn to clock on, then weaved her way through the machines towards her office.

The cleaners were busy sweeping up threads, lint and remnants, and the day shift was settling in, exchanging a bit of gossip as they shed their coats and bags and checked their machines over. Peggy returned their greetings but didn't stop to chat, for time was of the essence if the government orders were to be filled on schedule.

She could see Winnie Holman patiently instructing one of the new women on how to thread the baffling industrial sewing machine, so she smiled and returned her nod of acknowledgement and looked around for Gladys Bright. But Gladys was nowhere to be seen, and someone else was sitting at her machine, which was very odd.

Peggy changed course and approached Winnie.

'Good morning,' she said brightly, nodding and smiling to the other women in the line. 'How are you managing, Winnie?'

'Phyllis will get the hang of it soon enough,' she replied. 'It's only her second day, so I can't expect too much yet.'

'I hope you and Gladys haven't fallen out,' she said quietly, nodding towards the seat Gladys usually occupied.

Winnie's expression darkened and her mouth compressed into a thin line.

Oh, lawks, thought Peggy. *They've had one of their flaming rows and Gladys has taken umbrage and gone off to sit somewhere else*. 'Where is she?' she asked, looking round. 'Only I wanted to see how she's doing with Angela Smith.'

'Me and Gladys ain't fallen out,' she snapped. 'She's been put on nights.' Her expression soured further. 'She's not happy about it, and neither am I.'

Peggy frowned, for Gladys never did nights. 'But if she doesn't want to do nights, she doesn't have to.'

Winnie shrugged and the corners of her mouth turned down. 'Seems she ain't got no choice now that bossy bitch is in charge,' she said, jerking her head towards Peggy's office.

Peggy glanced across at the shadowy figure moving about behind the glass partition and gritted her teeth. 'I'm in charge, Winnie – at least during the days. I'll have a word with Mrs Whitlock and sort this out.'

'Won't do you no good,' the other woman replied. 'Gladys made me promise not to make a fuss about it, and that Anderson cow is as stubborn as a bloody mule when it comes to getting her own way.'

'We'll see about that,' Peggy muttered under her breath as she headed for her office.

She opened the door just as Mavis slammed the filing cabinet drawer shut. Peggy knew she'd locked that drawer last night. 'Those files are private,' she said, dumping her bag on the desk and shedding her coat. 'And you have no business going through them without my permission.'

'I have every right,' said Mavis coolly. 'I'm as much in charge here as you, and I need to know what sort of women I have to deal with.'

'Those files in that drawer relate only to the staff who work the day shift,' said Peggy, 'which is why I locked it and took the key home. The night-shift files are in the bottom one.'

'I need to have an overall understanding of all the staff,' said Mavis. 'In case you're absent.'

'No, you don't,' retorted Peggy, examining the drawer. She pointedly ran her finger over the deep scratches around the lock where Mavis had forced it open with the nail file she'd just slipped into her pocket. She held Mavis's glare. 'I shall get maintenance to change the lock today, and if you need to get at those files, then you'll have to ask me or Mr Goldman for the key.'

'It's not difficult to see that a little bit of power has turned your head,' Mavis said with a sniff. 'But then you always did have a smug sense of self-importance.'

Peggy gave her a withering look and refused to rise to the bait. 'I understand you've put Gladys Bright on night shift,' she said instead. 'Would you like to explain why?'

'I felt she was better suited to keeping check on things than that insolent Rawson girl Loretta put in charge. She's disruptive, won't take orders and is inclined to stir the others up.'

In other words, thought Peggy, *she's stood up to you.* 'I want Gladys back on days tomorrow morning, and Fanny Rawson back in her assistant role on nights.' She cut Mavis's protest short. 'And before you go running to Mr Goldman telling tales, you should know that he regards both women very highly, which is why he approved of their appointments.'

She looked at the clock and sat down behind the desk. 'Your shift is over, Mavis. Shut the door on your way out.'

If looks could kill, Peggy was certain she'd have been stone dead before Mavis had slammed the door and stalked off. She waited until she was out of sight and then blew out the breath she'd been holding. It hadn't been a pleasant way to start the day – yet it had confirmed her suspicions that Mavis was snooping.

She sat there for a moment to look through the office memos, and then went to the filing cabinet and pulled out the files on Gladys and Fanny Rawson. She hadn't really had a chance to go through any of them properly, and it would be interesting to discover what Mavis had found out about them which had brought about this deliberate change in routine. But most intriguing of all, why weren't both women complaining long and loud about it? Neither was known for holding their tongues when they thought an injustice had been done to them, and they had a perfect right to refuse the change of shift. Fanny would be losing the extra ten bob a week, and Gladys had worked alongside

Winnie for years. In fact, they were practically joined at the hip. And yet there hadn't been a peep out of either of them.

Peggy discovered that Loretta had kept very detailed files on both of them, with medical records, school and work records and any other information she'd managed to dig up over the years – and it all made for very uncomfortable reading.

Half an hour later, Peggy knew why both women had kept quiet. She closed the files, feeling quite grubby at having pried into such personal and painful secrets. She couldn't begin to understand why Loretta had delved so deeply into their lives, but if all the files were like this, then they should be locked away more securely, for they were a treasure trove for someone like Mavis. She stared unseeing out of the window, her heart aching at the thought of the burdens those two women were carrying, and yet sickened by how callously Mavis was exploiting them.

Gladys had never been one of nature's happiest souls, but now Peggy understood why that was. At the age of fifteen Gladys had been locked away and treated with electric shock for severe depression after a traumatic back-street abortion. Her parents had disowned her when she'd been discharged, so, homeless and alone, she'd rushed into an abusive marriage to a much older man who, over the years, had broken nearly every bone in her body. He was currently serving a long prison sentence for armed robbery in which a policeman had been injured, and Peggy hoped fervently that he'd stay in there until he rotted.

As for Fanny Rawson, she'd had an affair with a black GI whilst her husband was away with the fleet and had been forced by her mother to have the child put in an orphanage. The husband had come home on leave, somehow got wind of what had happened and thrown her out. He'd sold the house and gone back to sea, and she'd been forced to share a room at the overcrowded hostel because her deeply religious parents had refused to take her in. Leading up to her getting the job at Solly's it was suspected she'd survived abject poverty by going on the game.

Peggy knew she could never look at either woman again without a twist in her heart for what they'd gone through, and knew also that she had to do something about those files. God only knew what else Mavis had uncovered, and she needed to put a stop to it before things went any further.

She was startled from her dark thoughts by someone tapping on the glass partition. It was Winnie, and she looked troubled. Peggy beckoned her in and stood to greet her. 'How can I help, Winnie?'

Winnie looked at the files on the desk and gave a trembling sigh. 'So you knows it all, then,' she said flatly. 'I warned Loretta they'd only bring trouble. But she said she needed 'em for some university degree she were doing and promised to keep it secret.'

This was news to Peggy – but it did explain a lot. 'I haven't read all of them, Winnie,' she replied to reassure her. 'But I will certainly see to it that they're secure from now on.'

'You should burn the lot of 'em,' said Winnie, her many chins quivering in her distress.

Peggy put her hand lightly on the other woman's plump shoulder. 'Gladys will be back tomorrow, I promise, and I'll see to it personally that none of this gets out. You have my word on it.'

'Thanks, Peggy. I know you'll do yer best, but there's no telling what that bitch has found out, so Gawd knows who she'll turn on next.' She dabbed her eyes with a grubby handkerchief. 'I knows Gladys ain't always easy to get along with, but she's my friend, and I hate to think what this is doin' to her. She don't deserve it after all she's been put through.'

'I know, Winnie,' Peggy agreed softly.

Winnie sniffed back her tears and folded her meaty arms tightly beneath her large bosom as if trying to hold back the raw emotions she was battling with. 'We all done things we ain't proud of,' she said gruffly. 'And a woman like that will use 'em to get 'er way. You mark my words.'

'You leave Mrs Whitlock to me,' said Peggy. 'Now, dry your eyes and take a break. I expect you could do with a cup of tea and a fag. But don't take too long,' she added. 'Angela Smith could be struggling without Gladys to help her, and I need you to keep an eye on Phyllis before she wrecks the machine or sews herself to it.'

'I'll sort 'em both out, never you mind.' Winnie shot her a watery smile, then waddled off to the canteen.

Peggy noticed that many pairs of curious eyes were watching them both and tapped on the window to remind them they had work to do. Satisfied they were once more gainfully occupied she went to the cabinet and looked again at the many files squashed in there.

Coming to the conclusion that she had only one course of action open to her, she lifted out a handful at a time and placed them on the desk. She decided not to telephone down to maintenance to arrange a new set of keys, for by the time she'd gone through this lot there'd be no need for them. Sitting down, she lit a cigarette and began the long task of trawling through every file to weed out anything she considered to be unnecessary or inappropriate.

Peggy kept the work histories, contact addresses, references and the most basic medical records which she put back in the folders. Skimming the pages of notes Loretta had made on the deeply personal histories of the women, she set them aside.

Once all the files in the top drawer had been dealt with, Peggy carried this armful of dark and dangerous secrets down to the furnace in the basement and watched the janitor throw it all in. She waited until they'd been consumed by the flames and then returned to her office to deal with the files for the night-shift workers and casual labourers, which would also be carefully whittled down and burned.

The hours had flown by the time she'd finished, and she closed the cabinet with a sigh of satisfaction. She might have missed lunch, but she'd achieved something far more important, and would now celebrate with a fag, a sandwich and a cuppa.

However, as she made her way to the canteen she knew she still had to deal with Mavis, and as much as she hated telling tales, Solly had a right to know what had been going on.

14

Ron opened his eyes to utter darkness and the snuffling of a cold wet nose. He tried to lift his head but a sharp pain shot up his back and into his neck. Spitting and snorting dirt from his nose and mouth, he felt Harvey's tongue rasp across his face.

'Gerroff,' he spluttered. 'Will yer not be slobbering over me?'

Harvey whined and dug around Ron, nudging his nose through the dirt and debris that threatened to smother him before returning to wash his face.

'Good boy,' Ron managed. 'Thanks be you're in one piece, but that's enough washing for now.' He tried to push him off but found he could move no more than his hands – anything else sent terrible pains right through him. His head was throbbing, and his searching fingers found an egg-sized lump above his forehead, which had been neatly sliced into two and was probably bleeding.

He decided he couldn't just lie here in the hope that someone might come and find them. It was a miracle they were still alive, and now it was up to him to get them both out of here. He steeled himself to bear the pain and attempted to sit up – only to slump back down as a knife of searing agony ripped through him. Something large and extremely heavy was pinning him firmly to the floor.

Determined not to let the growing fear overwhelm him, he counted the seconds until the pain ebbed, and then tried to wriggle his toes and move his legs. They didn't respond, and that's when he knew he was in very serious trouble.

He lay in the dirt and darkness fighting against the claustrophobia and the rapidly growing terror that he and Harvey would die down here.

Every sound was magnified in that all-pervading black void and although he couldn't see, his other senses were heightened. He could hear the drip, drip, drip of water, the sigh of shifting earth and the groan of the supporting props; could smell the skittering, scampering creatures that lived down here, and the sour stench of his own sweat – and could feel the depths of the earth that almost entombed him, and the heavy weight on his spine that pinned him down on the unyielding floor. His imagination began to feed on those sounds. He needed light, had to have light.

But where was the torch? He hadn't had time to switch it off when he'd been blown through the tunnel, but there wasn't a glimmer to be seen.

'Don't let the battery be dead,' he whispered, his fingers frantically scrabbling through the debris around him. 'Please God if you're really there, don't let the battery be dead.'

He felt the edge of it, but it slid from beneath his fingers and skittered away out of reach.

'Fetch it, boy,' he gasped. 'Fetch the torch.'

Harvey snuffled and scrabbled around him, his breath hot on Ron's face, his heavy paws trampling painfully over Ron's shoulders as he desperately tried to do his bidding.

Ron bore the pain, for surely it was better to feel something that kept you alert, instead of that awful numbness in his legs and the silent creeping darkness that was beginning to sap the life from him.

He winced as Harvey dropped the heavy torch on his nose. 'Good boy,' he rasped, making a painful grab for it and fumbling for the switch more in hope than expectation that it had somehow switched itself off when he'd dropped it.

And it had, it had. Ron gloried in the light after all that darkness, but the beam was frail and wavering as he swept it over Harvey. The dog was filthy but seemed unharmed, which was a huge relief, so he aimed the beam in front of him and discovered he'd come to rest against something hard. He dug away the dirt that covered it and discovered it was the generator.

That small effort proved too much and he paused to catch his breath and deal with the deep, throbbing ache in the small of his back. He had his bearings now: he was lying in the left-hand corner of the main bunker, with his back to the tunnel which led to the steps and the hatch.

Harvey licked his face and nuzzled his ear as he whined and pawed at his shoulder to encourage him to get up.

There was nothing Ron would have liked more than to do just that, but he could barely move. Harvey had made a fair stab at clearing enough dirt away from his face so he could breathe, and Ron shoved away more until his head was resting on the cracked concrete. Then he switched off the torch to try and save the battery whilst he rested.

Plunged back into absolute darkness, Ron could feel it wrap itself around him and begin to sink its way right to his core.

Unable to bear it any longer, he turned the torch back on and quickly inspected the ceiling and walls. The concrete had come down, leaving exposed tree roots and great clods of earth that were precariously hanging from them, but he couldn't see even a hint of sky, or feel a breath of air coming from the air vents that were beyond the torchlight. He could only pray those vents were still open.

He switched off the torch, closed his eyes against that all-pervasive darkness and nestled his cheek against Harvey's muzzle, his mind working furiously.

How the *hell* was he going to get them out of here when he was unable to move more than his arms and hands? Even if Harvey barked himself hoarse no one would hear him, for they were a long way from any of the buildings on the Cliffe estate, deep within a remote valley and at least two miles from the nearest gun emplacement. The escape tunnels had probably caved in, so the only way out was through the trapdoor, and he'd closed that on their way in.

But perhaps those explosions had loosened and shifted the earth away from it enough for Harvey to be able to dig his way out? The thought lightened his spirits a little. 'Harvey,' he murmured, 'I want you to go home.'

He switched on the torch and, with a groan of agony, twisted towards the sharp bend that led to the tunnel and the steps which seemed to be clogged with dirt. 'Go home that way, Harvey. Try to get home,' he gasped before passing out from the unbearable pain.

When he came to again, it took a moment to get his thoughts back into order. Whether Harvey had tried and failed to get out, or not tried at all, Ron would never know, for he could feel Harvey's muzzle against his cheek and hear the soft, fretful whines in his throat.

'It's all right,' he muttered as the stark reality of their situation pierced his confusion and pain. 'We'll get out somehow.'

Harvey snuggled closer, and Ron could feel him trembling. He tried to switch on the torch, but the battery had died along with Ron's last vestiges of hope.

Fumbling back his sleeve, he saw the illuminated hands on his watch. Twelve hours had passed since he'd left Beach View, and now it was almost three in the afternoon. Surely, by now, someone must have noticed that he and Harvey had disappeared?

He held Harvey's paws and pressed his face into his filthy fur to comfort them both, for he already knew the answer. As he'd brought Harvey with him, neither of them would be missed until tonight. Peggy would think they were with Rosie, and Rosie would assume they were at Beach View. And even when they did realise both man and dog were missing, no one would know where to start looking for them.

The claustrophobia was closing in again and he fought to overcome it, determined to keep his mind clear despite the terrible throbbing in his head and the deep pain in his back. If only he could shift whatever was pinning him down, he might stand a chance of getting out of here. He reached back as far as he could, and his fingers scrabbled over what felt like a huge lump of rough concrete, and by the width and weight of it, he had absolutely no chance of shifting it.

He rested again, counting the seconds until the pain eased a little, his mind working furiously. There was a glimmer of hope – a tiny one – and he clung to it desperately, knowing it was their only chance of rescue.

Stan and Frank and the others would be waiting for him at the Officers' Club at seven, and when he didn't show up, there was one man amongst them who might, just might, have the wits about him to put two and two together and realise where he was. But it was a long shot, and even if he did suspect what had happened, would he remember the way after all this time?

Ron patted Harvey's paws and felt the reassuring softness of his nuzzling cheek against his face. 'We just have to be patient, boy. To be sure, he'll find us,' he whispered as the foul air seemed to thicken and a heavy drowsiness crept over him.

Peggy hadn't had the chance to speak to Solly. According to Madge, he'd been called to an emergency meeting at the main synagogue in the next town and couldn't say when he'd be back.

'If it's important, then I'm sure Rachel wouldn't mind coming in,' Madge said. 'Or perhaps I can help?'

Peggy had known Madge for years and could trust her implicitly, but the things troubling her were not for her ears, and she didn't want to disturb Rachel who she knew was hosting a fund-raising tea party this afternoon in aid of homeless refugees.

The files had been rendered harmless, and Mavis was welcome to pry if she dared. 'It'll keep until tomorrow,' she said. 'I hope you haven't forgotten it's Rosie's send-off do tonight.'

'I'm looking forward to it,' said Madge, patting the fresh shampoo and set she'd treated herself to in her lunch break. 'I haven't had a decent night out in ages.'

'See you at seven in the Anchor then, and don't forget to bring something to help with the food and drink. Rosie might have a pub, but it wouldn't be fair to expect her to give us all free drinks.'

Peggy shot off to collect Daisy, who was now in her usual dungarees, sweater and wellington boots, and quite happy after having had jelly and ice cream as a birthday treat. She noted that the doll had been carefully wrapped in the knitted cardigan and was buried in the string bag beneath the good dress and shoes. As Daisy seemed to have forgotten about the doll, Peggy thought she might hide it away until she was older and less likely to tear it to pieces.

They arrived back at Beach View to find that everyone but Danuta was home and dressed up to the nines for the party. Daisy demanded she put on her birthday finery again and Cordelia obliged whilst Peggy dished up a plate of supper for herself and Daisy and the girls finished making the pile of sandwiches they would be taking to the Anchor.

'I suppose Ron's already gone to the Officers' Club,' said Peggy, noting his and Harvey's absence. 'I hope they let dogs in, or there'll be ructions like there were before that parade.'

'None of us have seen him,' said Sarah, 'but then we haven't been home for long.'

'He's probably getting ready at Rosie's,' said Ivy with a wink. 'You know what them two are like with their billing and cooing.'

Peggy rolled her eyes and made no comment as she tweaked the tea towel more firmly around Daisy's neck and over her new dress to save it from food droppings.

Robert came into the kitchen a while later looking very smart in a suit and tie beneath his tweed over-coat, his shoes highly polished. 'Well, I'd better be off,' he said, giving Fran a hug and kiss before hand-ing her the violin case which she'd left upstairs. 'Have fun, girls, and I'll try not to wake you up when I bring Ron home.'

'Chance'd be a fine thing,' said Rita. 'Anyway,' she added with a cheeky grin, 'we might still be out having a fine old time ourselves.'

Peggy remembered Brendon's send-off on his last leave home, and had a sudden fleeting image of Frank face down in Ron's compost heap while Ron lay snoring on the cellar floor, and poor Brendon try-ing to wheelbarrow Frank indoors. It had been very funny, but not something to be repeated when they all had to be at work the next day.

'You'd better bring Frank with you as well,' she said to Robert. 'He'll never make it to Tamarisk Bay in the dark, and I don't want him falling off a cliff.'

Peggy finished her supper, and left Daisy under the watchful eye of Sarah to go and pack an over-night bag and get changed. She and Daisy would be sleeping in Rosie's spare room tonight, so they'd both need nightclothes and something clean for the morning.

With the case packed, she opened her underwear drawer and looked in disgust at her old corset. The elastic was threadbare and sagging, the satin virtually falling apart. And she'd lost so much weight since the start of the war, the damned thing swum on her.

Tossing it aside to put in the dustbin later, she decided to flout convention and go without it – after all, she reasoned silently, she had nothing to hold in, so she was hardly going to wobble about and cause a scandal like Gloria Stevens, who'd been a stranger to corsets all her life.

She smiled at the thought of Gloria, who had the nerve not to care what people thought of her and carried on in her own brash way. It was lovely of Rosie to invite her tonight, and Peggy was glad they'd become friendlier since the incident of the soot fall, for she'd always secretly admired Gloria.

Peggy changed into clean underwear and pulled on her yellow linen dress which had short sleeves and a square neckline. Fastening the buttons down the front, she buckled the cloth belt and eyed her reflection in the wardrobe mirror. The dress was an old favourite and definitely showing its age now, but the colour cheered her up and was just right for a celebration.

Standing by the mirror, she brushed her thick, dark curly hair into neat waves, dabbed some powder on her nose and carefully eked out the last of her lipstick and mascara. Happy with the result, she clipped on the sparkling earrings she hadn't been able to resist at a jumble sale and hunted out her one and only pair of low-heeled black shoes. They needed a bit of polish to hide the scuffs, and she'd have to have them resoled soon at the cobblers, but they would do for tonight.

She had one pair of decent stockings, but was saving those for the wedding, so she slipped her bare feet into the shoes, grabbed the evening bag that had done her such sterling service since the Christmas of 1932 and draped her gorgeous Indian silk stole over her shoulders. Jim had sent it as a Christmas present the first year he'd been abroad, and as she rarely went out, this was only the second time she'd worn it. Grinning with delight and eager for the evening to begin, she returned to the kitchen.

Coats, gloves and scarves were pulled on to ward off the bitter cold. Fran picked up the violin, and bottles and plates of sandwiches were gathered up amidst a great deal of chatter and laughter. Once they were all ready, they trooped out of the front door, none of them wanting to scuff their good shoes by going down the back alley.

Peggy held Daisy's hand and went arm in arm with Cordelia whilst the four girls paired off and hurried on ahead with the food and drink. Danuta had promised to join them once she'd finished her district rounds, and Peggy could only surmise that she must have been held up by some emergency or other.

Rosie had taken her time dressing carefully for this special evening, and knew she looked very glamorous in the black velvet cocktail dress and high-heeled silver sandals. This was a night to celebrate, and she was determined to enjoy every last minute of it, which was why she'd closed the Anchor for the night and put a big notice on the door to that effect.

Now the fire was lit in the inglenook, sending the sweet scent of apple wood into the room. Sprays of holly and ivy had been entwined with tinsel into wreaths which hung from the sturdy beams, and candles flickered in glass jars on the mantelshelf. There were more candles on the linen-covered tables which had been pushed together to form a line from one end of the room to the other. The curtains had been drawn to add to the sense of cosiness, the old piano had been polished, and to complete the picture, Monty was sprawled in front of the hearth fast asleep.

Rosie turned to her barmaid Brenda and they clinked glasses. 'Cheers, Brenda, I couldn't have done all this on my own.'

'Glad to help,' she replied after taking a healthy slug of gin. 'I must say, Rosie, it does all look lovely. I bet the stuffy old Officers' Club won't be half as nice.'

Rosie laughed. 'I doubt any of them will notice. Men are terrible at that sort of thing at the best of times, and after a lot of beer they could be in a mine-shaft for all they cared.'

'I'll just shoot upstairs and get changed,' said Brenda. 'Won't be a tick.'

Rosie nodded, and as she waited for her guests to arrive, prowled around the room, admiring the way the horse brasses glinted in the candlelight, and how Monty's brushed coat gleamed in the firelight. She felt calmer than she'd done in years, for within two days she would be Mrs Ronan Reilly and at the start of a whole new life. And it would be an exciting one, for she had plans to do a great many things once she'd sold the Anchor, and had even picked out the house she'd like to buy.

The only shadow marring her happiness was the fact she hadn't seen Ron since yesterday afternoon, but she supposed he'd been busy at Beach View doing the last-minute jobs still on Peggy's list. Still, it would have been helpful if he'd come to take Monty for his walks when she'd had so many things to do.

Her thoughts were broken by the arrival of the Beach View girls, who were soon followed by Peggy, Cordelia and Daisy. She hurried to greet them with kisses and hugs, and made a huge fuss of Daisy who was looking very sweet in her lovely new outfit.

The first round of drinks had been poured when Brenda came downstairs looking quite youthfully carefree in a pink frilly blouse and navy skirt to join in the fun as she wasn't serving behind the bar tonight; and then Madge turned up looking very glamorous in a dark green dress, wielding a huge bottle of gin courtesy of Solly, and a cake from the bakery.

Doris arrived at the same time as Peggy's sister-in-law, Pauline. They studiously ignored each other as they greeted Rosie, handed over their offerings and then promptly chose to sit at opposite ends of the table. Rosie was sad to see this for Peggy's sake, but there was nothing much she could do about it except hope the alcohol loosened them up enough to at least talk to one another – but not enough to have them falling out. She didn't want them to ruin Peggy's rare night off.

Alf's wife came in with Fred's Lil; Danuta rushed in having finished her district rounds and quickly gone home to change into a pretty white blouse and pleated skirt. She was swiftly followed by Stan's niece April, and Ruby.

'Oh, Ruby, April,' cried Peggy. 'It's so lovely to see you both.' She hugged the girls who'd once been her evacuees, and regarded them with deep affection.

'What have you done with little Paula?' Rosie asked April. 'She could have stayed here, you know.'

'That's really kind, Rosie, but Vera Gardener's looking after her, bless her. I don't know how I'd cope without her, to be honest.'

Peggy smiled. 'I told you when you first went for that interview at the telephone exchange that her bark was worse than her bite,' she said warmly. 'Being on her own now that revolting dog has gone, I expect she's very happy to mind little Paula.'

Rosie turned to Ruby, who was looking quite stunning in a simple dark blue dress. 'How's your Mike doing up there in the wilds of Scotland?'

'Getting very bored, but that could all change if he's sent home to Canada.' She gave a small sigh. 'It's what we've both been dreading, and of course I don't want 'im to go, but anything 'as to be better than watching puffins and gulls all day, I s'pose.'

'Oh, Ruby, I am sorry,' murmured Rosie.

'It ain't all doom and gloom,' the girl replied, ''cos once this war's over, he's coming back for us to get married.'

'How exciting,' said Rosie. 'So you'll be moving to Canada with him, then?'

'I'm willing to give it a go,' Ruby said brightly. 'At least there, I won't have to worry about me rotten mum turning up on the doorstep to cause trouble.'

Rosie patted her arm, thinking of the ghastly Ethel who'd spitefully pinched her letter to Ron and was now serving a prison sentence for stealing from the Red Cross. In her opinion, the further Ruby went from her mother, the better.

At that moment the door crashed open and Gloria Stevens made her entrance, holding aloft two bottles of champagne. She had some holly pinned in her peroxided hair, jewellery jangling, bosom and hips quivering beneath a very tight, short red dress.

'Wotcha, Rosie, gel,' she yelled. 'You can get this party going proper now I'm here.' She came down the step and nearly sprained her ankle in her high heels.

Rosie almost burst out laughing as all conversation stopped and everyone held their breath to look at her and see how she'd react. She had only told Peggy she'd invited Gloria, wanting it to be a surprise – and most clearly, it had been.

Without missing a beat, Rosie hurried towards Gloria and relieved her of the champagne before she dropped it. 'Glad you could make it, Glo,' she giggled, grabbing her around the waist to stop her toppling over. 'It looks like you've been having your own party. Steady the Buffs, girl, we've got a long way to go yet.'

Gloria shot her a sloppy grin and, before Rosie could stop her, plumped down next to Doris, who shrank away, pursing her lips.

'Blimey,' said Gloria, breathing gin fumes and cigarette smoke over Doris as she peered at her more closely. 'You made yer mouth look like a tight bumhole. Swallowed a wasp, 'ave yer?'

Doris went puce as Gloria screeched with laughter at her own joke and everyone else collapsed into helpless giggles.

Rosie quickly steered Gloria away from Doris and sat her between Ruby and Ivy who'd also come from the East End and welcomed her gladly. 'Try and behave, Glo,' she said through her giggles. 'Not everyone appreciates your sense of humour.'

Gloria knocked back half of someone else's gin and winked. 'I always said you and Ron were made for each other,' she slurred, raising the glass. 'The best woman won, Rosie. Here's to yer, gel.'

Rosie didn't point out that it had always been a one-woman contest. Raising her own glass, she downed it in one. This could turn out to be quite a night.

15

Stan the stationmaster looked at his pocket watch and checked it against the clock above the guests' bar in the Officers' Club. They'd all arrived promptly at seven and now it was almost eight and still there was no sign of Ron, which was so out of character it was beginning to worry him.

'It's not like Ron to be late when there's free drink to be had,' he rumbled. 'You don't think something's happened to him, do you?'

Frank and the others looked uneasily at the clock, and then down at the table loaded with empty glasses. They'd been in high spirits when they'd arrived, looking forward to giving Ron a rousing send-off, but after two rounds of drinks without him, their enthusiasm was flagging and Stan had voiced their growing concerns.

'I'll nip down to Beach View and see what's keeping him,' said Frank. 'He's probably fallen asleep and forgotten the time.'

'He might have gone to the Working Men's Club first by mistake,' said Sergeant Bert Williams. 'I'll pop over and see if he's there.' He pulled some notes from his pocket and handed them to Alf the Butcher. 'Get another round in, Alf. I shouldn't be long.'

Alf got the round, but no one felt like drinking as they sat in a tense silence watching the clock and waiting for the others to come back.

'You don't think he's done a bunk, do you?' asked Bertie Double-Barrelled. 'Chaps can get cold feet, don't you know.'

'He wouldn't do that to Rosie,' said Stan firmly.

'He wouldn't dare,' Fred put in. 'Rosie would kill him.'

'Aye, and I wouldn't blame her,' muttered Chalky White. 'But I wish I'd done a bunk before marrying my missus, and that's a fact,' he added gloomily before sinking half his pint.

Colonel White, Robert and John Hicks exchanged glances but said nothing, knowing that any encouragement would send Chalky off into one of his long, moaning monologues.

'He's not at the Working Men's Club or the Fishermen's,' said Bert Williams, plumping down in a chair to catch his breath. 'I saw Frank on my way back and there's no sign of Ron or Harvey at home. So he's going to the Crown to see if he's sneaked in there for a quick half with Gloria.'

'I doubt he'd risk that,' said Alf. 'Rosie would cancel the wedding and have his hide.'

'She'd have more than that,' said Fred with a snort. 'I know that if my Lil caught me in there, I'd end up singing soprano for the rest of me life.'

There was a half-hearted chuckle at this before they settled into a gloomy silence, waiting for Frank to come back. As the minutes ticked away, they sipped their beer and the older amongst them began a desultory conversation about the standing down of the Home Guard, and how much more time they'd now have on their hands.

The Colonel, John Hicks and Robert discussed the war news and what they would do once it was all over, and Bertie just sat thoughtfully, ignoring his beer and watching the clock.

He let the conversations drift around him. Something was nagging at him from the back of his mind and he needed a clear head to work out what it could be. And then the talk of the Lancaster bomber coming down to explode on the old farmhouse brought a scene from the past flooding back and it suddenly dawned on him as to where Ron might be. And if he was there, then they didn't have a minute to lose.

He was about to tell the others when he realised he could be mistaken. It was a long shot, and probably quite misguided, but it deserved some serious consideration before he spoke up. He didn't want to send them all on a wild goose chase – and besides, he wasn't at all convinced he could find his own way there after all this time.

But the thought kept nagging away at him, the possibility growing stronger and the dire consequences of doing nothing becoming more vivid.

If he didn't follow this up, his old pal could die. This was not the time to dither.

Unobtrusively, Bertie left the gathering and went in search of the club chairman to ask if he could use the telephone in his office to make a private long-distance call.

Peggy was feeling a bit tipsy after an hour and a half's solid drinking, so she'd left the party to check on Daisy. Her daughter was fast asleep despite the racket coming from below, so she tucked the blanket over her shoulders, softly kissed her brow and carefully made her unsteady way back down the stairs.

'Peggy!' Frank hissed through the partially opened side door.

Startled, Peggy spun to look at him and nearly fell over. She grabbed the telephone table to steady herself. 'What *are* you doing hiding behind that door, Frank?' She giggled. 'You do look silly.'

'Is Da here?' he hissed urgently.

'Of course he's not,' she hissed back. 'And neither should you be, Frank Reilly. You're supposed to be at the Offishers' Club.' She blinked and tried to focus on him, but he seemed to be shifting about in a most confusing manner. 'Is this some sort of daft game you men have thought up?'

He ignored her question. 'When did you last see him, Peg?'

Something in the urgency of his tone broke through the effects of the drink, but it took a while to think straight. 'Yesterday,' she replied. 'In the morning. Or it could have been teatime.' She shook her head. 'I'm really not sure. He comes and goes. Why do you want to know, anyway?'

'It's not important,' he replied, almost dismissively. 'Is Harvey here?'

She shook her head, still not really too concerned about this very odd conversation. 'Is he supposed to be? Won't that posh club let him in?'

'It doesn't matter,' he said impatiently and shut the door.

'That's all right then,' she said, turning to weave her way down the narrow hall back to the bar. *Frank can be very odd at times*, she thought. *And if it didn't matter, then why come at all?* 'He must be drunk,' she muttered, bumping into the coat stand and apologising to it until she realised what it was and had a fit of the giggles.

She forgot about Frank and his silly games, for the party was now in full swing, with Gloria bashing out a tune on the piano for a singalong, and Fran accompanying her on the violin.

'Was that Frank I saw you talking to?' asked Rosie when Peggy flopped into the chair beside her, took a good swig of wine and lit a cigarette.

'He was looking for Ron,' she replied.

'Why, where's Ron got to?'

'I don't know, do I? I haven't seen him since yesterday – and Frank said it didn't matter anyway.' She took another sip of the lovely cold wine. 'I bet

Ron put him up to it, and they were all outside sniggering to see how their silly prank was going down.'

She took a bigger sip. 'They'll probably start banging on the door and running away in a minute, silly devils.' She grinned at Rosie. 'Honestly, Rosie, men just never grow up, do they?'

'Yesterday?' Rosie took the glass from Peggy's hand and put it firmly on the table and out of her reach. 'Didn't he sleep at yours last night, Peggy?'

Peggy frowned. 'I'm not sure,' she admitted, trying very hard to sober up enough to think straight. 'His bed was made – so that could have meant he hadn't slept in it, I suppose. When he didn't come home for Daisy's birthday breakfast, I assumed he'd come over here and stayed the night.' She gave a lopsided smile and reached to get her glass back for a refill. 'It's all very confusing, Rosie,' she said, pouring more wine. 'I never know where he's sleeping.'

Rosie drummed her long red fingernails on the table. 'I'm beginning to wonder that myself,' she muttered. She leaned towards Peggy and took both the bottle and the glass from her. 'If his bed hadn't been slept in at yours and he wasn't with me – then where the hell was he?' she hissed.

'How on earth should I know?' Peggy protested, rather miffed that Rosie kept taking her drink away.

'I bet there's someone who does,' Rosie retorted, her blue eyes shooting daggers at Gloria.

'Oh, no, Rosie, don't even think that,' Peggy said sharply, grabbing her wrist to keep her in her chair.

'He promised not to go near her again, and he would never break that promise.'

'So where did he get to last night? Where's he been all day – and why isn't he with the others?'

'You're making too much of this,' Peggy said firmly. 'It's just some stupid practical joke the men are playing to wind us up. Forget about it, and let's get on with this lovely party.'

'But I can't forget it, can I?' Rosie snatched her wrist from Peggy's grasp, her voice louder as panic set in. 'Not now the doubt's been put in my head. What if Frank wasn't joking? What if Ron really *has* gone missing?'

All conversation faltered into silence around them. Gloria stopped bashing the piano keys and the singing petered out at the sound of Rosie's raised voice. Peggy was now quite sober.

'What's bitten your bum, Rosie?' Gloria asked, moving away from the piano.

'You might well ask.' Rosie got to her feet to square up to her and Peggy quickly darted between them to avert a row.

'Ron hasn't been seen since yesterday, and according to Frank, he hasn't turned up at the Officers' Club,' she said. 'Now, the whole thing could be a hoax dreamed up by the men, but if not, then it's serious.' She took a breath. 'I hate to ask, Gloria, but have you seen him at all?'

Gloria folded her arms. 'And why should I? What you insinuating, Peggy Reilly?'

'I'm insinuating nothing,' she replied with some exasperation. 'But if Ron and Harvey really have gone missing we need to think about where they might have gone.'

'Well he ain't 'iding in my pub,' said Gloria. 'I'd've given him the boot if he'd so much as put his nose round the bleedin' door now me and Rosie are mates.' She looked round at the other women. 'What about you lot? Anyone seen either of them today or last night?'

She was met with silence and shaking heads. Gloria slammed the lid shut on the piano and looked around at the wide-eyed gathering. 'Well I fer one ain't gunna sit here twiddling me thumbs, so get yer coats. We're going out to try and find the silly old bugger.'

'I suggest we stay here,' said Doris firmly above the scrape of chairs and general chatter. 'It's no good rushing off like headless chickens when we don't know the truth of the matter. It would be far more sensible for Rosie to telephone the Officers' Club and ask to speak to Colonel White. He'll tell you if it's a prank or not.'

There was a mutter of agreement and everyone sat down again as Rosie headed straight for the telephone to ask for the number of the club. She listened and then put down the receiver with a clatter. 'The number's engaged,' she said crossly.

'Leave it a few minutes and try again,' said April, who worked at the exchange. 'Better still, let me talk to Vera.' She quickly got through. 'Hello, Vera, it's April. We've got a bit of a problem here and urgently need to speak to Colonel White at the Officers' Club. Would it be possible for you to break into the conversation going on, or at least ring us back the moment the line's free?' She listened, thanked her, and put down the receiver.

'Vera's going to ring us back. She can't break into the conversation because it's long distance to a classified number in London. So we'll just have to be patient.'

'Let's have another drink, then,' said Gloria, 'and hope whoever it is on the phone ain't got verbal diarrhoea.'

'I don't really want any more to drink,' said Peggy confidentially to Rosie. 'This has sort of put a dampener on the evening.'

'You can say that again,' said Rosie. 'And if I find out it was all a prank, I will kill the lot of them.'

Frank had only just returned to the club having trawled the town for any sight of his father. It was now a quarter to nine.

'I don't know where else to look,' he said after downing a pint to quench his dry throat. 'But if he was up on the hills with Harvey and had some sort of accident, Harvey would have come back to alert us.'

'But he'd have found no one at home,' said Chalky. 'We're here and the women are at the Anchor.'

'He'd have followed their scent there,' said Frank stubbornly. 'He's a clever dog.'

'We should get a search party together,' said John Hicks. 'I'll round up some of my officers who are on duty, and take one of the fire trucks up into the hills.'

'We'll need torches,' said Bert Williams. 'It's pitch-black up there, and we could break our necks falling into some rabbit hole. I'll fetch them from the police station, and suggest the rest of you start searching the bomb sites around town, and all the alleyways.'

'I've already done that,' said Frank, his face drawn with worry.

'As a military man I've learned that search parties need to be properly organised,' piped up John White. 'Otherwise people will be going off in all directions, and places will be searched twice, whilst others are overlooked. We'll need to focus on one place at a time. Don't you agree, Bertie?' He looked round but Bertie wasn't there.

'He left shortly after Frank went down to Beach View,' said Chalky. 'I don't know where he went, but he's been gone a long time.'

'Whatever he's doing, he must feel it's more important than finding Ron,' said Stan. 'Perhaps he knows something we don't.'

At that precise moment, Bertie strode into the bar looking every inch the army major he'd once been. 'I know where Ron is,' he declared, his expression solemn.

'How's that then?' Frank snapped.

Bertie stiffened to attention. 'Need to know, old chap. Sorry, can't say. But there's no time to waste, because he's in great danger.'

He ignored the questions this elicited and turned to John Hicks. 'We'll need your fire truck because it has a flatbed at the back, as well as digging equipment, blankets, ropes, torches, drinking water, oxygen, first-aid kit and a stretcher. As there are so many of us, you'd better bring your jeep as well.'

'But where are we going?' Frank asked.

'Into the hills,' said Bertie with the fire of a fighting man lighting his eyes. 'I suggest you change out of those fancy shoes; there's some rough walking to do.' He checked his watch. 'It's now ten to nine. We'll meet outside here in fifteen minutes, so chop chop.'

Bert lumbered off to change his shoes at the station, Robert ran back to Beach View, and John Hicks went straight to the telephone to pass on the orders to Andy Rawlings who was in charge this evening. Chalky, John White and the others quickly finished their drinks and went to the cloakroom to fetch their coats. It was too far to get home to change their shoes, and in a crisis like this it really didn't matter.

Bertie got the steward to supply three flasks of very hot sweet tea and they all trooped outside to wait for the fire truck, which arrived minutes later with two crewmen on board. It pulled up outside, followed by the jeep John used to get about quickly in an emergency. Bert Williams was red in the face and puffing like a steam train as he arrived a minute later wearing his sturdy policeman's boots and carrying extra torches.

Bertie regarded the overweight and elderly man with some misgivings. 'Perhaps it would be better if you stayed here, old chap,' he said. 'You'll be no use to us if you have a heart attack.'

'You don't tell me what to do, you little pipsqueak,' Bert replied gruffly and shoved past him to clamber into the jeep.

Unfazed by his rudeness, Bertie Double-Barrelled climbed up into the front seat of the fire truck. 'Don't ring the bells, but head for the Cliffe estate on the fastest route you know,' he said to the driver. 'I'll tell you where to turn off.'

Curious faces peered from the windows of the Officers' Club as the fire truck and jeep screeched away.

The telephone rang at the Anchor and Rosie dashed to answer it.

'Mrs Braithwaite? Brigadier Arthur Pendleton here, Officers' Club chairman. How may I help you?'

'I need to speak to Colonel White very urgently,' she replied.

'I'm sorry, but Colonel White has just left with his guests.'

'Left? Left for where?'

'I'm really not terribly sure, but they went in a great hurry and were travelling in a fire truck and jeep, heading out of town.'

Rosie just managed to thank him before slamming the receiver down and grabbing her coat. 'They've all gone off in a fire engine and John Hicks's jeep,' she announced to the gathering. 'No one seems to know where they're heading, but it was in a tearing hurry, so something's up. I'm going to the club to see if I can find out anything more.'

'Then we'll all come with you,' said Gloria, who'd drunk herself sober.

'I doubt they'll let *all* of us in,' said Doris snootily. 'One does have to be a member, you know.'

'Yeah, I do as it 'appens,' snapped Gloria. 'I've been a member for years. And before you ask, I got it through my son what was an officer afore he was killed fighting fer his country – so put that in yer bleedin' pipe and smoke it.'

'All right, Glo, no need to take on so,' soothed Ivy. 'Let's get going.'

'I think we should stay here,' said Sarah. 'The men know where we are, and they'll ring here the minute they have any news.'

'Actually,' said Peggy, 'that's a good idea. What do you think, Rosie?'

'I agree,' she replied, discarding her coat and slumping back down into a chair. 'And I'm sure that if the people at the club hear anything, they'll ring here.'

'D'you want us to stay and keep yer company, Rosie?' asked Gloria.

'That's very kind, but there's little point, Glo. The party's over, and I'm not up to being sociable any more.'

'Fair enough. Ring me the minute you hear anything.' Gloria stood up. 'Come on, you lot, there's a drink on the 'ouse at my place for those what want it.'

Doris, Pauline and the Beach View girls turned down the offer, wanting to stay with Rosie, Peggy and Cordelia. As everyone else donned their coats and scarves and said goodnight, Rita grabbed her coat, shot out the side door and ran down the road to the fire station. If John Hicks had called out a truck, then it must be serious, and as Ivy's boyfriend, Andy, was duty officer tonight, he might have some inkling as to what was going on.

Ron's eyelids felt as heavy as lead, and he had to force them open. He felt so very tired; exhausted in fact, but the air didn't smell right, and it seemed to be getting humid down here.

Harvey was snoring beside him and hardly stirred as Ron struggled in vain to get his poacher's coat off. Had the air vents become blocked? Was that black damp gas he could smell, or just the natural marsh gas and methane of an underground chamber? Either way it smelled foul.

Ron groaned. He couldn't think straight, his head hurt and he was feeling nauseous. He'd lost all feeling in his body, and he'd remembered too late that he had a box of matches in his coat pocket, so they could have had a little light after all. But if that was gas, then lighting a match would finish them both off.

He sank his chin back to Harvey's still paws, but there was merely an answering twitch of his whiskers and a soft grunt to acknowledge him. Ron knew then that the vents were blocked and they were slowly being gassed by something.

At least it will be a gentle death, Rosie, he thought before he fell asleep again.

16

Amid all the excitement, Bertie realised he'd forgotten to ring the Anchor to tell the women what was happening – but it was too late now. He could only hope the club chairman would inform them when they phoned the club, which they were bound to do at some point after Frank's visit.

Bertie sat between the driver and the two silent firemen as they raced along. His long telephone call to Dolly Cardew at SOE HQ had finally elicited the information he'd been dreading, and he knew there wasn't a minute to lose if Ron and Harvey were to be rescued alive.

'Go past the main entrance to the estate and then turn onto the track and go up the hill,' he shouted above the noise of the engine.

The driver slowed as they passed the imposing gates, found the chalky track which ultimately led to Tamarisk Bay, and swung the heavy, high-sided vehicle onto it. The sturdy tyres gripped the uneven surface and the engine didn't seem to struggle at all with the very steep slope, but everyone clung on because they were being rocked back and forth and jarred with every turn of the wheels.

Bertie could see the burned-out skeleton of the Lancaster sitting amid the shattered remains of the old farmhouse, and suspected that when it exploded, it had set off a chain reaction in the bunker that lay directly beneath it. It could very well have been the cause of Ron getting trapped – but had he survived? Were they already too late to rescue him and his dog?

They reached the southern corner of the high wire fencing that surrounded the woodlands and farms of the estate. 'Slow down,' said Bertie, 'and follow it as far as you can. We won't be able to get right to the site, because it's hidden in that deep valley amongst the trees, but try and get as close as you can.'

The bright headlights lit up the valley as the fire truck bounced and jounced along the rough ground. They weaved between the trees, thudding over exposed roots and tearing their way through thick gorse until they came to the impenetrable barrier of chalk outcrops, more gorse and closely grouped trees.

The driver drew to a halt, the headlights penetrating the deep black of this hidden valley. 'Now what?' he asked.

'Leave the sidelights on so we can find our way back easily. We have to walk the rest of the way,' said Bertie. 'But first I need to speak to you all.'

He didn't miss the glances exchanged between the three firemen, and knew they thought him a rather silly old buffer who was enjoying himself despite the occasion.

They were right in a way, he silently admitted as he slid down from the high truck. But it wasn't enjoyment – it was pride in knowing his skills and experience were being brought into play again, and that, under his charge, they would find Ron.

He stood ramrod straight with his hands clasped behind his back as he waited for the others to join him. He was impatient to be getting on with it, but also suddenly nervous that he might not remember exactly where to go to find the entrance – and yet knew he must not allow the others to see that, for they would lose confidence in his leadership.

'All right, chaps,' he began when they'd all assembled. 'The place where we're heading is classified as top secret. As such it is imperative that no one talks about it afterwards – not even to our nearest and dearest – and I shall have to ask you to sign the Secrets Act on our return.'

He waited for them to agree, and then pointed to the trees. 'We will have to carry the equipment into there,' he said. 'It's difficult terrain, and the walk will take a good twenty minutes of hard going. If any of you feel you are unable to continue then you must speak up now.'

His gaze trawled across Fred, Alf, Chalky and on to Bert Williams, who still looked liverish, but belligerent – and to Stan who'd recently had a mild heart attack. They were younger than him, but unfit and overweight, and he really hoped they'd see sense and stay here.

But they all stood firm so, with reluctance, Bertie turned to John Hicks. 'Will you be able to manage with your prosthesis? Only it is very rough underfoot in there.'

'I've coped with worse,' he replied flatly.

Bertie nodded and checked his pocket watch. It was almost nine-thirty. 'Then let's get the equipment divided up between us and move out. Time is of the essence.'

The firemen took the heavy oxygen cylinder, jerry can of water and coils of rope, and the rest was divided up between the others. Bertie saw to it that Bert Williams was in charge of the blankets and flasks, and Stan, the stretcher. He took a pickaxe and hefted it onto his shoulder. 'This way.'

'Where exactly are we going, and what will we find when we get there?' asked Frank.

'We'll find underground storage bunkers and a lot of tunnels,' replied Bertie. 'Why they're there, you don't need to know, but your father and I are familiar with them, and I'm sure Ron will come out of this all right.'

'How can you possibly tell?' Frank persisted. 'What if he's trapped miles underground where we can't reach him?'

The same thought had occurred to Bertie, but this was not the time to be pessimistic. 'We'll deal with that scenario if and when it arises,' he replied briskly. 'Until then, I suggest we all remain positive.'

They walked for a while with the bright lights of the fire truck showing the way, but as they went deeper into the woods, their pace slowed and they had to switch on the torches.

Chalky White was the oldest man, and he was beginning to flag, but Alf and Fred took charge of the heavy first-aid box he was carrying and made sure he wasn't left behind. John Hicks grimly kept pace even though it was clear he was struggling with his false leg. Robert, who was the youngest, and Colonel White silently matched Bertie step for step, with Frank close behind them.

Bertie's night sight wasn't as good as it had once been, and the bobbing torchlights merely cast confusing shadows, making it more difficult to gauge his whereabouts. His last foray into this valley had been almost four years ago, and he'd done it in absolute darkness, confident he had the route firmly drummed into his head – now he had the noise of the others, the sense of urgency that could make him careless, and the lights to contend with.

He came to a halt and flashed the torch from side to side to get his bearings, and then moved on, slower now and concentrating hard on that hazy map he'd learned by heart so many years before.

Danuta had seen Rita dash off, and suspected where she might be going. As the others settled in by the fire to wait for the telephone to ring, she hurried down Camden Road towards the fire station.

Rita was in earnest conversation with Andy Rawlings, and they both turned to stare at her as she hurried towards them.

'If it is an emergency they will need a nurse,' she said. 'Where have they gone?'

'I'm really not sure exactly,' said Andy. 'John just said to prepare the fire truck with emergency equipment and get to the Officers' Club.' He rubbed his chin. 'I suspect they've gone into the hills somewhere, because they wanted digging equipment, oxygen, water and ropes – and his sturdiest boots – but I can't be certain.'

'We must find them,' said Danuta. 'Rita, we will take bike.'

'Fine by me,' said Rita. 'But we'll freeze up there in this lot.' She flicked at the flimsy tea dress rippling in the wind against her bare legs.

'So we will borrow fireman's clothes,' said Danuta, heading straight for the line of waterproof coats and trousers hanging above a shelf of sturdy boots.

'I don't think John will ...' began Andy.

'John won't mind,' said Rita, pulling the trousers on over her dress and hunting out her working boots. She tossed a second pair to Danuta, hoping they might fit, and within two minutes they were dressed.

'I don't like the thought of you girls going up there on your own,' said Andy.

'Don't be daft, Andy,' Rita said. 'You're on duty, and I know my way about up there.' Grabbing her crash helmet, she gave it to Danuta, and donned Peter's. It was a bit big, but it was better than nothing. 'Phone the Anchor and tell Rosie what's going on, she's out of her mind with worry.'

'I must go home for medical bag,' said Danuta.

'Righto.' Kicking the starter on her motorbike, Rita waited for Danuta to sit behind her. 'Hold on,' she yelled above the bike's roaring engine.

Danuta clung to Rita as they shot out of the fire station and headed for Beach View. Leaping off at the end of the alley, she rushed as best she could in the ill-fitting boots into the house and up the stairs. Grabbing her medical bag, she kicked off the boots and stepped into her black lace-up shoes, then raced back down and within seconds was back behind Rita.

Rita took off like a rocket, leaning the bike at nerve-shattering angles around corners and opening up the throttle on the straight.

Danuta pressed into her back, her head tucked down, the medical bag tight between them, her heart thudding wildly. She hadn't felt a thrill like this since the last time she'd been parachuted into France.

It was now after ten o'clock. They'd drunk enough tea to sink a battleship, worried themselves to a frazzle, and although Andy had telephoned, they were still none the wiser as to where the men had actually gone or what had happened to Ron and Harvey.

'I wish there was something we could do instead of hanging about waiting for the damned phone to ring,' muttered Peggy in frustration.

'There's nothing we *can* do,' Rosie replied, pale and drawn with worry. 'Until we know for sure where they've gone, or what's happened, we're stuck. And even if we *did* know where they were, how would we get to them?'

She scrubbed at her face with her hands. 'Oh, God, Peg,' she rasped, on the brink of tears, 'what if Ron really is in serious trouble?'

'We have to stay positive, Rosie. There's no point in letting your imagination run riot – it'll only make you feel worse.'

'Our men will find him,' said Fran.

'Of course they will,' Doris piped up. 'John is an experienced soldier, as are Bertie and Frank – and the others all possess local knowledge. They'll track him down.'

'Let's hope so,' muttered Ivy. 'All this hanging about knowing nothing is driving me round the bend.' She looked at the gathering. 'Where's Rita and Danuta? Why aren't they back from the fire station?'

'They've been gone a long time,' Sarah murmured.

'You're right, they have,' said Peggy. 'But I know those girls too well. And I wouldn't mind betting they've gone after them on that blessed motorbike.'

She took a trembling breath at the thought of the reckless way Rita drove the thing, and could only pray there wouldn't be any more dramas tonight.

Bertie was very much afraid he might be lost. This secret valley had changed so much over the last four years that it was barely recognisable. Small trees had grown tall, saplings had seeded themselves amid the tangles of briar, creeper and gorse, and once sturdy trees had been brought down by high winds or succumbed to old age and fallen down to rot away.

The skyline was different too, the canopy much thicker, which blotted out the moon and stars he might have used as a compass, and served to deepen the darkness beneath it.

Bertie came to an abrupt standstill, the sound of breaking twigs, soft oaths and trampling feet of the others dwindling away as they caught up with him. His inborn sense of direction must not fail him now, he thought desperately. He'd been so positive he was following the right path, but his confidence was ebbing away rapidly as he'd gone further into this unfamiliar landscape.

'Which way now?' asked Frank. 'By my reckoning we've been walking for over half an hour and you said it would only take twenty minutes.'

'Frank, I know you're anxious, but I need a moment of quiet to check my bearings.'

'You mean you've got us lost?' Frank shone the torch into Bertie's eyes.

Bertie swiped it away. 'I'll be of no use to Ron if you blind me with that,' he snapped. 'And I am *not* lost. I just need time to reconnoitre the area.'

There was a deep muttering of discontent from the others as they crowded round him. The older ones were tired and sweating, the younger ones were losing patience, and he could see the Colonel was beginning to have serious doubts about his leadership.

Bertie knew that if he didn't pull himself together, he'd have a mutiny on his hands, and any hope of finding Ron would be lost. He blocked off the noise of the men arguing amongst themselves and concentrated hard as his sight adjusted once more to the darkness.

Ron was an expert tracker and poacher. He knew this place like the back of his hand and would leave no sign of his passage, but there had to be something to follow – a broken twig, a footprint in a clump of weed, or bent grasses. However, there had been nothing so far, and Bertie was beginning to despair.

He determinedly bucked up his spirits and his belief in himself, and slowly trained the beam of the torch across his surroundings. This was the right way, he was sure of it now, for he was seeing the trees as they had once been, and he recognised an outcrop of chalk half-hidden beneath the spread of gorse.

The beam drifted over gorse and brambles, skimming over a scrape in the earth and a pile of dead leaves. He quickly shone the torchlight on that scrape again and realised no rabbit had done that. He bent to examine it and the leaves behind it.

'What's that?' asked Frank.

'It's where an animal had a crap and scraped the leaves over it,' muttered Bertie, prodding the leaves with the toe of his shoe and uncovering the stinking mess. 'I'd say that was dog, wouldn't you?'

'It's certainly big enough. But was it Harvey?' Frank muttered.

'It's fresh, so it's a very real possibility,' replied Bertie, cleaning his shoe on a clump of long grass.

He was about to move away when he heard something very faint that didn't belong in these woods. Freezing on the spot, he held up his hand for silence. 'Listen,' he breathed.

None of them moved, their heads cocked, straining to hear what Bertie had heard.

And then it came again, so faint that only those with excellent hearing could make it out.

'That's Harvey,' gasped Frank. 'And it came from down there.' He tramped off, calling to the dog, the sound of his voice ringing through the trees as the weak, irregular barks spurred him on.

Bertie was so relieved he hadn't led them all astray that he happily let Frank take the lead – and yet it troubled him that Ron hadn't replied to his son.

The barking stopped as they reached the trapdoor to the underground bunkers and tunnels, and it was clear to them all that Ron had had to hack his way through the undergrowth to get to it.

'Good boy, Harvey,' shouted Frank. 'It's all right, boy. We're coming to get you.' He put his hands round his mouth and shouted for his father. 'Da! Da! Are you down there?'

There was no reply and Bertie took charge again, pointing to the trapdoor. 'There's a bunker to the right at the bottom of the steps, and behind that are five miles of tunnels and two more bunkers. I should warn you,' he said quietly to John Hicks, 'that I have it on the highest authority there is ordnance stored down there that mistakenly has not been cleared.'

'How much ordnance?' asked a grim-faced John.

'Enough to blow up most of this hill and half the Cliffe estate.'

John Hicks turned to the others. 'We'll deal with this,' he said. 'You civilians must go back to the fire truck and stay there.'

'I'm not going anywhere until I find my father,' Frank protested.

'None of us are,' said Fred the Fish and they stood purposefully where they were.

'I should warn you there's ordnance down there, and after all this time it's probably highly volatile.'

'Then we shouldn't be wasting time,' said Alf. 'And the more hands there are, the quicker we'll get them out.'

John Hicks knew there was little point in arguing. 'Let's see what we've got to deal with,' he said, taking charge of the lever and drawing back the trapdoor.

Everyone edged forward as he shone his torch down on the wall of earth and broken concrete that blocked their way.

Harvey's weak howl came from beyond it. 'We're lucky,' said Bertie. 'They're in the first main bunker and not half a mile down one of the tunnels. But whatever you do, don't try digging through that mound. It's the roof of the bunker, and below that is a concrete ceiling.'

'What's holding the place up?' asked John Hicks.

'Corrugated iron sheeting and wooden props at this end,' Bertie replied. 'Just dirt, iron cladding and props the further down you go. But by the look of that, the whole thing has collapsed. I'll see if the air vents have been blocked and try to clear them.'

It took a glance to discover that the drainage pipes forming the air vents had cracked, slipped and shifted, the earth and forest detritus falling into them from all sides and blocking them entirely. Bertie knew the dangers of deadly gases building up underground, particularly if there had been an explosion. 'Help me clear these,' he said to Robert. 'They need fresh air down there.'

As Harvey's whimpers grew fainter and there was still no sound from Ron, the firemen got busy dismantling the trapdoor and widening the opening. Once that was achieved, every man picked up a spade or pickaxe and began to dig determinedly away at the rubble that blocked the way in.

They saw the fire truck lights immediately they breached the hill, and Rita swung the bike towards them and raced over the undulating ground, almost losing Danuta from the back as she was lifted from the seat. She slowed the bike and then drove into the valley until they could go no further.

Sliding off the bike, her legs trembling from clinging on, Danuta pulled off the crash helmet and regarded the woods. 'We should have brought torches,' she said. 'But if we turn off the headlight, it will only take a moment to get our night eyes.'

As Rita switched off the bike's headlight, Danuta quickly laced up her sturdy shoes. Hitching up the waterproof trousers that swamped her small frame, she gripped her medical bag. 'You are ready, Rita?'

'I can't see a bloody thing,' she replied.

'You prefer stay here and I go?'

Rita looked at her surroundings and shivered. 'No fear.'

'Then take my hand. I will lead the way.'

They set off into the ever-deepening darkness, and although Rita constantly tripped and stumbled, Danuta could see the way clearly. The men had been careless as they'd set out to find Ron, and it was easy to see which way they'd gone by the trampled weeds, the freshly broken branches and snapped twigs.

It was ten-thirty when the club chairman telephoned the Anchor to say that he'd heard nothing from the men and would be closing up for the night. He promised to keep an ear open for any call that might come through and let them know immediately.

'I feel terrible that I didn't think to go with Danuta,' said Fran. 'If there has been an accident, then they'll need medical attention.'

'Danuta's quite capable, and the firemen will be trained in first aid,' soothed Peggy. 'You have absolutely no need to feel guilty about anything.'

'I have to be on duty at six tomorrow morning, so if you don't mind, I'll go back to Beach View and try to get some sleep,' Fran said. 'But ring me the minute you hear anything.'

'Of course we will,' said Peggy. 'And I suggest you take Sarah, Pauline and Ivy with you. There's no point in all of us hanging about here twiddling our thumbs when you've got work in the morning.'

'I'll make my way home as well,' said Doris. 'John will let me know what's happened when he gets back.' She kissed Peggy and gave her a hug. 'I suggest you try and get some sleep, although I know it won't be easy.'

She turned to Rosie, who was now quite haggard with worry. 'Ron's a tough man. He and Harvey will pull through. You'll see.'

They trooped outside to discover it was raining again and so quickly made their way home, each of them knowing they would have little sleep tonight.

Peggy encouraged Cordelia to go to bed in Rosie's spare room, where mercifully Daisy was fast asleep with Monty snoring on the rug between the two single beds. Once Cordelia was settled, Peggy went into Rosie's sitting room and, finding her sitting forlornly by the dead fire, set about getting it alight again.

'Here, drink this,' she encouraged, handing her a glass of brandy. 'It might make you feel a bit calmer.'

'How can I be calm?' Rosie replied tightly. 'My Ron's out there somewhere, hurt or worse, and I have absolutely no idea what the *hell* is going on.' She tossed back the brandy, lit yet another cigarette and began to pace back and forth.

Peggy sipped her brandy and remained silent. There was nothing she could say that would ease Rosie's fears, or her own, for that matter, so as Rosie paced endlessly back and forth, smoking one cigarette after another, she listened to the clock ticking away and tried not to imagine what might be going on up in those hills.

But it was the not knowing which bred the growing, terrible fear that she might never have the chance to tell Ron how much she loved and admired him.

Rosie kept pacing, her imagination running riot, her heart aching for the man she loved so much. She knew he was strong, and capable of surviving almost anything. But what if, this time, he'd come across something he couldn't beat?

She threw the cigarette butt into the fire and sank onto the couch, curling into herself as the tears finally came. 'Oh, Peggy, I can't bear the thought I might lose him,' she sobbed.

'I know,' Peggy replied, drawing her close until their tears mingled and hope began to dwindle away as the clock kept on ticking.

Stan, Chalky and Bert had to admit defeat after a while and leave the digging to the younger and more able. John Hicks was clearly struggling with his false leg, but he refused to give up and wielded the spade alongside his three crew members.

The tunnel was narrow, so only one man could work at a time, shovelling up the dirt to the next man, who shovelled it back through the opening and out amongst the surrounding trees. They were making good headway, for Bertie had counted the steps and his spade had just clanged against the concrete floor at the bottom.

Harvey's whines were louder and clearer now the air vents were open. But what drove them harder was the fact there had still been no sound from Ron.

It had started to rain, which only made their task harder. Bertie took a breather and looked at his watch as he let another man take his place in the line. They'd been digging for nearly an hour and he knew for a fact there was still quite a way to go before they broke into that main bunker.

He was aching all over, unused to such strenuous exercise, and dolefully regarded the angry blisters on his hands. They wouldn't do much for his golf swing, he thought sadly, and he was supposed to be playing an important match tomorrow. He pushed back his shoulders, ignoring the rain hammering down on him, picked up the spade and got digging again. Cordelia would never forgive him if he didn't get Ron out alive.

'What's happening?'

Danuta and Rita clambered down into the dip, looking incongruous in oversized firemen's kit.

'What are you two doing here?' shouted John from the depths of the entry tunnel.

'We've come to help,' said Rita, grabbing a spade. 'And Danuta's got her medical kit. How far down is Ron buried?'

'We need to break through here,' said John. 'Bertie reckons we've got about fifty feet before we reach the bunker.'

Without further questioning, the two girls joined in. They all worked with a will and in silence, for none of them had the breath to talk and the rain was now thundering down through the trees, turning the earth to mud which made their footholds treacherous.

And then they heard a scrabbling, and before any of them could react, Harvey pushed his way through the wall of earth and almost twisted himself in half in his delight at seeing them.

Frank made a terrific fuss of him, but the dog wriggled away and headed back through the hole he'd made. He began to bark urgently.

'It must be clear on the other side,' said Frank. They began to dig even faster, and suddenly the wall of dirt subsided, and they were in the bunker.

Harvey continued barking as he stood guard over Ron. The torch beams lit up the place to show a collapsed ceiling, thin sheets of rusting iron, lead pipes, wooden props, and great chunks of concrete amid at least four feet of earth. And in the corner by an ancient generator lay Ron in a cleared circle of that earth, with an enormous slab of concrete pinning him down.

'Don't try and move him,' warned Danuta. 'His back must be injured and we could damage his spinal cord.'

The men cleared a hasty path through the dirt and she hurried to him. The concrete slab was heavy and it took two men to remove it.

'He is alive, but his pulse is very weak,' she said. 'We must get him to hospital. Call for ambulance, Mr Hicks. It's urgent.'

'No ambulance can get anywhere near this place, and my radio has no signal from here. We'll have to carry him out ourselves.'

Danuta thought for a second and then nodded. She'd been in a situation like this before when an escape tunnel had collapsed on the group of French partisans she'd been hiding with. 'Okay. We make his back safe first.' She looked round and grabbed a long, thin sheet of flat iron cladding.

Frank was kneeling beside his father, and Harvey was next to him, quiet now he knew Ron was being looked after. 'What are you going to do with that?'

'Protect his back when we put him on stretcher,' she replied, digging in her medical bag for bandages. 'You have first-aid box, Mr Hicks?' At his nod, she continued. 'Please, you have something to brace his neck? He should also have a little water to wet his lips and wash his face and eyes, and he needs oxygen.'

Danuta made a makeshift neck-brace with wads of cotton wool and yards of crepe bandage and fastened it firmly with a nappy pin. Ron didn't stir as Frank held the oxygen mask over his face, so she checked his pulse again and felt his forehead. He was cold and clammy and his mouth was tinged blue despite the fresh oxygen being pumped into him. She would have to hurry and get him out of here.

She didn't attempt to remove the many layers of clothes, but injected a shot of morphine into the back of his hand and then quickly tied his ankles tightly together.

'What are you doing that for?' asked Frank.

'To stop him moving his legs,' she muttered. 'Now you help me put iron sheet under him to stabilise his spine.'

The firemen brought the stretcher, and with the help of Robert, took a corner each of the sheet of iron, and under Danuta's precise instructions, carefully slid it beneath Ron's belly and lifted him onto the stretcher.

'Leave iron in place. It will keep him flat and not sink in middle,' Danuta said, tying him firmly to the sheeting by winding yet more crepe bandage around him. Satisfied he was being held as fast as possible, she stepped back. 'Now we go.'

They carried Ron back the way they'd come, thankful for the clear path they'd made earlier, and the bright torchlights, but all too aware that if one of then slipped or jolted the stretcher, they could cause further damage to a badly injured and far too silent Ron.

Harvey was clearly suffering from exhaustion and the lack of oxygen, so Alf lifted him up and settled him across his broad shoulders.

When they came to the motorbike and fire truck they stopped.

'Put stretcher in back of truck on floor,' said Danuta. 'Have you got radio signal yet, Mr Hicks?'

John nodded and pressed the button to speak to Andy back at the station. 'We're on our way. Have the hospital on standby, and call the vet. Ron has suspected back and neck injury, and he and Harvey have been exposed to gas. Oh, and tell Rosie, will you? She'll be out of her mind with worry by now.'

Danuta clambered into the back of the truck and Alf eased Harvey from his shoulders so the faithful dog could lie beside Ron.

Danuta was very businesslike as she took charge of the oxygen bottle and mask. 'Frank, you will sit there and hold your father very evenly – no, I mean firmly – by the shoulders so he is not rolled about when we move. Robert and Fred, you are to hold his legs to keep him very still.'

Rita kicked her motorbike into life as the others climbed wearily into the fire truck and jeep, and they set off very slowly over the rough ground. They held onto Ron and kept him from being rolled around or jerked as the truck carefully negotiated the dips and rises and then could relax a little as they reached the smooth main road.

With the bell ringing urgently, they raced into Cliffehaven and turned into the hospital forecourt where the medics were waiting alongside Rosie and the entire Beach View household.

It was now one in the morning, and once Danuta had given the doctor in charge her report on Ron, she quietly stood by as Rosie and the others swarmed towards the stretcher and followed its passage into the emergency department. Harvey, she noticed, had found a new lease of life after a dose of fresh oxygen, and the second the vet finished treating him, he'd shot off to join the others.

Danuta gave a weary sigh of satisfaction. Ron would be safe now in the hands of the real experts, and whatever the outcome, she was glad to have been able to repay him – albeit in a very minor way – for all the love and care he'd shown her from the moment she'd arrived at Beach View.

17

Rosie was almost on the point of complete collapse when the call had come through from Andy to say the rescue party was on its way to the hospital. He hadn't explained what had happened or where Ron had been found, but it was clear he'd been badly injured.

She'd sent Peggy to wake Cordelia and Daisy, telephoned Beach View with instructions to let the others know what was happening, and then quickly changed into slacks and a warm sweater. She was all fingers and thumbs, her pulse racing so fast she could scarcely breathe.

Without waiting for the others, she'd pulled on her coat and raced to the hospital just in time to hear the urgent ring of the fire engine bells and the roar of a motorbike and jeep approaching from the distance.

She was quickly joined by everyone else, including Gloria, April and Ruby, and her heart was in her mouth as she stood in the hospital forecourt watching the filthy, rag-tag assembly of rescuers clamber wearily down from their vehicles and the medics rushing to lift the metal-lined stretcher from the back of the truck. She couldn't begin to imagine what had happened, but the sight of Ron lying so still on that rusting bit of metal made her feel quite ill.

Now, as she followed the stretcher into the examination cubicle, her whole focus was on the beloved man who lay there, silently praying over and over that he would pull through.

'You'll have to wait outside,' said the resident doctor.

'I'm not going anywhere,' she retorted. 'We're getting married tomorrow.'

The doctor rolled his eyes as the ties were cut and the four nurses and two orderlies carefully lifted Ron from the metal sheet onto the examination bed. 'I doubt that very much,' he said brusquely. 'Stay if you must but keep out of the way – and if you are going to have hysterics, have them outside.'

Stunned by his rudeness, Rosie edged into a corner, out of the way of the nurses who were working on Ron. She watched as his filthy clothes were cut from him, lines of tubing were inserted into his arms, and he was hooked up to a fresh oxygen supply.

He looked so vulnerable lying there, with half his face covered by the mask and the base of his spine cruelly bruised, but at least he finally seemed to be coming round. She managed to stem her tears, but her legs were trembling as she watched the doctor examine Ron's spine. This elicited a deep groan from

Ron, and she very much feared she might faint, for the doctor's expression didn't bode well.

He muttered to one of the nurses to fetch Ron's medical notes and inform Mr Armstrong of the situation, and then ordered the others to turn him onto his back, being very careful not to bend him in any way.

Once Ron was on his back, the doctor ran a pencil along the soles and outer edges of his feet, and having seen a slight reflex in his toes, continued across the top of them and over his shins, up to his knees. Getting only a minor reflex reaction, he fixed the stethoscope into his ears and listened to Ron's heart. When he finally turned to Rosie, he was unsmiling.

'This man needs urgent surgery,' he said. 'I've sent for Mr Armstrong, our consultant orthopaedic surgeon, to come and examine him. Is there any medical history we should know about before we operate?'

'He's got a shard of shrapnel in his back from the trenches,' Rosie replied, determined to keep her wits about her. 'Apart from that he's extremely fit and strong for a man in his sixties, with no history of heart or lung problems.'

She swallowed her nervousness. 'Has he damaged his spine? Is that why you have to operate?'

'We'll know more once Mr Armstrong has examined him and we have a chance to X-ray the area. Until then, I suggest you join the others in the waiting room.'

'I want to stay with him,' she said stubbornly.

'He's been heavily sedated and won't know you're here,' he replied, clearly not used to being disobeyed.

'I don't care,' she retorted. 'I'm staying.'

The doctor muttered something under his breath that Rosie suspected was rather rude, and swept out of the cubicle.

Ignoring the shocked expressions on the nurses' faces as they began to sponge away the muck clinging to Ron, Rosie stepped forward to take his hand. 'It's all right, my love,' she murmured against his grubby, bristled cheek. 'I'm here with you. You're safe now.' She doubted he could hear her, or even knew she was there, but it made her feel a little better to be able to touch him at last.

Mr Armstrong arrived like a potentate prince, followed by his entourage of scurrying nurses and stately Matron. Tall, silver-haired and imposing, he swept in, ignoring Rosie, and focused on Ron.

There was a deathly hush and Rosie could hardly breathe as she studiously ignored Matron's furious glare of disapproval and waited for the consultant's verdict.

He finally stepped back from the examination table and held out his hand for Ron's medical notes, which a little nurse quickly provided. Having read them, he turned to Matron. 'Take him to X-ray immediately and have my theatre prepared. See to it that the most experienced theatre nurses are available. This will be a long, complicated operation requiring the highest standards, and I shall probably need a second team of nurses standing by to take over should it go on too long.'

'Sister Goodyear is available,' said Matron, 'but as she shares a house with the patient, I don't believe it would be ethical for her to participate in the operation.'

'That is a nuisance,' said the consultant. 'Have her on standby anyway. We've a long morning ahead of us.'

'Is it the shrapnel?' Rosie dared ask.

He looked startled to see her there, and regarded her from his great height, his grey eyes gleaming with what looked suspiciously like relish. 'It very well could be. But I think the X-rays will confirm my suspicion that the patient has suffered two crushed lower vertebrae, and if the shrapnel has embedded itself there, it will require ground-breaking surgery to remove it.'

Rosie's heart hammered with fear. 'Will he come through?'

'That is something I cannot tell you until I've opened him up,' he replied with rather too much enthusiasm for Rosie. 'Spinal injuries are always tricky and can lead to complications with the kidneys, and even paralysis if the spinal cord is damaged. It depends entirely upon what the X-rays show.'

'And if the cord has been damaged?' Rosie persisted.

'Then there is every chance Mr Reilly might not walk again.'

'Oh, God, no,' she whispered through her fingers.

His smile softened his expression. 'But it seems that Sister Danuta has done extremely well in stabilising his spine, so there is some hope. Medical advances have greatly increased since the First World War, and as long as any fracture is stable and the kidneys function, he has a chance of surviving.'

Rosie felt her legs buckle, and she had to steady herself against the examination bed. 'You mean he might die?' she managed.

'Had this happened ten years ago, then that would have been my prognosis,' he said darkly. 'However, Mr Reilly is otherwise supremely healthy, and as I am confident in my skills as a surgeon, we do stand a small chance of getting him through – although he may be confined to a wheelchair.'

Rosie almost sagged with relief at this tiny spark of hope. She didn't care if he ended up in a wheelchair, she just wanted him alive. 'Thank you,' she breathed.

'Don't thank me yet,' he replied. 'We have a long day to get through first, and so I suggest you go home and rest.'

Rosie had no intention of going anywhere. 'How long will the operation take?'

'How long is a piece of string?' he replied. 'It's impossible to gauge.'

She found herself being gently but firmly steered out of the cubicle by Matron, closely followed by Armstrong and his entourage. She would have liked to have kissed Ron again, but he was already being wheeled away – still silent and far too inert.

Rosie left the emergency department and found the others filling the waiting area. Peggy embraced her immediately and Rosie saw that everyone from Beach View was there, as well as Gloria, Ruby, April and Doris. The men from the search party were there too, looking as grubby, damp and exhausted as Rita and Danuta, and Harvey was slumped in a soggy, muddy heap beneath the line of chairs.

Inundated by questions she couldn't really answer, she sank down in a chair next to Peggy and gratefully accepted a cup of stewed hospital tea which she sipped as she tried to absorb the doctor's prognosis and then tell them what was happening to Ron.

'He'd be better off dead than left a cripple,' muttered Gloria, who never knew when to keep her mouth shut. 'A man like Ron could never cope with that.'

'I know you mean well, Glo,' said Rosie, 'but that's really *not* what I need to hear right this minute.'

'That surgeon sounds a bit pompous,' said Frank. 'Jim had the same op in India to get the last bit of shrapnel out of his back, so it's not ground-breaking as that man put it.'

'I think it very much depends on where it is and what other damage has been done,' said Rosie fearfully.

'What shrapnel?' Peggy asked sharply.

Frank reddened and earned a dig in the ribs from his wife Pauline. 'Sorry, Peg,' he said. 'I thought you knew.'

'Knew what?' she demanded.

'Jim got some shrapnel in his back and most of it was removed at the field hospital, but he went down with a fever and had to wait until he was flown out to India for the doctor there to retrieve the rest.'

'I'm sorry to put a dampener on things,' said Fran who was now in her nursing uniform and ready to go on duty. 'But it will depend entirely on how close to Ron's spine the shrapnel is, as well as the size of it. Mr Armstrong is the best surgeon there is, but if the shard is small and has been embedded in Ron's spine, it *will* take ground-breaking surgery to get it out.'

'We mustn't give up hope,' breathed Rosie, gripping Peggy's hand for comfort. She regarded Frank, who seemed so sure of himself. 'Jim's pulled through all right, hasn't he? And if he's well enough to go back to his regiment, then there's a real chance Ron will recover fully as well.'

'That's what I believe,' said Frank firmly. 'We Reillys are a tough, stubborn lot. A bit of shrapnel doesn't stand a chance of beating us.'

Rosie could only pray that was so. 'What happened out there, Frank?' she asked. 'Where did you find him?'

Frank looked shifty, and the other men moved about uncomfortably in their chairs. 'I can't rightly say,' Frank replied. 'We can only speculate that when that Lancaster came down it must have shaken the ground and made some sort of sinkhole and Da fell into it.'

'But that Lancaster came down at about four in the morning,' Rosie protested. 'What on earth was he doing up there at that time?'

Frank shrugged. 'Who knows? Da's always up to something or other. We're just thankful we got him out.'

Rosie had a lot more questions, but Matron bustled into the room at that moment and brought the conversation to an end. She looked askance at the mess from the muddy boots and dripping coats on her floor – and the presence of a damp, filthy dog in her waiting room.

'I suggest you men go home, take that animal with you, and clean up,' she said sternly. 'I dread to think of the germs you've been trailing into my hospital.'

Her gaze swept to Danuta and Rita. 'You did very well tonight, Sister, and probably prevented further damage to Mr Reilly's spine; but I believe you have to be back on your district rounds soon. You should both have a bath and see to your other duties, rather than sitting about here risking pneumonia and spreading germs.'

She marched off and began issuing orders to the nurses to clean up the mess and see to it that the dog was immediately removed from the premises.

'Well,' muttered Rita, 'that's told us. But she's right. We're both due on duty and I don't know about Danuta, but I'm so cold I can hardly feel my feet.'

'Aye, and poor old Harvey needs a scrub-down too,' muttered Alf. 'I'll take him home with me and keep him for as long as needed.'

'I'll look after Monty, if you'd like, Rosie,' said Fred the Fish. 'The boys will love having him, so he'll be no bother.'

The men shuffled about, clearly loath to leave, but aware they too needed hot baths and to get on with their day.

Rosie realised it was up to her to send them on their way. 'I want to thank you all for rescuing Ron, and for being so kind in taking on the dogs,' she said. 'But Ron could be in theatre for hours, and although I really appreciate your love and support, it's probably best if you all go home. You have work to do, shops to open and a pub to run. I promise I'll keep everyone posted the minute I hear anything.'

One by one they hugged Rosie and took their leave, Harvey reluctantly being led away by Alf on a length of string, until only Peggy, Doris and Cordelia remained, along with Daisy who was dozing in her pushchair.

An hour passed, and then another before Fran came in to tell them Ron was out of X-ray and was about to go into theatre.

They sat in silence and watched the clock tick away another two hours.

'I hate to leave you like this,' said Peggy as the Town Hall struck six. 'But Daisy needs her breakfast, and there's a bit of a crisis at the factory, so it's vital I go into work this morning. But I promise to call in during my lunch break. If you hear anything, ring the factory. Madge will pass a message on.'

'I should go and make sure John gets a good breakfast inside him before we have to be in the office,' said Doris. 'Unless you want me to stay, Rosie?'

Rosie managed to dredge up a smile. 'None of us are really doing any good here,' she said quietly. 'I appreciate the offer, Doris, but I'm all right, really.'

Doris squeezed Rosie's shoulder in sympathy and went to join the Colonel, who'd unexpectedly appeared in the doorway.

'I'll keep you company, Rosie,' said Cordelia. 'And young Fran has promised to keep us informed with any news from theatre now she's on duty.'

Rosie clasped her hand in gratitude and then lit a cigarette. Now Peggy had left, she was very grateful for Cordelia's company, and for all the wonderful kindness she'd been shown by everyone, but her mind was on what the X-rays might have revealed, fretting over the possibility that the shrapnel might have crippled Ron for life – or worse, that he might die whilst he was under the knife.

'That surgeon better have very steady hands,' she muttered to Cordelia. 'Or he'll have me to answer to.'

Peggy arrived home to discover that Sarah was cooking breakfast, and Ivy had stoked the fire and laid the table whilst Danuta and Rita were having their baths. She told them Ron was still in theatre, then saw to Daisy, who was a bit grumpy at having had a disturbed night's sleep. Although she didn't feel at all hungry, Peggy managed a boiled egg and a piece of toast with a very welcome cup of tea and a fag.

Robert dashed downstairs and rushed off to Castle Hill Fort with barely a word, shortly followed by Rita and Danuta, who'd bathed and changed, and now tucked into the food ravenously.

'So, what exactly happened last night?' asked Peggy. 'The men would tell me nothing, and Rosie and I need to know.'

The girls shared a glance, and it was Rita who replied. 'Ron had an accident in the hills,' she said. 'He got trapped in a landfall. That's really all I can say.'

'What the heck was he doing out there at that time in the morning?'

'I don't know,' said Rita. 'He never came round, so couldn't tell us.'

Peggy suspected that the rescuers had rehearsed their story and were hiding something from her, but she was determined to get to the bottom of it. 'If he was trapped underground, then how did anyone know where to find him?'

Rita shrugged and Danuta kept her head bent to her breakfast. 'Someone did say that Bertie Double-Barrelled led them to him,' said Rita eventually, succumbing to Peggy's level stare. 'I'm sorry, Auntie Peg, but we were all told not to breathe a word of what happened last night, because it would be a breach of the Secrets Act.'

'Good grief!' gasped Peggy. 'What on earth was the old devil up to out there?' She realised it was a rhetorical question, for she now knew she'd get no answer from anyone that had been involved. 'I suppose I should just be grateful you got to him at all, and that he's in the best place to be treated properly,' she said with a sigh. 'But, oh, God, the waiting to hear if he's pulled through is killing me. Lord only knows what it's doing to poor Rosie.'

Both girls gave her a hug, then cleared their dishes and rushed off, leaving Peggy none the wiser. The house felt strangely deserted and horribly silent without Ron, Harvey and Cordelia, and so she turned the wireless on for company and quickly made a flask of tea and a pile of sandwiches to take to the hospital for Rosie and Cordelia.

Wrapping the sandwiches in newspaper, she then went down to the basement with Daisy to see to the ferrets and feed the chickens. Returning to the kitchen some time later, she switched off the news broadcast, which didn't really have anything new to say, and prepared herself and Daisy to leave the house.

With Daisy snugly protected beneath the waterproof covers of the pushchair and happily dozing, Peggy tied her headscarf under her chin, buckled the belt on her raincoat and opened her umbrella. The driving rain came at her in horizontal sheets and she found she really had to struggle against it – especially when it blew up from the sea as she crossed over into Camden Road.

It was a foul day and her spirits were at their lowest ebb. She couldn't bear the thought of Ron going under the knife. He'd looked so helpless lying there, his face ashen beneath the oxygen mask, and suddenly looking old and frail – not the Ron she knew at all.

And the thought of poor Rosie having to sit and wait while her imagination must be running riot was hard to take as well. Peggy felt awful about leaving her there with Cordelia, who was far too old to be sitting about after a poor night's sleep, but it was imperative she speak to Solly today before Mavis's troublemaking went any further.

As she reached the Anchor, she was surprised to see the lights blazing in the bar. Thinking they must have left them on in their rush to get to the hospital, she hurried inside and took in the sight of Brenda and the other two barmaids busy clearing up the abandoned party.

'Oh, Brenda, that is kind. Rosie will be so grateful.'

'It's the least we can do in the circumstances,' Brenda replied. 'Fred came to fetch Monty, so he's all right, but if you could tell Rosie we'll keep the pub going for her. She doesn't need the worry of this place with everything else going on.'

Peggy nodded and promised to keep them informed on Ron's progress, then went back out into the rain. She hurried to the hospital and found Rosie and Cordelia where she'd left them. 'Any news?'

'He's out of theatre,' said Rosie, her face drawn and pale with worry. 'Fran popped down and told us, but she doesn't know how the operation went.' She took a tremulous breath. 'He's in recovery now, but she warned us not to expect much more information for at least another hour or so.'

'At least it seems he's come through,' Peggy said soothingly. 'I've brought you sandwiches and tea,' she added, fishing them out of her string bag. 'I'll pop back later with something hot from the factory canteen.' She looked at Cordelia, who was clearly very tired. 'Would you like me to take you back to the Anchor so you can rest?'

'No, thank you,' she replied, sitting a little straighter in her chair. 'I'm staying put until I know that old scallywag is on the mend.'

Peggy knew better than to argue. She told Rosie what Brenda and the other two barmaids were doing.

'That's so typical of Brenda,' said Rosie, once more on the verge of tears. 'How very kind everyone has been. I seriously don't know how I can ever repay all their love and care.'

'You don't need to,' Peggy assured her. 'They love you and Ron, and are only too pleased to have something to do that might help you both.' Daisy was starting to wriggle and grizzle, so Peggy quickly kissed Rosie and Cordelia, then wheeled the pushchair back outside before it became a full-blown tantrum.

Hurrying to the crèche, she explained to Nanny Pringle what had happened to bring them so early to her door, and was greatly relieved when she took it all in her stride and promised to look after Daisy and make sure she had a sleep.

Peggy had noted Solly's Rolls-Royce parked at the kerb. The day shift was yet to begin, so this would be the perfect time to have a quiet word with him about Mavis. Not wishing to be seen by Mavis or the girls on night shift, she ran through the rain to the fire escape and let herself into the outer office.

Madge had yet to arrive, so she dumped her wet umbrella in the stand by the coat rack and hurried through to tap on Solly's door.

'Come in.'

Peggy was surprised to hear Rachel's voice, for she rarely arrived at the factory before nine – but in fact was rather relieved, for Rachel would be easier to talk to. She went in and found her alone behind the large desk.

'Hello, Peggy,' she said, getting to her feet in surprise. 'I'm sorry we both missed the parties last night, but Solly was held up late at the synagogue, and I got called in here to deal with Fanny Rawson, who'd taken a nasty fall and had to be rushed to hospital with two broken ribs and a badly twisted ankle.'

Peggy was startled by this piece of news and decided her own, however monumental, could wait. 'Fanny's not usually clumsy,' she said, undoing her coat and taking off her headscarf. 'Is she all right?'

'They strapped up her ribs and ankle and are keeping her in for the day to make sure she isn't suffering from concussion. She took a nasty blow to her head, you see, and had been knocked out cold.'

'How did it happen?' asked Peggy.

Rachel poured them both a cup of strong, aromatic coffee from the percolator that sat on a nearby filing cabinet, and added milk and sugar. 'That's the odd thing,' she replied as they both settled into the chairs. 'Fanny said she'd tripped on the stairs leading up to the offices, but when I asked around, no one would admit to seeing her fall. It beats me what on earth she was doing coming up here at all.

She had no cause to know neither Solly nor I would be here.'

'What did Mavis say? I'm assuming she was in attendance?' asked Peggy.

'Of course she was,' said Rachel. 'She confirmed what Fanny told me. Why do you ask?'

Peggy sipped the delicious coffee and decided not to answer directly. 'It's strange no one else saw her fall,' she said finally. 'Most of the women down there have eyes like hawks.'

'Yes, I know, and that does bother me,' murmured Rachel. She sat back in Solly's creaking chair and regarded Peggy evenly. 'Do you think there's more to this, Peggy?

'I'm very much afraid there might be,' she replied. She put down her coffee cup and told Rachel about the personal files, Mavis's snooping, and the switch of personnel. 'I burned everything except for the work records, basic medical information and their references,' she finished.

'You did the right thing, Peggy,' Rachel sighed. 'Loretta should have destroyed all those notes once she'd finished her social history degree. I can't believe she's been so careless.'

She opened the silver cigarette box, offered it to Peggy and then lit up. 'I have no doubt your suspicions about Mavis are correct – I never trusted her from the start. But what on earth do we do about it? We have absolutely no proof of anything unless one of those women talks to us.'

Peggy remained silent, for she really didn't know what to suggest.

'Do you think there was some sort of confrontation between Mavis and Fanny?' Rachel asked. 'Is it possible she and Mavis were fighting on the stairs and Fanny really did lose her footing – or do you think she was pushed?'

'I strongly suspect the latter could have been the case,' said Peggy. 'But if there was a confrontation, it was in full view of the entire night shift. So why isn't anyone speaking out about it? Fanny has lots of friends down there, and Mavis isn't popular. It doesn't make sense.'

'Who is Fanny's best friend? Perhaps she can be persuaded to speak out.'

Peggy thought for a moment, remembering the notes in Fanny's file. 'Julie Raymond shares her room at the hostel and they've become very close. But it wouldn't be a good idea to approach her here. Better to wait until she's gone off shift.'

'Would you do that, Peggy? She might be afraid to talk to me as I'm the boss's wife. I'll keep Mavis here on some pretext at the end of the shift so you have time to whisk Julie off somewhere quiet.'

Rachel reached into a drawer and pulled out a ten-bob note from a tin cash box. 'Take her to the Lilac Tearooms and treat yourselves to some scones or something.'

Peggy took the money and slipped it into her handbag. 'When's Solly due in?' she asked.

'Not until this afternoon,' said Rachel. 'My car's broken down, so he's waiting at home to pick it up from the garage.' She thought for a moment, and then stubbed out her cigarette. 'I think it's best if we clear this up together, Peggy. Solly has a great deal on his plate at the moment, and I don't want him blowing a fuse over Mavis and her shenanigans. His blood pressure simply won't stand it.'

She smiled at Peggy's worried expression. 'Don't fret, Peggy. I know how to handle him. He'll thank us in the end, believe you me.'

'I hope so,' said Peggy, who doubted it very much.

Rachel became businesslike. 'Now, Peggy, what can I do for you? It's still very early, so something must be up.'

Peggy told her about the night's dramas.

'Oh, Peggy, I'm so sorry,' Rachel gasped. 'I've been rattling on about Mavis and Fanny and you must be in a terrible state. Forget about talking to Julie, and get yourself back to the hospital.'

Peggy shook her head. 'I'm of no use there, and Cordelia's keeping Rosie company until the others can pop in,' she said. 'If you don't mind, I'd rather deal with what's happening here. It'll give me something else to think about.'

'Well, if you're sure,' Rachel murmured.

'Quite sure,' she said firmly. She glanced at her watch. 'I'll slip outside and wait for Julie. The end of the shift is only five minutes away.'

Rachel nodded, and as Peggy pulled on her coat, she pressed a button on the intercom connected to the shop floor office.

'Mrs Whitlock. Would you be so kind as to come up to my office at the end of the shift? There are some time sheets I need to go through with you before you leave for home.' She disconnected the line without waiting for a reply and winked at Peggy. 'It's up to you now. Good luck.'

Peggy grabbed her umbrella and hurried through the fire-escape door to avoid Mavis. Making her way down the rattling iron staircase to the factory forecourt, she stood beneath her umbrella, waiting for Julie, her mind working on how to approach the tricky subject of Fanny's fall.

As the men and women began pouring out of the factory, and others poured in, it was quite a task to pick her out, for Julie was small and slight, with pale brown hair and ordinary features which didn't make her stand out in a crowd. But eventually Peggy spotted her, and as she came out of the gate, followed her down the street for a little way and then tapped her on the shoulder.

'Hello, Julie, Remember me? Peggy Reilly.'

'Course I do.' The girl grinned, making her sallow face light up and her pale eyes shine. 'You helped me get the job here, and I'm ever so grateful.'

'I'm just glad you're happy here,' said Peggy, tucking her hand into the crook of Julie's arm. 'Why don't we have a cup of tea and a bit of cake or something at the tearooms? My treat.'

The girl's expression was immediately guarded, and she eased her arm away. 'Why'd you want to treat me, Mrs Reilly? What you want?'

'Just a chat,' said Peggy. 'I thought it might be nice to catch up on all your news and hear how you're getting on now you're on night shifts.'

Peggy could see the girl was tempted, so she encouraged her with a friendly smile and a nudge against her shoulder. 'Come on, Julie. It's cold and wet out here, just think of a lovely cup of tea and bit of cake sitting by that fire in the tearoom where it's all warm and cosy.'

'Well, all right,' she replied with obvious reluctance. 'But only for a bit. I'm tired and need me sleep.'

Peggy steered her along the road to the teashop which had stood in Camden Road for years, and chivvied her inside to the jolly sound of the tinkling bell above the door. 'Good morning, Bella,' she said to the owner. 'A pot of tea and a plate of cakes, please.'

Julie was clearly overawed by it all. Peggy suspected the girl had never set foot in the place before today, and rather regretted having to spoil her treat by pumping her for information. She chose a table at the back of the room where they couldn't be seen by anyone passing the window, and slipped off her coat and scarf.

She held her hands out to the fire in the hearth. 'This is nice, isn't it?' she said. 'Much more pleasant than standing about in the wet and cold.'

Julie nodded warily, perhaps already suspecting where this meeting was heading. She too shed her coat and warmed her hands, and stared in appreciation at the plate of delicious-looking cakes Bella had just placed on the table. 'Blimey,' she breathed. 'I ain't seen the like since I don't know when.'

Peggy encouraged her to choose the large slab of chocolate cake, whilst she selected the Victoria sponge. 'Bella does the best cakes in Cliffehaven,' she said. 'But then her uncle owns the dairy, so she can always get butter and cream.'

She waited for Julie to tuck into her slice. 'It's just such a shame Fanny couldn't be here to share it. Perhaps we should ask Bella to wrap up that piece of sponge for her so you can take it to the hospital?'

Julie paused in her chewing and then nodded and carried on eating, the temptation of such a delicious treat too great to resist.

Peggy wasn't in the least bit hungry and nibbled at the cake as she surreptitiously watched Julie eat a second slice and wash it down with the hot, strong tea. When she'd gauged the girl was ready, she began to probe.

'Mrs Goldman tells me that poor Fanny will be staying in hospital for a while. I do hope her injuries won't stop her from working.'

'She'll be back tomorrow,' said Julie, her gaze firmly fixed away from Peggy. 'Fanny's not one to shirk because of a few bumps and bruises.'

'It was rather more than that, Julie,' said Peggy. 'She's got two broken ribs and a very nasty bump on the head as well as a twisted ankle. She's lucky she wasn't killed after falling down those stairs.'

'Yeah, I know, but like I said, Fanny ain't one to make a fuss.'

Peggy chuckled. 'Now, Julie, we both know Fanny enjoys making a fuss when she thinks someone's playing unfairly, and I wouldn't mind betting she'll get the union representative on to Mr Goldman for having such a dangerous staircase.'

The girl looked back at her like a startled fawn. 'Oh, she wouldn't do that, Mrs Reilly, not with ...' She clamped her mouth shut.

'But Gladys Bright is a very good and helpful union leader. I'm sure ...'

'You're not to say nothing to no one about them stairs. Especially Gladys Bright, she won't do nothing about it anyway, and none of us want trouble.' Her little face crumpled as she burst into tears. 'I knew I shouldn't've come here.'

Peggy reached across and took her hand. 'Oh, Julie, I'm so very sorry. But you see I *am* on your side. I think I know what happened to Fanny last night, but unless you can be straight with me, then there's absolutely nothing I can do about Mavis Whitlock and the trouble she's causing everyone.'

The girl's eyes widened and she stopped snivelling. 'You know about her?' she breathed, wiping her nose on her sleeve.

Peggy nodded and gave her a clean handkerchief. 'Probably more than you'll ever realise. I know she's causing unrest and making some of the girls' lives a misery – particularly Fanny's, and I need your help to stop her.'

Julie blew her nose and wiped her eyes and thought about this whilst she poured a second cup of tea. 'Does Mrs Goldman know too?' she asked eventually. 'Only I saw you and her talking earlier.'

'We both suspect something is very wrong,' Peggy said carefully. 'You see, nothing happens on that factory floor that isn't seen by everybody. And yet Fanny went tumbling down those stairs, apparently unseen by anyone.'

'This won't get me into trouble with Mr Goldman, will it? Only I don't want to lose me job.'

'He'll be very grateful to you for being honest,' said Peggy, 'and could very well reward you for it.' She didn't know that for sure, but a word in Rachel's ear might bring about ten bob or so.

'Me and Fanny are real good mates,' said Julie. 'I know what happened to her and how she earned a living before she got the job at the factory, but then I been down the same road as her, so we understand each other.'

She took a sip of tea and then lit a cigarette. 'We was all getting along really well until that woman come along and demoted Fanny, making her lose out on the extra ten bob a week. Fanny told me she'd somehow found out about her past from Loretta's files and threatened to tell Mr Goldman, who would then sack her on the spot. But if Fanny paid her half a crown a week and didn't make a fuss over being demoted, she'd keep quiet about it. Fanny said there weren't nothing she could do, but she'd heard from Gladys Bright that the same sort of threat had been made to her.'

Peggy simmered with fury but remained silent as Julie's anguish poured out of her in a stream of words and more tears.

'Fanny told me the Whitlock woman probably knew all about me being on the game before, so I had to keep me mouth shut or I'd be out on me ear too.' She mopped up her tears again and drank more tea.

'I dunno what got into Fanny last night, but she saw that bitch up in Mr Goldman's office, and decided to go up there and have it out with her once and for all. We all saw her storming up them stairs and into Mr Goldman's office, and it wasn't long before they was yelling at each other and pushing and shoving. I don't know how it happened, but Fanny was shoved by that woman out of the offices and onto the landing.'

Julie took a restorative sip of tea and a puff on her cigarette. 'Fanny was yelling blue murder about how Mavis had no right to snoop in Solly's office and that she'd tell him about it the moment he came in – and that she's been bullying everyone and making them pay 'er ter keep 'er mouth shut. That's when Mavis pushed her, and she fell down them stairs.'

Julie shivered. 'She made the most awful noise, tumbling down there, and when 'er head hit the floor, it was like a ripe pumpkin being dropped on concrete.'

Peggy felt sick, for she could well imagine the sound. 'But why on earth did everyone keep silent?'

'The bitch knew she'd done wrong, 'cos she ran down the stairs and tried to wake Fanny up. When it was clear Fanny was out cold she got scared and ordered someone to fetch an ambulance whilst she rang Mrs Goldman. Then she said that if anyone spoke about what had happened, she'd fix the time sheets so everyone's pay was docked by at least two hours.'

Julie's hand trembled as she stubbed the cigarette out. 'To be fair, none of us can afford to lose any pay, so we did what we could for Fanny before the ambulance and Mrs Goldman arrived, and then went back to work.'

'Thank you, Julie, for being so honest.'

'This won't get me into trouble, will it?' she asked anxiously. 'Only if that bitch gets to hear I've been telling tales, me life won't be worth living – and neither will Fanny's.'

'I can promise you she won't know anything, and I'm very certain that when the night shift comes back this evening, there will be no sign of her.'

'Really?' The girl's eyes shone with hope. At Peggy's nod, she grinned. 'Would it be all right if I had another bit of cake, then? Only it seems a shame to waste it.'

Peggy pushed the plate towards her and managed a tight smile. Mavis would certainly be confronted over her wrongdoing, but she doubted she'd go quietly. And despite the promise she'd made to Julie, she very much feared that Mavis could not be got rid of quite so easily. She needed to get back to Rachel and have a council of war.

She paid for the tea and cake and an extra slice for Fanny, which was placed in a brown paper bag. 'I must get back to work, Julie,' she said, pulling on her coat. 'Please give Fanny my best regards when you deliver that cake.'

'Thanks, Mrs Reilly,' Julie replied. 'I do feel better now for telling you.'

Peggy hurried across the road to the hospital, to discover that Bertie was now keeping Rosie and Cordelia company, but there was no further news on Ron's recovery.

Returning to the factory, she clocked in and shed her raincoat and umbrella in her office, then went up the wooden stairs to talk to Rachel.

Rachel listened as Peggy relayed the conversation she'd had with Julie. 'I'll certainly see she's rewarded,' she said. 'But I've been on the telephone to Solly's brother in London, and it made for a very interesting exchange. It seems he really has pulled a fast one by sending her down here – and now we're stuck with her.'

'You've got to be joking!' gasped Peggy. 'What she did last night was bordering on criminal. She's damned lucky she didn't kill Fanny.'

'That's as maybe,' said Rachel, 'but she's as slippery as an eel and will somehow wriggle out of it.' Rachel lit them both cigarettes and leaned her elbows on the desk. 'It appears that she's been up to the same sort of thing in London too, but when he told her he was going to sack her, she threatened to take a complaint to the union, accusing him of assault.'

'What!?'

'Like a fool, he'd had a bit of a fling with Mavis, which he ended when his wife found out and threatened to divorce him and take all his money. Mavis had had ambitions and never forgave him for breaking it off, so when he threatened to sack her, she got her revenge, accused him of assault and threatened to call a full strike and walk-out.'

'No wonder he wanted to be rid of her,' breathed Peggy.

'He knew Solly was in a bind, so managed to pay Mavis off with a hundred pounds and the promise of getting her the job here. And like a soft fool, Solly agreed to take her on without asking any questions,' said Rachel. She gave a deep sigh. 'We'll have to

347

handle this very carefully, Peggy. We simply can't afford a strike at this crucial point in that demob suit contract.'

'Then what do you suggest?' Peggy asked. 'We can't keep her on, not now we know what she's capable of.'

'I don't know,' Rachel admitted. 'But Solly will have to be told, and I dread to think of the fallout it will cause between him and his brother.'

'I'd better get back down there,' said Peggy, noticing that work had almost stopped on the factory floor as the women gossiped amongst themselves. 'It looks as if trouble's already brewing.'

'Keep me posted, Peggy. And thanks for taking the time to deal with Julie when you have so many other things to worry about.'

There was a good deal of muttering on the shop floor as Peggy slowly made her way back to her office, and from the snatches of conversation she heard along the way, it seemed that news of Fanny's altercation with Mavis had spread – which was worrying.

'Fanny is being well looked after in the hospital and expected to be back at work tomorrow,' she said as the women looked to her and fell silent. 'The events of last night are being dealt with, so I'd appreciate it if you got on with your work.' She turned to Winnie and Gladys. 'Would you come into my office, please?'

They followed her in and shut the door. She waited until they were seated, and then lit them both cigarettes.

'If you don't do something about that woman, we're going to call a strike,' said Gladys.

This was what Peggy feared. 'Mrs Goldman and I are dealing with it,' she said firmly. 'The night shift has refused to discuss what happened, so the gossip going round is merely hearsay, and not to be acted upon until we know for sure what we're dealing with.'

'We've heard enough to know that woman has to be got rid of,' said Winnie, 'and if a strike's the only way, then so be it.'

'Will you at least give me and Mrs Goldman the rest of the day to sort things out?' begged Peggy.

Winnie and Gladys conferred in murmurs and then nodded. 'You've got until the end of the shift,' said Gladys. 'Then it's an all-out strike.'

Peggy watched them leave and sank back into her chair. This was turning into a nightmare day, and it had only just begun.

18

Rosie was almost at the end of her tether. The hours had ticked away and there was still no news from the recovery room. She'd started to worry about Cordelia too, and in the end persuaded Bertie to take her back to Beach View so she could sleep.

Peggy had popped in with a bowl of hot stew from the factory canteen, Rita had come to sit with her through her mid-morning break, Danuta dashed in and out during her district rounds, and Frank had put in an appearance at midday before he was due to start his shift at the tool factory.

Rosie was exhausted from stress and worry and the need to reassure everyone that she was all right and would let them know as soon as she heard anything from the doctor. Now she was sitting alone, a quiet island in the busy waiting room, glad of a moment's respite and the chance to be silent and still for a while, and not have to talk, worry about everyone else and keep up a stoic front.

Rosie had never been stoic – she wore her heart on her sleeve and was not ashamed to cry or give vent to her emotions – and at this moment she felt like running screaming through the hospital and beating down the doors of that recovery room to demand answers and see for herself what state Ron was in. How much longer would she be forced to wait? Just what on earth were they doing to him?

She checked her watch against the large clock on the wall and heaved a sigh of frustration. Ron had been in recovery for over six hours, and as Fran had been ordered to another ward, she was absolutely in the dark as to what was going on.

She stood up and began to pace, ignoring the surrounding babble of voices and crying of young children that seemed never-ending. Lighting yet another cigarette, she stood in the entrance porch and watched the rain coming down from a gloomy sky, and wondered if this torturous day would ever end.

'Mrs Braithwaite?'

She whirled to face Matron. 'Is he awake? Is he all right?'

'He's still in recovery, but he'll be moved to a side room off Men's Surgical once he's come round fully.' Matron's smile made her look younger somehow, and less fierce. 'Mr Armstrong is very pleased with how the operation went, although it proved to be a very long and complex procedure.'

'How so?'

'The impact of the blow to Mr Reilly's spine crushed two of the lower vertebrae and left a hairline fracture in his hip.'

'And the shrapnel?'

Matron's smile was positively beatific. 'Mr Armstrong's magnificent skills have once again saved the day,' she eulogised, 'but of course his humility would never allow him to boast about it,' she added confidentially. 'The shrapnel was needle-thin, but Mr Armstrong possesses a delicacy in his steady hands which is unmatched, and he was able to retrieve it.'

'Thank God,' Rosie breathed.

'It is Mr Armstrong you should be thanking,' said Matron firmly. 'Without his skill and dedication, Mr Reilly would not have survived.'

Rosie was sure God had something to do with it but didn't argue, since the woman was clearly in awe of the surgeon. 'So my Ron's going to make a full recovery?'

'We won't know until he comes round fully,' Matron hedged. 'I suggest you go home and come back at six. All being well, Mr Reilly should be on Men's Surgical by then.'

'I'd prefer to stay,' said Rosie.

'As you wish,' said Matron, 'but I really don't advise it. You'll do him no good by wearing yourself to a frazzle.'

'We were supposed to be getting married tomorrow,' said Rosie, on the verge of tears. 'And we've waited so long for that day. It doesn't seem fair for this to happen now.'

'I know, my dear,' Matron soothed, 'but life rarely is fair. At least he's come through the operation, and plans can always be remade, you know.'

Rosie nodded in agreement, but felt that she and Ron had been fated never to marry. She watched Matron bustle off, her starched apron crackling, and then caught sight of her reflection in a nearby window. She looked like some mad woman who hadn't slept for a month and then been pulled through a hedge backwards. Deciding she would go home to bath and change and do something about her face and hair, she grabbed her coat and headed out into the rain. She didn't want Ron waking up to see her like this – she'd scare the living daylights out of him.

There had been strange comings and goings amongst the men and women on the shop floor throughout the day, and Peggy wondered if they were hatching some sort of plot, but when she'd questioned them, she was fobbed off with 'gone for her tea break ... gone to the lav ... had to nip out to see to a fractious child in the crèche'.

Peggy's nose for trouble was twitching, and even though she'd warned Rachel about the ill-feeling, strike threats from the shop floor and the deadline which had been agreed, Rachel took it in her stride and went home to tell Solly in the privacy of their home so that she could calm him down before they returned to the factory at the end of the shift.

Peggy was in her office going through the work sheets when Rosie telephoned to say that Ron had come through the operation and although she hadn't been able to speak to him yet, it seemed everything had gone well. Feeling hugely relieved, Peggy promised to meet her at the hospital the minute she could get away.

The mood in the factory was ugly as the end of the shift drew nearer, and as Peggy made her rounds of the machinists and cutters, she knew there was trouble ahead, and had absolutely no solution to it.

Ten minutes before the end of the shift she saw Solly and Rachel enter the upstairs office. Delighted she was no longer alone to deal with this looming crisis, she went to join them.

Solly was still simmering with rage, puffing on a cigar and stalking around the office like a bear with bellyache whilst Rachel sat quietly at the side of the desk. 'She's got to go,' he rumbled. 'I can't afford a strike – not now – not until we've fulfilled this damned contract.'

Peggy glanced across at Rachel, who lifted a shoulder as if to say she had no idea what to do about it either. They watched the hands on the clock move towards six and the end of the shift.

'Oh, Lord,' breathed Peggy as she looked down onto the shop floor. 'You'd better come and see this.'

The entire shift got to their feet as one, whilst the night shift came in and stood in solidarity with them. Every eye was turned to Mavis as she came into the factory and was met with absolute silence.

'What are you all doing standing about?' demanded Mavis.

A heavy, ominous silence was her reply as they stood firm.

'I'll deal with this,' said Solly, grim-faced and determined.

'Wait,' advised Rachel, grabbing his arm to stop him rushing off. 'I have a feeling they've got a plan of their own to get rid of Mavis.' She quickly switched on the two-way address system which the office used to make announcements to the workers down below and hear what was being said by them.

Rachel and Peggy stood beside Solly at the large window that overlooked the shop floor.

'You on the day shift, get out of here,' snapped Mavis. 'The rest of you, get to work, or I'll dock your pay.'

'We're not moving until we've had our say,' said Gladys, stepping forward with Winnie and the other two union representatives from the night shift. 'We know what you've been up to and we aren't going to stand for it no longer.'

'I've done nothing,' protested Mavis. 'Fanny fell, and that's an end to it.'

'She didn't fall,' shouted one of the women. 'We all saw you push her.'

'Yeah,' shouted another. 'And we know you've been threatening people too, poking about in Loretta's notes and taking money off them what can't afford it.'

'And what was you doing in Mr Goldman's office last night?'

355

Mavis drew herself up stiffly and faced them, although she no longer looked quite so sure of herself. 'I ... I'm in charge. I have a perfect right to go where I please.'

'Are you going to do anything about her, Mr Goldman?' shouted Winnie up to the window. 'Only time's up and we're going on strike if you don't.'

There were mutters of agreement, and Solly spoke into the microphone. 'Mrs Whitlock, my office – now.'

Mavis was ashen-faced as she caught the ugly mood of the women and saw Solly's furious glare. She ran up the stairs, ignored a tense and wide-eyed Madge, and hurried into Solly's office.

'It was an accident,' she blurted out. 'Fanny assaulted me. I was merely defending myself.'

'There have been powerful accusations made against you, Mrs Whitlock,' he said, his voice ominously quiet. 'What do you have to say in your defence?'

'It was an accident, and I immediately made sure that she got proper medical attention.' She glanced at Rachel. 'Mrs Goldman will confirm that.'

'I can confirm the ambulance was in attendance,' said Rachel, 'but the real reason for her so-called "accident" has only become clearer over the last few hours.'

'What do you mean?' Mavis was flustered, and she glanced down at the belligerent gathering on the shop floor, perhaps suddenly realising that someone must have talked. 'You don't want to listen to them,' she snapped. 'They're all liars.'

Solly waved away this blatant attempt to besmirch everyone else and glared down at her, the colour slowly rising in his face. 'We all know who the liar is. And the bully. So what is your excuse for using my niece's notes to blackmail the women in my employ, and for being in my office last night?'

'I thought I heard the telephone ringing,' she stammered.

'Liar!' he shouted into her face. 'The phone is put through to your office during the night.' He was breathing heavily, clearly fighting to keep his temper in check.

'You have no call to speak to me this way,' she protested. 'I am innocent of all the charges made by those women, and I'm shocked you should listen to the likes of Peggy and that Gladys with their filthy insinuations.'

There was an angry buzz from the factory floor and Solly seemed to grow taller and broader as he loomed over her, but his voice was deceptively soft. 'You have two choices, Mrs Whitlock. You either resign, or I dismiss you without reference. What is it to be?'

'I'm not resigning,' she retorted, showing more bravery than Peggy would have given her credit for. 'And if you dismiss me, I shall inform my union and have the entire factory brought to a standstill.' She smirked as she once again glanced down to the gathering on the factory floor. 'It seems that either way, you won't be fulfilling that contract.'

'Oh, we will,' rumbled Solly. 'I've spoken to my brother and know what sort of woman you are. He paid you off to keep you quiet, but I won't be doing that. And if you go to the union with some cock and bull story, you'll regret it. You see, I have already spoken to the union president and given him the facts of the matter. So, what's it to be? Resignation or dismissal?'

'Go, go, go,' came the chorus from the shop floor, accompanied by stamping feet and clapping hands.

Mavis crumpled. She knew that she'd completely lost control of the women she'd thought she could bully, and had no chance of getting the better of Solly Goldman. 'I'll hand in my resignation, then,' she said quietly.

'A wise decision,' said Solly. 'Consider it accepted. I'll have the wages due to you sent on.' He leaned closer to her. 'And if there's one hint of trouble from you, I'll have a word with Sergeant Williams about your blackmail attempts.'

The men and women cheered as, red-faced, Mavis left with all the dignity she could muster through the emergency door and down the outside fire escape to the loud shouts of, 'Good riddance to bad rubbish!'

Solly mopped his hot face and smoothed back his hair, then went out onto the landing and looked down on his workers with affection. 'It's good to see you being so supportive of one another,' he boomed. 'I've always prided myself on the fact I have the very best and most loyal workers. In future, should there be a problem – any problem – you mustn't hesitate to tell us. We're here to listen and to help. Now let us carry on, and begin another shift in the knowledge that if we stick together, we are invincible.'

Peggy glanced at Rachel as she switched off the public address system, and they exchanged a smile. Solly was getting quite Churchillian in his old age.

Rosie hadn't slept since leaving the hospital. First off, she had telephoned the registry office to cancel the wedding, and the Officers' Club to cancel the wedding reception. That done, she'd shed more tears as she'd packed away her wedding outfit in a trunk and stowed it beneath one of the spare beds. She would wear it one day, God willing. But for now she had to forget weddings and champagne and concentrate on getting her beloved man back on his feet.

She had a bath and changed into a dark blue dress and matching jacket, then carefully made up her face and brushed her hair so that when Ron woke up, he wouldn't see how tired and frightened she was. She left the Anchor shortly before five-thirty and hurried across Camden Road to the hospital, where she found Frank sitting in the waiting room.

'I thought you'd gone to work,' she said, sitting down beside him.

His face was drawn and grey with worry. 'I did, but I couldn't concentrate. Where's Peggy? I thought she'd be here with you.'

'She told me at lunchtime that some sort of crisis had blown up at the factory, and she might be late,' Rosie explained. 'But I'm sure she'll be here soon.'

They sat there in mutual worry and frustration, and were soon joined by Ivy, Ruby, Sarah, Pauline, Cordelia and Bertie. Alf the butcher and Fred the Fish arrived minutes later, swiftly followed by Peggy, Doris and the Colonel. Rosie was pleased to see them, but wished someone would come and tell her what was going on, for all this hanging about was sending her quite mad with worry.

Matron came into the room and headed straight for her. 'He's out of recovery and in a side room off Men's Surgical,' she said quietly.

Rosie's legs almost gave way. 'He's all right?'

'He's not fully awake, and will probably not make much sense if he tries to talk, but yes, it appears that the operation went well.' Matron looked at the others. 'Only one visitor tonight, I'm afraid.'

'I'm his son,' said Frank, getting to his feet. 'I demand to be allowed to see him.'

Matron looked up to meet his steady gaze. 'Very well,' she said reluctantly, 'but only for five minutes – and that goes for both of you.'

'But that's not long enough,' Rosie protested.

'It's all you can have,' said Matron firmly. 'Mr Reilly is a very sick man and needs all the peace and rest he can get. Visiting hours are from two to four, and six to eight. You can see him tomorrow – but again, only two visitors at a time.'

Rosie and Frank meekly followed her down the endless corridors until they came to a single room set to one side of the men's surgical ward. 'I shall be back in five minutes,' she said before bustling off.

The room was very warm, lit by a low wattage lamp, and with a machine bleeping softly by the bed where a nurse was taking Ron's temperature and noting it down on a chart. She put her finger to her lips and gestured to them to come in and close the door.

Rosie only had eyes for Ron, who no longer had an oxygen mask over his face, but seemed to be lying half-naked on his side beneath a sheet, his bandaged back smeared with some sort of red lotion.

'What's all that for?' she whispered.

'He has a minor pressure sore from being trapped beneath something heavy,' the nurse murmured. 'The zinc lotion will help it heal and prevent further sores.' She gave Rosie a reassuring smile. 'He's as comfortable as possible and heavily sedated against any pain.'

Rosie approached the well-cushioned bed and took Ron's hand. Kissing it, she touched his face and bent close to his ear. 'Hello, darling man,' she whispered. 'You've come through. You'll be all right now.'

It was then that she noticed the clear, empty bag hanging down at the side of the bed and the red rubber tube disappearing up his pyjama leg. 'What's that for?'

'It's a catheter,' the nurse explained. 'It's very important we monitor his urine output to make sure his kidneys are working properly.'

'And are they?'

'It's a bit soon to tell yet,' she replied carefully. 'But Mr Armstrong will explain everything.' She pressed a soft hand on Rosie's shoulder. 'I know how silly this sounds in the circumstances, but do try not to worry. Mr Armstrong and we nurses will be looking after him day and night. He really will get the very best care.'

'How long will he be confined to bed?' Frank muttered.

The nurse bit her lip. 'Each patient is different,' she hedged. 'There's no real set time.' Seeing their horrified expressions, she quickly added, 'But Mr Reilly is a very fit man for his age, so he could be up and about quite soon. We can only wait and see.'

She left the room and quietly closed the door behind her.

Frank stood on the other side of the bed and looked down at his father with such love and dread that it twisted Rosie's heart. 'We'll just have to be patient, Frank,' she murmured. 'And be thankful that he's still alive.'

Frank cautiously touched his father's hand. 'Da, it's me, Frank. You'd better wake up, old fella, because all this lying about is wasting good poaching time.'

Ron groaned and his eyelids fluttered. 'Salmon for Christmas,' he mumbled. 'Where's Harvey?'

'He's with Alf, being a real butcher's dog,' said Rosie with a lightness she didn't feel. 'I expect he'll be as fat as lard by the time you come home.'

'Aye,' he sighed. 'That he will.' His eyes opened and he gazed blurrily at Rosie and gave a weary smile. 'Darling wee girl. What ... doing ... here?'

Rosie lifted his hand to her cheek, careful of all the things sticking out of the back of it and attached to drips. 'I've come to make sure you're all right,' she managed through her tears. 'What on earth were you doing out there, Ron? You've given me the fright of my life.'

'Ach. Not cry, wee Rosie. Tired,' he sighed before drifting back to sleep.

She and Frank sat there in numb silence for what felt like only seconds before Matron came in. She checked Ron's chart, the bag beneath the bed and the drips hanging above it. 'Mr Armstrong wishes to speak to you both,' she said. 'Follow me.'

Rosie kissed Ron's cheek and Frank squeezed his hand, then they followed Matron outside.

Mr Armstrong was in a well-appointed office overlooking the rear gardens of the hospital. He rose to greet them from behind a polished mahogany desk cleared of everything but a large model of the human spine.

He waited until they were settled on the edges of the comfortable chairs before speaking. 'You will have noted that Mr Reilly is being treated for a pressure sore. It is quite shallow, so I expect it to heal quickly without the need for a skin graft, but from now on he will be turned every two hours to prevent any more developing. He will eventually have a plaster jacket applied to aid the healing of the fracture, and if all goes well then he will begin a course of physiotherapy. But there is a long road to negotiate before that can happen.'

He pointed a ruler at the model. 'This is the human spine,' he said unnecessarily, 'and these are the lumbar vertbrae that have been compressed.' He pointed to the two largest at the base of the spine and made sure he had their full attention before carrying on.

'Mr Reilly is fortunate in that the ligaments at the back of the vertebrae are intact, and therefore any damage to the nerves in this lower region can recover. The fracture is what we call stable, and there are definite signs of reaction to stimulus in his feet and lower legs, so there is hope that his partial paralysis will be temporary, and that he might – just might – be able to walk again after a long course of intensive physiotherapy. But every patient is different, so nothing is certain.'

Rosie's emotions went from utter joy to plunging despair within seconds, but Armstrong was still talking and she had to force herself to concentrate.

Pointing to what Rosie would call the hip bone, he said, 'This is the ilium, which has suffered a hairline fracture.' The ruler moved to the top lip of the ilium. 'The shard of shrapnel was driven like a nail into the ilium here, causing the fracture.'

He regarded them solemnly. 'Mr Reilly was extremely fortunate that its passage was stopped by the ilium, for if it had progressed further into the compressed vertebrae and severed his spinal cord, not even my skills could have retrieved it or prevented complete paralysis.'

'Thank you so much,' breathed Rosie. 'I can scarcely believe how lucky we are to have had you to save him.'

'Yes, thank you,' growled Frank, who'd gone as white as a sheet.

Armstrong bowed his head in gracious acceptance of this praise. 'However, there is more, I'm afraid.'

Rosie and Frank clasped hands tightly as they tensed themselves for bad news.

'I won't bore you with the medical names for them, but the hips and spine are protected by muscles and sinews, which form a sort of corset. These are what help us to bend, sit and walk, and twist and turn. These muscles are connected to others throughout the human body to protect vital organs – such as the kidneys and intestines.

'When the spine is damaged, the kidneys can go into shock and stop working, so it is now vital that we keep an eye on Mr Reilly. If the kidneys don't function, then he will not be able to empty his bladder, except by being manually expressed when it becomes full, or with the use of a catheter, which can bring about the risk of infection if done too often.'

He rested his forearms on the desk and entwined his long, graceful fingers. 'I have every hope that Mr Reilly's kidneys will recover to the point where he can urinate without intervention; however, in cases like this, one should be prepared for the worst. If the kidneys fail, then I'm afraid Mr Reilly will not survive.'

Rosie burst into tears. 'No. You can't let him die. Not after all this.'

'I'm afraid it won't be up to me, Mrs Braithwaite. It will be up to fate, and the condition of Mr Reilly's kidneys.' He stood to show the interview was over. 'I'm sorry not to have been able to give you better news, Mrs Braithwaite. I understand you and Mr Reilly were due to be married tomorrow?'

'Yes,' she sobbed.

'We can provide the facilities to go ahead with a wedding here, if you so wish. In the circumstances, I would advise you do so.'

Rosie fell against Frank, bereft of strength and crippled by the loss of hope.

'Thanks, Mr Armstrong,' said Frank, holding Rosie close. 'We'll get back to you on that. My da's a strong wee man and he'll pull through, you'll see.'

'I very much hope so,' murmured Armstrong as he accompanied them to the door. 'But I shouldn't delay in arranging things with the hospital padre. Time could be of the essence.'

Rosie fell in a dead faint, and Frank's face was grim as he gathered her into his arms and carried her out of the room.

Matron appeared as if she'd been waiting for them, and quickly showed Frank into a side room where there was a bed. 'This is for the doctors when they're on nights,' she explained. She poured a glass of water. 'Give this to her when she comes round, and then take her home.'

19

Huddled into her furs, Dolly Cardew drove as fast as she dared through the teeming rain. It was a foul night, the damned heater wasn't working again, and the pale headlights were barely picking out the winding, narrow lanes. The journey from London felt endless, but it was one she had to make, for she could no longer bear the thought of not being with Ron and seeing for herself how he really was.

She had known Ron since she was a girl, and loved him as the big brother she'd never had. He was a kindred spirit who enjoyed walking on the wild side of life, and fed on the excitement of being involved covertly behind the lines. They'd both found themselves in dangerous situations during the First War, and Ron's experiences back then had bred in him a need to be useful and to hone his hard-earned skills when war had been declared again. Now his life seemed to be hanging by a thread – and the thought filled Dolly with dread.

She opened the quarter-light window and fumbled to light a cigarette as she peered into the dark night and felt the gusting wind rock the little car. She'd thoroughly enjoyed her First War, working covertly in France, and had been thrilled to be called into service again when the SOE had been formed at the start of this one. Her task this time kept her mostly at Bletchley, where her fluent French and German and knowledge of France helped to prepare the secret agents and saboteurs who were to be parachuted into Europe.

But the fun had lost its allure when her agents were betrayed or killed, and had definitely faltered when young Danuta had been captured by the Gestapo. Her escape had been miraculous, her recovery from her injuries a testament to the girl's strength of purpose to never be beaten, but Dolly knew that Ron shared her guilt over what had happened to her, for it had been they who'd encouraged the girl to risk her life.

And now it was Ron who was in danger. She'd found out last night, when Bertram Grantley-Adams had telephoned her London office. It was by sheer chance that she'd been there, for she'd only just returned from Bletchley Park that afternoon. She'd listened to Bertram's theory as to where Ron might have been, and after making a series of urgent telephone calls, she'd soon confirmed that his suspicions were spot on, and swiftly gave Bertram the go-ahead to set up a rescue team.

Being buried alive was the stuff of nightmares, Dolly knew how Ron hated being in enclosed, dark places after his tunnelling experiences in the First War, and she had spent the night in an agony of frustration and anguish waiting for Bertram's call to say he'd been found alive. When it had come at five in the morning, she'd gone straight to her superior, Sir Hugh Cuthbertson, to ask permission to drive to Cliffehaven.

Dear Hugh had been very understanding, even though she'd woken him at the crack of dawn in a blind panic. He was a wily old fox, but a wise mentor and counsellor, and he'd advised her to wait until tonight. She'd protested at first, and then realised he was right, for her sudden arrival in Cliffehaven would elicit awkward questions she had no way of answering without giving away the part she and Bertram were playing with the SOE – for how else would she have known about Ron's accident? There had been no other calls from Peggy, or even Danuta.

So here she was, in the middle of nowhere, the rain hammering on the roof and the windows misting up despite the fact she'd cracked open the window.

She slowed down to take a series of particularly sharp bends, lit yet another cigarette and peered into the murky darkness until she reached a straight stretch and put her foot down on the accelerator. Hugh had let her borrow the car from the London office pool, but it didn't have much go in it, which was very frustrating, and now the rain was coming in through the window. She threw the cigarette out, shut the window and smeared away the instant veil of mist which spread across the windscreen.

'Damn, damn, damn,' she swore softly. 'I should have come down whilst it was still light.' Gripping the steering wheel, she sat forward and slowed the car again as she reached a huge puddle that spread the width of the road. Knowing the dangers of flooding the engine by driving through the middle of it, she crawled along at the very edge, praying there wasn't a deep pothole lurking there that might damage the underneath of the car or twist the wheels out of alignment. She certainly didn't fancy breaking down out here at this time of night.

'This is as bad as blasted Devon,' she muttered, remembering the narrow, twisting lanes that she'd navigated on her last visit to her younger daughter, Carol.

At the time, Carol had only just returned to her little cottage in the village of Slapton, after a spell of living at the farm where she worked as a land girl when she'd been evacuated during the American rehearsals for D-Day.

Darling Carol had forgiven her for being a lousy mother as well as the far more heinous sin of keeping her father's identity secret. Felix Addington turning up in Slapton had been a terrible shock, and Dolly was eternally grateful that both he and Carol had been so understanding about it all – and that she'd found love again with the man she'd thought she'd lost all those years before.

Carol's understanding and love was a far cry from the way her elder daughter, Pauline, had reacted. She was sour-faced and needy at the best of times and saw everything Dolly did as a personal slight, and had cut her mother out of her life. Dolly was not the sort of woman to put up with that kind of nonsense, and she had come down here to have it out with Pauline and try to mend fences – between them and between Pauline and her beleaguered husband, Frank Reilly.

'Poor old Frank got the worst of it all, as usual,' Dolly murmured, opening the window again to clear the fog on the windscreen. 'I do hope Pauline actually listened to what I had to say and did something to repair that train-wreck of a marriage – if only for his sake.'

The tiny dashboard clock showed it was now after three in the morning, and as she breached the hill and headed down the High Street and into Camden Road, it soon became evident that poor old Cliffehaven had come off quite badly from the recent V-2 attacks that Peggy had written to her about. The block of flats next to the hospital was gone, and there were gaps all down the street past the Anchor. *At least that's still standing*, she thought, looking up at the darkened windows. *I hope Rosie is managing to get some sleep tonight – though I very much doubt it.*

Dolly drove the car into the hospital forecourt and round to the car park at the side. She switched off the engine, killed the lights and sat for a moment, deep in thought.

Bertram had telephoned again this afternoon, reporting on Ron's condition. He clearly hadn't known much, but it was enough to make her extremely worried. Now she was here, she was not at all sure she wanted to see what had happened to Ron, for he was very dear to her, and the thought of losing him was simply too dreadful to bear.

However, she might not get the chance to see him alive again, and she'd never be able to live with herself if she turned round and went back to London without doing so. Cross with herself for even considering such a thing, she grabbed her handbag and ran through the rain to the hospital entrance.

Shaking the rain from her fur, she patted her expensively coloured and set hair, and headed for the information desk, where an elderly man sat behind a sliding window sipping from a mug of tea. 'I am Mrs Cartwright, and I have an appointment with Matron,' she said once he'd slid back the glass.

She could see by his expression that he was about to give her an argument, and held up a letter addressed to Matron and clearly marked with the portcullis of government and the letters MOD stamped in red at one corner. 'She is expecting me,' she said firmly.

'Look, lady, you ain't coming in here to see anyone at this hour. You can wave that envelope about as much as yer like. It don't mean nothing to me.'

'That will do, Simms.' Matron appeared, duly starched and rustling even at this ghastly hour of the morning. Tall and slender and rather elegant, she had an attractive face, rather marred by untamed eyebrows and a sour expression.

'Mrs Cartwright?' she asked, looking Dolly up and down as if she was a rare and exotic specimen in a laboratory.

'I'm so sorry to disturb you at this ridiculous hour,' said Dolly. 'But I couldn't get away from London any sooner.'

'I really don't understand why you couldn't have waited until the usual visiting times,' grumbled Matron, leading her towards her office. 'My hours are very long as it is, and I don't appreciate all this cloak-and-dagger nonsense.'

Dolly closed the door behind her. 'There's a war on, Matron,' she replied blithely. 'Sometimes these things are necessary if we are to safeguard our national security.'

'I fail to see how Mr Reilly could affect such a thing,' said Matron with a sniff.

Dolly made no reply and remained standing.

'Oh, well, I suppose I'll just have to put up with it,' sighed Matron. 'But it's all most inconvenient.' She folded her hands neatly over her silver belt buckle. 'Your colleague mentioned a letter of introduction from Whitehall.'

Dolly handed over the letter which had been signed by her boss, Sir Hugh Cuthbertson, in his guise as Minister for Internal Security at the Home Office.

'What is it you want, exactly, Mrs Cartwright?' asked Matron when she'd read the letter and noted the signature with a raised brow.

'I wish to see Mr Reilly and to speak to his surgeon,' she replied.

'Mr Armstrong is not to be disturbed,' Matron bristled. 'The surgery on Mr Reilly took several hours and he has a full theatre list starting at seven this morning.'

'Then he won't mind being woken a couple of hours early,' said Dolly.

Matron's bushy brows rose in horror. 'That is out of the question,' she snapped.

'When you spoke to Sir Hugh on the telephone, didn't you understand the gravity of the situation, Matron?'

'I understood that I was being ordered about by some titled toff in London,' she retorted stiffly. 'This is *my* hospital, Mrs Cartwright, and *no one* tells me what to do.'

'I'm afraid we all have to obey orders, Matron – whether we like it or not. I've just spent four hours driving down from London in the most appalling weather, and will have to drive back again before the night is over. I'm here to see Mr Reilly and the surgeon, and will remain until I do so.'

The two women looked evenly at one another, both aware they'd reached an impasse. It was Matron who blinked first. 'I'll take you to Mr Reilly,' she said with great reluctance, 'but it may be some time before I can reach Mr Armstrong. He lives outside Cliffehaven.'

'I'm prepared to wait,' said Dolly, opening the door to encourage the woman to lead her to Ron.

Matron's starched apron crackled as if giving voice to the wearer's brittle mood, and she hurried along a maze of brightly lit corridors until she reached the last door.

'He's in the side room to guard him from infection,' she said. 'A nurse is to stay with him at all times to monitor his vital signs. Please do not do anything to disturb or upset him.'

Dolly's heart missed a beat at the woman's stern expression, but she managed to nod before stepping inside. The light was very dim and it took a moment for her eyes to adjust after the bright corridors, but the sight of Ron was all too clear, and she had to stifle a gasp of horror as she acknowledged the nurse and stepped over to the bed.

She was barely aware of a muffled conversation going on between Matron and the nurse before the woman left, for her whole focus was on the pitiful sight of the man in the bed. 'Oh, Ron,' she breathed. 'What on earth have you done to yourself this time?'

His eyes moved beneath the lids and flickered open. 'Dolly? What you doing down here?'

'I came to see how you are, you old rogue,' she whispered fondly.

He moved his head against the pile of pillows. 'Got to get out, Dolly. Caving in. Gases coming.'

The nurse rushed over but Dolly waved her away, for she'd realised he thought he was still in the tunnel – or even perhaps in one of those he'd dug to lay explosives in the first shout. She gently stroked back the hair drooping over his forehead. 'You're in hospital, Ron,' she soothed. 'The tunnel was yesterday and we're both quite, quite safe.'

He became still and tried to focus on her. 'Can't move,' he rasped. 'Buried.'

'You've hurt your back,' she explained softly. 'And they've tucked in the sheet very tightly, which is why you can't move.' She continued to stroke back his hair and hold his hand as he struggled to absorb what she was saying.

'Don't tire yourself, Ron,' she murmured. 'Go back to sleep. I'll be here for a while yet.'

'Ach, Dolly. To be sure, 'tis good to see you,' he sighed.

'It's good to see you too,' she replied, her heart breaking at the sight of him, 'but it might be better if you said nothing about my visit to Peggy and the others.' She leaned to whisper in his ear so the nurse couldn't hear her. 'I'm Mrs Cartwright for now and Dolly's not supposed to be in Cliffehaven.'

He gripped her fingers with surprising strength. 'Still up to your old tricks, eh?' He gave a sigh and fell back into a morphine-induced sleep.

Dolly sat with him for an hour, but he didn't wake again. She made no attempt to question the nurse, but watched closely as the girl monitored his temperature and pulse rate, and kept checking the drips.

At a quarter to five, a tall, handsome man appeared in the doorway, immaculately dressed in a three-piece suit, but clearly in a filthy temper. He jerked his head at Dolly, indicating she should follow him, turned on his heel and walked back into the corridor.

Dolly took an instant dislike to him. 'I'm assuming that was Mr Armstrong?' she said to the nurse. At her nervous nod, she turned back to a comatose Ron. 'God has summonsed me,' she whispered. 'I'll pop in again before I leave.'

She took her time to gather up her fur coat, gloves and handbag, smiled at the nurse and slowly walked out of the room.

Armstrong was nowhere to be seen.

The blasted man's playing games, she thought crossly. *And I'm in absolutely no mood to pander to what appears to be a vast ego.*

She began to walk back down the corridor, her high heels tapping on the polished floor, until she reached an open door and saw him sitting behind an enormous and expensive-looking desk – *another sign of his perceived self-importance*, she thought sourly.

She strolled in, noting that he hadn't stood to greet her – another black mark against him – and eschewing the two chairs standing in front of that ridiculous desk, made herself comfortable on the couch. It stood beneath the window off to one side of the desk, and therefore forced the man to turn round to face her.

'I do not appreciate being summonsed at this time of the morning,' he snapped.

'You have rather made that clear,' said Dolly, lighting a cigarette. 'I have to say that your manners are far from what I'd have expected from a man of your education and eminence.' She smiled at him sweetly. 'But then none of us are at our best at this time of the morning, are we?'

He gave an irritated sigh, fetched an ashtray and placed it on the arm of the couch. 'Indeed we are not,' he said by way of apology as he looked down at her from his great height. 'What is it you want from me, Mrs Cartwright?'

'I'd like you to tell me about Mr Reilly's operation, and your prognosis for the future. And please don't patronise me by glossing over things. I might be a woman, but I'm an intelligent, level-headed one and have probably experienced more blood and gore than you ever will.'

His eyebrows rose at this and a smile twitched at the corners of his mouth. 'Somehow,' he murmured, 'I don't find that remotely surprising.' He reached for the telephone. 'May I offer you some coffee?'

'That would be utter bliss,' sighed Dolly, relieved the games were over and they'd called a truce.

Armstrong had just finished going through every detail of Ron's operation when a nurse arrived with a tray set with a bone china coffee pot, sugar bowl and milk jug, and delicate cups and tiny silver spoons which rattled on their saucers as she nervously placed the tray on the desk.

'Thank you, dear,' murmured Dolly when it became clear Armstrong wasn't going to say anything. *Really*, she thought in exasperation. *The man's a Neanderthal.*

The nurse scuttled out like a frightened rabbit and softly closed the door. Armstrong poured the coffee, and Dolly refused the milk and sugar. She liked her coffee strong, fragrant and satisfying – just like her men.

'So,' she said after taking a reviving sip. 'What is your prognosis, Mr Armstrong?'

'He has a long road of recuperation ahead of him as long as he can empty his bladder on his own,' he replied. 'Unfortunately, there seems to be no progress in that direction, and if it continues, then I'm very much afraid he will not survive.'

She almost spilled her coffee and had to put the delicate cup and saucer down on the arm of the couch. Clasping her trembling hands tightly in her lap, she ignored the wild beating of her heart and regarded him evenly. 'Surely there must be something you can do to force the bladder to work?'

'Sadly, medical science has not advanced to that degree,' he replied. 'The only two options I have are manual expression, for which my senior nursing staff and I have been trained, and the catheter. I'm loath to use it too often as it can infect the kidneys, so do so only when the bladder is full.'

'I see,' she murmured, fighting hard to hold back the tears which she was damned she'd let fall in front of this pompous oaf.

'If the bladder cannot be emptied of its own accord then infection will quickly follow and result in kidney failure,' he carried on, seemingly oblivious to her distress. 'Spinal surgery is one of the most complex procedures, but the research into its aftermath is sadly lagging.'

'How long does he have?' she asked quietly.

'A matter of days if his kidneys don't function,' he said bluntly. 'I'm sorry, Mrs Cartwright, but you did ask me to be honest with you.'

'Do Mrs Braithwaite and the rest of his family know?'

'I don't think they fully understood the severity of his situation when I spoke to them yesterday, so I shall be speaking to them again today to prepare them. I have suggested that if Mrs Braithwaite wishes to have a wedding ceremony here in the hospital, it can be arranged at very short notice. But she was too distressed to discuss it.'

'I'm not surprised,' said Dolly, the image of a distraught Rosie flashing in her mind's eye. She got to her feet. 'Thank you, Mr Armstrong, for all you've done for Ronan. I'll pop in to see him again, just for a minute, and then I must go back to London.'

Without waiting for his reply, she hurried out of the room and down the corridor to the Ladies' she'd spotted earlier.

Dolly rarely cried – in fact, she prided herself on managing to keep her emotions tightly under control in any given situation – but as she shut the cubicle door and sank onto the lavatory lid, she buried her face in her hands and shed hot, desperate tears as her heart broke into a thousand pieces.

Half an hour had passed by the time she'd recovered enough to think straight. Having come to a decision, she quickly repaired her make-up and steeled herself to return to Ron's room. She was now absolutely determined to get him through this.

The nurse seemed to be doing something to Ron which involved a rubber tube and a clear bag – the catheter Armstrong had been on about – and she looked startled and very unhappy to see her as she quickly pulled the sheet over Ron's nakedness. 'You can't come in now,' she hissed. 'I'm just about to ...'

'That can wait,' said Dolly imperiously and firmly nudged past her to get to Ron.

'Wake up, Ron. I need to talk to you,' she said urgently.

Ron stirred and reluctantly opened his eyes. 'Dolly? What ... doing ... here?'

'I'm here to tell you to buck up and have the biggest piddle of your life.'

Ron frowned. 'What?'

'You heard,' she retorted, waving away the fretful nurse and reaching for the bottle on the bedside cabinet. 'You need to pee on your own, Ron. If you don't you'll die – and I'm damned if I'll let you do that, so you'd better listen to me for once and do as you're told.'

She ignored the desperate protest from the nurse and shoved the bottle at him. 'Use this,' she commanded, 'and think about running water; imagine you're standing by a fast-flowing river, and a gushing tap.'

She spied the washbasin in the corner and hurried over to turn on both taps until the water was splashing everywhere. Returning to Ron, she gripped his hand, desperately drawing him back out of his medicated stupor so he could hold the bottle firmly and in the right place.

'Concentrate, Ron. Concentrate on your bladder. Feel how full it is; put every ounce of that amazing strength of mind to emptying it. Listen to the water, Ron. Listen to how it splashes and think how wonderful it will feel to wee.'

'What is going on here?' Armstrong strode into the room.

'Be quiet,' ordered Dolly. 'Ron needs to concentrate.'

'I really must protest,' he stormed.

'Then do it outside,' snapped Dolly. 'Come on, Ron. You know you want to pee, so let it go. Relax, concentrate and pee as long and loud as you want. It will save your life – I promise.'

Ron seemed to have got the message. He gripped the bottle and closed his eyes, his face a mask of concentration.

Dolly held her breath, but moments later he gave a quavering sigh. 'I can't,' he murmured. 'I want to, but I can't.'

'Of course you can,' she said bossily. 'Come on, Ron. We won't look if that's what's bothering you. But you must wee if you're to get through this and marry Rosie.'

'If you don't leave immediately, Mrs Cartwright, I shall call security,' rasped Armstrong. 'I will *not* have my patient bullied, and you have no right to be in here.'

Ron had closed his eyes again, and Dolly didn't know if he was asleep or putting his mind to emptying his bladder. Either way, the bottle remained empty.

'I thought it might help,' she capitulated in despair. 'Ron has a strong will and can set his mind to anything.' She reluctantly began to collect her handbag and furs when she heard a dribble of urine go into the bottle.

'That's it,' she yelped. 'Yes, Ron. Yes! Come on, you can do it. More, more, more.'

Armstrong hurried over and watched in astonishment as a steady stream continued to flow unaided into the bottle. 'I don't believe it,' he breathed.

'You'd better believe it,' crowed Dolly. 'This is a prime example of the power of mind over matter.' She almost laughed at Armstrong's stunned expression, but was so happy she really didn't care what he thought.

She handed Armstrong the bottle, grasped Ron's hand and kissed his cheek. 'Well done. Oh, Ron, so very well done. You've saved your life. Really you have.'

Ron's face was suddenly a better colour as he winked at her. 'To be sure, I've never been applauded for peeing before,' he rumbled. He looked blearily at Armstrong and managed a ghost of his usual bright smile. 'She's a wonderful woman,' he sighed, and promptly went to sleep.

Dolly kissed his cheek again and collected her things. 'That's my job done here,' she said cheerfully to a stunned and speechless Armstrong. 'It's up to you now to get him back on his feet.'

Danuta had been called out to help the midwife with a breech birth, and was wearily cycling back to Beach View, her thoughts on breakfast and a couple of hours of sleep before she checked on Ron and had to begin her daily district rounds.

The startling sight of her mentor and tutor, Dolly Cardew, coming out of the hospital, made her wobble to a halt. Fearing her visit to Cliffehaven General could mean only one thing, she dashed after Dolly as she hurried to her parked car.

'You have come to see Ron?' Danuta asked breathlessly when she caught up with her.

Dolly turned sharply and stood stock-still. 'Yes, Danuta. But you haven't seen me. Understand?'

Danuta nodded – of course she understood. 'Is very bad, I think, for you to come all this way,' she murmured.

Dolly shot her a beaming smile. 'Well it was until I made the old so-and-so wee for England,' she said in delight. At Danuta's baffled expression, she laughed and went on to explain.

'Of course, his kidneys might very well have recovered on their own,' she admitted, 'and he could have been on the verge of peeing for himself, and it was just good timing on my part. But I like to think I helped – and I thoroughly enjoyed putting a spike in Armstrong's inflated ego,' she finished with a giggle.

'But that is wonderful,' Danuta breathed. 'Ron must have very strong will.'

'Indeed he has,' replied Dolly with an affectionate smile.

'You are going back now?'

'Yes, things are moving rapidly on the other side of the Channel and I'm needed back at Bletchley.' She gave Danuta a hug. 'But I'll come back as soon as I can. Just remember that I was never here. It was a certain mysterious Mrs Cartwright who turned up and had the impudence to defy Mr Armstrong and get Ron on the road to recovery.'

Danuta was quite baffled. 'But how did you know what had happened in the first place?'

Dolly tapped the side of her nose. 'Contacts, Danuta, I'll say no more.' She kissed her cheek and gave her another swift hug. 'I'm so glad you've settled back in here again. Will you stay once the war is over?'

'This is my home now, and I enjoy very much my work, but there is much I can do in Poland. I am thinking I might return there to nurse for a while.'

Dolly nodded. 'I did wonder if that might be the case,' she murmured. 'Peggy will miss you horribly, but if there's anything I can do to help you, just ring or write, and I'll be straight onto it.' She looked at the delicate watch on her slim wrist. 'Now I must go.'

Danuta stood in the hospital forecourt and watched her drive away with a cheerful toot of the horn and a wave. She grinned. Dolly Cardew was a force to be reckoned with – as was Ron – and if between them they'd beaten all the odds and got him on the road to recovery, then it wasn't far short of a miracle.

Jolyon Armstrong stood by the side of Ron's bed as the nurse carefully measured and tested the contents of the bottle. The Cartwright woman was a sophisticated glamour-puss, and would have been just his type if she hadn't irritated him intensely with her sense of entitlement and her refusal to be cowed by his eminent position in the hospital. But by God, the woman had to be admired. She was quite fearless;

sure of herself and absolutely determined to do what he'd failed to achieve these past twenty-four hours.

'Mr Reilly has a urinary tract infection,' said the nurse, holding up the test tube of cloudy and discoloured urine.

'Start him immediately on oral sulphonamide. We can't risk the infection getting into the kidneys.'

He wrote the prescription down on the chart and smiled at the nurse, startling her, then dug his hands into his trouser pockets and strolled back to his office. The events of this early morning had to be recorded. It would make a fine article for the *Lancet*, and provoke a great deal of debate amongst his peers.

He lovingly stroked the polished surface of his beautiful desk and sat down. He'd always been a realist, and of course it was possible that Mr Reilly's kidneys had recovered from the shock of the operation quite naturally. Yet the case for mind over matter was definitely one to explore further. There would be no need to mention the part Mrs Cartwright had played in Reilly's recovery, for she was not the sort of woman to ever read anything more challenging than *Vogue* magazine, let alone a medical journal.

20

Rosie hadn't been able to sleep, and after tossing and turning in her bed, she'd thrown back the covers and got dressed. She could hear Frank snoring in the spare bedroom and left him to it. He'd been so kind after she'd fainted, and had brought her home, insisting on staying with her for what remained of the night.

Pauline had looked po-faced about it, but Frank had been firm and told her to spend the night at Beach View with Peggy, who was distraught by it all and needed her family around her – though what earthly good Pauline would do was beyond Rosie.

Making a cup of tea, she watched the sky lighten from her sitting-room window, and heard a car screeching round the corner into the High Street and roar off into the distance. She saw Danuta cycling along Camden Road, looking rather perky for this hour, and concluded that she must have been called out to some district emergency that had turned out better than she'd expected.

Rosie lit a cigarette although she didn't really want one. She'd smoked too much and worried herself silly over these past two days, and was now suffering from a thick head and a bit of a sore throat. But this should have been her wedding day, with all the fuss and laughter and nerves such a thing entailed, and the knowledge that it could now be months away – if at all – was just one more stress added to all the others she was trying to deal with.

What was happening to Ron? Was he holding his own, or fading? She could only take comfort in the fact there had been no telephone call, for it would have meant the worst possible news. And yet, if he really was clinging to life by a thread, why wouldn't they let her sit with him? It was too cruel, really it was.

She turned from the window and paced the room. The questions had plagued her to the point where she thought she might go mad. It was all so frustrating, and the only place she really wanted to be was in that hospital with Ron; not wearing a damned hole in her sitting-room carpet.

Startled from her thoughts by a sharp rap on the side door, she hurtled downstairs to find Fran on her doorstep. Her throat constricted. 'What's happened?' she managed. 'He's not …? He hasn't …?'

'He's on the mend, Rosie,' she replied, grabbing her hands, her face wreathed in smiles.

'But how? That doctor said …'

'Well, he was wrong,' said Fran firmly. 'And thank God for it. Ron's kidneys have recovered, his bladder has emptied naturally, and although he has a slight infection, he's sleeping like a baby.'

Rosie had to sit down. 'Oh, Fran, that's the best news I've had in days,' she whispered. 'I was so frightened. I really thought I was going to lose him.'

'We all did,' murmured Fran, her voice not quite steady. 'But he has a long road ahead of him, Rosie. You do understand that, don't you?' she warned softly.

'Yes,' she breathed. 'And I can bear anything as long as he's alive.'

Frank came thundering down the stairs barefooted, with his shirt barely tucked into his trousers, his hair tousled and his face grey and drawn with anxiety.

Fran quickly explained the reason for her visit, and Frank sagged onto the bottom step with relief. 'To be sure, the old fella has nine lives,' he managed gruffly. 'I knew he'd pull through – really I did. But for a moment there ...' He got to his feet and held out his hand to Rosie. 'We must go and see him for ourselves.'

'I wouldn't advise it,' Fran said quickly. 'Mr Armstrong's in theatre all day, but Matron's on the warpath this morning, and if she catches you, there'll be hell to pay.'

'She can do or say what she wants,' said Rosie, who was quite prepared to go into battle now she knew Ron was on the mend. 'We're going to see Ron and that's that.'

She gave Fran a hug. 'Thank you so much for coming straight over with your news. Now go home and tell the others, and then get a good long sleep. You've more than earned it.'

Peggy hadn't been able to sleep either, and she'd spent the remainder of the night sitting on Ron's bed waiting for the sun to rise, and dreading the sound of the telephone ringing.

She gave a sigh as she finished cleaning out the ferrets. Bert Williams had promised to take care of them until Ron was well again, and she couldn't help but admire him for defying that awful wife of his for once because he wanted to do something to help his old pal.

Bert's wife wasn't the only one who was making life difficult in this time of crisis. Pauline had not been at all helpful with her prophesies of doom and gloom, and her constant moaning about Frank spending the night at the Anchor. Eventually, Peggy's tolerance had snapped and she'd told her rather sharply to shut up and go to bed.

When the telephone had rung at two in the morning the entire household had responded, white-faced and tense as Peggy had rushed to answer it. The relief that it was a summons from the midwife to Danuta was almost tangible, and they'd returned to their beds in the desperate hope that it wouldn't ring again and Ron would survive the night.

Peggy was alerted by the sound of hurrying footsteps and the opening of the back door. She rushed out to see Fran's beaming smile, and once she'd heard that Ron was expected to recover, they collapsed into one another's arms and shed tears of relief and thankfulness.

'I've told Rosie and Frank,' Fran said eventually. 'They're determined to visit Ron, but I have warned them there could be trouble from Matron. Something or someone clearly upset her last night, and she's being snappier than ever. The poor nurse who was looking after Ron was given a terrible ticking-off – I don't know what about – but I saw her running back to the nurses' home at the end of her shift in floods of tears.'

'Hmph. I'd like to see her try it on with Rosie and Frank,' muttered Peggy. 'Or with me, for that matter.' Galvanised into action now there was good news, she went up to the kitchen and put the kettle on the hob. 'Tell the others,' she said, 'and then go to bed. You look worn out.'

Fran ran upstairs and Peggy went into her bedroom to wake up Pauline who was snoring fit to burst in the double bed. She waited until she was fully aware of what was going on and told her the marvellous news.

'I'm going to the hospital,' she said, 'and as it's Saturday, would you mind looking after Daisy until I get back?'

'Well, I don't know,' Pauline muttered. 'I feel wrung out with so little sleep and all the worry I've been through, and I need to get home and change my clothes.'

Peggy regarded her with disdain. 'We're all wrung out and on the point of collapse, Pauline,' she said through gritted teeth. 'And if you're that exhausted, you certainly won't manage the long uphill walk back to Tamarisk Bay. I'm just asking you to mind Daisy until one of the girls can take over.'

'All right,' she said with great reluctance. 'I'll wait here until Frank gets back to walk me home.'

Peggy swiftly changed into her outdoor shoes and pulled a cardigan on over her jumper and skirt. She kissed Daisy's brow as the child slept peacefully in her cot, then left the room to fetch her raincoat and umbrella. Hearing the delighted chatter from upstairs, she smiled, then slipped out of the house.

She was halfway down Camden Road when she saw Rosie and Frank emerge from the Anchor. 'Wait for me,' she called, breaking into a run.

'Oh, Peggy,' breathed Rosie. 'Isn't it the most wonderful news?'

Peggy slipped her hand through Rosie's arm and hugged it. 'It most certainly is. I was almost on the point of telephoning Anne and Cissy to tell them to come home immediately when Fran told me. I can hardly believe we're so lucky to still have him.'

They trooped across the road and made their way into the hospital. 'His room's down this corridor,' said Frank, leading the way. 'Keep an eye out for Matron – if she spots us we're done for.'

The corridor was busy with porters pushing patients on trolleys or in wheelchairs and nurses bustling back and forth with breakfasts, bedpans and bedlinen. No one took any notice of them as they approached the door, and after a brief hesitation, Frank dared to push it open.

Matron was standing by Ron's bed.

Rosie ignored her and went straight to Ron and took his hand. 'Hello, darling man,' she murmured, noting his better colour. 'I hear you're on the mend.'

'How *dare* you come in here?' spluttered an appalled and furious Matron. 'Nurse. Get rid of them immediately.'

'I'm sorry,' the girl said fearfully. 'But you really will have to leave.'

'Not until I've seen my father,' said Frank, standing like a monolith in the doorway.

'Please,' she begged, shooting terrified glances at the stormy-faced Matron who was now bearing down on her.

'To be sure, I'm sorry, wee girl,' muttered Frank. 'But neither you nor that woman will see the back of me until I've spoken to Da and seen how he is for meself.' With that, he brushed past Matron and approached the bed.

Peggy could see the girl was frantic and close to tears. 'Don't worry, dear,' she soothed. 'I'll make sure you don't get into trouble.' She shot Matron a glare that would have withered a fainter heart – but it seemed Matron was made of sterner stuff, for she stood her ground and glared back.

'This is *my* hospital and *my* nurse,' she hissed. 'Should I choose to discipline her, then it's none of your business. I will *not* put up with these disruptions. What with visitors disturbing him in the middle of the night and ordering Mr Armstrong around, and now you causing trouble, I have every right to throw you out. And if you don't leave, I shall call for security.'

Peggy frowned. 'What visitors in the night?'

Matron's lips thinned to a tight line, and although it was clear to Peggy that she wished to say more, something was preventing her from doing so – which made her even more curious.

'Dolly?' mumbled Ron from the bed.

Peggy realised the mystery could be explained and rushed to his side. 'Has Dolly been here?' she asked him.

Ron's eyes were closed as rolled his head on the pillow, mumbling something incoherent.

'He's heavily sedated and doesn't know what he's saying,' said Matron. 'If you would come into the corridor – now – I will explain his treatment in more detail.'

Peggy could see that Matron was getting as jittery as the nurse – probably dreading the sudden arrival of Armstrong, who would no doubt blow a fuse on finding them all there. She suddenly didn't feel quite so bold.

'Come on,' she urged the other two. 'At least we know he's all right now. We can come back this afternoon.'

Rosie kissed Ron's cheek, and Frank squeezed his hand before reluctantly following Peggy out of the room.

Matron was positively bristling, her starched cap trembling with suppressed fury. She shut the door and turned to face them. 'Mr Reilly has made great progress during the night,' she said flatly. 'But you bursting in like that will not improve his chances of recovery.'

'Then you should have kept us informed,' snapped Rosie. 'Can't you even *begin* to imagine what we've been through these past few hours by being kept in the dark after being told he might die?'

'I am not in the habit of making unnecessary telephone calls,' said Matron stiffly. 'Mr Reilly's condition was improving.'

'What do you mean, "was"'?' demanded Rosie. 'He looked very much better to me.'

'That's because he has a slight fever brought on by an infection,' said Matron.

'So, what are you doing about it?' asked Frank.

Matron drew herself up to her full height and took a deep breath. 'We are treating him with sulphonamide.' On seeing their bafflement, she gave a sigh of annoyance and explained. 'It is an antibacterial compound of potassium nitrate which should make his urine more alkaline and thereby stop the infection from progressing to the kidneys.'

'And if it doesn't?' asked Frank.

'Infection is the greatest barrier to recovery, and until very recently there has been little we could do about it. The infection either cleared naturally, or it didn't.'

'You mean Ron still might die?' gasped Rosie in horror.

'Not at all – especially with Mr Armstrong in charge of his case,' Matron replied sharply. 'There have been great advances in the field of antibiotics over the past few years, and they have been used to great success in the military. Mr Armstrong is taking part in a trial set up by Mr Fleming who has developed a drug called benzylpenicillin. So far the results have been highly satisfactory, and should the sulphonamide fail to halt the infection, then he will prescribe the penicillin.'

'So you're using my Ron as a guinea pig?' snapped Rosie.

'Absolutely not,' said Matron hurriedly. 'Benzylpenicillin has been tried and tested for a number of years, and it has been decided to expand its use. Very few hospitals have so far been supplied with this drug, but as Mr Armstrong has friends and colleagues in high places, he has managed to obtain it.'

'So,' said Peggy, 'Ron will get better?'

'Oh, yes. I'm quite sure of it,' said Matron. 'But there is still the question of his partial paralysis, which cannot be cured by medication. You must be patient and adhere to the hospital rules. They are in place for a reason. The smooth running of this hospital and the health of our patients depends upon them.'

'We do understand,' said Peggy, 'and will stick to visiting times from now on. But please don't take it out on that little nurse. She really was not at fault.'

Matron pursed her lips and gave a sharp nod before turning away and sweeping down the corridor.

'Do you think we dare nip back in and say good-bye to Ron?' whispered Rosie.

'We're going home,' said Peggy firmly. 'That poor nurse is in enough trouble as it is because of us.'

They left the hospital and kissed and hugged Rosie goodbye as they parted at the Anchor, before walking back to Beach View with a lighter step. Ron was on the mend if Matron's prediction was right.

They were stopped repeatedly by concerned shopkeepers and friends as they went along Camden Road, and had to tell Ron's story over and over again. It never ceased to amaze Peggy how quickly news travelled through this town, but it was wonderful to know how much people cared about Ron and how eager they were to offer their help and support.

There was no sign of Monty at the fish shop, for he was being taken for a long walk by the four boys Fred and Lil had adopted – and it seemed Harvey was being equally spoiled by Alf's family.

Peggy saw Bert Williams coming out of the alley-way at the back of Beach View with Robert, lugging the ferrets' enclosure between them. 'It's very kind of you to take them,' she said as they met on the pavement.

'It's the least I can do,' he said, placing the heavy wooden box on the ground. 'Though the wife has put her foot down, and I'm having to house them in the shed behind the police station,' he said with a grimace. 'How's Ron doing?'

Peggy let Frank explain, and hurried indoors to see to Daisy and pass on the news to the others. Having done this, she poured a cup of tea to whet her whistle after all the talking, and lit a fag before going into the hall to ring Cissy and Anne.

Much to her frustration, she had to leave a message for Cissy as she was on duty, and when she rang the farm down in Somerset it took an age for anyone to answer. She could only think they must all be busy in the fields and was about to hang up when Anne said a rather breathless 'Hello?'

'Oh, Anne, I'm so glad to have caught you,' said Peggy, settling into the hall chair for a good chat.

'You nearly didn't,' said Anne. 'I just happened to be passing the kitchen on the way back from the milking parlour when I heard the phone ringing. Has something happened for you to be ringing so early?'

Peggy relayed the long and distressing saga of Ron's accident and hoped-for recovery, which was greeted with some distress and a few tears. 'I know it's a lot to ask,' she said, 'but is it at all possible you and the boys could come home to see him? And then stay on for Christmas? I'd so love to see you all again, and Ron's bound to recover quicker with his family around him.'

Anne gave a long sigh. 'I wish I could, Mum, but the girls have got chicken pox and are still very much in the catching stage as well as being horribly fractious with it. I doubt we'd do him any good at all. As for the boys, Bob's embroiled in farm work and his duties with the army cadets, and Charlie has finally made the county junior rugby team and is away with them on a training jolly.'

Peggy could have wept with disappointment, but she managed to stifle the urge and put a smile in her voice. 'Oh, well, it can't be helped, I suppose. These things always come at the worst time, don't they?'

'Indeed they do,' said Anne. 'The school had to close early because of the chicken pox outbreak, so the Christmas concert we've worked so hard to arrange had to be cancelled. But there is some good news. I've heard from Martin again.'

'Oh, Anne,' Peggy breathed. 'How is he?'

'He says he and Roger are still with Allan Forbes – the young chap who saved Martin's life when he was shot down – and are doing fine. Martin has received a couple of my letters and is delighted that the girls and I are safe and doing well.'

She hurried on. 'Of course he has no idea of what's happened to Cissy's Randy or Charlotte's Freddy since they were transferred to another camp – and doesn't know if Freddy has received the news about the twins. Roger is over the moon about little Faith's safe arrival and he and Martin are as well as can be expected, but they're all champing at the bit at being held prisoner instead of playing their part in bringing the war to an end. They send their love to everyone and really appreciate the letters once they get them – which seems to be very sporadically.'

'Oh, that is good to hear,' sighed Peggy. 'I'll ring Kitty and Charlotte later to tell them.' She stubbed out her cigarette. 'Your father's done very well and thoroughly enjoyed his leave in India. He's been sent to retrain now he's an officer, and expects to be in Burma again by Christmas.'

Anne giggled. 'I can't imagine Da as an officer. I bet he's furious at having to leave his mates, but we're all so very proud of him. I had a short letter from him last week, and it seems he and his friend, Big Bert, are a recipe for disaster. I wouldn't mind betting they'll lose those pips before the war's ended.'

'Neither would I,' murmured Peggy. 'I just wish he could come home.'

'I am sorry we can't be with you, Mum. It won't feel like Christmas for you without us all there – but perhaps this really will be the last one we have to spend apart. What about Cissy? Will she be able to visit, do you think?'

'I really have no idea,' Peggy said sadly. 'Things are winding down at Cliffe and she's not even sure she'll have a job by Christmas. I'm hoping to speak to her later when she comes off duty.'

'I'd better go, Mum. Rose and Emily are having a set-to and I need to sort them out. It's been lovely talking to you. Give Grandad my love, and if there's any more news on him, please let me know. I'll try and ring on Christmas Day.'

'That would be wonderful.' Peggy could hear the background noise of two little girls squabbling. 'Give the girls a kiss for me when they've calmed down, and send my love and hugs to the boys.'

She replaced the receiver and sat there for a moment thinking about her beloved children and grandchildren whom she missed so much it was a physical pain in her heart. They'd been apart for too many Christmases, and now it seemed this was to be another. How long would it be before she could hold them again?

She pulled herself together and tried to get through to Kitty and Charlotte, but the line was engaged.

Looking at her watch, she realised it was almost time to go to the Red Cross distribution centre for her voluntary two-hour shift, so she'd be able to speak to them then.

21

Ron had no idea how long he'd been stuck on this bed and in this hushed and darkened room, for the days and nights had blurred into one another, and the curtains over the window had remained closed. Routine seemed to be the order of this torturous place: being rolled from one side of the bed to the other every couple of hours, having stuff slathered over his pressure sore, medication injected into his numb backside, humiliating enemas, and doctors' rounds where he was peered at and prodded whilst being surrounded by medical students who didn't look old enough to have left school.

He'd been vaguely aware of Frank hovering over him with such a look of pity on his face he'd wanted to shake him and tell him to pull himself together – if he'd only had the energy – and of seeing Peggy, Cissy and his old pals who seemed to float in and out of here like fretful ghosts.

It was very warm in this room, especially now they'd incarcerated him in a plaster jacket that reached from just below the neck to the base of his hip and held his spine in a stretched and rigid grip. He lay there suffering the indignity of having his private parts washed by a young nurse, his eyes closed to spare both their blushes – although she didn't seem at all bothered by her task – and he couldn't actually feel what she was doing.

He was getting used to the hospital routine now that he was capable of staying awake for more than five minutes. The kidney infection had made him delirious in the beginning, and everything had passed in a colourless haze of sound and senses, and there had been times when he wondered if he was actually awake or just imagining things. However, several scenes from that time were very clear in his mind and he clung to those, determined to keep some sense of reality in this very strange world he'd found himself trapped within.

He was uncomfortable, to say the least – especially when the physio came in to manipulate his legs and make him do exercises to strengthen the flaccid muscles and keep them supple so they didn't atrophy and twist out of shape. When it came to the back exercises the pain was often excruciating – which was a good sign, according to Armstrong – but the medication brought blessed relief.

He had some feeling in his lower legs, ankles and feet, and enjoyed the way the nurses massaged the cream into his heels, shoulders and elbows to prevent bed sores, but unusually had not become aroused by their touch, which was more than a bit worrying – but he'd put that down to the medication, and not feeling the full ticket, certain the feeling would return at the most inappropriate moment.

Ron kept his mind on other things as the nurse rubbed a soapy flannel round his neck and dried it off with a rough towel. He was almost certain that it had been Dolly who'd come to bully him about emptying his bladder. Who else but Dolly could be so bossy and demanding when all he'd wanted to do was float in a void of painless darkness? Of course, she'd had to be obeyed, and it had indeed been a blessed relief to do her bidding if only to be left in peace.

Then there was his darling, sweet Rosie. He'd woken several times to find her sitting by his bed, pale of face, her lovely eyes dimmed by worry as she tried so very hard to appear cheerful. There were things he needed to say to her – important things – if only he could stay awake long enough to express them.

He lay there with his eyes closed as the nurse pulled up his pyjama trousers and then started lathering his face in preparation for a shave. *I hate all this fuss and mucking about,* he thought as the cut-throat razor rasped over his chin. *It makes me feel so damned useless. But I suppose anything's better than being dead – and neither Dolly nor Rosie would forgive me if I just gave in and turned up my toes.*

I should be so lucky, he thought grimly. *I can't do much more than twitch a toe or two at the best of times, let alone wriggle them about.*

The knowledge that he still had no sensation in his hips and thighs was something he didn't care to dwell on, for he'd heard enough of the nurses' chatter to know it could lead to a lifetime in a wheelchair. Armstrong had been fairly positive that once the nerves in his lower back had recovered, the feeling would return, but as time had gone on, he hadn't been quite so cheerful about it.

The real trouble with this place, he thought crossly, is that no one told him anything he could really latch on to. The nurses prevaricated and jollied him along, the doctors rushed in and out saying very little, and Armstrong mumbled to himself as if he wasn't even there. And when he did arrive with his blasted entourage, it was always shortly after he'd been dosed up to the eyeballs and couldn't take in a word.

'There we are, Mr Reilly,' said the nurse brightly, breaking into his dark thoughts and fears. 'All lovely and fresh for Mr Armstrong's visit. Now, do you need the bottle?'

At his nod she bustled about clearing up towels, flannels and bowls, then hurried out of the room, returning minutes later with the bottle.

Ron sighed with deep satisfaction as he filled it and when she'd disappeared once more, felt himself drifting off again, but deliberately jerked himself awake. He wanted to hear what Armstrong had to say today, and ask him straight what was actually going to happen to him.

Ron hadn't taken to Armstrong at all. He was an obnoxious sort who'd clearly been very unkind to poor Rosie when she'd been so distraught. But Dolly had sorted him out good and proper. He grinned at the memory of them bickering over him as he'd tried to concentrate on peeing – determined to show the man that together, he and Dolly were invincible. And yet that could have been a dream – one of many he'd had just lately, and Armstrong had called her Mrs Cartwright.

'Good morning.' Armstrong swept into the room accompanied by Matron, a flutter of nurses and a scuffle of student doctors.

Ron simply nodded in acknowledgement, then wondered why he'd bothered as Armstrong didn't even look at him, but stood with his back to the bed expounding at length about Ron's progress to his eager and fawning audience.

'This patient has recovered very quickly from the kidney infection, thanks to the sulphonamide,' the man intoned. 'But we must now wait to see if he fully recovers from his back injury.'

He pulled a slim phial from the pocket of his suit jacket and held it up. 'I retrieved this from the iliac. As you can see, it is a needle of shrapnel which had been buried in the patient's back since fighting in the trenches back in 1917.'

'I am here, you know,' rumbled Ron crossly. 'And it was the end of 1916 when the field doctor left that in there. I'd be obliged to have it back, if you don't mind.'

Armstrong looked at him as if surprised to see him there. 'Quite so,' he muttered, before handing over the phial and turning back to his audience.

'As I was saying, Mr Reilly does appear to have suffered some nerve damage, which I had hoped would have repaired itself by now. Whilst he can move some of his toes and raise and drop his right foot, and there are certain areas of skin in his lower legs which respond to stimuli, there is no such reaction from the waist to his knees. He's receiving daily physiotherapy to stop the muscles atrophying, but if the nerves in his back don't recover soon, Mr Reilly's condition will probably not improve.' He paused. 'There is also the likelihood that his erectile function will not return.'

'Hold on right there,' snapped Ron who was now fully alert. 'What's all this about erectile function? Do you mean I can never have sex again?'

Armstrong at last deigned to approach the bed and talk to Ron directly. 'That is a distinct possibility if the paralysis continues,' he said coolly. 'But we can always hope it will be temporary.'

'That's easy for you to say,' Ron protested. 'I was supposed to be getting married again.'

'You're very fit and have made great progress, but I'm sure that at your advanced age the lack of sex will not bother you too much. You'll succeed in finding other pleasures when you are up and about in your wheelchair.'

'Over my dead body,' muttered Ron. 'I'll walk on me own. You'll see – and enjoy making love to my Rosie.'

Armstrong turned to Matron and the others. 'Our patient seems very determined,' he said with a smug smile. 'It will be interesting to see if his will is stronger than medical science.'

'You can bet your damned life on it,' muttered Ron, sticking two fingers up at the man's retreating back as he swept out.

Ron regarded the sliver of shrapnel which had caused him so much discomfort over the years. 'To be sure, 'tis a miracle you didn't kill me,' he muttered. 'But if I don't get out of here on me own two feet and with everything working properly, you might as well have done.'

He closed his eyes, weary and with little hope despite his earlier brave defiance. Armstrong's prognosis haunted him, bringing visions of a bleak future in which he was tied into a wheelchair, never to walk the hills again or feel the freedom of the wind in his hair as he went out with Frank in his fishing boat, and – worst of all – never to make love to Rosie again.

He couldn't marry her. Not like this. What use was he if he couldn't be a proper husband to her? How could he possibly saddle her with the drudgery of nursing him day and night until he became a withered, dried-up, bitter old man? That wasn't the life he'd envisioned for them.

He felt the hot tears well and let them fall. The pain of knowing he had to set Rosie free was far more agonising than the one in his back – but lose her he must if she was to have any sort of life.

He must have fallen back into a medication-induced sleep, for when he next opened his eyes the scenery had changed and there was the lovely sound of soft singing in the background. Had he died? Was that angels he could hear?

He blinked to clear his vision and was almost blinded by the bright light which, he at first thought, must be from the gates of Paradise. Then sense returned and he realised he was still very much alive and that he'd been moved into the ward with the other men, and the man sitting on his right-hand side was most definitely not Saint Peter, but Father O'Leary.

'What's going on?' he muttered.

'It's very early on Christmas morning, Ron, and the heavenly choir is the nurses doing their bit to cheer everyone up.' His brown eyes twinkled. 'You didn't think you'd died, did you?'

'Not at all,' he fibbed. 'Heaven would hardly be smelling of disinfectant, now would it?' He rested back into the pillows after a glance round at the paperchains and tinsel which had been strung every-where. There was even a Christmas tree standing in the corner. 'It can't be Christmas,' he muttered. 'I only came in here the other day.'

'It's been two weeks, Ron,' replied the priest. 'Since you came in here, the Battle of the Bulge has been raging, General Patton is set to relieve Bastogne, and the Russians have started besieging Budapest.' He gave Ron's hand a consoling pat when it became clear he was finding it difficult to absorb the news. 'They've relaxed the rules today, so visiting hours have been extended. Your family will be here soon, which is why I've come in so early.'

Ron's brain was still fogged with medication and could take none of it in. 'Early? But Armstrong was here on his evening rounds a minute ago.'

'That was yesterday,' Father O'Leary replied gently. 'I managed to speak to him then, and he said you were progressing slowly.'

'Holy Mother of God, I'm losing the hours and days of me life lying here,' Ron said on a trembling sigh.

''Tis sorry I am you've got yourself in this mess,' the priest replied rather too cheerfully. 'But I understand you're recovering well and will soon be sent to the Memorial to recuperate and start intensive physiotherapy. I have no doubt you'll be up and about and causing mischief again before too long.'

'I wish that was the truth of it, Father,' he replied sadly, the conversation with Armstrong coming back with shocking clarity. 'I doubt I'll be going too far just yet.'

Father O'Leary eyed him questioningly, but Ron wasn't about to tell him anything so personal. This wasn't the confessional, Father O'Leary liked to gossip, and he didn't want half the town knowing his problems.

O'Leary placed two paperback books on the bedside locker. 'I thought these might help to fill in some time,' he said.

Ron saw the lurid covers of half-naked women being threatened by snarling men with blood-soaked knives, and raised a brow. 'To be sure, Father, you never cease to surprise me.'

'There's nothing better than a good murder mystery to keep you occupied,' he replied with a glint in his eyes. 'Now I must go. This is a busy day for me and your family will be here soon.'

He stood and made the sign of the cross over Ron to bless him before eyeing him with curiosity. 'Did you feel closer to God when you were trapped underground, my old friend?'

''Twas the devil calling to me out of the darkness, Father, and me dog that dug me out before I smothered. If God had anything to do with it, He wasn't in evidence then, and certainly isn't now.'

Father O'Leary gave a mournful sigh. 'Still a heathen, even after all that. To be sure, Ronan Reilly, you're beyond saving – but I admire your courage in facing your adversity.'

Ron watched him leave the ward and wondered whether it was courage or stupidity that kept him so determinedly a heathen. But when that final trumpet call came he'd no doubt find out if he'd backed the winning side or not.

Rosie was humming quietly along to the church service on the wireless as she finished wrapping her Christmas presents. She hadn't had much time for shopping, and the shops were almost bare of anything remotely interesting or properly festive. But she'd persevered and had managed to find some lovely pyjamas for Ron, a winter coat with a velvet collar for Daisy, and some little trinkets for the girls and Cordelia – and there was a bottle of real French perfume for Peggy that she'd managed to get on the black market.

It didn't really feel like Christmas without Ron at her side, and she fully understood now how badly Peggy must have suffered during all those Christmases she'd spent without Jim and the rest of her family. But like Peggy, Rosie was determined to make the best of things as they put on a brave face for little Daisy, and enjoyed the special dinner Peggy and Doris were laying on that evening at Beach View.

They'd arranged a sort of visiting roster for today because it soon became clear that everyone wanted to see Ron to wish him well. His old pals, Fred, Alf, Chalky, Bert and Stan, would take the first shift, with Bertie Double-Barrelled and Cordelia going in next with Peggy, and possibly Daisy – it would depend on how overexcited the child was – and Cissy if she'd managed to get leave from the airfield.

The Beach View girls would go in with Robert once Ron had had his lunch, and then Doris and the Colonel would take over before Frank turned up with Pauline – and then Rosie would have him all to herself until suppertime.

Rosie placed the presents in a basket which she'd decorated with bits of holly and mistletoe she'd found whilst out for a solitary walk in the park. There had been a lot of those recently, but they'd helped clear her head after the stuffy heat and dry atmosphere of that hospital room, and given her the energy she'd needed so badly to keep up her spirits.

With the basket packed, she sank into the couch and glanced at the mantel clock. The pub was shut for the day; the street below her window was unusually quiet; there was no dog to walk and no housework to do that couldn't be left for another day. She was becoming restless – which was danger-ous, for it gave her time to dwell on things she didn't really want to think about.

Ron had slept through her visit the previous evening, and she'd sat watching him, fretting over the fact he still couldn't move his legs or feel any-thing much below the waist. Having managed to finally snare Armstrong and make him tell her what was going on, she had learned that Ron was far from out of the woods yet, and if something didn't happen soon, he could very well never walk again.

She remembered how she'd been so happy to have him alive that she'd blithely said she could accept anything as long as he was still with her. But how would Ron feel about being tied to a wheelchair for the rest of his life? And how would she cope?

Rosie determinedly blanked out that thought. She hadn't been able to care for her husband James when he'd become mentally ill, but she would knuckle down to give Ron the very best love and care that she could. And besides, she reasoned, Ron was not the sort of man to accept such a terrible sentence and just give in. He would fight tooth and nail to prove the doctors wrong, she just knew it – but she was also realistic enough to know that there were some battles which simply couldn't be won.

Did they both have the strength of purpose to see this through together? Was their love for one another strong enough to withstand the many problems which were undoubtedly ahead?

Rosie took a trembling breath and prayed that it was, and that they could forge a new and very different life together after this. However hard it might be.

Ron had been delighted to see everyone this morning, and to hear that Harvey and his ferrets were being so well tended, but now he was exhausted, and grateful for a bit of respite. Christmas lunch had been served, but he had little appetite for chicken and soggy potatoes and pushed it away, wanting only to sleep before the nurses came to turn him on his other side, and the hordes descended again.

'So, this is where you're hiding,' said a cheerful and wonderfully familiar voice.

Ron breathed in her light, flowery perfume as her soft lips kissed his cheek. He smiled and opened his eyes. 'Hello, Dolly,' he murmured. 'Or is it Mrs Cartwright?'

Dolly chuckled and shrugged off her fur coat. 'So you do remember. I hope you kept my visit to yourself?'

'I think so,' he replied. 'I'm not really sure of anything much.'

'Well I'm no longer here in disguise. Peggy wrote to me, so I thought I'd pop in to wish you Merry Christmas and see how you're getting on,' she said, pulling off her leather gloves and giving him a naughty smile. 'Still managing to fill that bottle on your own?'

'Of course,' he replied with as much dignity as he could muster.

'I'm surprised they haven't put you in traction yet,' she said, glancing down at his feet, which were sticking out from under the sheet. 'I've been reading up on things and thought the idea was to stretch the spine to get it back into shape.'

Ron fought to keep his voice steady as he answered her. 'They'll not be doing that now they've put me in this plaster jacket. Traction doesn't work when there's no feeling from the waist down.'

'Oh.' Dolly's bright smile faded and she reached for his hand. 'But they must be able to do something to help you get the feeling back, surely?'

'The physio comes in and mauls me about, but nature has to take its course,' he muttered. 'Or not, as the case might be,' he added gloomily.

'And if it doesn't?'

There had never been secrets between them, and Ron had to swallow hard before he could reply. 'I'll be finished as a walking man. And fit for nothing – let alone a proper husband to Rosie.'

Dolly gripped his fingers and leaned closer, her expressive face showing her anguish at the realisation of what he'd meant by that last statement. 'Rosie will love you regardless,' she said firmly. 'I can't have you thinking like that, Ron. It's still very early days and things could change.'

'I'll not be marrying Rosie and condemning her to a life of little pleasure and endless drudgery,' he muttered. 'Best to finish it today, and let her find someone else who can give her a better future.'

Dolly's eyes hardened. 'Don't you *dare* talk like that, Ronan Reilly. This is not the time to wallow in self-pity and I won't allow it.'

Ron almost smiled at her bossy tone, but he was hurting inside too much, and couldn't even look at her, so he closed his eyes and tried to block out the sound of her voice.

'Ever since I've known you, you've been a fighter,' Dolly continued firmly. 'Determined to have your way against all the odds, you raised your boys single-handedly after Mary died; survived the trenches and being buried alive in that damned bunker. I will *not* let you just roll over and give in.'

When he refused to respond, she prodded him sharply in the arm. 'Do you hear me?'

'To be sure, the entire town must hear you,' he grumbled.

'Then have the decency to look at me whilst I'm talking to you,' she said crossly.

He opened his eyes. 'You're talking *at* me, not to me. And I don't take kindly to it, Dolly. I'll not be marrying Rosie if I can't be a proper husband to her. She deserves better than to be burdened with a useless cripple.'

She prodded him again with a very sharp fingernail. 'Oh, for heaven's sake, Ron, pull yourself together,' she said in exasperation. 'Rosie will make up her own mind as to whether or not she wants to be tied to a self-pitying, weak man who has neither the will nor the courage to buck up his thinking and get on with the fight.'

She sat back in the chair and regarded him steadily. 'Although, at this minute, I wouldn't blame her for dumping *you* if this is the way you plan to carry on.'

'Hell's teeth, woman. Do you never give up?' he retorted. 'I never took you for a hard-hearted harridan, and to be sure, I don't envy that Yank you're planning to marry.'

Dolly giggled. 'That's more like my old Ron,' she said affectionately. 'Now promise me there'll be no more talk of finishing it with Rosie. It's Christmas Day, and she's had enough to contend with these past two weeks without you hurting her even more. And you would hurt her, Ron, deeply and irrevocably.'

'I can't make that promise, Dolly,' he said, wearily accepting she was probably right about the unwarranted pain he would cause his beloved girl. 'But I won't say anything today.'

'Good. It won't hurt to wait a bit and see how the land lies before you burn your boats with Rosie. Miracles do happen, Ron – as you and I both know.'

She dug in her handbag and pulled out a beautifully gift-wrapped box. 'A little something to enjoy when you're off the medication,' she said softly.

Ron fumbled with the wrapping and discovered it was a quarter-bottle of cognac. 'I'll have to give it to Rosie to keep until then. If Matron spots it she'll confiscate it.'

He slid it beneath the sheet. 'Will you be staying on to bully me further, or going back to London to boss someone else about?'

Dolly smiled as she gathered up her things and bent to kiss him. 'I've decided to stay a couple of days to make sure you're doing as you're told. It will probably annoy the devil out of Pauline, but I'm hoping that as it's the season of goodwill, some of it will have rubbed off on her. I'll see you tomorrow.'

Ron noticed how every man's admiring gaze followed her slow sashay out of the room and couldn't help but grin. Dolly was very aware of the effect she had on men and played it to the hilt. That American general would have one hell of a woman on his hands, and he could only hope the poor man was well prepared for her.

Dolly left the hospital, deep in thought. She'd never seen Ron so depressed before, and although she fully understood the reason, it worried her. She had always seen Ron as the epitome of what a man should be: strong of build and mind; intelligent, magnetic and handsome with a twinkle in his eye and a soft spot in his heart for those he loved. To even think of him as impotent and tied to a wheelchair was simply too awful to bear.

'And what of Rosie?' she murmured as she reached her car. She looked over at the Anchor, wondering what was going through her mind at this moment. Rosie was an intelligent woman and would surely have guessed that the paralysis had affected other things – but in her anxiety and the trauma of these past two weeks, had she fully digested the ramifications of impotency in a man who'd always been so physical?

Dolly stood there in a quandary. She'd come down on the spur of the moment as it had been quiet in London, and she had hoped to see Ron on the mend. The realisation that he was far from improving, but had regressed to the point where he was talking of ditching Rosie, had shocked her to the core – which was why she'd been so harsh with him.

Yet she'd meant every word, and had hoped she could stir him up enough to make him see that if he gave in now, then he'd only be fulfilling Armstrong's prophecy. But the fight seemed to have left him and he could only see the very worst outcome.

Dolly came to a decision. She would talk to Rosie and find out what she knew or had guessed, and get some sense of what she was thinking. It wasn't really her place to interfere in other people's business, but then she'd never been one to stand on the sidelines when something needed to be done – and if Ron had lost the will to fight, then it was up to her and Rosie to get him out of this slough of despond and back on the road to recovery.

As she approached the Anchor she wondered how Rosie would react to her turning up unannounced. They'd met infrequently over the years, but had never become close friends, and Dolly had accepted that was probably because Rosie was wary of her, and rather jealous of the long special relationship she shared with Ron, and in which she'd played no part. She pulled the collar of her mink coat up to her chin to stave off the bitter north-east wind and knocked on the side door.

A minute later it opened and Rosie stood there, her reddened eyes widening at the sight of her visitor. 'Hello, Dolly. This is a surprise.'

'I hope you don't mind me turning up like this,' she said with an apologetic smile. 'But Peggy wrote and told me what had happened to Ron, so after visiting him, I thought I'd pop in and see how you're doing.'

'Oh, that is kind.' Realising how cold it was to be standing on the doorstep, Rosie stepped back and opened the door wider. 'Do come in,' she said distractedly. 'To be honest, I could do with some company until it's my turn over there.'

Dolly noted how hard Rosie was trying to appear cheerful and stoic, for gone was the dazzling blue in her eyes and the vivacious light in her face. She was clearly struggling, and if Ron let her down now, the consequences could be shattering.

Dolly followed her up the narrow wooden stairs to her sitting room, and as she'd always been curious about Rosie's living arrangements, was rather impressed by how pretty and neat it was – although there was a distinct lack of any Christmas decorations apart from the basket by the fireplace.

'I expect you'd like a drink,' said Rosie. 'Tea, or gin and tonic?'

Dolly smiled and took off her gloves. 'I could certainly murder a gin. After all, it is Christmas, and the drive from Bournemouth was ghastly, and the atmosphere in that hospital as dry as a desert.'

Rosie told her to make herself comfortable whilst she poured the drinks. 'I'm sorry it's a bit chilly in here, but coal is as rare as hen's teeth and I have to keep what I can get for the fire in the bar.'

To show Rosie that she was entirely comfortable with the chill, Dolly draped the fur over her shoulders, settled into the couch and gazed around at the feminine room, trying, without success, to imagine Ron sitting there in his scruffy clothes and old boots. 'This is a lovely room,' she said, taking the glass from Rosie.

Rosie glanced round as if seeing it with fresh eyes. 'It's not too bad,' she agreed, 'but of course it won't be at all suitable once Ron comes out of hospital.'

'Why's that?' asked Dolly carefully. 'I should think Ron would be like a schoolboy trapped in a sweetshop. Isn't it every man's dream to live over a pub?'

'Not if he's in a wheelchair,' said Rosie, sinking down into the chair opposite her.

'So, you know about the paralysis?'

Rosie took a sip of her drink and nodded. 'The doctor told me eventually – but only after I had to almost bully it out of him.'

'Men can be so annoying, can't they?' said Dolly. 'Why is it that we have to force things out of them? Do they think we're too empty-headed and feeble to be told harsh facts?'

Rosie shrugged, took another sip of gin and then gave a sigh. 'Ron's just the same, and there have been times when I could have cheerfully throttled him.'

'I can well imagine,' murmured Dolly, who'd often had the same urge. 'Still, it is early days and there is still hope those nerves will recover and he'll get full use of his legs again.'

'That's what I've been praying for,' Rosie admitted. 'But I have to be realistic, Dolly, and think about the future – however it may turn out.'

Dolly drank the gin, and decided this was the moment to bring up the most delicate subject of all. 'It will be an uphill struggle for both of you to adapt to a whole new way of life,' she murmured. 'Especially if Ron's paralysis has affected more than just his legs.'

Rosie averted her gaze from Dolly and nodded. 'That's something the doctor warned me about last night.' She took a sip of her drink. 'But sex isn't everything, is it?' she said bravely. 'We'll be all right.'

Dolly had to admire her courage, but words were easy; it was what was going on in her head and heart that really mattered. 'I'm sure you will,' she replied softly. 'You're both strong people, and once Ron has come to terms with things, you'll soldier on as before.'

Rosie gave a soft grunt. 'Soldiering on seems to be my role in life,' she said with profound sadness. 'What with James and now Ron. But, yes, I am strong, Dolly, and I won't let this beat me.'

'Good for you. So, what are your plans?'

'When Ron and I got engaged, we decided I'd sell the Anchor once the war was over and there was a bit of money about, so we could spend more time together. But as that seems to be dragging on endlessly, I'll have to think about bringing my plan forward into the New Year. This place isn't at all suitable if he's confined to a wheelchair, so I thought I'd start looking for a large bungalow.'

Dolly almost choked on her drink. 'Good grief, Rosie,' she spluttered. 'Can you really envisage you and Ron in some bungalow surrounded by a hundred others and full of old people? It would be too ghastly for words.'

Rosie managed a smile. 'I agree. But if Ron can't walk, it's really the only option.'

Dolly put down her glass and sat forward. 'Look, my dear,' she said softly, 'don't make any rash decisions now. You're exhausted and frantic with worry, and you might make the most awful blunder by buying something just because it's convenient.'

'I know you mean well, Dolly, but I really have little choice.'

'I do understand, and if the worst comes to the worst, then of course you must be practical about things. I'm just urging you not to be too hasty. Armstrong could be wrong, and although Ron's feeling very down at the moment, there is still hope those nerves will recover and he'll be back to his old self.'

'I am clinging to that hope, Dolly, but as each day passes ...' She drew herself up and regarded Dolly squarely. 'Ron might be feeling low at the moment, but at heart he's a fighter – and so am I. Neither of us will give in, regardless of the outcome, I can promise you that.' To stave off any argument, she took the empty glasses and refilled them.

Dolly offered her cigarette case and lit them both a Lucky Strike before raising her glass. 'Here's to you both.'

They drank in silence and Dolly became aware of Rosie surreptitiously admiring her silk blouse and tailored skirt. Rosie had always made the best of herself on what Dolly suspected might be a tight budget, and she wished she'd thought to bring her something to cheer her up – and then remembered the little hat she'd packed. It would suit Rosie perfectly.

She dragged her thoughts back to more practical matters. 'I wonder, Rosie, if you'd mind very much if I asked you a favour?'

Rosie frowned. 'What sort of favour?'

'It's a bit cheeky, I know, and you must say immediately if it's not convenient, but you see this visit was very much on the spur of the moment, and now I've seen Ron, I'd like to stay on for a couple of days. I was wondering if I could bunk in here on the couch?'

'But won't Frank and Pauline expect you to stay with them?'

'That wouldn't be a good idea. Pauline's still very off with me.' She could see Rosie was hesitant and so hurried on. 'Don't worry, Rosie. I'm sure I can find a hotel or B & B for a couple of nights.'

Rosie smiled. 'Don't be silly. Of course you can stay – and you won't have to sleep in here, I have a spare bedroom.'

'Are you sure?'

Rosie nodded. 'To be honest, I'll be glad of the company. This place has been far too quiet lately.'

'Then I'm glad I asked,' said Dolly, shooting her a bright smile. 'It will only be for a couple of nights, but Christmas is no time to spend alone, and as we both care for that infuriating old scallywag, we can work together to buck up his spirits and stop him from being difficult.'

Rosie raised her glass and giggled. 'I'll drink to that,' she said. 'God help him with both of us on his case – he'll be running for the hills just to escape us.'

Dolly chuckled. 'Amen to that,' she replied.

22

It was New Year's Eve and Ron was exhausted as well as hopeful. Bill Watson, the sturdily built middle-aged physiotherapist, had just put him through the torturous back exercises and was now working on his legs and feet.

'I felt that,' he said gruffly as the man finished massaging his legs and began to manipulate his right knee in an effort to straighten it out.

'Where did you feel it?'

'In my knee and up my thigh.'

Watson said nothing and turned his attention to the other leg.

'Ow! Watch what you're doing,' Ron said sharply. 'That hurts.'

'But that's good,' Watson replied, continuing the manipulation. 'It means those nerves in your back are starting to recover.'

'Do you really think so?' Ron asked, hardly daring to hope. 'Is that why I've suddenly got pins and needles in my feet?'

Watson grinned and nodded. He tested the soles of Ron's feet, and although the reaction was sluggish, it was still a reaction. 'Push against my hand as hard as you can.'

Ron concentrated and felt the man's large hand beneath his foot as he tried to push it away. The movement was minimal, but it was there, and the same thing happened with the other foot.

Bill Watson smiled and drew the sheet back over Ron. 'That's splendid,' he said. 'Now I want you to practise pushing your feet up and down and pressing your knees into the mattress using your thigh and calf muscles. Do it as many times and as often as you like; it won't do any harm, but will strengthen those muscles, get the blood flowing properly and help you to walk again.'

'To be sure, I'll be working on them every minute from now on.'

'Good. Because I shall be getting you out of this bed tomorrow and on your feet.'

Ron looked at him in amazement. 'Really? But I feel as weak as a kitten, and to be sure, these legs will not be holding me up.'

'You'll have me to hold onto,' Watson soothed. 'You'll probably feel light-headed and a bit nauseous at first, but now the feeling has come back we need to work hard at getting you mobile.'

He dug his large, soft hands into the pockets of his white coat. 'If all goes well over the next day or so, I shall propose you be transferred to the Memorial, where they have special facilities for recuperation from the sort of injuries you've sustained.'

'Aye, I'm aware of that,' said Ron. 'A couple of our evacuees were treated there.'

'So you have some idea of what you're in for,' said Watson. 'They'll have you up and about in no time – but I warn you, it won't be a picnic. The army physical training instructor is a hard taskmaster and takes no prisoners.'

Ron grinned and flexed his feet beneath the sheet. 'Aye, so I've been told, but if he gets me walking again, I'll not be arguing with him.'

He looked up at the other man. 'Tell me straight, Bill. How long will it all take before I can get this plaster jacket off and go home?'

'The jacket will have to stay in situ for about three to four months, but you should be walking unaided by then, and able to go home. You'll have to return to the Memorial for regular physio and check-ups, and then for an X-ray to see if the fracture has healed properly and there are no deformities. If all is well, the jacket will come off then.'

Ron stared at him in shock. 'Three to four months?' he gasped.

The other man nodded. 'These things can't be hurried. Concentrate on getting back on your feet, and you'll find the time will pass very quickly.' He pulled back the curtains surrounding the bed and left the ward.

Ron yanked the sheet off his feet and tried wriggling his toes. They weren't responding very well, so he attempted to flex his feet up and down.

There was definite movement, but far too little for his liking, and as he'd never been a patient man, he felt frustrated by the thought it could be months before he was free of the plaster cast and up and about again.

And then there was the not-so-minor problem of impotency. There was no life down there at all and he was beginning to wonder if there ever would be again. He should have asked Bill when and if he could expect a change, but it was all a bit embarrassing and he hadn't liked to broach the subject.

Ron passed the rest of the morning doing his exercises and found that his appetite had returned as well as the feeling in his legs. By visiting time he was tired, but the ache in his legs was a pleasant and very satisfying one after not feeling very much at all for almost three weeks.

He watched Rosie and Dolly come through the swing doors and couldn't help but preen a little in the knowledge they were there to see him, for he knew the other men envied him. They were beautiful and glamorous and certainly brightened up the place as well as the patients, going by the admiring looks they garnered as they came down the ward to his bedside.

He hugged his secret to himself as they kissed him and then told him what they'd been doing that morning – preparing the Anchor for a New Year's Eve party, which had, of course, involved a trip to Plummer's to buy a new dress by way of celebration. He listened to their chatter with an indulgent smile, and then, unable to resist any longer, he tugged off the sheet and wriggled his toes and feet.

'Oh, Ron!' they gasped in unison.

'But why didn't you tell us straight away instead of letting us chatter on?' Rosie protested. 'Does this mean you'll soon be walking again and coming home?'

'It's early days,' he replied. 'But I'll soon be up and about, you'll see.' He went on to explain about the Memorial and the months it might take before he could be rid of the hated jacket.

'I know the Memorial can work wonders, Ron,' said Dolly. 'But it won't be easy for Rosie and the others to get up there every day.'

'I'll get my car out of storage,' said Rosie, whose eyes were brimming with happy tears. 'It will need new tyres and a good service, and of course I'll have to apply for petrol ration stamps. But if I only use the car to get to the Memorial and back, it shouldn't be a problem.'

She leaned forward and took his hands. 'Oh, Ron,' she breathed excitedly. 'Just think, we could get married once you're back on your feet. And April is such a lovely month for a wedding.'

Ron couldn't meet her eye. 'Aye, well, don't be getting ahead of yourself, wee girl. I've a long way to go before we can make those sorts of plans.'

'They're better than the ones she had before,' said Dolly dryly. At Ron's questioning look, she gave a chuckle. 'Rosie was planning to buy a bungalow.'

Ron looked at them both aghast. 'A bungalow?'

Rosie and Dolly collapsed into giggles. 'You sounded just like Lady Bracknell in *The Importance of being Ernest*,' spluttered Dolly.

Ron had no idea what she was talking about. 'To be sure, 'tis no laughing matter,' he grumbled. 'I'll not be living in a bungalow and that's an end to it.'

'And you won't be, my darling,' soothed Rosie, trying to stifle her giggles. 'We'll get married and stay in the Anchor until there's some money about, and then sell to the highest bidder and find a lovely house somewhere.' She shot a conspiratorial glance at Dolly. 'In fact, there is a house I'm interested in, and although we both agree it needs a lot of work, it would be the perfect place to start our new life together.'

Ron didn't want to upset her, and certainly didn't have the courage to talk about his intimate problem in the middle of a busy ward to the two women who had been clearly plotting behind his back. But he had to say something to stop them from rushing headlong into things.

'We'll not be marrying until I can walk properly and carry you over the threshold,' he said, taking the sting out of his words by kissing Rosie's hand. 'We both have to be patient, my love,' he murmured.

Rosie blinked as her smile faltered. 'Yes, of course,' she managed. 'I just thought that as ... That's to say ...' She gave a trembling sigh and fell silent.

Ron could tell she was trying not to show her disappointment and felt like an absolute heel. But for her own sake, he couldn't let her arrange another wedding and have to cancel it. Because he was damned if he'd marry her if he stayed as he was and couldn't be a proper man for her.

He decided to change the subject and turned to Dolly. 'I thought you were only staying for a couple of days.'

'You don't have to sound so grumpy about it,' she replied tartly. 'Rosie very kindly asked me to stay on and I thought you were enjoying my little visits.'

'To be sure, you've bullied and cajoled me until I'm worn to a shred,' he teased. 'I hope you haven't been the same with Pauline.'

'My daughter is still finding it hard to talk to me, but we've mostly kept out of each other's way over Christmas, and as I'm going home first thing tomorrow, you'll no doubt both be pleased to see the back of me.'

Ron grinned and took her hand. 'Ach, Dolly, you were always so easy to rile – you rise to the bait quicker than a leaping salmon. Of course I've loved seeing you, and I'm glad you and Rosie got to know each other better. But don't you have more important things to do than hospital visiting?'

'I certainly do,' she retorted. 'And now you're on the mend I shall see to them with great pleasure.'

'Dolly has been wonderful company,' said Rosie. 'I shall miss her when she leaves.'

Ron saw the women exchange warm smiles and was delighted that whatever barrier had existed between them had been well and truly broken through this past week.

Peggy hadn't expected to enjoy Christmas, what with the family scattered, Ron so poorly in hospital and the unsettling news coming out of the Western Front where the Battle of the Bulge was still raging amid bitter winds and thick snow, but the day itself had been a surprisingly jolly one.

Cissy had come for the day and sixteen of them had sat around the table in the dining room that evening to enjoy Peggy's two roasted chickens which had been sacrificed for the occasion, and as everyone had brought something for the table, they'd had a veritable feast. Perhaps the atmosphere had been helped along by Daisy's innocent joy, the telephone call from everyone in Somerset, and the fact that at last everyone seemed to have heard from their men in the POW camps – they'd ended up singing along to the wireless and then dancing until midnight to records on the old gramophone.

Peggy wrapped herself in her overcoat and thickest scarf, hat and gloves and walked briskly down the hill towards the promenade. Daisy had a cold, so she'd left her at home with Sarah and Rita, and she was finding it quite liberating to be able to walk at her own pace unhampered by a pushchair and enjoy the simple – and quite rare – pleasure of having time to herself.

The weather had closed in during the week, with a bitterly cold wind and a threat of snow in the leaden skies, but now the seafront had been cleared of gun emplacements, barbed wire and mines, it was a huge delight to stride along and then stop for a moment to lean over the railings and simply enjoy the view. These little pleasures had been missing for too long, and although the war was still being fought on the other side of the Channel, there was a definite feeling of expectancy in the air. Things were going the Allies' way at last, with General Patton relieving Bastogne, and the Soviet troops besieging Budapest, and once the battle in the Ardennes was won, there would be a clear road to Berlin and victory.

Peggy buried her chin in the woollen scarf and dug her gloved hands deeper into the pockets of her overcoat as the icy wind made her eyes water and burned her cheeks. She hardly dared hope that 1945 might at last bring peace, but the evidence that things were changing was everywhere. There had been no air raids for two weeks, some men were coming home having been released from their war duties, the trappings of war, such as the barbed wire and gun emplacements, were gone, the blackout diminished to the point it was almost normal again with street lights and thinner curtains. If only the rationing would become less strict, life would be very much easier, but now the winter was proving to be so harsh, there were rumours flying about that bread and potatoes might soon be rationed for the first time. If these two staples became harder to get, then the British housewife would really struggle to feed the family.

Peggy determinedly turned her thoughts to happier things as she pushed away from the railings and headed towards the westerly cliffs that dropped down to the sea.

Rosie had telephoned her earlier to tell her the wonderful news about Ron getting the feeling back in his legs, and the fact she was getting her car prepared so the daily visits to the Memorial wouldn't involve a long bus journey. Doris's stalled relationship with Colonel White seemed to be back on and firing on all cylinders now he'd realised life was too short and perilous to risk losing something that had become very precious – and Doris was now walking about with a beatific look on her face and a sapphire ring on her engagement finger.

And then there was the party tonight to celebrate the arrival of 1945, and the very real hope that this would be the last New Year spent parted from their loved ones. Her thoughts drifted to Anne, the boys and granddaughters down in Somerset before turning to Jim in Burma, to Rita's dad and Peter Ryan, Cissy's Randy and Charlotte's Freddy, and then on to Martin, Roger and the young Allan Forbes who, according to Danuta, had played such a heroic part in saving Martin's life. To see their faces again, to hear their laughter and feel their arms about her, was something she hadn't dared to dream about until now.

'Please God,' she breathed as she reached the shelter at the very end of the promenade and sat down. 'Bring an end to it and let them all come home.'

23

Asch, Belgium
1 January 1945

The sixteen Allied air bases in Belgium, the Netherlands and France had been supporting the ground forces fighting the Battle of the Bulge on the Western Front. The weather had closed in with thick snow which prevented both sides from flying, and brought the hostilities on the ground to a temporary stalemate.

Like his fellow officers, Peter Ryan was glad of the respite, for they'd been flying numerous daily sorties ever since he'd been seconded to the American 9th Air Force 366 Fighter Group based at Asch in Belgium. This was home to the P-47 'Hun Hunters' and the blue-nosed P-51s that were on loan from the 8th, and he'd become deeply attached to the Mustang that he'd been assigned, not only for its speed, but for its agility in the air and smooth handling.

Apart from supporting the Allied ground forces, their other main task was to bomb German cities and industrial zones, destroy the heavily guarded V-2 sites, shoot down German training craft, and make sure there were no safe areas for the young and very inexperienced enemy pilots to be trained without being attacked.

After five long years of war and heavy losses both in planes and ace pilots, the Luftwaffe was not the same as the one that had blitzed through the Low Countries in 1940. Fuel supplies were at a premium, their planes were being shot down by Allied anti-aircraft fire having been caught flying too slow and too low by their barely trained and nervous young pilots, and the factories building replacement aircraft were constantly being destroyed.

The New Year celebrations had left Peter Ryan with a bit of a fuzzy head, but nothing that a good fry-up and a gallon of tea hadn't been able to cure. He'd been scheduled for a bomber escort mission later in the day, but had managed to wangle permission for a pre-dawn combat patrol should the weather prove clement, which was why he was up at this unearthly hour.

The forecast was good, and although it was still dark, the sky was clear, the air bitterly cold. Eager to be back in the air after the lay-off, he and the other pilots hurried over to their readied Mustangs and with cheerful shouts of 'Good luck!' clambered in.

Peter had learned to fly his father's crop-duster in the outback of Australia, and was as at home in a cockpit as in a comfortable armchair. The war years had proved to him that he'd been born to fly, and when the fighting was over, he planned to find a way to continue to do so. But for now he must concentrate on the job in hand.

Once he'd gone through the usual checks, he tightened the straps on his seat belt, blew a kiss to the snapshot of Rita he'd stuck above the controls, and then raised his thumb to the aircraftsman to signal he was ready. The chocks were pulled away and he eased the Mustang towards the runway to await his turn for take-off.

He'd left the runway behind him as the Mustang climbed into the night sky, but as the wheels thudded up into the undercarriage, his heart missed a beat. There were at least fifty Focke-Wulf 190s coming out of the east and heading for the airfield.

With the adrenaline rushing through him, and the excited chatter from the other pilots in his headset, he turned towards them and got off a two-second burst of gunfire before he swooped away. Looking down, he saw he'd hit an enemy plane's fuselage and wing root, and as it half-rolled, it caught a wingtip on the ground and cartwheeled across the field, narrowly missing a squadron of Thunderbolts which were taking off.

But there was no time to be a sightseer, for more 190s and 109s were bearing down on them from the north. The dogfight was fast and furious, the pumping of adrenaline sharpening his senses and keeping him focused as he twisted and turned the Mustang to avoid collision and give chase.

His next target began smoking profusely and then plummeted to the earth where it exploded, but there was no time to celebrate, for life was being made very difficult by the intensity of the Allied ground-fire which forced them to break off their attacks to avoid being hit by their own side. It was utter mayhem in that crowded, deadly sky as bullets rattled, engines screamed and the airfield was lost in the thick cloud of black smoke rising from the bombed buildings and burning planes.

Peter felt the thud of bullets in the wings and air cooler as a 190 came out of nowhere but was then shot down by his wingman 'Birdie' Flemming. He saw no reason to land immediately as he was over friendly territory, so turned the Mustang to join in a large dogfight to the west.

In the melee he scored hits on a 190 and a 109. His Mustang was still flying well despite the damage, so when he saw a 109 strafing the northern end of the airstrip, he went after him.

The 109 turned to meet him and they roared headlong towards each other until the very last second to break away, turn and come back again. They made two more head-on passes, guns blazing, before Peter scored a hit in the nose and wings and the 109 crashed and burned at the side of the runway.

What he didn't see was the 190 swooping down at him out of the rising sun, and as the bullets thudded into him he looked down in surprise at the blood blossoming through the holes in his leather jacket. 'Strewth, Pete, mate,' he muttered. 'The bastard's shot me.'

Strangely, he felt no pain, and was clear-thinking enough to fire back, avoid a head-on crash with a Thunderbolt and make a reasonably decent landing off to one side of the runway, hitting his head sharply on the windscreen as he slewed to a skidding halt. However, as he switched off the engine and the rescue crews clambered up to get him out, the world went black.

Peter came to and found he was in a hospital bed and a raging headache was making him feel sick. 'What the flaming hell happened?' he mumbled upon discovering he was tightly bandaged from head to hip, and could barely move.

'You got shot, mate,' came the laconic reply from his friend and fellow Aussie, George 'Birdie' Flemming, who was sitting in a chair next to his bed.

'Yeah, I gathered that, Birdie. How bad is it?'

'You banged your head, so they're flying you back to England later tonight. Can't do much more here now the place has been shot up.' Birdie finished rolling his smoke and stuck it behind his ear for later. 'You'll be right, mate,' he said, his hawk-like features breaking into a broad smile. 'And you'll get to see that little Sheila of yours, I reckon, 'cos you're off to the Memorial at Cliffehaven.'

Peter liked the sound of seeing Rita again, but if he was being sent to the Memorial then his wounds must be serious. He thought about asking Birdie again about his injuries and then decided not to. He'd only fudge the truth, and when it came down to it, there wasn't much he could do about anything anyway.

'So what happened out there today, Birdie?'

Birdie shifted in his chair and looked away. 'It was three days ago, mate.'

'Three days?' Peter tried to absorb this piece of shocking news and simply couldn't.

'Yeah, they took you into theatre to get the bullets out, and although you came round for a bit you weren't making any sense, so they dosed you up again and left you to sleep it off.'

'Strewth,' breathed Peter, still unable to take it all in. 'So what happened to the raid? I'm assuming we beat them off?'

'Too right, we did.' Birdie gave a broad grin. 'It was all over by midday, and those that were left scurried back to Germany with their tails between their legs. We all reckon it was the Luftwaffe's last big effort to get us out of their skies, 'cos they hit all sixteen Allied air bases that morning with everything they had.'

Birdie fell silent and concentrated on rolling a second smoke, but Peter noticed that his hands weren't quite steady, and that despite his cheerfulness, there was something brittle behind that smile. He said nothing, for they were all at the end of their tether and no one needed reminding of it.

Birdie stuck the second cigarette behind the other ear. 'Le Culot in Belgium and Heesch in the Netherlands got off almost scot-free, because the squadrons were off elsewhere, but altogether, two hundred and fifty of our planes were destroyed and another one hundred and fifty damaged, with very few pilot casualties on our side.'

'And Jerry?' Peter asked.

'Jerry didn't come out of it at all well considering it had to be their largest single-day mission, and they'd thrown everything into it. They lost more than two hundred pilots, killed or captured, including wing commodores, group commanders and fourteen squadron leaders.'

His smile didn't reach his eyes. 'Most of them were shot down by their own flak because no one had given them the proper co-ordinates or warned the gunners down below of the raid.'

'What a shambles,' Peter sighed.

Birdie rallied his spirits and sat straighter. 'Ah, yes, but you haven't heard the best of it, mate. There's a story going round that one of the captured Germans was being interrogated by the CO and pointed out of the window at some of the wrecked Thunderbolts burning away on the field and asked him with a smug smirk what he thought of that for a good day's work.'

Birdie chuckled. 'The CO didn't reply, but waited until this morning when the man was to be shipped off to a POW camp and took him out to see the fleet of shiny new replacement P-47s that had just arrived from Paris. "What do you think of that?" he asked. By all accounts, the bloke just looked at all those planes and replied sadly, "That's what's beating us."'

Arakan Peninsula, Burma

Jim had been sent to Calcutta when he'd left the training camp, and it was here that he'd learned the shocking news that the Chindits were being disbanded and the battalions dispersed. His orders had been to join XV Indian Corps, so he'd taken a series of hair-raising short flights to the western coast of Burma to take part in Operation Talon. This would involve a series of amphibious assaults on the Arakan Peninsula, the objective being to clear the area of the remaining Japs and to build airfields on Ramree and Cheduba islands to support the Allies' ops in central Burma.

To Jim's great delight, the first man he saw on his arrival was Big Bert. Larger than life and twice as ugly, Bert had been seconded to 3 Commando Brigade, which would be leading the amphibious assault on the peninsula. They'd spent half an hour catching up with each other before the orders came to move out, and in the weeks that followed they'd seen each other only in passing.

On the last day of December 1944 they'd advanced on Akyab island to very little resistance as most of the Japanese had retreated, and so had occupied the island and its airfield at no cost to themselves on the 3rd of January.

On the 12th of January they'd landed on the peninsula and carried the advance inland until they'd come under heavy enemy machine-gun fire. The mixed brigades had fought back hard, but it seemed the Japs were determined to fight to the death, so air support had been called in and the tanks from the 19th Lancers brought up to resume the assault. The attack had finally been successful, with few casualties on their side and all the Japanese dead.

For the next couple of days XV Corps and 3 Commando had carried out patrols throughout the peninsula to clear out the last of the enemy, and now they were preparing to capture the village of Kantha as a preliminary move on Kangaw, which could only be reached across a number of waterways on the mainland.

Jim sweltered in the tropical heat as he listened to the commander warning them of what they could expect. There would be no roads; the terrain was mostly mangrove swamps and rice paddies, which would initially prevent tanks or artillery coming ashore. The whole area was dominated by a high wooded ridge known as Hill 170, which was currently in the hands of the Japanese 54th Division. It was vital they took and held the hill, for doing so would cut off the supply and escape route of the Japanese to Rangoon, and ensure the safety of the Allied troops landing on the Myebon Peninsula.

From past experience, Jim knew that the Japs would defend that escape route to the death, so that night he wrote long letters to Peggy, Ron and Frank. He'd been shocked to the core to get the news about his father, and could only pray that the doctors hadn't taken into account Ron's strength of will and stubborn determination to prove them wrong. To imagine him in a wheelchair was too much to bear, and the frustration of not being granted leave to go and see him burned deeply. He wrote encouraging words to his father in the hope they'd help keep his spirits up, and demanded every scrap of news from Frank and Peggy so he could be kept up to date with his da's progress.

They left the beachhead at dawn in inflatables, and then had to wade waist-deep in the murky water to gain the beachhead two miles south of Kangaw. To keep their arrival a surprise, they had no naval or air bombardment to support them.

Each unit within the brigade was given a different objective: 1 Commando, supported by Big Bert's 3 Commando, would lead and secure Hill 170, code-named Brighton; 42 Commando would secure the beachhead between two tidal creeks, codenamed Thames and Mersey; and Jim's unit was to secure two valleys to the east of Hill 170 codenamed Milford and Pinner.

It was now almost dawn of the 23rd of January. Jim was amazed and thankful that all objectives had been taken with minimal Japanese resistance, and he and Bert were just congratulating themselves on a job well done when the silence was shattered by a bombardment of heavy artillery and machine-gun fire. The Japs were attacking – and in strength.

The mortars exploded with deafening blasts that sent fountains of earth and jungle detritus showering down on the men in the shallow trenches. The barrage of enemy machine-gun fire increased and it was clear that the Japanese had gathered all their resources to defend their escape route and take back Hill 170.

Jim and the twenty-four men in his platoon survived four days of ceaseless barrage, and when it had finally fizzled out, were relieved to see their brigade, supported by a troop of Sherman tanks, coming to take over their position. The following night, Jim's brigade attacked Kangaw, and the two hills dominating the road east, and despite strong resistance from the Japanese managed to capture Kangaw and occupy the hills.

Jim and the rest of his brigade were taking a well-earned breather and looking forward to withdrawing from the area now that it was securely in the hands of the British when they were once again woken at dawn by a fierce artillery bombardment and heavy machine-gun fire. The focus of the Japanese surprise counter-attack seemed to be the northern end of Hill 170 which Jim's platoon and Big Bert's commando unit were defending with the aid of a tank troop.

Everyone dived into the shallow trenches and began to fire back, Big Bert working with the ease and efficiency of experience on his forward Bren gun. They all knew this was only the warm-up to a major assault, and steeled themselves for what was to come.

The noise of the bombs and continuous gunfire rang in Jim's head as he fired back, keeping an eye on his men, and moving from trench to trench to encourage them, keep them alert and distribute ammunition. He had no idea how many Japanese there were advancing on his position, but they were coming at him in an unceasing stream, throwing grenades and rattling off bullets less than ten yards away.

Jim was almost blinded by the sweat stinging his eyes, but in order to get a better field of fire, he stood exposed to the enemy's heavy barrage so he could lob grenades more accurately, and fire down at the Japs in the dead ground at the base of the hill. He needed to hold them back whilst the medics attended and evacuated his wounded.

A small number of Japanese had managed to break through one of the positions and had made a suicidal attack on the Sherman tanks with charges fixed to the ends of bamboo poles. After a hand-to-hand battle in which most of them were killed, the survivors climbed on top of two of the three tanks and exploded their charges, killing themselves as well as the men inside.

The crew of one of the forward Bren guns had been wounded, so Big Bert had taken it over until a replacement crew could be sent up from troop HQ. This second crew was wounded on the way up, so Bert continued his barrage until he ran out of ammunition and then picked up a two-inch mortar, which he fired from the hip like some western gun-slinger.

Jim followed his example some time later when a fresh attack came in, and in spite of being under heavy fire with the enemy too close for comfort, he once more stood exposed and fired the mortar, killing six enemy with his first bomb. When they were all expended, he went back through heavy grenade, mortar and machine-gun fire to get more.

Big Bert was doing the same, and they caught one another's eye and grinned as they hurried, under fire, back to their positions with their fresh ammunition.

Once those bombs had run out, Jim went back into his own trench and, with bullets whizzing over his head, lobbed off several grenades and used his Tommy gun to fire back. He was too occupied to see how Big Bert was doing.

The battle for Hill 170 lasted thirty-six hours and ended in victory for the British, ensuring that the 54th Japanese Division's escape was cut off. Further landings by the 25th Indian Division and the overland advance of the 82nd (West Africa) Division made the Japanese position in the Arakan untenable and they made a general withdrawal to avoid the complete destruction of the 28th Japanese Army.

Jim didn't feel like celebrating, for fourteen men in his platoon of twenty-four had been injured, and six of his positions had been overrun by the enemy. He was nonetheless inordinately proud of his men, for they'd held on through twelve solid hours of continuous and fierce fighting until reinforcements had arrived. The combined brigades had lost 45 men with 90 wounded; the Japanese had lost almost 400.

Jim joined the other officers in brigade HQ, which had been set up on Hill 170, and looked around for

Big Bert. Bert was big and burly enough to stand out in any crowd, but Jim couldn't see him, and the first pang of dread began to gnaw at him. About to ask the man sitting next to him if Bert had been injured, he was silenced by the loud voice of his commanding officer calling for order.

The man began to speak, his expression solemn. 'The battle of Kangaw has been the decisive battle of the whole Arakan campaign, won very largely due to your magnificent defence of Hill 170.' He went on to talk of the number of decorations for gallantry that would be awarded, including a posthumous Victoria Cross for Lieutenant George Knowland.

'Mention should also be made of the posthumous George Cross to be awarded to First Lieutenant Albert Cummings – or Big Bert, as he was affectionately known by us all.'

Jim sat there, stunned, as the man continued. 'Big Bert was a larger-than-life character who could always be relied upon to do his duty. He fought bravely and without thought for his own safety, and was last seen standing defiantly on the top of his trench firing his rifle at the advancing enemy. When he ran out of bullets, he snatched up a Tommy gun and fired at will to protect his men in the trench, and was mortally wounded by returning enemy fire. The magnificent heroism shown by men like Lieutenants Knowland and Cummings ensured that our successful counter-attack could be launched from the vital ground which they had played such a gallant part in holding.'

Jim had to swallow the lump in his throat and maintain a stiff façade until the man had finished talking. The moment he was dismissed, he hurried outside and went to snatch up his backpack and find an isolated spot down by the water where he could mourn in private.

He couldn't believe that Bert was dead – that all that brawn and courage and downright pig-headedness had been wiped out; that they'd never get drunk together again, or swap tall stories. He stared out over the water, his eyes brimming as he remembered the fun they'd had in India on their last leave, and all the things they'd gone through since their arrival out East.

As the sun dipped below the horizon and the land was plunged into tropical darkness, he pulled the small flask of whisky from his pack and raised it in a toast.

'Here's to you, my friend. Try not to cause too much mayhem up there, big man. You've earned those wings. *Sláinte.*'

Stalag Luft III
Sagan, Eastern Germany

Air Commodore Martin Black pulled up the collar of his ragged flying jacket to try and ward off the bitter cold as he trudged through the deep snow covering the sixty acres of compounds. The temperature had plummeted to below zero before Christmas, and now that it was late January it seemed to be getting colder by the day. With their clothes rotting on their backs and their stomachs constantly growling from hunger, the prisoners were struggling to cope with the icy weather.

Stalag III was administered by the Luftwaffe, and housed captured Allied airmen from Britain and the Commonwealth as well as a huge number of USAAF personnel who'd been arriving in droves since the previous October. The camp had grown considerably since Martin and the others had been snatched from the jaws of death at Buchenwald, for it now had five separate compounds, North, South, East, West and Central, each housing *kriegies*, as they called themselves after the German word for prisoners of war, *Kriegsgefangene*. Each compound consisted of fifteen huts, measuring ten by twelve feet, each of which housed fifteen men in five triple-deck bunks, and it was rumoured that there were now around ten thousand inmates.

Martin was duty pilot that evening, which meant it was his turn to follow one of the guards, or goons, as they called them, so he could warn the others of his location and then carefully record his movements in a log book. The eight-hundred guards were either too old for combat, or young men convalescing after long tours of duty or from wounds. Unaware of the connotation of their nickname, and having been told it stood for German Officer Non-Com, they accepted it happily enough.

Due to the fact these men were Luftwaffe personnel, the prisoners had initially been accorded far better treatment than they'd expected, and Deputy Commandant Major Gustav Simoleit had even ignored the ban against extending military courtesies to POWs by providing full military honours for Luft III funerals. However, the last few months had seen less food and medicines coming into the camp, and the guards had become jittery and much stricter.

Martin's boots were leaking and he could no longer feel his toes, but as the goon hurried into the administration hut to join the large group already in there, his curiosity was piqued. The atmosphere in the camp had felt charged these past few days, and something had definitely stirred up the commandant and his leading officers.

Rumours were flying about, as they always did, but this time perhaps there was some element of truth in them, which was deeply worrying. There had been stories of Hitler ordering mass evacuations of the camps in Eastern Germany, with thousands of *kriegies* being forced to march for miles in appalling weather, because the Russians were rampaging towards Germany, determined to conquer Berlin.

Martin crept closer to the hut and huddled out of the wind to try and overhear what they were saying, but although he'd learned a good deal of German during his long incarceration, the voices were too low and muffled to catch anything helpful.

He gave up and trudged back to his crowded hut where the presence of fourteen other bodies at least raised the temperature a few degrees, and there was the possibility of a cup of hot tea from the last of the Red Cross rations.

'What ho, Martin,' said Wing Commander Roger Makepeace through his hacking cough. 'Have you found out what the goons are up to?'

Martin shook his head and poured himself a cup of very weak tea. There was no milk or sugar as usual, but as it was hot and wet, he didn't really care. Cradling the cup in his cold hands, he let the steam of it thaw his face. 'How's young Forbes?'

Roger grimaced. 'Sick bay is full to the rafters and there's not much the medic can do without proper medicines. Forbes is fighting the fever, though, and as he's young, he stands a chance of getting through it.'

Martin nodded and sipped his tea. Allan Forbes had saved his life when he'd been shot down, and although he'd been young and full of energy when they'd been captured, dysentery, the poor rations of late and a chest infection had turned him into a shadow of the boy he'd been. Martin could only hope he wasn't about to follow the legion of dead prisoners who now lay beneath the snow in the camp cemetery.

He was about to climb into his bunk when the bells for *appell* began to clang urgently throughout the camp. The men looked at one another, for it was almost eleven at night, and most roll-calls were in the morning.

'Perhaps we're about to find out why they've had ants in their pants these past two weeks,' muttered Roger, scratching at his head lice.

'That would be a first,' someone else piped up. 'They don't tell us anything.'

'Perhaps the Russians really are on their way,' said another.

They trudged down the steps to find that the wind had dropped to a freezing stillness and it was snowing again. Lining up, they saw that each compound was doing the same, and knew that something was definitely up.

Their fears were soon confirmed. They had an hour before the camp was to be evacuated.

Roger and Martin spent the time making sleds from the bed slats so they could carry any of the injured through the snow, whilst others collected the thin blankets for extra cover, stuffed their pockets with every last morsel of food and packets of cigarettes, and stashed the precious letters from home in their inside pockets. Every stitch of clothing, however threadbare, was pulled on, and boots were stuffed with paper in the hope it would keep out the wet.

On the stroke of midnight the entire camp, including the sick, was ordered to assemble once more. It was snowing hard and the temperature had plummeted even further, and they stood there shivering as they were divided into groups of three-hundred with goons to guard them. Martin, Roger and the others from hut 8 stuck close together, making sure young Forbes was safely strapped to one of the homemade sleds, and swathed in blankets.

The barriers between the compounds were opened, and at the commandant's signal, the ten thousand prisoners began to trudge slowly through the main gates and, in the darkness, start the long trek down the snow-covered avenue of trees.

None of them knew where they were being sent, but for the next six days they were force-marched over sixty-three miles, struggling through thick snow in temperatures as low as minus seven. They rested at night in factories, churches, barns, or in the open, and with little or nothing in the way of food, decent clothing or medical care, the effect on already weakened bodies was devastating.

On arrival at Spremberg, they were crammed into cattle trains and taken nearly four hundred miles north-west to a naval camp in Bremen.

During this mass exodus their numbers were quickly decimated by starvation, frostbite leading to gangrene, and typhus which was spread by body lice and the general unhygienic conditions. To Martin and Roger's despair, the dead had to be left behind in ditches, forests and by the roadsides – and when young Allan Forbes succumbed on the third day, they were both too dispirited and weak to even feel sorrow or shame as they stripped his body of blankets, boots and coat and left him beneath a scraping of snow.

Stalag Luft IV
East Prussia (now Poland)

It was now early February, and deep snow covered everything as the temperature continued to drop. Freddy Pargeter and Randy Stevens had thought Stalag Luft VI was bad enough, with its sadistic guards and lack of decent food and medical care, but Stalag Luft IV had shown them they'd truly arrived in hell.

The guards were inclined to bayonet or kick the POWs on the slightest whim, their dogs were vicious, and captured escapees were shot immediately. The forty wooden barrack huts were surrounded by high fences of barbed wire and each housed up to two hundred men. They'd managed to stay together, but in their section of the camp, there hadn't even been bunks for them to sleep in. None of the huts had been heated, latrines were out in the open and there were no proper washing facilities, so they were plagued with lice and dysentery as well as hunger. The distribution of Red Cross parcels and clothing was rare and the medical supplies less than adequate.

Freddy and Randy had long since lost the energy and enthusiasm for escape attempts. It was all about survival now, and as they could clearly hear the sound of the Russians' heavy artillery fire in the distance, it seemed that liberty was at long last in reach.

However, they'd also heard the rumours that tens of thousands of POWs were being force-marched west, and so it had come as no surprise when the *appell* had been called, and the eight thousand prisoners were sent off in blizzard conditions for a destination unknown.

They were carrying all their possessions in bundles on their backs as they helped one another through the thick snow. Both were very weak, for they'd lost a lot of weight from starvation and dysentery. Randy also had frostbite in his feet and hands, but they both knew that should they fall or lag behind, one of the guards would put a bullet in their head.

The ordeal they shared with their fellow prisoners would last for almost three months, cover over nine hundred miles and cause over one thousand deaths. It would become known as the Black March, and those who survived were haunted by it for the rest of their lives.

24

Cliffehaven

It was mid-March, and Ron had just finished an exhausting two hours of exercises in the gym and the physiotherapy room. He walked with a bit of a limp, and his back really hurt if he tried to lift anything heavy, but he was feeling positive and much stronger now the prospect of going home had become a reality.

He'd washed and pulled a dressing gown over his shirt and trousers, and was now sitting beside Peter Ryan in the day room overlooking the Memorial's dreary back garden, which was only just recovering from the harsh winter. The sun was bright and the sky clear, but having poked his nose out through the door, Ron knew it was still bitterly cold.

He had arrived at the hospital the day before the young Australian pilot was brought in, and because Peter was Rita's friend, Ron had made it his business to visit him every day. The lad was very poorly and a long way from home, but despite the age difference, they'd got on well, and as bones and scars had begun to heal, they'd whiled away many a pleasant hour talking about their families, the women they loved, and the lives they'd led before the war.

However, the head injury Peter had sustained on that crash-landing meant that he still suffered from severe concussion, which caused mood swings and dizzy spells, and when he wasn't feeling quite the ticket, he would become morose and uncommunicative. Today was one of those days.

'We're a couple of old crocks, I reckon,' muttered Peter once the squadron of planes had flown over and they could hear one another again. 'I'm fed up with sitting here with nothing to do all flaming day.'

'Speak for yourself,' Ron said. 'I've got more than enough to do just getting myself up and about – and it wouldn't hurt if you did the same. You'd certainly feel better about things if you stopped moping about and let Rita visit you.'

'There's no point, mate. What use am I to a girl like that? She's better off finding someone else.'

Ron had had the same thoughts about Rosie when he'd first been hospitalised, but it was worrying to hear such things voiced by one so young. Peter was in his late twenties, and although his injuries had been quite severe, they were no longer life-threatening. These dark moods were doing him no favours. 'To be sure, it's time to stop feeling sorry for yourself and start thinking about what Rita might want,' Ron told him.

'You're a fine one to talk,' scoffed Peter. 'What about you and Rosie?'

'She'll have her wedding when I'm fully fit,' he said firmly. 'I admit I thought like you at first, but I never refused to see her, not even in the darkest days. Poor little Rita was devastated when you turned her away and told the nurses she wasn't to visit again.'

'I don't want her to see me like this,' Peter grumbled, sticking out his plastered leg and plucking at the bandage that swathed his head.

Ron grunted. 'As if she cares what you look like. She was just relieved you weren't dead like poor young Matt.' He regarded Peter evenly. 'It took a long time for her to get over him, you know, and when she finally allowed herself to fall for your dubious charms, how did you repay her?' He shook his head. 'I'm disappointed in you, Peter. I thought you were made of sterner stuff, and I don't like the way you're treating her.'

Peter sighed. 'I don't mean to be a mongrel,' he admitted, 'but I had plans for me and Rita, and now I've got this weakness in my head and can't fly again, what have I got left to offer her?'

'Your skills as a mechanic,' said Ron, who was fast losing his patience. 'Look, son, it might feel as if the world has ended because you can no longer fly, but there are a hundred and one things you can do instead. If you're really serious about Rita, then talk to her, for goodness' sake. She can't read your mind.'

'I'll think about it,' he mumbled.

'You do that,' Ron replied shortly. He grabbed his walking stick and got to his feet. Waiting until he was quite steady, he walked slowly out of the room, his left foot still drooping slightly and dragging. It wasn't the boy's depression that was making him restless, but the need to keep exercising so he could go home to Beach View at the end of the week. This place, and everyone in it, was getting on his nerves.

He was still encased in a plaster jacket, and his legs and back ached from the physio's pummelling, but at least he was upright again, and the erotic dream he'd had last night had definitely brought about a significant stirring down below. It might not mean he was back to his old self, of course, but it was a definite sign that he was on the mend in more ways than one. The real test would come when he and Rosie were alone together.

Peggy and everyone at Beach View had really missed not having Harvey in the house since Alf had taken him in, and so when Alf had brought him in this morning after his early walk, it had been a joyful reunion. She'd been tempted to keep him, but knew she simply didn't have the time to walk him twice a day, what with having to visit Ron, look after Daisy and go to work, and so there had been a few tears as Alf had taken him away again.

Poor old Harvey had looked quite bewildered, but Alf had promised to call in more often, and to try and sneak him up to the Memorial this afternoon so he could see Ron.

'I don't fancy his chances,' said Rita. 'Matron's a proper tyrant, and if she catches him there will be an almighty row.'

Unfortunately for the patients at the Memorial (but making life considerably easier and calmer for the staff and patients at Cliffehaven General), Matron Billings had been transferred back to the Memorial and had swiftly imposed her iron regime there.

'Harvey's pining for Ron,' said Peggy, 'and I'm sure Ron's missing him too. Alf will be wise enough to keep out of Matron's way.' She cupped the girl's cheek, noting the sadness in her expression that had been present ever since Peter had sent her away from the hospital. 'And what about you, Rita? Have you decided what to do about Peter?'

Rita took a deep breath. 'I'm going up there to have it out with him,' she said firmly. 'This state of affairs has gone on too long already, and we need to have a proper talk.'

'You have to be very certain of your feelings for him, Rita,' Peggy warned. 'The bump on his head has changed him and ruined any chance of the plans he had to keep on flying. And although I under-stand what an emotional storm you're going through, it won't do either of you any good if you rush into something just because the situation seems to demand it and you mistake pity for something much deeper.'

'I do know that, Auntie Peggy, and I'm quite, quite sure of how I feel about him.'

Peggy drew her into a hug and held her close. Rita was like a daughter and she wanted only the best for her – to see her happy and settled with the right man who would love her unconditionally and care for her into old age. Peter had seemed perfect until he'd been wounded, but his refusal to see Rita had rocked Peggy's faith in him. He'd have to change his attitude radically for Peggy to trust him again.

She said none of this as she cuddled the girl, for it would be up to Rita in the end to decide whether he was right for her or not. But there was a rocky road ahead if she tied herself to Peter, for he was bound to want to return to Australia after the war, and Peggy wasn't at all sure that little home-bird Rita would settle well so far from her father and all she knew.

She kissed the top of the girl's head, then, after a long moment, let her go. 'Rosie's coming to pick me and Daisy up at two. Do you want to come with us?'

Rita grinned impishly. 'I'll make my own way, thanks. Rosie's driving scares me half to death.'

Peggy giggled. 'Not at all like you on that motorbike,' she teased. 'But yes, Rosie is a bit inclined not to watch where she's going. Still, she's managed to get us all there in one piece so far, and thankfully there's not a lot of traffic on the roads yet.'

Rita pulled on her old leather flying jacket and wrapped a woolly scarf around her neck in preparation for the cold motorcycle journey over the hill. She kissed Peggy's cheek. 'Wish me luck. I'll see you later.'

Peggy smiled as Rita ran down the stairs to the cellar and slammed the back door behind her. Peter didn't stand a chance if she was that determined to have him for her own, and it rather reminded Peggy of when she'd chased after Jim, intent upon marrying him, despite the fact half the girls in the town were on the same mission.

Men really could be very dim at times, she thought with a soft smile. Didn't they realise how deadly a really determined woman could be?

Rita dashed into the garden, but instead of removing the tarpaulin cover from her Triumph, she hurried down Camden Road to the fire station. Minutes later she was astride Peter's motorbike and roaring up the hill towards the Memorial at top speed. If turning up on his precious bike didn't get a reaction from him then nothing would. And if he blew his top, so much the better, for at least he'd be talking to her at last and they could have a jolly good row to clear the air.

She realised she wouldn't get very far if she arrived through the front gate of the Memorial on the bike, so she took the steep, rutted lane which wound up the hill through the woods. This was one of Ron's favourite walks, and he'd brought her here as a little girl to hunt in the deep, dark pool at the centre of the woods for the eels that gathered there at certain times of the year. He'd also taken her to look for birds' nests in the spring and, when she was a bit older, to lie very still in the long grass to watch fox cubs emerge from their dens to play like puppies in the evening sunlight that filtered through the trees.

She smiled at those happy memories, hoping they could do such things again once he was back to his old self. But for now she had a pig-headed and very irritating Aussie to deal with.

Peter had been dozing when he thought he heard the familiar roar of his motorbike. Opening his eyes, he sat up sharply and watched in fury as Rita came pelting down the lawn towards him. By the time she'd spun the bike to a skidding halt outside the window, he'd grabbed his crutches and was on his feet.

'What the flaming hell do you think you're doing?' he shouted through the window.

Rita took off her crash helmet and grinned at him mischievously as she ruffled her dark curls. 'Can't hear you,' she shouted back.

'Flaming women,' he muttered, thumping his crutches on the floor as he swung his plastered leg and tried to hurry to the door. 'Flaming leg,' he cursed when he almost tripped and fell in his rush. He grabbed his coat and yanked the door open. 'What are you doing on my bike?'

'What does it look like?' Rita enquired sweetly. 'Seeing as I've been the one to service it and get it going properly, I've earned a ride or two.'

'I never said you could mess about with it,' he retorted, struggling into his coat and making his careful way across the paved area.

'I have *not* messed about with it,' she replied tartly. 'It's running as sweet as a nut – which is more than I can say for the job you did on it before you went off to Belgium.'

'I'll have you know I was going to sort it out properly when I got back.'

'Well, I saved you the bother.' She grinned at him. 'If you weren't such a grump, I might even have offered you a pillion ride.'

Peter saw the glint in her lovely brown eyes and knew she was teasing him. His bad mood fled and he grinned back. 'I don't reckon even you'd dare risk that.'

Rita regarded him from bandaged head to plastered leg, the glint in her eye suddenly challenging. 'Oh, I don't know. You took me for a ride on the Triumph when I had my leg in plaster.' She reached into the pannier for the spare helmet and held it out to him. 'What's the matter, Pete? Lost that Aussie thirst for adventure, have you?'

He snatched the helmet from her and fumbled to get it over the bandages. 'I'll show you,' he muttered.

'Better get a move on then,' she replied, looking over his shoulder. 'I spy an advancing Matron.'

He glanced back. For a big woman she was moving fast, and her furious expression didn't bode at all well. He dropped the crutches, sat side-saddle behind Rita with his plastered leg stuck out, and grabbed her around the waist. 'Chocks away, Rita. Put your foot down.'

Rita spun the bike round and headed past the startled woman, down the side passage, across the gravel driveway and out onto the main road. It was wonderful to hear Peter's yell of sheer joy, and to feel his arms around her, but she suddenly came to her senses and realised that what they were doing was utter madness.

She slowed the bike and carefully turned off down a narrow lane.

'What are you doing?' asked Peter as she brought the bike to a halt.

Rita switched off the engine and kicked the stand into place so the bike didn't topple beneath him. 'I shouldn't have done that,' she said, easing off the bike to stand and face him. 'It was dangerous and stupid, and I could have killed you.'

'Oh, Rita,' he sighed. 'That's the most exciting thing to happen to me for weeks.' He put his hands on her waist and looked into her eyes. 'I don't care if it was stupid, because it's made me realise how much I've missed you. I'm sorry I've been such a gallah, Rita.'

'I don't know what a gallah is, but if it's something stupid and Aussie, then it suits you,' she replied without rancour. 'I've missed you too,' she added softly. 'Please don't shut me out again.'

He awkwardly drew her to him. 'Never again, I promise,' he murmured before kissing her passionately.

Ron had heard the motorbike and gone out onto the far end of the terrace to watch the scene on the lawn with a certain amount of admiration and relief. It was certainly time those two young things sorted out their differences, but he wasn't at all sure about making that sort of exit with Matron now well and truly on the warpath. There'd be hell to pay when they came back, but Ron had the feeling that neither of them would care a jot.

'That was one of your girls, wasn't it?' Matron snapped. 'I can't say I'm surprised. You're not exactly the ideal role model.'

Ron ignored her sniping and she stormed off in high dudgeon. They'd had their differences over the years and her venom rolled off him like water over a duck's back. He dug his free hand into his dressing-gown pocket, glad of its warmth as he leaned on his walking stick and slowly headed along the terrace to the wooden bench where he'd had to tie Harvey when he'd come to visit Danuta the previous year.

Harvey's visits to the hospital in those days had been a bone of contention between him and Matron, as had Queenie, who'd escaped from his pocket one day and run riot around Danuta's room. *It's all fun and games, really*, he thought. *But it is a shame the silly woman takes things so seriously.*

Settling down to fill his pipe and enjoy the crisp fresh air after the stifling atmosphere of the hospital, he eyed the tyre tracks that ran down the otherwise pristine lawn and smiled. Rita had always been a girl to rise to a challenge, and throughout her short life she'd certainly had to contend with rather a lot.

Her mother had died when Rita was only a toddler, leaving a grieving Jack Smith to raise her with a good deal of help from Peggy. And then he'd been sent off to war, their home and garage business was destroyed in a fire-bomb attack and Rita had really struggled to find her place in the world, until Peggy had once more taken her under her wing. The loss of Matt, her first love, had hit hard, but it seemed she'd found something very special with that young Australian, for they were very alike in so many ways.

He got his pipe going and puffed contentedly. He and Peggy would miss her horribly if she went off to Australia, but then the young ones had their own lives to lead, and all they could really do was wish them well and hope the future held all they hoped for. But Australia was a very long way away, so once she was gone, then they'd probably never see her again.

He gave a deep sigh as his thoughts turned to the changes they would all have to face after this war was over. Danuta was talking about returning to Poland to nurse; Sarah and her sister Jane would either go to their mother in Australia or meet her back in Singapore to await news of their father and Sarah's fiancé, Philip; Ivy and Andy were making plans to return to London to set up home; and his granddaughter Cissy seemed absolutely determined to marry her young American and go to live over there. That, however, depended entirely upon whether he'd survived the POW camp, and still wanted to marry her. They had, after all, been apart for almost three years, and their separate experiences were bound to have changed them both.

The same held for his other granddaughter, Anne, and the two girls living in Briar Cottage with their babies. Their men would be very different from the ones they'd last seen, and he suspected that after the first flush of joy at having them home, they'd have to learn to fall in love again.

As for Jim and Peggy, he could only hope for the best. Jim had been away for too long, and Peggy had found an independence he suspected she'd find impossible to let go. It could cause a great deal of friction between them, but in Ron's opinion, Peggy had a right to do what she wanted and enjoyed, and although his son could be stubborn, he would surely realise that Peggy was a bright, intelligent woman who needed more than being tied to the kitchen sink.

Ron gazed out across the garden to the past when he'd returned from war and tried to pick up the pieces again. After the noise and the horrors of the trenches, it had felt as if he'd been transported into a world he no longer recognised or understood – or even fitted into.

He'd so longed for peace and to be back in those familiar places he'd once called home, that he'd thought he could just step back into his old shoes and carry on as if nothing had happened. But he'd discovered that he missed the excitement and the chaos – and every day stretched before him endlessly, the nights spent in tormented dreams. Only his sons and the other survivors understood what he was going through, for it seemed that the rest of the world was too busy getting on with life to care.

Ron realised he was getting maudlin as well as rather chilled. He knocked the dottle from his pipe, shoved it into his pocket and heaved himself off the bench. He'd see if there was a chance of a cup of tea and a biscuit before Rosie came to visit. Little Nurse Brown was on duty, and she was usually very amenable to a wink and a smile.

'Harvey, stop!'

Ron looked round at Alf's desperate shout and saw Harvey hurtling towards him down the lawn. He didn't have time to sit down again or brace himself before his dog threw himself at him, knocked him to the ground and tried to lick him to death as he crawled all over him.

Winded by his fall and unable to push the heavy dog off him, Ron lay there on the grass and let Harvey do his worst. He hadn't seen him since the tunnel collapse and was so delighted that he seemed as daft and energetic as ever that when he got his breath back, he put his arms round him and buried his face in his fur. 'To be sure, 'tis good to see you too, old boy,' he chuckled. 'But you weigh a ton and I can hardly move.'

Harvey licked his face and ears and gave little whines of pleasure as he resisted Alf's tugging on his lead.

'What is going on out here?' Matron demanded. 'Get that dog away immediately!'

Harvey growled, his hackles rising in recognition of the woman who'd shouted at him before.

'I'm sorry,' panted Alf, desperately trying to haul Harvey away from Ron. 'He was pulling so hard the lead slipped out of my hand, and there was no way I could catch him once he saw you.'

Ron was still on his back beneath the dog. 'Aye, leave him be, the pair of you. Seeing my dog again is the best tonic I could have.' He ruffled Harvey's ears and the dog reciprocated by dribbling down Ron's neck.

Matron shoved Alf out of the way and grabbed Harvey's collar, giving it a nasty tug.

Harvey's head whipped round and he gave a deep growl which revealed a set of wickedly sharp teeth.

'There, there, Harvey, she won't be biting you,' soothed Ron. 'Be a good dog and let me back up onto me feet. To be sure, it's cold on this damp grass.'

Alf pulled Harvey away and held tightly to both lead and collar as Matron tried and failed to get Ron onto his feet.

'Blast and double blast,' Ron spluttered, flailing like a beached turtle in the plaster jacket. 'Alf, give us a hand up, for pity's sake.'

Alf fixed the loop at the end of the leash around his ankle, and at the risk of having his leg whipped from beneath him by an overexcited Harvey, managed to get Ron back up and sitting on the bench. His face was as red as a beetroot, and he was sweating profusely from the effort, his frightened gaze darting frequently towards the furious Matron.

'I'm sorry, Ron. I wouldn't have brought him if I'd known what trouble he'd cause – but he was pining, you see, and off his food.'

'Aye, you did the right thing, Alf,' he murmured, taking charge of the lead. 'Now sit and behave, you heathen beast,' he said firmly to Harvey. 'Or Matron will have us both for the high jump.'

'Oh, you're way past the high jump, Mr Reilly,' stormed Matron. She turned with a furious glare to Alf. 'You will leave immediately and take that animal with you. I do not wish to see either of you here again.'

Despite Ron's encouragement to Harvey to go home, Alf had to virtually drag him along the terrace and out of sight through the side entrance. It wouldn't have surprised Ron at all if Harvey appeared again, having escaped Alf.

Matron turned the full force of her rage on Ron. 'This is not the first time you and your animals have disrupted the smooth running of my hospital, and I will *not* stand for it. Do you hear?'

'Aye, I can hear you – and so can they,' he replied sourly, nodding towards the many faces at the windows. 'To be sure, I'm much better from the visit, so I really can't understand why you're in such a lather.'

'Get indoors, Mr Reilly,' she rasped. 'You will need your plaster checked for any damage, and if there is, then one of my nurses will have to attend to it – despite the fact there is more than enough for them to do as it is.' She drew a shallow breath. 'I shall be reporting you to the board of governors – and if you give them as little respect as you've shown me, they'll see you're sent to an RAF rehabilitation unit in Loughborough along with Wing Commander Ryan.'

Her mouth twisted into an unpleasant smirk. 'I doubt very much your dog will find you there, and as all visiting is strictly off limits, there will be no more repeats of this afternoon's disgraceful carrying-on.'

Ron regarded her with loathing. 'You're a disgrace to your profession,' he growled, 'and about the most unpleasant woman I've ever had the misfortune to meet. The board will certainly hear from me too, and with any luck they'll get rid of you so that this hospital can be run efficiently by someone who is not a stranger to kindness and understanding.'

Matron stood there with her mouth opening and closing like a fish out of water, and Ron winked to those watching at the window. What Matron didn't know was that the chairman of the board had been his commanding officer during the last big push in 1918, and had personally recommended Ron for a bravery award. Ron didn't usually rely on past glories to influence people, but this seemed the perfect time to break that rule and use every ounce of influence he had to get rid of her.

25

Ron had been released from the Memorial the following week, and although Matron had clearly not reported him and Peter, Ron had written a letter to his old CO, outlining his complaints, which had been counter-signed by nearly every patient.

Peter, who'd had to stay on, told him that Matron had been swiftly replaced by a very pleasant, motherly woman who possessed a marvellous sense of humour and fun, which enlivened the place no end. Ron had been very glad to hear it, for now the atmosphere was lighter, the patients would recover much more quickly.

He was certainly feeling much better now the hated plaster jacket had been removed. The X-rays had shown that the hairline fracture had knitted well and there was very little deformity in the lower vertebrae. His left foot still drooped a little, but intensive physiotherapy sessions at the hospital were slowly improving it, and although it still pained him to lift anything heavy or walk too far, he was able to get about without the hated walking stick – and even managed to take Harvey and Monty for short walks on the lower and easier slopes of the hills.

Ron had moved back into his old basement room at Beach View with Harvey, but as he was capable of walking to the Anchor now, he quite often spent the night with Rosie. The first time had been quite stressful as he'd worried he might not be able to make love to her – and if he could, he might disappoint her. But Rosie, darling Rosie, had let him take his time, and afterwards they'd lain back and grinned at one another like two naughty teenagers before repeating the delightful exercise all over again.

Ron had proposed again that night, and the following morning they'd gone to the Town Hall and booked their wedding for the 7th of May, determined that this time absolutely nothing would happen to stop it.

As March drifted into April and the news from Europe brought hope that the war might really be close to ending, the atmosphere in the town became electric. Every wireless was tuned to the BBC, the makeshift cinema was constantly packed to the rafters with people eager to watch the Pathé newsreels, and newspapers were pored over and discussed at length.

Since the start of the New Year, the Germans had withdrawn from the Ardennes; the Allies had taken Cologne and established a bridge across the Rhine at Remagen, and the Russians had captured Warsaw and Danzig. Dresden had been destroyed by a firestorm after sustained Allied bombing raids, and whilst there was an Allied offensive in northern

Italy, the Americans had encircled the Germans in the Ruhr.

There had been other shocking revelations which made the newsreels almost too horrific to watch, for the Russians had liberated the concentration camp of Auschwitz; and the Allies had liberated Buchenwald and Belsen. Ron had thought he'd seen the worst of man's inhumanity to man, but the horrific scenes had brought him to tears even though he was filled with utter revulsion and rage for what the Nazis had done.

He and a sobbing Rosie had left the cinema before the feature film and gone down to the seafront. They needed fresh air and the soothing sight of the sea to dispel the horrific images that now haunted them.

'How could people do such things?' sobbed Rosie. 'I know there have been rumours for months, but I put them down to propaganda and never really believed such horrors were actually happening.'

Ron had no reply, but put his arm round her and held her close, his vision blurred with tears as he stared out across the calm waters of the Channel. The Red Cross had kept people informed of what had been happening in Europe, but they'd clearly not been given access to those death camps – or if they had, had kept shamefully quiet. They had also had no access to any of the POWs held by the Japs, and he dreaded to think what sort of tortures they must be suffering. He thought of Jane and Sarah, who'd kept the spark of hope alive that their father and Philip would come through, but after reading Jim's letters about how the Japs behaved, and seeing that newsreel, he doubted very much if any of the prisoners had survived.

They'd walked slowly back to the Anchor and gone to bed where they simply held one another for comfort and reassurance, but mostly in the hope that this really would be the war to end all wars, and scenes like the ones they'd seen that evening would never again be repeated.

Fanny Rawson had been promoted to shop floor manager on the night shifts, and the work at the factory was proceeding at an even faster pace, spurred on by the hope the war was about to end and their men would be coming home. The wireless was on day and night, and when the news came on the machines fell silent – something Peggy and Solly turned a blind eye to in the knowledge they'd work even harder afterwards.

A huge roar of approval almost lifted the rafters when the Americans took Nuremberg and the Russians began to attack Berlin. No one believed the spurious Nazi report that Hitler had died heroically of his wounds at his post in Berlin, for everything they'd learned about him over the past six years pointed to a man who was far from heroic.

There was even greater jubilation when the Germans surrendered in the Ruhr; the Allies took

Venice; the Russians entered Berlin and Mussolini was captured and hanged by Italian partisans.

It had taken a while to get them settled back to work after that, but when it was announced on the last day of April that Hitler's body had been found by the Allies alongside his mistress Eva Braun, and Goebbels, and that it was clear they'd committed suicide, they were on their feet cheering and dancing around the machines in unbridled delight.

Peggy decided they'd earned the celebration and left them to get on with it. She climbed the stairs to the offices and found that, unusually, Madge wasn't at her desk. She went through and found her with Solly and Rachel, celebrating the news with large glasses of whisky.

'Come in, come in, Peggy,' Solly boomed. 'We have something to celebrate at last.' He poured a generous measure and handed her the glass. 'He's escaped punishment like the coward he is, but the world is rid of him and he will rot in hell if there's any justice.' He raised his glass. 'Here's to the victory that is now so nearly within our grasp.'

They drank in silence, and Peggy noticed that Solly had lost weight since the liberation of Auschwitz, and that his smile no longer lit up his eyes. Her heart went out to him – and to Rachel, for the preliminary lists of prisoners had shown that several members of his family had been slaughtered there, with others as yet to be found amongst the thousands of displaced people now wandering all over Europe. She couldn't imagine how painful that must have been for them both, but the shadows of their sorrow were clearly marked in their eyes.

'How are the wedding arrangements going?' Rachel asked. 'I hope Ron's not going to do anything silly to postpone it again.'

Peggy dredged up a smile. 'He's being very well behaved for a change,' she replied. 'And he's decided not to have a drinking session this time, but to spend his last night at home with us. I think that accident really did knock the stuffing out of him, and although he's almost back to his old self, he's aware that any more damage to his back could cripple him.'

'He was very lucky to recover so well,' murmured Solly. 'I look forward to being there when they at last make their vows.' He drained his glass and put it down on his desk before glancing out of the window that overlooked the shop floor.

'It looks as if there's no work being done down there, Peggy. We'll be celebrating again very soon, I'm sure, but there are orders to fill, and we can't afford to lag behind.'

Peggy nodded, drained her own glass and went rather tipsily down the steep wooden stairs. A word here and there soon brought order, and the happy chatter mingled with the whirring machines as the wireless broadcast jolly music to sing along to.

Peggy was so excited she could barely sit still on that extraordinary Monday morning. Not only was it Ron and Rosie's wedding day, but the Germans had reportedly surrendered totally and unconditionally to the Allies, and General Slim's 14th Army had advanced the four hundred miles down the Irrawaddy River from Mandalay to take Rangoon. The Japanese had at last been all but routed from Burma, and her brave, darling, wonderful Jim had been there playing his part.

'He'll be coming home,' she squeaked in delight. 'Jim will be coming home before we know it – and so will Anne and the rest of the family.'

'Aye, once the Yanks have cleared the islands in the South China Sea and the Pacific, the Japs will have to surrender,' said Ron, struggling to fix the stiff collar to his best shirt. 'Can you help me with this, Peg? To be sure, I'm strangling meself.'

Peggy was all fingers and thumbs, so left the task to Fran and shot off to find the old bunting and flags she'd been storing under the stairs ever since the war had begun. Churchill had promised to broadcast to the nation on the 10th, but the news-reader had said that Victory in Europe Day would probably come before that, so if it really was the end, he'd probably speak to everyone tonight or tomorrow morning.

With her heart full of joy at the knowledge she'd soon have all of her family home again, she brought the box into the kitchen and dumped it on the table. 'We've got at least three hours to get this lot up,' she said, dragging the dusty and rather ragged strings of bunting out. 'Come on, everyone, we don't want to be the only house in Cliffehaven not to be decorated. And, Cordelia, what did you do with the balloons I kept back after Daisy's birthday?'

Cordelia chuckled and shook her head. 'I don't have baboons, dear. All this talk of peace has clearly gone to your head.'

Peggy was too excited and happy to correct her, and as the bunting was unravelled and given a good shake, and everyone helped to tether it above the front door and windows and along the back wall, she couldn't resist hugging and kissing each of them in turn. When it was done and they stood back to admire their handiwork, she swung Daisy onto her hip and held her close. This was the happiest day of her life, and from now on there would always be sunshine.

Rosie's hairdresser had come in very early to do her hair and nails, and had then stayed on to help Brenda and the other two barmaids string the bunting above the door and windows. Rosie had stood on the pavement in her nightclothes to watch as her nails dried, for on this very special day, it was wonderful to see that every shop was bedecked in flags and balloons, making the whole town look very gay. It was as if Cliffehaven was celebrating not only the promise of victory in Europe, but her wedding to Ron.

She'd returned the happy greetings, waving and smiling at those who wished her luck, then when

Dolly had driven up and emerged bearing a large and mysterious box, she'd followed her indoors.

'Oh, Dolly,' she breathed after giving her a hug of welcome. 'I can hardly believe this really is our wedding day.'

'It most certainly is,' she replied, 'and I suspect that if victory is announced, it will be a day that everyone will remember.' She drew off her gloves and fur wrap before reaching for the box. 'I know you have something old, new and blue, so I wondered if you'd like to borrow this.'

Rosie gasped at the sight of the stunning mink wrap nestled in tissue paper. She drew it almost reverently from the box and draped it over her shoulders. 'Oh, Dolly, it's perfect,' she sighed, running her fingers through the thick caramel-coloured fur. 'But it must be worth a fortune and I'll be terrified of damaging it.'

'Nonsense,' said Dolly. 'When you described the dress you'd decided to wear instead of the other outfit, I just knew this would add the finishing touch. Your white fox is beautiful, and would have been ideal with the pale blue – but this will set the right tone, don't you think?'

Rosie gazed at her reflection in the mirror above the mantelpiece and grinned. 'It's glorious, but I think the dressing gown rather lets the side down, don't you?'

They both giggled like schoolgirls as Rosie did a twirl.

Dolly looked at her watch. 'You'd better start getting ready, Rosie. You don't want to be late and give the old rogue a scare.'

'It would serve him right after all the times he's kept me waiting,' she replied. 'Help yourself to tea or a drink whilst I get dressed.

Rosie took her time, for she wanted everything to be perfect – or as perfect as it could be. Her underwear wasn't at all alluring, but she'd sewn on strips of lace and tiny blue ribbons to make it prettier and less utilitarian. The silk dress was new because the blue dress and coat brought back too many sad memories. It had been beautifully made by the seamstress that lived behind the Town Hall, and once she'd slipped her feet into the gold sandals and placed the mink over her shoulders, she dared to look at herself in the wardrobe mirror.

Delighted with what she saw, she picked up the small brown leather-covered Bible she'd been given by her mother on her first communion, and went into the sitting room.

'Oh, Rosie, you look so lovely,' said Dolly with a sigh. 'Ron will be bowled over.'

Rosie felt herself blush. 'It's not too much, is it?'

Dolly gently held her arms. 'It's perfect.' She softly kissed her cheek. 'You and Ron are a perfect match, and if the old so-and-so misbehaves, you call on me, Rosie. We sorted him out last time, and we can do it again.'

Rosie giggled, caught sight of her reflection in the mirror and was quite stunned by how sophisticated, calm and radiant she suddenly appeared to be. 'Oh, Dolly, I'm so very happy. Thank you for being such a good friend.'

'It's my pleasure,' said Dolly, picking up her own fur from the couch and glancing out of the window. 'Brenda's been up to take Monty home with her, and Bertie's waiting downstairs with his car, so I must fly if I'm to get to the Town Hall before you.' She blew her a kiss and ran down the stairs.

Rosie stood in the silent room for a moment, and then fetched the single rose Stan had brought from his allotment earlier this morning. 'Well, Rosie, girl,' she murmured. 'This is it. This is the day you've been waiting for. The sun is shining, the war looks to be at an end, and with any luck Ron will be waiting at the Town Hall by now.'

She winked at her reflection in the mirror and went down the stairs, the butterflies of excitement fluttering just a little even though she felt calmer than she'd ever done before.

Ron was feeling nervous, but also excited as he slipped on his suit jacket and pinned the single rosebud onto the lapel. Rosie wanted to make an entrance on the arm of Bertie Double-Barrelled, who would also be driving her car up to the Town Hall, so he was planning to walk there with everyone from Beach View.

The house was in chaos and Harvey wasn't making things any calmer by dashing about and getting in everyone's way. Frank arrived with Pauline in time for Ron to take him outside for a quiet drink before they had to leave and to check that Frank hadn't forgotten to bring the ring Rosie had taken so long to choose at the jeweller's.

'Don't worry yourself, Da. I'm not that addle-headed,' Frank said, patting his shoulder with a heavy hand. 'It's grand to see you in one piece and all ready for this special day, and when Jim and the rest of the family come home we'll have an even bigger knees-up.'

Everyone had made a special effort for the day, the girls wearing their prettiest frocks, the men freshly barbered and shaved and in their smartest suits. Cissy was wearing her uniform as she'd yet to be discharged from the WAAFs, Cordelia was in her favourite lilac and white outfit, and Peggy was in the blue silk suit that she'd worn for Anne's wedding to Martin. Daisy was dressed in a frock of white lace with a coronet of flowers in her hair, and would carry a basket of confetti once the service was over.

They left the house together, Harvey trotting alongside Ron in a smart new collar decorated with a green ribbon. The town was a riot of colour with flags, balloons and bunting everywhere, and they arrived en masse at the Town Hall to find a young bride and groom posing on the steps for photographs. After congratulating them, they trooped inside and up the red-carpeted stairs to the largest of the wedding rooms which was redolent with the scent and colours of the many flowers Stan had provided from his allotment as his wedding present to them both.

Ron walked towards the front row of chairs and grinned in delight when he saw Dolly sitting alongside his old pals. 'This is a pleasant surprise,' he murmured, admiring the elegant silk suit and outrageous hat before carefully kissing her scented, powdered cheek.

'Well I couldn't miss the wedding of the year, could I?' she teased, kissing him back. 'I don't need to wish you luck, Ron. You've struck gold with Rosie, and I just know you'll be very happy.'

Ron ordered Harvey to sit and be quiet as he took his seat beside Frank and looked back towards the doors where Fran was waiting with her violin to serenade the bride as she walked down the aisle. He gave her a wink, which she returned, and then let his gaze roam over the gathering. Although Jim, Anne and the others were missing, these were the people he loved best in the world – even Doris now she'd changed for the better – and his heart swelled as he took in the happy faces. They were here for him and Rosie, he thought in a haze of joy. And then he looked at his watch and began to panic. Where was she? It was now five minutes past eleven.

He was about to send Frank to look for her when the sweetest violin note trembled and soared, bringing a breathless hush to the room.

It was the opening notes of an old Celtic song, the name of which he couldn't remember, but he knew it told the story of Ireland's mountains and valleys and majestic sea shores, and spoke to his heart just as Fran and Rosie had known it would.

His legs were trembling with emotion as he got to his feet and turned to look at his beautiful bride slowly coming towards him on Bertie's arm. Her long shot-silk dress gleamed gold and green and copper in the bright lights as it fell in a sheath over her curves to the gold sandals. The pale brown mink stole was draped elegantly over her shoulders, held in place by a sparkling clip. A band of green velvet decorated with shamrocks of silk and lace nestled on her crown, the delicate veil not quite hiding her glorious blue eyes and radiant smile. She carried a single red rose and the leather-bound Bible he knew she'd been given on her first communion.

Ron was stunned by her beauty, her grace and the fact that this glorious woman was about to be his wife. 'You look … You're the most beautiful woman in the world,' he managed as she came to stand beside him. 'Are you sure you want to be tied to an old wreck like me?'

She took his hand and giggled. 'It's too late for you to back out now,' she whispered. 'We're in this together, come what may.'

They shared a loving smile and gazed into one another's eyes as the registrar began the service. They exchanged their vows almost in a daze, and before they knew it, the ring was on her finger and he was kissing her.

Fran struck up a lively Irish jig, accompanied by Robert on the saxophone, and four members of the local band on tambour, flutes and a penny-whistle. Everyone got to their feet to clap and tap their feet in time, and once the registers were signed and witnessed, Ron tucked Rosie's hand into his arm and proudly walked with her back down the aisle, where Daisy was enthusiastically tossing confetti in her wake. His heart was bursting with pride and happiness, and when he gazed into Rosie's lovely eyes, he could see his adoration reflected there.

The wedding celebrations went on late into the night, and when they were finally able to slip away from the Officers' Club to the Anchor, it was to find that their bedroom had been strewn with flowers and rose petals. Ron couldn't carry her over the threshold, or up the stairs, but as they stood in the bedroom doorway he took her hand and kissed her. 'I will love you to me last breath,' he whispered against her lips.

'And I you,' she replied.

Ron swept her into his arms, kicked the door shut behind him and with a swooning, overwhelming passion made love to her as if it was for the first time.

Dear Reader,

Another few months have flown by and, although we've been blessed with a wonderful summer here in England, I have been deeply immersed in the winter and spring of 1944/45 which was cold and wet. I did get time to sit in my garden and enjoy the sunshine, but the Reilly family and all at Beach View kept bringing me back to my desk.

Overshadowing the roller coaster of Ron and Rosie's wedding plans are the overseas events in January and February 1945 in which we find our POWs and our servicemen facing severe challenges in order to survive. Victory in Europe is at hand, but Jim is still fighting the Japanese in Burma and, with the harsh winter hindering the POWs on their death march across Germany, nothing is guaranteed.

Peggy has her own trials to deal with – not least the worry over her scattered family and the continued V-2 attacks. Although there are challenges ahead for her too, her indomitable spirit keeps her going even through the darkest days when tragedy strikes at Beach View and it seems she might lose someone very close to her heart.

I've had many lovely letters and emails from fans telling me how much they love the Reilly family, and how good it feels to be back in the love and warmth of Peggy's kitchen. I feel the same, for they are my family too, and I shall miss them when the series ends. But there are two books still to come, so it's not over quite yet.

I do appreciate the lovely emails and encouraging messages on Facebook, and I feel very blessed to have made so many friends through social media. Writing can be a solitary occupation, and it's a great boost to know that all the effort and hours of writing and research is being cheered on by so many well-wishers.

I hope you had a wonderful Christmas, and that the New Year of 2019 will bring health and happiness to each of you. With all best wishes,

 x

WELCOME TO

Cliffehaven

ELLIE DEAN

A Map of Cliffehaven

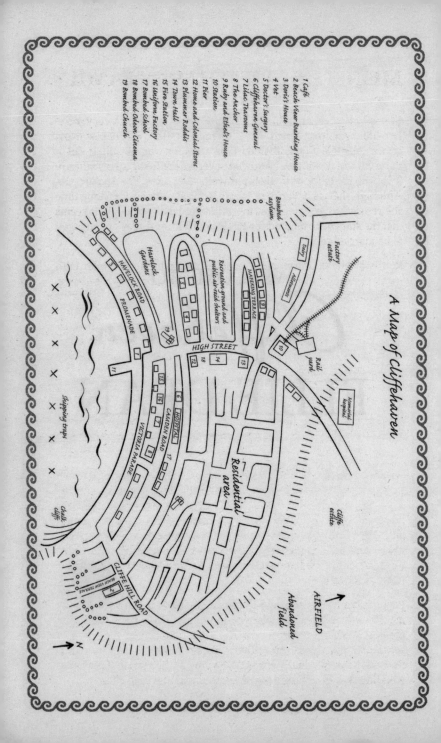

1 Café
2 Beach View Boarding House
3 Doris's House
4 Vet
5 Doctor's Surgery
6 Cliffehaven General
7 Lilac Tearooms
8 The Anchor
9 Ruby and Ethel's House
10 Station
11 Pier
12 Home and Colonial Stores
13 Plummer Roddis
14 Town Hall
15 Fire Station
16 Uniform Factory
17 Bombed School
18 Bombed Odeon Cinema
19 Bombed Church

Bombed asylum

Factory estate

Dairy

Allotments

HAVELOCK ROAD

Havelock Gardens

PROMENADE

MAFEKING TERRACE

Recreation ground and public air-raid shelters

Rail yard

Memorial hospital

Cliffe estate

HIGH STREET

CAMDEN ROAD

HOSPITAL

VICTORIA PARADE

Residential area

Chalk cliffs

Shipping traps

BEACH VIEW TERRACE

CLIFFE HILL ROAD

AIRFIELD

Abandoned field

N

MEET THE CLIFFEHAVEN FAMILY
RONAN REILLY

Ron is a sturdy man in his mid-sixties who often leads a very secretive life away from Beach View. It turns out that the contacts, experience and skills Ron gathered in the previous war are still useful in these current hostilities. Widowed several decades ago, he's fallen in love with the luscious Rosie Braithwaite who owns The Anchor pub. Although she has never been averse to his attentions, for a long time she refused to let things get too intimate. Finally, though, it seems that the stars have aligned for Rosie and Ron, and they are engaged to be married soon.

Ron is a wily countryman; a poacher and retired fisherman with great roguish charm, who tramps over the fields with his dog, Harvey, and two ferrets – and frequently comes home with illicit game hidden in the deep pockets of his poacher's coat. He doesn't care much about his appearance, much to his daughter-in-law Peggy's dismay, but beneath that ramshackle old hat and moth-eaten clothing beats the heart of a strong, loving man who will fiercely protect those he loves.

ROSIE BRAITHWAITE

Rosie is in her early fifties and in love with Ron, though for many years she had to remain married to her first husband, who was in a mental asylum.

She took over The Anchor twenty years ago and has turned it into a little gold-mine. Rosie has platinum hair, big blue eyes and an hourglass figure – she also has a good sense of humour and can hold her own with the customers. She runs the pub with a firm hand, and keeps Ron at bay, although she's not averse to a bit of slap and tickle. And yet her glamorous appearance and winning smile hides the heartache of not having been blessed with a longed-for baby, and now it's too late.

Peggy is her best friend, and the family living in Beach View Boarding House has taken the place of the family she'd never had. Her greatest wish is to start a new life with Ron – even though he's exasperating at times. And now, with the passing of her husband, Ron and Rosie are finally engaged. So long as they can make it to the wedding day, their future together looks brighter than ever.

PEGGY REILLY

Peggy is the middle sister of three, in her early forties, and married to Jim, Ron's son. She is small and slender with dark, curly hair and lively brown eyes, and finds it very hard to sit still. As if running a busy household and caring for her young daughter wasn't enough, she also did voluntary work for the WVS before getting a job in the local uniform factory, yet still finds time to offer tea, sympathy and a shoulder to cry on when they're needed.

She and Jim took over the running of Beach View Boarding House when Peggy's parents retired – her older sister, Doris, thought it was beneath her, and her younger sister, Doreen, had already established a career in London.

Peggy has three daughters, two sons, and two grand-daughters. When war was declared and the boarding house business became no longer viable, she decided to take in evacuees. Peggy can be feisty and certainly doesn't suffer fools, and yet she is also trying very hard to come to terms with the fact that her family has been torn apart by the war. She is a romantic at heart and can't help trying to match-make, but she's also a terrible worrier, always fretting over someone – and as the young evacuees make their home with her, she comes to regard them as her chicks and will do everything she can to protect and nurture them.

DORIS WILLIAMS

Doris is Peggy's older sister and for many years she has been divorced from her long-suffering husband, Ted, who died very recently. She used to live in the posh part of town, Havelock Road, and look down on Peggy and the boarding house.

But her days of snooty social climbing and snobbishness are behind her. Having lived with Peggy at Beach View Boarding House after bombs destroyed her former neighbourhood, Doris has softened in her ways and although she's still proud of her connections to high society, she's also on much better terms with her sister and the rest of the family.

But despite all this, Doris is still rather lonely, especially with her only son now married and moved away. Could her recent change of heart also lead to a new romance?

LOOK OUT FOR THE NEXT
CLIFFEHAVEN NOVEL

ELLIE DEAN

With Hope and Love

PRE-ORDER NOW IN
PAPERBACK AND E-BOOK

Out 22nd August 2019

Lose yourself in the

Find Love. Find Hope.
Find Cliffehaven.

world of Cliffehaven

Ellie DEAN

Can love survive in a time of war?

Where the Heart Lies

United by love, separated by war…

Ellie Dean

Always in my Heart

It was a time of friendship, family, love and loss…

Ellie Dean

All My Tomorrows

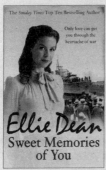

The *Sunday Times* Top Ten Bestselling Author

Only love can get you through the heartache of war

Ellie Dean

Sweet Memories of You

The *Sunday Times* Top Ten Bestselling Author

Wartime can bring friendship and love as well as heartache

Ellie Dean

Shelter from the Storm

The *Sunday Times* Top Ten Bestselling Author

Does absence make the heart grow fonder?

Ellie Dean

Until You Come Home

The *Sunday Times* Top Ten Bestselling Author

ELLIE DEAN

The Waiting Hours

Can the tide of war heal her broken heart?

The *Sunday Times* Bestselling Author

ELLIE DEAN

With a Kiss and a Prayer

Can she bring her loved ones home?

The *Sunday Times* Bestselling Author

ELLIE DEAN

As the Sun Breaks Through

Amid the war, hope burns brighter than ever

Hear more from

ELLIE DEAN

SIGN UP TO OUR NEW SAGA NEWSLETTER

Penny Street

Stories You'll Love to Share

Penny Street is a newsletter bringing you the latest book deals, competitions and alerts of new saga series releases.

Read about the research behind your favourite books, try our monthly wordsearch and download your very own Penny Street reading map.

Join today by visiting
www.penguin.co.uk/pennystreet